MW00574392

Devils Kill Devils

Also by Johnny Compton

The Spite House

Johnny Compton

Devils
Kill
Devils

NIGHTFIRE

TOR PUBLISHING GROUP

NEW YORK

DEVILS KILL DEVILS

A Nightfire Book
Published by Tom Doherty Associates / Tor Publishing Group
120 Broadway
New York, NY 10271

www.torpublishinggroup.com

Nightfire™ is a trademark of Macmillan Publishing Group, LLC.

The Library of Congress Cataloging-in-Publication Data is available upon request.

ISBN 978-1-250-84168-1 (hardcover)
ISBN 978-1-250-37505-6 (international, sold outside the U.S., subject to rights availability)
ISBN 978-1-250-84169-8 (ebook)

Our books may be purchased in bulk for promotional, educational, or business use. Please contact your local bookseller or the Macmillan Corporate and Premium Sales Department at 1-800-221-7945, extension 5442, or by email at MacmillanSpecialMarkets@macmillan.com.

First U.S. Edition: 2024
First International Edition: 2024

Printed in the United States of America

0 9 8 7 6 5 4 3 2 1

Devils
Kill
Devils

1

She clicked the light switch on the hotel room wall, and in the infinitesimal space between the absence and arrival of light, a space undetectable to the mind, much less the eye, Sarita Bardales saw someone who could not be in the room. A tall shadow standing near the window, featureless but facing her and Frank, nonetheless. Watching them enter.

The shape disappeared before the click of the light switch left Sarita's ears, too quickly for anyone to have ever been there. Sarita told herself that it had been a product of her inebriation, but she had still recognized the man within the silhouette in the fraction of an instant it had appeared to her. She took this recognition as additional proof that she imagined it. Imagined him. He had no reason to be there now, at the close of this perfect day.

Six months ago, after watching mutual friends suffer restless children, condescending relatives, and unhelpful friends at their wedding, with hypnotized smiles on their faces, Sarita and Frank promised each other that their nuptials and reception would be different. They would set rules and see to their own wants first, and anyone who wouldn't be happy to attend under their guidelines would be free to stay home. Sarita had gone so far as to co-author her maid of honor's brief speech, though that was primarily due to Tori admitting she was concerned about saying the wrong thing.

Given Tori's state of mind the past few years, her obsessions with the "flexibility of reality" and the power of prayers and "spells," Sarita thought it prudent to help Tori find words appropriate to the occasion.

Frank's biological mother, Harrah, took issue with their plans. She wanted to be first in line to dance with her son at the reception, but he had every intention of giving his stepmother, Misty, that honor. The latter had been in his life for twenty-two of his twenty-seven years, during which time his birth mother had been fitfully present, which was, arguably, for the best. The faint scar that divided his right eyebrow, and the deeper, curved, and jagged rows of scars on his left forearm, strengthened that argument. Still, Harrah had insisted on having the first dance because she was his "real" mother, and that, to her, was that. Frank told her he loved her, but she could either accept what he wanted or not attend. She formally declined the wedding invitation soon after, as did most of his family, save for his grizzled bulldog of an uncle, Everett, who attended as an ambassador of the Stallworth clan rather than an eager guest, although he broke down as the reception ramped up and danced almost enough to make up for the rest of the family's absence. Sarita and Frank agreed it was all for the best.

Simple resoluteness had guided them through a terrific day. An ideal day. Everyone in attendance, so far as Sarita could tell, had had a wonderful time. No stress, no pressure, no awkwardness, no drama. It had been, as she'd desired, a carefree celebration. Now the wedding was in their rearview mirror, overtly pleasant, colored in the warmth of a generous buzz. Just ahead of them, close enough to kiss, was their first night together as husband and wife.

Frank brought her to the large bed, tried to set her down but fell forward himself and pushed her away to keep from falling on her. She laughed so hard she briefly lost her breath.

The shadow man she'd imagined a moment earlier was as close to forgotten as could be. She rolled toward Frank as he turned onto his back.

"Next time," he said, "I think maybe we should go a little easier on the vino. Just a thought."

Her fingers toyed casually with a lock of his brown hair. "Next time? Next time we get married?"

He looked at her, his smile widened. "You know this is all a practice run, right? It has to be. People talk about the day they got married as being their best day, but it's not really supposed to be that. Nothing's ever this good. So, we'll have to break up at some point and start this over again. Just a little more down-to-earth and realistic next time."

"Makes sense," she said. His cologne and the wine on his breath comforted her in ways she wouldn't want explained, like she wouldn't want to read a textbook study of why cocoa tastes sweet, and then why sweetness is coveted, and what receptors of the brain get placated and whatnot when you eat chocolate. Some things were enriched by a little mystery. Love, she thought, was among those things.

"I've told you I love you today, right?" Frank said. "Not counting the vows. Wait, I put 'I love you' in the vows, right?"

"Don't ask me to remember too much right now, babe," Sarita said. "Best I can tell you is I know you said, 'I do.' That happened. Oh, and then right after that you started shouting, 'My chick is hotter than yours' at everybody in the room."

"I'm almost sure you're making that up."

"It happened. I was shocked, but flattered. I don't think my mom appreciated you yelling that at my dad, though."

He chuckled, then kissed her. She had changed into a sleeveless, white, knee-length dress following the ceremony. He was still in his black tuxedo, but he'd lost the tie and unbuttoned his shirt collar hours ago. Now she removed his jacket and untucked his shirt. He sat up, back against the headboard, and she straddled him. They kissed intermittently until he started to laugh at her inability to get the first button open. She laughed, too, looking down at the button near his waist.

"Are you wearing a chastity shirt? What the hell . . . ?" When she looked up at him the seriousness of his expression startled her so much that she needed an extra second to realize he was not looking at her. He was looking at something behind her.

Then Sarita sensed it. A dimness had stolen into the room. Something else, as well. A third party. *Him.*

Gooseflesh rose on her skin, and she had an unconscious urge to scratch all over to make her nerves go away. *It can't be,* she thought. *Why would he be here?* When she looked back, she saw him.

Angelo stood at the foot of the bed, dressed in black. Strands of his long, flaxen hair hung over his face. Through the thin curtain of hairs he met Frank's gaze with an ash-hot glare.

Sarita had never actually seen him this close, she realized. The only other time she'd been this close to him, she'd been unconscious in his arms. Every other sighting had been at some distance. Now she appreciated how muscular and simply *immovable* he looked. He was a stone-skinned statue, well over six feet tall, hulking and unnaturally lean all at once. Even through his clothes, this could not be more evident.

His fists were balled tight. He made no sound, seemed not even to breathe.

Is the hotel on fire? she thought. *Fire. Or a bomb. Active shooter. Something. We've got to get out of here.*

Before she could begin to explain this to Frank, to find the words that would convince him, he took Sarita by the shoulders and moved her to the side, then moved ahead of her. He tried to speak, croaked, cleared his throat, tried again. "If you want money, you can have it. I won't fight you over it. I have credit cards and I have a little cash on me, too. All right? My wallet's still in my pocket. I'm just going to take it out. I'm not trying anything, as long as you don't try to hurt my w—"

Before Frank could reach for his wallet, Angelo reached for his throat. His massive hand clamped around Frank's neck and lifted him from the bed, took him toward the balcony windows. Sarita leapt toward Angelo, grabbed his arm. She wasn't a slight or weak woman. She still carried a little of the muscle she had acquired in high school, playing softball. Nowadays, she ran, did a home-boot-camp workout somewhat routinely, and also wasn't too particular about what she ate. Despite all of this, she hung from Angelo's arm like she was a child. Smaller. She was a doll. So, too, was Frank, at the mercy of Angelo's strength.

"What the hell are you doing? Angelo, listen to me. He's my *husband*. He's not going to hurt me! *What are you doing?*"

Frank tried to pry Angelo's hand free with one hand, punched him repeatedly with the other. He may as well have been punching a wall. Angelo slammed Frank into the window. The glass cracked but held. Frank's pupils rolled up. His face was turning blue.

"Angelo, stop! Listen to me, damn it! *Angelo!*"

He flung her away, more forcefully than she could have expected. She tried to hold on, lost her grip, flew over the bed, and fell headfirst into the side of the honeymoon suite's oversized, heart-shaped bathtub. A heavy, dull ringing enveloped her head, pushing all other sound into the far distance, like she was wearing a vibrating church bell for a helmet. Darkness overtook her for a moment, then receded to reality.

A voice called to her. She couldn't truly hear her name through the stuffy haze of her concussion, but she knew the voice, sensed its urgency. It was Frank. Something was wrong. He was in trouble, and still on the other side of the room. The face before her, staring at her with concerned, guilty eyes, was not her husband's.

"Why—?" she said to her guardian angel.

A hand with a gold wedding band on the ring finger came over Angelo's face, tried to claw at his eyes. Angelo turned, raised a fist, brought it down. Frank's pained scream sliced through Sarita's head. She tried to lift herself up from the floor and the room tilted. Her stomach contracted and she almost vomited. There was no strength in her arms or legs, but she couldn't let that stop her. She needed to move. She needed to do something, because Angelo's fist was up again, down again. Up, red and wet, then down. Again. Again. And now Sarita could hear the impact of each punch, a mallet crushing a sack of sticks and mud. She crawled forward and grabbed Angelo's back.

He stopped, turned to her, eyes swimming with insanity and hate, and then shame. He looked away from her, stood. The room went black as though he had commanded it to, then the lights flickered on again. Angelo was gone.

Sarita wished she could follow him, disappear with him, partly to keep fighting him, beat him until he answered her question—*Why?*—but, more than that, she wanted to go away with him to avoid confronting what remained with her in the hotel suite.

She could see Frank's legs where he lay on the floor, but his upper body was blocked by the end of the bed. She called his name. He did not respond, did not move. She called it again, more urgently this time, as though he were playing a cruel prank and she meant to let him know with her tone that it had gone too far. Still, he did not move. She crept over to him.

"No, no, no. Frank . . . Oh God. Oh God."

The pulped ruin of her husband's skull made her gag. A wealth of blood spread across the floor from beneath what little of his head was left. She wanted desperately to deny what she saw, tried to will it to disappear the way Angelo had. Instead it stuck in her vision like a broken claw. When she tore herself away its scar remained in her mind's eye.

"God, please," she said, eyes still shut, begging for a miracle. She'd believed since she was a child that anything was possible. That Heaven sometimes intervened to save a life that should have been lost. She'd been the direct beneficiary of this four times. Now she pleaded for one more miracle—just one—for Frank.

She looked at him again and nothing had changed. He was still dead. Defaced. Unrecognizable. She screamed loud enough to be heard beyond a room designed to contain a different kind of screaming. It was raw and powerful, purposeful. It was as though she was trying to call a weapon into existence through sheer force of horror, anguish, and rage. Something sharp, heavy, and hellish enough to gut an angel.

2

Sixteen years prior, on an overcast Thursday at the beach, nine-year-old Sarita Bardales had her first brush with death.

José and Janelle Bardales had passed their love of sand and sea on to their children. That day, Janelle drove Sarita and her brother, David, from San Antonio to Malaquite Beach near Corpus Christi for a day trip, something they tried to do at least twice each summer, supplementing the week-long annual vacation they spent at South Padre Island.

Janelle was alone with the children on this trip because José's job had pulled him out of state at the last minute. Janelle had suggested they reschedule, but hadn't really wanted to, and was glad when José objected to cancelling their little getaway. She pulled the kids out of school for the day and drove two hours to one of their favorite places to be, at one of the best times of year to be there.

It was the week before Memorial Day, just ahead of the annual crush of visitors that came with the beginning of summer vacations. The weather was warm and there were far fewer people at the beach, especially on a weekday, than would be present once school was out. José not being there just meant they were guaranteed an extra trip to the beach this summer to make up for his absence, which was fine by everyone.

The kids were easy to handle. As easy as a laid-back thirteen-year-old boy and his tireless little sister could be, anyway. They seldom fought. When they did it was almost always due to Sarita trying to badger David into doing something lively, something that required running and shouting and getting scraped up, anything other than sitting around listening to music through headphones or playing video games, David's two favorite pastimes. Most of the time one or the other would relent before an argument flared up and José or Janelle had to intervene. They got along even better at the beach. They both loved to play in the water and made games of challenging the modest waves.

Sarita and David were both very good swimmers for their respective ages, with David even making it onto his school's swim team. His sister, naturally, was already hoping to emulate him and routinely begged him to take her to the public pool in their subdivision to teach her how to "get as good as you are." When the pools had reopened in March of that year, he obliged a few times, with Janelle and José even allowing them to go by themselves on one occasion. They respected the water as much as they loved it, and Janelle trusted them not to do anything too reckless. They knew better than to dive into the shallow end of the pool, or to drift too far out when they were at the coast.

On that day in May, the waves were coming in steadily, and were active enough to be fun, but not fierce enough for the beach patrol to raise the red flags warning of potentially dangerous currents. Instead, the yellow flags were up, which carried the more generic warning that just because the current was calm or moderate, "Do Not Assume Safe Water."

Janelle went out into the water with the kids when they first got to the beach, played with them some while also privately gauging the strength of the current. After several minutes she judged it to be safe—*No assuming here, thank you kindly, yellow flag*—and returned to the sand to do some sunbathing, leaving the kids to enjoy themselves in the Gulf.

It was Sarita's first time at the beach since she had turned nine and, perhaps more importantly, since David had turned thirteen and started looking like he had a few muscles. Not only was her mom a little more trusting of her in the water, but her parents also trusted her big brother to take care of her.

He'd gotten strong enough to lift her up from under her armpits and toss her into the air, letting her splash back into the water, with a pretty big assist from her jumping along with the throw to get as much height as possible. Mom was more open to them doing this than Dad was. They'd had a small argument over it when they went to the pool together in April, their mother only objecting to them doing it if too many other people were nearby because it wasn't fair to be jumping into other people's space, while Dad wasn't too keen on it overall, telling David, "Be careful with her" or "Not so high" after almost every toss.

Later, Sarita overheard Dad explain to Mom why it concerned him so much. When he was younger, he'd seen a couple of kids doing something similar at a lake, until the smaller kid landed on a large stone with a sharp edge under the water and cut his leg open.

"I'm just saying, things can happen," Dad had said.

"Yeah, but we don't take them to lakes," Mom replied. "I mean, you can see what's underwater at the pool, and they don't really have rocks like that at the beach."

"I know, I know." And, like a lot of their little arguments, at least the ones Sarita eavesdropped on, that was it. Short, simple, and easily resolved when one or the other conceded with "I know" or "I get it."

As much fun as it had been at the pool, Sarita couldn't wait for David to throw her into waves at the beach. They tested it out a couple of times while Mom was in the water with them, and couldn't get as much height and distance here as they could in the pool. It was harder for Sarita to get her footing for a jump in the loose sand and with the current constantly nudging her, and David was dealing with the same thing. The way it felt when she landed on the waves, however, more than made up for it. Hitting the water and immediately feeling it push her around was like being on a carnival ride she didn't have to wait in line for, especially when it was a nice, strong wave with a little bit of a monster's roar preceding it.

The lower height and shorter distance on the jump-throw probably made Mom more comfortable with them doing it here in the Gulf of Mexico, which Sarita still called "the ocean," no matter how often David or her parents corrected her, because what was the difference, really?

Knowing that David would tire out soon, Sarita tried to put more effort into the last jump she would make for a while, at least until he had a chance to rest, and she felt like she hung in the air for an extra second before joyfully screaming on her way back down. She crashed into a wave that was a bit weaker than expected, but that was okay. When she popped back up she wiped the salt water from her shut eyes with one hand and reached blindly for David with the other, as she always did.

This time, when David grasped her hand he also immediately pulled her forward. The water in her ears cleared enough for her to hear that the wave coming up behind her was stronger and larger than any other they'd felt at any of the other times they had been allowed to get in the water at Malaquite.

She opened her eyes in time to see how wide and anxious David's eyes were, and to see that even on a cloudy day this wave cast a shadow over most of him. Which meant its shadow covered all of her.

The undertow lifted her feet up, pulled her legs back. The wave slammed down onto both of them, but seemed to target her. She hit the sand, got the wind knocked out of her, bounced up about a foot or so, not high enough to break the surface and take a breath, and then the sea yanked her backward, out of her brother's grip, into depths she was not prepared to tread.

David's cry, a stunned yelp, came a half second ahead of his sister's, which was not the exhilarated shriek Janelle was accustomed to hearing, but had a scraping edge to it that immediately told her that her child was scared. The brevity of each cry brought Janelle to her feet.

She looked to the spot in the water where she'd last seen her children, where their voices had come from. She saw what appeared to be foam and turmoil on the surface, but no sign of Sarita or David. She looked around for them, hoping that they had just gotten farther away from her than she had realized, and that she would see them unharmed some distance to her left or right, heads obscured by swells that had grown in the last few minutes. In two seconds she went from worried to panicked as she didn't spot them, and they did not answer when she called out their names.

She ran into the water, and as she came to the edge, David popped up, a little too far out from shore for Janelle's liking but still close enough for him to stand. He wiped his face with both hands, and now Janelle noticed there was blood trickling from his nose. She continued running toward him.

"David, what happened? Where's your sister?"

"Mom?" David's eyes were still closed. "Mom, where's Sarita? Do you see Sarita?"

"What happened, David?" She took him gently by the shoulders to comfort him, but also to calm him enough for him to answer her.

"It was a wave," he said, talking fast, eyes open now, reddened by salt water, his head on a swivel like he was looking out for an attacker. "They weren't that bad I thought but then one big one came in and hit us harder than I thought it would and I hit the bottom and I was holding Sarita but I couldn't hold on. Where is she? Mom, do you see her?"

A knot of fear sprouted in Janelle's throat. She thought of undertow, rip currents, and everything else she'd been told to be mindful of when she was in the sea, and that she'd tried to teach her own children to respect. Her father had loved to surf in his birth city of Cape Town, in his youth, and was the reason Janelle had a Mami Wata tattoo on her leg, similar to one he'd had as well. He'd taught her, through various anecdotes, some more believable than others, to treat the water almost like it was alive and always watching, waiting for the moment when it could abduct you.

The worst thing she'd experienced in the waters of the Gulf of Mexico, however, was a jellyfish sting, and not even a particularly painful one. Nothing close to the monster waves, close encounters with sharks, or sudden riptides her father had warned her about. She realized now that this had made her complacent, willing to risk her kids being on their own with such dangers as though they didn't truly exist.

Janelle was almost chest-deep in the waves now. The tug and push of the current was rougher than it had been when she'd been in the water with her children. She felt the sand loosening and sifting away underfoot. Noticeable as it was, it did not feel strong enough to her to be unmanageable. Then again, she wasn't the scrawny child that Sarita was, and she hadn't seen the freak wave that David had described.

She hadn't seen it.

She hadn't been watching them.

Lord forgive me, please, please let her be okay. Help me find her, please.

Janelle looked up and down the beach. They had chosen this time of year to avoid the crowd and enjoy the space. A week later—even a few days—and they would have had dozens of people in the water with them, within speaking distance. They would have had an impromptu search party immediately available. Now they were virtually isolated.

A party of ten that had been drinking and listening to country music under a large tent twenty or thirty yards away was closest to them. A man and woman from that group had come to the edge of the water, looked toward Janelle and David with curiosity, but neither rushed to help. And what help could they provide now that wouldn't be too late? Sarita needn't have been under for very long for it to have been *too* long already.

No. NO. I'll find her and she'll be all right, she has to be.

Janelle looked for any sign of Sarita, called her name again. David joined her, calling for his sister. Janelle felt like she should be moving, running, rushing in one direction or another, feeling through the water for her daughter, but what if she went the wrong way? What if, in her rush, she went right past Sarita without noticing her? She had already let this happen—

Stop it!

—what if she made another mistake?

Stop it! Please, Lord in Heaven. Please help me find her.

One of the watchers from the shore shouted, "Hey, are you guys okay?"

"My daughter! Have any of you seen—"

"Mom, look!" David took hold of Janelle's hand and pulled her in the direction he was pointing. Janelle turned to see a large man in wet, dark clothing walking from the water—already in the knee-deep shallows. He was so pale he looked ghostly. In his arms, he carried a young girl's limp body.

To Janelle, everything in the world except for the man walking away with her daughter seemed to freeze and become a blur. It was impossible for her to have missed the man in the water before. He was too tall and broad for her not to have seen him, his attire too stark and out of place as well. Besides that, even if he were much smaller, even if he were a child, he was walking to the spot where Janelle had been lying on the beach. She would have run past him on her way into the water. She either could not have missed him, or he could not be there at this moment, holding Sarita, but she had, and there he was.

Sarita had no real memory of being saved, but she dreamt of it repeatedly throughout her life.

In her dreams the water is black, and she's so deep that there's more of it above her than there is below her. She hears something stirring beneath her, feels a plume of disturbed sand from the seabed push up toward her. She knows that something has come from under the ocean floor to get her. She swims harder now, no longer just trying to get to the surface, but trying to get away from whatever creature is coming from below, which surely has teeth and an empty stomach to fill.

When she feels hands, her heart goes light, like she doesn't have a real heart at all, but one of those heart-shaped helium balloons she and David gave Mom for Mother's Day just weeks before that day she almost drowned at Malaquite.

The hands are strong. The arms cradling her feel even stronger. The speed with which she is carried to the surface causes her to black out before she is brought out of the water.

For years she wonders how true to life this dream is.

By the time Janelle was running toward him, screaming for him to wait, screaming for others to help her, to stop him, the pale man had stooped to set Sarita down on Janelle's beach blanket. If he heard Janelle's cries, he did not show it. He didn't acknowledge her at all. He knelt over Sarita and placed his palm to her forehead as though checking for a fever. He watched and waited for a few seconds, then Sarita coughed, expelling water from her lungs. The man in black helped her turn to her side as Sarita vomited the seawater she'd swallowed. As the girl gulped in a deep breath, rubbed her eyes, and started to cry for her mother and brother, the pale man stood and walked away.

Janelle was close now, David right behind her, and their nearest neighbors from the party tent were making their way to see about the commotion as well. Janelle dropped to her knees and pulled Sarita to a seated position, rubbing her back.

"Oh, thank God. I'm here. Momma's here. It's okay. You're okay."

David caught up, saw that his sister was alive, and burst into tears. "I'm sorry, Sarita. I didn't mean to let go. I tried to hold on. I didn't mean to let go."

Janelle took David's hand, told her boy it wasn't his fault, then attended to Sarita, patting her back, trying to tap the remaining coughs out of her body. Janelle wanted to apologize for even bringing them here and letting them enter the water, but choked the words down before they could come out. They would do no good. Sarita had started to calm down and breathe easier already. David wiped his eyes and composed himself. Janelle knew she might start crying if she apologized now, and that would only agitate the children.

A woman from the tent approached Janelle and said, "Do you need help?"

"Momma, my throat hurts," Sarita said. "I got sand in my eyes."

Janelle smiled at the helpful neighbor and said, "We have water in our cooler. Could you please?"

The neighbor opened the cooler, grabbed a bottled water, and handed it to Janelle, then said, "Do you know that guy?" She nodded toward the pale man, who now walked past one of the large, grassy dunes that formed a barrier between the beach and the nearest road.

You see him, too, Janelle thought, but didn't say aloud, fearing she would sound crazy. She started to call out to him, then reconsidered, though she could not understand why.

"He saved my daughter," Janelle said to the woman, and the woman understood this as a sufficient answer. Janelle's mind, however, repeated the question—*Do you know that guy?*—and then rephrased it to lead her to the answer it sought. *Who was he?*

A guardian angel. Sarita's guardian angel.

Janelle put her hands together and thanked the Lord for hearing her prayers.

3

A mountainous headache had grown through Sarita's skull. Stronger than the medication the nurses plied her with, it was a ponderous pain that she thought she'd have to scale, rather than let pass. It magnified the phantom roar in her ears that had been with her since the day Angelo lifted her from the Gulf. Every doctor she'd seen about it told her it was a form of tinnitus, and each said it in a way that also told her they were somewhat unconvinced, but this was the only explanation that made sense to them. It sounded like waves in the distance, and was typically so faint she only noticed it when she was in a perfectly quiet room. Other times it was pronounced enough to make her feel like she was actually at the beach, and even *in* the water. She could shut her eyes and summon a floating sensation based on the sound alone. On rare occasions it could almost deafen her to what someone right beside her was saying. This was one of those occasions.

The combination of hangover and head trauma had done this to her, and she couldn't even sleep through it. The doctor told her it was safe—the deadly danger of post-concussion sleep was somewhat overstated, depending on certain conditions, it turned out—but Sarita couldn't do it. When she closed her eyes for longer than a second, she saw Angelo's bloody fist rising, and the unrecognizable horror it had made of her husband.

Four hours had passed since she had come to the hospital. She hadn't shed a tear yet. She felt the sting of grief behind her eyes, but couldn't push it forward. Hatred and confusion overwhelmed her heartache, held her sadness behind a giant wall. She thought herself combustible, certain to ignite if she didn't get up soon and do something.

Do what, though?

Correct this.

How?

Find him. Get answers. Kill him.

But that would not "correct" anything. It's not like she could trade Angelo's life for Frank's. At least, she didn't think so. Then again, how could she be sure of that, or anything? She'd had a guardian angel once upon a time, something that most would dismiss as an absurd fantasy. Even the ardently religious paid mere lip service to the concept. And, a short time ago, the guardian angel who had saved her life four times before had beaten her husband to death. There was nothing she could be sure of now.

The door to her room opened and Sarita's mother entered carrying a small cup of black coffee.

"Where's Dad?"

Her mother spoke, but the phantom roar drowned her out. Sarita clenched her teeth, shut her eyes, and waited for the noise to subside. Her mother, recognizing the signs of this, waited for Sarita to open her eyes again.

"Sorry," Sarita said. "Where's Dad at?"

"He's in the lobby, talking to David."

"David's here?" Sarita said, accepting the coffee and putting it on the tray beside her bed. Her brother was a Coast Guard rescue swimmer, stationed in Alaska. He'd wanted to come to the wedding, but duty called, and Sarita had more than understood.

"Talking to him on the phone," her mother said. "But once your father explained things, he said he'd get here as soon as he could."

Sarita nodded. Part of her wished they hadn't told David, though she knew that was unrealistic. She could picture her brother pacing in his apartment, fidgeting, tortured by helplessness, already convincing himself that this somehow wouldn't have happened had he been here. Those sentiments, irrational as they were, would intensify once he found out who had done this. *If* he found out. Perhaps it would be better not to tell him. But she needed to tell someone. There were only two people besides David who knew of her guardian angel and truly believed in him, but only one was here. Telling her wouldn't do much good, but it would be doing something, and she couldn't stand doing nothing.

Sarita took Janelle's hand. "Mom, I need to tell you something. I know who did this. I told the police I didn't know, but that was because they wouldn't have believed me."

She paused to register her mother's response. In Janelle's eyes, subtle uncertainty gave way to a dawning, disbelieving realization.

"It was Angelo," Sarita said. "Angelo killed Frank."

Janelle stared at her for a time, forgetting to blink. Then she shook her head as if to break from a trance. She stroked Sarita's hair and spoke in her gentlest tone, reserved for delivering news that was hard to hear. "Dear. Dear . . . you were struck in the head. You took a very hard hit, you might have even lost consciousness. And you'd just seen Frank . . . oh, Frank, I can't believe he's gone. I can't believe someone would do this. But whoever did—"

"Mom, I told you who it was."

"Sarita, you're confused. The hit to your head, the stress of it all. God, I can't imagine. I can hardly begin to believe it's real myself, and I wasn't even there. For you to have seen it must have—"

"Exactly. I *did* see it. I went through it. It was him."

"I'm sure he must have been there. He was there to save you, just like always. But your memories of it are all jumbled because of what happened."

"I'm not confused," Sarita said, though some distant part of her wondered if she might be. Her mother's explanation made more sense than what she was saying, what she remembered. It prompted fewer questions and was more palatable. The only problem was that it was a lie.

"Listen to me," she said. "Angelo did it. I watched him. He killed Frank right in front of me."

Janelle, who had been strong for her daughter since arriving at the hospital, refusing to grieve until later, now cried the tears that Sarita could not. "And he hurt you, too? That's impossible. He wouldn't do that."

"He didn't mean to. I was trying to protect Frank and—"

"Why would he kill Frank?" Janelle said, her voice climbing. Sarita held Janelle's hand tighter, and Janelle shut her eyes and nodded, calming herself. "Why would he kill him? Frank wasn't hurting you, was he?"

"That's not it," Sarita said, adding force to her voice that wasn't there before, all but commanding her mother not to question this. "Frank never ever hurt me. He never would."

"And neither would our Angelo."

Our Angelo. Sarita was reminded that Angelo wasn't hers alone. Janelle had seen him before Sarita had. Janelle had prayed for a miracle that day on the beach, and the pale man had appeared with her daughter in his arms, and soon after that Janelle had named him. In her eyes, she owed him a debt she could never repay. He'd saved Sarita then, and two more times since that Janelle knew of. He was as good as family.

"It just doesn't make sense," Janelle said. "It's . . . it's impossible. He's never done anything like this."

But he has. Would it make a difference now if Sarita told her mother about the fourth time that Angelo had saved her? The incident she'd kept from her mother. So far as Janelle knew, Angelo was incapable of violence. Sarita knew better. David did as well. Sarita doubted telling her mother what happened that night at the party would change her mind. More likely, Janelle would take it as evidence that their Angelo must have known something about Frank that Sarita refused to consider.

Sarita lay back in bed and looked to the ceiling, the senselessness of the argument striking and exhausting her.

Janelle brought the guest chair closer to Sarita's bedside and sat down. "I just think maybe you're . . ." She shut her eyes, took a deep breath, and started again. "No, I'm wrong. I'm sorry. Everything you've dealt with tonight, and then to hear me doubting you. I don't know what's wrong with me. I believe you. I promise I do. If you say that's what happened, that Angelo did it, then that's what must have happened."

Sarita looked at her mother. Her throat tightened and ached, waiting for her to weep, but the tears remained locked behind her eyes. Her mother cried enough for the both of them. Sarita hugged her tight, like she was trying to pass some of her strength into her mother.

"Thanks, Momma."

"I'm so sorry."

"It's okay."

"No, no it's not." Janelle pulled back to hold her daughter's face, look her in the eye. "I can't understand how this could have happened, tonight of all nights, to my baby girl. Oh God, to Frank. His poor mother. His *mothers*. Oh God, why?"

Sarita pulled her mother close again, her body trembling as, at last, a thin stream of tears broke free.

4

Sarita was seventeen the second time Angelo saved her life. She was sitting in Mrs. Hughes's biology class. A test paper full of unread questions sat on her desk. She'd awakened that morning to a glowing pain on the right side of her abdomen that had grown to the point that it hurt just to hold her pencil.

Through most of the morning she managed to ignore the pain, but it intensified in the last half hour, blossoming from fist sized into something that occupied most of her torso. A frothing, bottomless nausea had settled in as well, and she wondered at last if she should go to the nurse's office. Her period ought to be two weeks away, and never induced pain like this, so that removed it from culpability. She had skipped breakfast, lunch was an hour away, and no one else in the family had complained of stomachaches this morning before Tori picked her up to take her to school, so she didn't think it was something she'd eaten. The fear of this being morning sickness—that she was pregnant—flashed through her head, but she hadn't had sex in six months, since her farewell fling with her ex, before he moved with his Air Force parents to Germany. Surely pregnancy symptoms would have arrived before now, wouldn't they? If not that, what else could it be? A stomach flu?

To her left, beyond the classroom window, something caught her eye.

She looked out, and for a moment there was no pain, no classroom or desk or test or anything in the world other than the wan, white-haired man looking back at her.

Underneath a gray sky and the darker shadow of a large tree, amidst relentless sheets of rain, stood a man she recognized only through her dreams and her mother's descriptions. Alone in the downpour, seemingly untouched by it, he did not move, and gave no indication that he knew Sarita could see him. He only stared ahead, and at a distance of fifty yards or more she couldn't see that he was looking at her, but she nonetheless knew.

Her mother had told her the story of her guardian angel a hundred times. Janelle had written poems and prayers about the tall, fair-skinned man she had named simply "Angelo." Sarita found the story harder to believe as she got older, and had asked David more than once to confirm it, but he wouldn't give her a direct answer, not wanting to speak of the day his little sister almost drowned on his watch. The only thing harder to believe than the idea that guardian angels were real was the possibility that her mother had made the story up for no discernible reason. Still, prior to seeing Angelo for herself, Sarita had begun to think the story was largely embellished, that her dreams were more the product of her mother's multiple retellings of said story than of something that actually happened to her.

Some heroic stranger must have pulled her from the water, sure, but he was no mysterious angel. Just a Good Samaritan who left the scene so soon to avoid extra attention. YouTube, the 'Gram, and more were full of videos of such unsung, random heroes who fled immediately, shunning any attempt to turn them into a public figure, and she was pretty sure at least half of those clips were genuine.

Seeing Angelo and immediately recognizing him put an end to her disbelief in him so abruptly she felt like she'd crashed into a building. Not only did she see him and know that he was a not a figment of her imagination, she knew why he was there. She bolted up from her desk, almost knocking it over.

"I have to go to the hospital," she said to Mrs. Hughes, then turned to Tori, seated two rows over, and said, "I have to go *right now*."

Ignoring the gazes of her classmates, and Mrs. Hughes's questions about what was wrong and whether she was okay, Sarita walked out of the classroom while imploring Tori to take her to the hospital. Tori shook free of the surprise caused by Sarita's outburst and followed her friend out the door.

Less than an hour later, Sarita was in an operating room having her appendix removed. The surgeon would later tell her parents that things might have been considerably worse had she waited even another half hour before coming to the emergency room.

Tori Weiss was Sarita's closest friend from the first day of first grade, when Sarita shared her crayons after Tori forgot to bring hers, through nearly their last year of college. They both played softball, loved the same rappers, and weren't the type to cry at movies, except for that one about the dog who still waited for his owner at the railway station well after the man had died. Even after drifting apart somewhat in more recent years, Tori had been Sarita's only choice for maid of honor. Tori had once helped save her friend's life, simply by listening to her, trusting and not questioning her when she said she needed a ride to the emergency room. Later, listening to Sarita, believing in her, would have a small hand in saving Tori's life.

This bond, however, was not what led Tori to intuit that something awful had happened when she saw the name Janelle Bardales pop up on her vibrating phone in the early hours the morning after the wedding.

The call itself had not awakened her. Her eyes had opened just seconds before, preceded by a hastening of her heartbeat that she'd felt even before waking.

She answered the call coming from the woman she had referred to as her "Bonus Mom"—barely in jest—since grade school, whose number Tori had saved in every phone she'd ever owned.

"Hello."

"Tori," Janelle said, "I'm sorry if I woke you up. But . . . I'm sorry . . . I've just been calling around because I don't want people to hear this some other way. You shouldn't hear it from . . ."

Pain snipped her voice. Emotional, but it may as well have been physical. May as well have been pincers digging through her esophagus.

"Is Sarita okay?" Tori started to ask, then stopped herself dead and said in an almost mesmerized, flattened tone, "It's about Frank."

"Oh, God, you heard already?"

"No, I just . . ."

I just knew. Which was true. Sometimes, information—*knowledge*—just came to her, although this occasion would prove another reminder that she had far more work, studying, and practice ahead of her if she was going to learn how to acquire such insight in time for it to do any good.

They kept very few secrets from each other, and after her surgery, Sarita felt an obligation to tell Tori about her guardian angel. Tori buried her skepticism, as well as a modicum of curiosity, underneath understanding and never let it show in front of Sarita. Privately, she wondered what must have come over Sarita to have invented—or hallucinated—such a story. In her quietest moments, she allowed herself to wonder what it would mean—for reality, for the world as she knew it so far, everything—for Sarita's guardian to be real. Ultimately, she decided that ascertaining Sarita's motivations or trying to determine how much truth there could possibly be to "Angelo's" existence didn't matter. Her friend needed to believe in her angel to help her process her brush with mortality, and Tori didn't think it was her place to question why.

Four years later, on Halloween night, Tori saw Angelo for herself, and discovered it was her place to question everything she thought she knew.

Sixth Street in Austin, on a Saturday night, is typically teeming with bar hoppers. Halloween night invites larger crowds. That year, Halloween fell on a Saturday, and there were sections of Sixth Street so choked with costumed revelers it took twenty minutes to walk two blocks. There were people dressed in meticulously crafted replications of popular characters, others wearing whatever outfit or mask was left on a store shelf that morning, still more who cobbled something together out of whatever they found on a Goodwill rack, and a subpopulation of fit college boys dressed as whatever allowed them to show off their arms, pecs, and six-packs. Then there were those like Sarita and Tori who eschewed costumes. In bar after bar, at least one man would approach Tori and ask where her Halloween spirit was, and she always answered that this year she decided to go out as Someone Dressed Comfortably.

They had met up with two friends and former softball teammates from high school who made the drive up to Austin from San Marcos, where they went to Texas State University. Deedra and Candace consumed alcohol like it was oxygen and held their liquor like a cask, far outpacing Tori, though Sarita fared a bit better. Shortly after midnight, the two Texas State girls started pitching the idea of leaving the Sixth Street strip to attend a house party in West Lake Hills twenty minutes away, where they could drink for free. Sarita seemed agreeable to it, but Tori was enjoying herself where she was.

She liked to dance and felt more comfortable doing so in the low lighting of a club or bar than at a house party. She had also picked up two numbers already tonight. The first was from a white guy from Dallas who was allegedly dressed as George Clooney. He looked nothing like the actor, but was attractive in his own right and wore his suit well. The other phone number was from a Black guy dressed as Frederick Douglass, which Tori admired for the hair commitment alone. She looked forward to seeing who else she might meet on the strip tonight, but the other girls outvoted her. The party was to be their next stop.

Sarita had hailed a ride via an app on her phone, and the driver waited for them on one of the side streets perpendicular to the pedestrian-clogged strip. Candace and Deedra entered the tidy white minivan and Tori was going to follow them in when a hand snapped shut around her wrist.

Sarita's grip was fierce, almost aggressive. She had grabbed Tori without looking, her head turned back toward Sixth Street. Tori, shorter than her friend, had to lean forward to look past Sarita and see what had seized her attention.

Under the moonless night, seemingly untouched by the myriad artificial lights of the strip, Angelo's ice-white skin was ethereal, almost translucent. A thick haze smothering a lightly flayed body. Despite this, and despite his size, Tori might have thought her eyes were playing tricks and that he was simply another partier in costume were he not staring at Sarita, and if the crowds were not passing hurriedly around him, maintaining fair space and avoiding any chance of eye contact with him, as though they knew he was a living omen. Perhaps they did know on some primal level, but were unconscious of it. No such shadow of ignorance hid Tori from her realization. Nonetheless, hoping to hear a refutation, she asked Sarita, "Is that him?"

Sarita relaxed her grip on Tori's wrist and said, "I can't go." Sufficient confirmation.

"Hey," Deedra said from inside the van. "What's wrong?"

"I don't think we should go to that party," Tori said.

"Oh, come on. I already texted Bryce to say we're on our way."

"Seriously. I think we should just stay here."

Candace sighed. "You know you're not tied to us. If you guys really want to stay, it's fine. Just stay."

"But I told Bryce specifically about Tori," Deedra said to Candace quietly, as if Tori were in the next room and not within a whisper's earshot.

"Well, you shouldn't have done that," Candace said. Tori looked at them, stupefied. Could they not see the distress Sarita was in? Had they not heard Tori say she was serious? Didn't they understand?

It occurred to her that no, they did not understand. They did not see Sarita's genuine distress, and had no cause to believe the situation was serious. They held their liquor well, but they were still miles beyond sober. Even if they had been clearheaded, the nature of the situation might have escaped them as it would have escaped almost anyone. As it would have escaped Tori had she not seen Sarita in this state once before. There was no way she could explain this to them. No chance that they would believe her. They were friends, but not close enough to take her at her word that harbingers and angels were real. Still, if there was a real danger in going to the party, she had to try.

"Listen, I think something bad is going to happen."

"We're going to go on ahead," Candace said.

"I seriously don't think you should. Listen—"

"We'll be fine. We know everybody there. I'll text you the address if you two want to catch up. And if not, we'll catch up later. We'll call you for brunch tomorrow or something."

The driver, silent and patient through all of this, looked in the rearview mirror and asked, "Are you ready?"

"We're ready," Deedra said. The driver pushed the button on his armrest to close the van's automated sliding door. Tori stood there, mouth slacked, unsure of what to do or say. *What if it's not even about them,* she thought. *Last time, Sarita had to go to the emergency room. What if you're wasting time talking to Deedra and Candace when you should be checking on Sarita, or calling an ambulance for her?*

Deedra and Candace waved goodbye through the van window as it pulled away from the curb and drove down the road. Tori noticed now that Sarita was moving back toward Sixth Street, toward the figure in black who had turned away from her as soon as the van door closed.

"Hey," Sarita called after him. "Hey!"

Tori caught up to her. "Sarita, how are you feeling? Are you sick? I think we should get you to a doctor, just in case."

Not hearing her, Sarita moved forward into the crowd. While it had parted for Angelo, the mass of people proved more difficult for Sarita and Tori to move through. Tori took her friend's hand.

"Sarita!"

"What?"

"We need to get you to the hospital."

Sarita looked at her like she'd said something singularly foolish. "What?"

"The last time you saw him you ended up needing surgery. You barely got to the hospital in time."

"That's not it. I feel fine, it's not like last time. That's not what he was warning me about."

"Then what is it?"

Sarita's voice rose like she was speaking to be heard above a storm. "I don't know."

"Well, what do you think—"

"I. Don't. Know. He doesn't fucking talk to me, Tori. He just shows up and then he's gone." She shook her head, squeezed Tori's hand, which Tori knew was her way of apologizing. "I think if it was about me being sick again he would have shown up earlier. I think. I can't know for sure. But he walked away after Candace and Deedra left. I think I just wasn't supposed to go with . . . them. Shit."

She pulled her phone from her purse and called Deedra.

"Something's going to happen to them?" Tori said.

"I think something happens at that party. Maybe." A couple of seconds later she was leaving Deedra a message urging her to call back. When Candace didn't answer either, she left her the same voice message, followed by text messages. *CALL ME ASAP!*

"I shouldn't have let them leave," Tori said.

"There wasn't anything you could've done. What were you going to tell them?"

"I don't know. I could have told them something."

"Shit . . . maybe we should go after them."

"You think?"

Sarita shrugged, but was already pulling up a different rideshare app on her phone and requesting a driver. "Come on. Maybe we can catch up, and if he shows up again I can point him out to them. I mean, you knew as soon as you saw him, right? You *knew*."

"Yeah," Tori said, almost like she hadn't been listening, too distracted by a blossoming realization.

Sarita took Tori's hand like her friend was a child who might wander off in a department store, and walked her back to the rideshare pickup area that Candace and Deedra had just departed from.

A black car waited for them. Tori tried to dispel the idea of it being an omen, but only managed to lose it in the mob of thoughts turning her brain into a confined space and threatening to choke out all of the oxygen, placing her on the brink of passing out. Angelo's supernaturality being self-evident seemed to have split into multiple considerations: Was it just the sight of him? Did he tap into a different sense she didn't know she had? If so, was that now permanently activated? Were there more like him around that she should be seeing, then? How could there not be?

Regarding the attempt to catch up to Dee and Candace, Tori couldn't help but think of a comedian who suggested that there should be a "reckless driver" option for rideshare services. For when you cared less about making sure you reached your destination safely than you did about getting there as quickly as possible—even if it meant risking never getting there at all. It was a silly thing to think of now, and inappropriate, yet somehow fitting as well. Long gone were the days, if they ever existed, of hopping into a cab, telling the driver, "Follow that car" and "Step on it!" She wished she could give those orders to the driver now and not have him look back at her like she'd asked him to run an old woman down at a crosswalk.

The urgency of the situation continued to build with each second that passed without a response from the girls. Tori shook her phone out as though it were holding back the messages she wanted to see, keeping them to itself just to torment her.

As they rounded the hill up to the house hosting the party and saw tendrils of smoke drifting like spirits in front of the full, large moon, the heat of their urgency disappeared, replaced by a cold so deep it was closer to pure pain, a bite and pull from something strong enough to rip you in half.

The white van never made it to the house. It met almost head-on with a speeding roadster that was coming downhill in the wrong lane. The van's driver swerved to dodge; the van was clipped nonetheless, then skidded off the road, rolling four times on its way down the embankment. Deedra died upon impact, thankfully spared from the ensuing fire. The driver died from his injuries shortly after reaching the hospital. Candace had been ejected from the vehicle through a side window. With extensive rehabilitation she regained most of her speech and motor skills two years later, though she slurred her words now and lived with chronic back pain and memory deficits. She got a tattoo of Deedra's initials enclosed in rose petals on her arm, the letters rendered as thorny vines. After her recovery, she dedicated herself to volunteer work with other accident victims.

Less than a month after the crash, before the semester was over and with just eighteen credits left before earning her bachelor's degree, Tori abandoned school. Remorse over not keeping the girls out of the van had stricken her with insomnia and illness for days. She couldn't open a textbook or any of her notepads to study. Something other than guilt left her unable to concentrate on coursework, however. A thick cloud of questions and curiosity had filled her mind.

Reality had been altered. Or it had been shapeless all along and she was seeing it now for the first time. She could hardly comprehend how Sarita had lived with this knowledge for so long. Accepted it and went on with her life as though it were normal.

In less than a week Tori gave up trying to force-fit Angelo's existence into the simple "facts" and "truths" she'd known up until she'd seen him. His appearance had not been a coincidence, he was not some stranger Sarita had mistaken for someone else, and he was not dismissible. Her heart told her that, and most of her brain as well, even if a stubborn portion of it had tried to cling to its notions of "logic" like a zealot.

"Even a genius knows less than there is to know," her grandmother had once told her, an axiom she had invented to keep her sharp-minded granddaughter humble and open-minded as she entered college. Tori wished her grandmother were alive today so she could tell her that she now had a small idea of how impossibly immense the unknown was, how flexible and alterable reality and nature were.

Then again, maybe she could tell her still. Maybe her grandmother could hear her if she simply spoke the words aloud, or said them just the right way. Who could say she couldn't? Angels and harbingers existed. What other impossibilities were real as well?

5

It wasn't the first funeral Sarita ever attended, but it was the first to make her contemplate the futility of the exercise. The ritualism and prayers, the formalized, communal engagement with sadness. Under these circumstances, especially, the service felt aimless. The ceremony would proffer no closure. The fellowship would assuage no grief, pacify no anger. The man in the closed casket to be lowered into the earth was in no way whole. His body was divorced from its spirit, and separated even from part of itself, though this last morbid fact was not fully understood by most of the mourners. They could only presume that his face was damaged too badly for an open casket to be suitable, not that it had been pulverized into the floor of the hotel suite. Not only was Sarita aware of this, she had *seen* it. Angelo's fists had permanently pressed the remains of Frank's head into her mind. She was the sole witness to it, and now here she was, expected to act as though everyone else's mourning was in any way comparable to hers.

Sarita knew that this was a cold viewpoint to have of Frank's funeral, but retreating into rationalism gave her an inch of refuge. It allowed her to cope with the unspoken accusations beamed at her by most of Frank's relatives, the rest of the Stallworth family. For once, the phantom wave in her ears proved useful. It was loud enough today to muffle everyone's words.

She could make out what they were saying, but was spared sharpness she knew must be in their tones as they tried to commiserate with her. Still, they could only mask the anger and suspicion in their eyes so much. Had she heard it in their voices, too, she might have snapped.

Only Uncle Everett had approached her with genuine warmth, actually hugged her instead of just leaning in to touch shoulders and pat her back before all but shoving her away, like she was a knowing, callous carrier of death itself.

Had her emotions reigned, Sarita might have shouted at one of the Stallworths, or all of them. His biological mother, Harrah, would have received the brunt of it. She had approached Sarita wearing a fixed scowl and with ire smoldering in her eyes. They did not hug, only shook hands, and even at that simple touch Harrah had stiffened and held back, as though holding an insect someone had forced into her hand.

You're the worst of them all, Sarita thought, and fought not to say. *You couldn't even show up for his best day.*

His best day.

Well, it *had* been . . .

Sarita thought of the day he proposed. Would Frank consider that his new best day? Sarita remembered it as a great one, at minimum. Harrah had actually been there for that, and had been pleasant to be around. She had gasped almost as loud as Sarita when Frank produced the ring box and dropped to a knee. In fact, Everett was the only one of the Stallworths in attendance at the party that evening—which Frank had told everyone was just a celebration of his well-deserved promotion at work—who knew ahead of time what Frank planned to do.

Sarita had expected Harrah to take offense to being kept out of the loop and the spotlight, and for her to barely conceal her displeasure. At the baptism for one of Frank's younger cousins, for instance, Harrah had wanted to hold the baby more than the child's own mother did, and went out of her way to say how hurt and insulted she felt when the boy's father told her, "Can you act like it ain't your show one goddamn time?" Frank had actually been the one to talk her down and console her, then, as even Everett's patience for her was thin enough to dodge raindrops on that occasion. Frank had brought her aside, said something, coaxed a laugh out of her, then walked her back into the fold. Sarita never asked what he told her—she felt like it wasn't her business—but right now it felt like something that could connect them. Something Sarita should be able to ask of her mother-in-law.

You remember that time at the baptism? What did Frank tell you?

That could open the door to discuss other stories, allow them to dwell on anything other than Frank being gone, and how he met his end. They could share something close to a smile while reminiscing. There was zero chance of that happening, however, with Harrah looking at Sarita like she'd shown up in clothes soaked with Frank's blood, dragging the cudgel she'd have needed to kill him.

The worst part about reading accusation in Harrah's eyes was knowing that she wasn't entirely wrong.

The harbor of rationalism demanded Sarita be understanding of the hate and suspicion flowing in her direction. She tried to be less judgmental of the Stallworths. They squinted when they looked in her direction, as if they could peer through her lies and press a confession out of her if they concentrated hard enough. Sarita tried not to blame their suspicions on simple bigotry, though it was inevitable that at least a few of these individuals had been assured that something like this would happen as soon as they heard that Frank was engaged to a girl that was both Black *and* Mexican.

Sarita's sober, stoic mind, unimpaired by the despondence and fury and fault she wanted to envelop herself in, told her she could only be so angry with Frank's family. It made sense for them to suspect of her some level of wrongdoing, even if they had no concrete reasoning for their distrust. She *was* withholding information from them, just as she had withheld information from the detectives assigned to Frank's case. They wouldn't have believed anything she told them, but that fact only amounted to one more relevant item that she knew and wasn't sharing with anyone who didn't already know of Angelo.

And, though she wanted to believe herself blameless, Sarita knew that she was the catalyst for what had befallen her husband.

It was good to be indoors and secluded now, with the service and reception finished, away from the acidic, peeling brightness of the day, to say nothing of the watchful in-laws. Clouds would have been welcome. Gray days had always made Sarita feel serenely unnoticeable, like she was one small piece of a massive, washed-out camouflage pattern. The sky today had instead been clear, and the temperature warm for late October, even by South Texas standards. A cold front was expected next week on the heels of an approaching two-day storm that partially motivated the decision to schedule Frank's funeral sooner than later. Many people had already been in town for the wedding, as well. No sense in pushing the service too far out. It was a practical decision that did not take the deceased into account at all, because the deceased had no feelings to account for. A practical decision that, to Sarita, only reinforced the futility of it all.

She could not know if Frank was now a ghost, or in Heaven, or in some other state of existence that she was no more aware of than the reason for his murder. She was confident, though, that wherever he was, nothing about today's rites and collective mourning impacted him in any material way. None of it would help him "move on" or find peace or find the road to his ultimate destination. None of it mattered.

All that mattered was summoning Angelo so he could answer for his crime.

Years before, after the incident at the party, and after she'd told her family she was going to travel the country, David had given her a small black .380 as a birthday present, told her to be careful with it, but unafraid of it. She'd left it home during her excursion, not wanting to be bothered with learning the gun laws in each state she traveled to, and not seeing any use for it given the personalized superweapon that followed her everywhere she went, but she held the gun by her side now as she stared at herself in the bathroom mirror. There was no ritual she knew of for conjuring her angel, and she didn't want to ask Tori about it, because Tori would just try to talk her out of it. She wished she could just speak his name a certain number of times, light a certain number of candles, wait a certain number of hours. Something basic. None of that would bring him to her, though. Save for the one horrible exception of her wedding night, Angelo only appeared when she was in mortal peril.

She put the loaded gun to her head and waited for him to come to her. She told herself she wasn't bluffing, said it aloud a few times hoping he would hear her. She even considered squeezing the trigger and relying on an angel being faster than a bullet, or able to use divine means to save her, but she wasn't quite ready to risk that. When he failed to show after several minutes, she put the gun down, went to her bedroom, and opened her laptop.

She couldn't be the only person to have experienced something like this, could she? Someone else out there must have their own story of a guardian angel to share. And maybe a story of one that went too far. One that misread a threat, hurt someone they shouldn't have. Worse. Killed someone. She knew she'd have to wade through dozens if not hundreds of pages of search results containing nonsense and frivolity before she found something authentic, if she found anything at all. It wasn't ideal, but it was a starting point, and she wasn't going to get any more sleep tonight than she had the last few nights anyway. Might as well try to make some use of her time. Then, if her search failed to produce anything, in the morning she'd call Tori to see what she already knew, or could find out, about angels, or things disguised as angels.

6

She was, to her followers, The Founder. To the few in her inner circle, and still fewer who knew her before she created her religion, her name was Cela.

The title that fit her best, however, was The Godmaker, and her centuries-long gestating plan to save civilization from human-borne crises had been a few years or less from culmination before Frank Stallworth's early demise.

Frank Stallworth. "The Devil of Devils," as she referred to him. As her followers came to know him, just as they knew Sarita Bardales as "The Godbride," or "The Martyred Mother."

Now, with Frank having been killed ahead of schedule, Sarita might never become The Martyred Mother. What, then, would become of the work Cela had devoted much of her extended, extraordinary life to?

Already, amidst much rejoicing at The Devil's death, there were whispers of The Founder's folly, and more concerning suggestions. Not merely her congregants, but the very priests she had handpicked and elevated privately alleged that her great, undone prophecy might not be an innocent mistake. They gossiped like they were less afraid of her hearing them—which she could—than they were of her deliberately misleading them.

What if she had, all along, been a false prophet, they wondered? A devil in secret?

How they could reconcile this with the fact that the religion would not exist without her, who could say? She had known and capitalized on the irrationalism of faith. That was part of what gave it such strength. It did not have to make sense to them that their Founder might also somehow be the ultimate heretic. They needed only to believe it—to *want* to believe it. Just as they had, all along, believed that Cela's doomsday prophecies could not be true.

And now, the one she had considered most faithful to her had submitted to impulse at best, conspired against her at worst, to make a liar of her.

The Devil of Devils was dead, killed by Sarita's own guardian.

News of his destruction reached Cela's congregation through a magnificent psychic light that inspired a spontaneous mass led by the high priest who nurtured their optimism, bolstered it through hymns he wrote that espoused the power of prayer to avert destiny. Now, it appeared, their steadfast devotion and pleas for The Martyred Mother to be spared had fallen on merciful ears.

The Godbride would live, her martyrdom prevented.

Now nothing would impede Sarita's union with The Viscount.

Their child, The Messiah, would not die in Sarita's womb with her. He would be born, and be the living peace, harmony incarnate who would enlighten humans so they could live well among the unliving.

And the prophetess Cela's visions were, at minimum, fallible.

So her flock now believed.

How many empires formed and fell in the time of Cela's planning, forecasting, and maneuvering of parts into places where they could interlock with other moving parts generations from being born? She contended with thousands of contingencies and adjusted to each accordingly. She lost her most trusted advisor—the old Greek who was, truly, her *sole* advisor—to self-administered excommunication. Without the one she now only thought of as "The Exile," she had to carry the burden of her visions alone. Yes, she had recruited others who developed limited predictive abilities, but nothing approaching what she and The Exile possessed. Still, she endured, and never strayed. Most impressively, The Godmaker had done it all without being suspected by her believers.

Now, all her work was undone at near zero hour by one of its most essential agents. And the fools comprising her flock thought it was a blessing. It was not fair for her to be as upset with them for this as she was. None of them—none who remained within the fold, at least—were privy to her visions of the future, and none knew why it was essential for Sarita and her unborn child to be killed by The Devil of Devils.

That Frank Stallworth was dead was trouble enough. The way he died further undermined Cela's standing. Sarita's "guardian angel" had crushed his skull in an unremarkable room of a quasi-metropolitan hotel. An ignominious place for a religion's supreme enemy to die. Better a filthy little motel in a beaten-down town, or an alley littered with the detritus of the city. She could spin poetry deserving of prophecy and parables out of that. Or, of course, out of a death in a grander or symbolically sound location. Anywhere from a palatial cathedral to a dank cave would have been better. The hotel room was banal and inadequate. It made Cela's Devil appear pathetic, which she had already made him out to be, albeit in a crucially different way. Her Devil—*their* Devil—was meant to be petty but cunning, and brave in his own foolhardy manner, and therefore still threatening. Not fragile. Not inconsequential.

Had she the luxury of time, she could have spent weeks, months, or even years raging at this unforeseen turn, her failure to have a contingency in place for such an occurrence, and at the audacity of figureheads she had ordained quietly questioning her integrity and decrees. Had she less self-control she would be chewing a prelate's heart at the moment, while forcing the others to select which of them would be next. She would flush The Exile from his hiding place, kill him, and display his head on a stake for setting an example of defiance. The exigency of the situation demanded she adapt and address immediate concerns, instead. When she sensed The Devil's death—too late to intervene safely or effectively—her mind went into motion, not just weighing how to react, but how to steer everyone else's reactions. It was never too late to regain control.

The believers were calling it a miracle. They had been ready to write and sing new hymns to celebrate the death of Cela's carefully crafted Devil. She needed to remind them that the threat had not passed. This new, unanticipated "miracle" might have brought them closer to their messiah than any of the prior prophecies deemed possible, but the threat could live on.

Cela was The Godmaker, but also The Devilmaker. The latter role was more crucial than the former with respect to transforming a faith into an uprising, a flock to turn into an army. Divine fury demands a galvanizing target.

Fortunately, her designated Devil was survived by a suitable—arguably superior—successor. His mother.

Harrah Stallworth would be on the road soon. Driving into as much isolation and desert as she could stand. Hardly the equivalent of Cela's own venture into the Bayuda ages prior, but Cela was confident she could replicate the most pivotal result of her excursion in a condensed timeframe for Harrah.

She would plant the seeds for Harrah's infernal enlightenments by ensuring Harrah saw her in places that reminded her of what she was fleeing from.

7

I can't believe I touched her hand, Harrah thought. It was one day after the funeral for her only child. His "homegoing" service the preacher kept calling it, and it had taken enough restraint to bind a storm for Harrah not to challenge the man, ask whether Frankie was going to be waiting for her then, home and whole and healthy, when she got back to her house. No? Then stop fucking calling it that. Frankie wasn't going "home." He wasn't even "going" anywhere. He was gone already. And that girl, Sarita, had probably killed him, or at minimum had a hand in it.

And I touched—shook—_that girl's hand. If she really did it, or had any part in it, I can't ever be forgiven for that. If God'll forgive me for it, I don't deserve it._

It just gave her one more reason to escape everything. Those closest to her knew this and understood. They hugged her, said they would keep praying for her while she was gone, told her they'd see her in a few days. People on the periphery, who mistakenly thought they had a foot inside her inner circle, judged her for it.

"You're really going to leave?" one of her aunts said to her. The one who came down from Idaho, who she hadn't spoken to in almost twenty years.

"Let her be," Harrah's uncle, Everett, had said to his sister.

"I just don't see how—"

"You don't have to see how. It ain't you that's going through it."

Her aunt kept the rest of her objections to herself, though Harrah still picked up on them as though she were a mind reader. How could she leave the day after the funeral? How could leaving her family and friends behind to be alone—to go to a Native casino, no less—be anything but selfish and cold?

Well, just like Uncle Everett said, anybody who wasn't going through it didn't have to understand. The only thing Harrah needed any of them to understand was that if they didn't like it, they could tell it to each other, write it in a diary, or, hell, put it online to tell the world about it, do one of those "Am I the Asshole" posts, as long as they didn't bring it her way.

The Lucky Eagle Casino in Eagle Pass was about a two-and-a-half-hour drive from Harrah's part of San Antonio. One hundred fifty miles away from the well-wishes, the forlorn faces, the awkward attempts to lighten the mood from her one cousin who would combust if he stayed serious for too long. Away from the Bible-thumpers who wanted to tell her Frankie was in a better place. Away from certain other relatives who used to offer to make her ex-husband, Don, pay for leaving her. "And that tramp he married, too," they would say of Frankie's stepmother, Misty.

That last group—which included the aforementioned aunt's son, Joey, and his favorite cousins—was the one Harrah needed to get away from the most. If she stuck around, they would tell her things she shouldn't hear—but wanted to hear—about Sarita Bardales.

That girl ain't telling us everything. She's hiding something. Just give us the word. We'll get it out of her and then some. Never liked her anyway. Always had a feeling about her.

Harrah couldn't trust herself around that, and knew it days before the funeral. She needed a distraction, or else she might give in to temptation. She would want to believe Joey when he brought up the bikers he supposedly knew, who allegedly owed him a favor, who he swore had basically made him an honorary member of their club. Harrah could imagine him promising that his biker buddies could snatch Sarita from her house, throw her in a trunk—presumably from a rented vehicle—and have her spilling her guts at gunpoint near a riverbank before the day was over. Even though she would know he was bullshitting her as much as himself, she might ask him to put in a phone call anyway, provided Everett didn't overhear and talk them both out of doing anything stupid.

Already on the road, Harrah made herself think of the back half of the drive to the Lucky Eagle, her favorite part. Flat and remote, especially that forty-mile stretch of Farm Road 481. There were areas out there where you could look so far to the right or left that the horizon might hypnotize you. Whisper in your head, *Try and chase me. See if you can catch me.* The only thing that sullied that part of the drive was seeing Border Patrol vehicles and passing the checkpoint. It made her wonder what kind of desperate souls would brave all that sun and nothing to try to break into a place where they were being waited on and watched for anyway. How hard could it be where you were from for you to risk getting found and arrested by the patrol out here, or worse, getting found by no one at all after you run out of food or water, and end up dinner for coyotes and vultures?

Before getting to Farm Road 481, however, something that Harrah had forgotten about made the first leg of the drive—through Highway 90—difficult for her. There were four roadside cemeteries along the highway. She did not remember this until she passed the first one, just outside of San Antonio. Had she thought of this ahead of time, she'd have picked an alternate route. As it was, when she passed that first cemetery, it served as an instant reminder that she'd buried her boy so recently the dirt smell was still fresh in her nostrils. The only way to keep from thinking of Frankie's name etched into the tombstone she'd have to buy for him was to picture that goddamned girl's name there instead.

SARITA.

Written in barbed, burning letters. Devil red. The color of stones in Hell. The color of the dress worn by a woman that Harrah now saw standing alone in the cemetery, facing a large sculpture of an angel, so that it looked like the inflexible, gray wings sprouted from her shoulders.

Harrah barely caught a glimpse of the woman just as the cemetery was exiting her periphery, and wondered how she could have initially missed her given how vividly she pictured her now that she was out of sight. This was supplanted by her wonder at having such a distinct mental image of someone she'd seen so briefly she could have mistaken them for a mirage. A strange projection of her grief. Somehow that made more sense the longer she thought of it. It was easier to believe that the woman had slipped free from Harrah's brain to appear before her eyes, and represented something she'd been suppressing.

Something. As if there were a field of candidates and not one thing, and only one, that she was trying to keep trapped and buried.

Buried. Damn it, she couldn't wait to get to the casino.

The woman in the cemetery represented the thing she was driving away from. The hard reality that she distantly hoped to escape forever. Not in the sense of never returning, but in the sense of returning to an altered world. She would immerse herself in lights and booze and games, and hopefully a little sex if she caught eyes with the right man, and then come back home in a few days to see her Frankie waiting at the door, wondering where she'd been. All of this pain and horror would prove to have been an uncannily realistic nightmare, and she'd never give another thought to how she was ever convinced it had actually happened.

The woman in the cemetery was the antithesis of this fantasy. She was the undeniability of the phone call informing her to come to the police station, the identification of her son by a tattoo on his arm, the open murder case, and, most of all, the closed-casket funeral service and burial. Time does not rewind or readjust. The past, no matter how recent, never autocorrects to a better alternative. Life cannot be undone, and death is even more stubborn.

Frankie was dead.

A stranger in a red dress—real or imagined—had reminded her of that. The woman's immaculately dark skin did not disqualify her from being Harrah's avatar any more than the suddenness of her appearance disqualified her from being a real, living person. Either way, what mattered most was that she'd been there. Harrah saw her, and the message her presence carried made Harrah consider turning the car around to go home, understanding the pointlessness of her attempted escapism.

Had she not seen the Black woman in the red dress a second time, she may have indeed turned around.

The woman stood closer to the gates of the next cemetery, nowhere near any large sculptures of immobile angels, or any other markers and memorials. She was not quite facing the road, and her braided locks veiled her eyes, but she could still have been watching Harrah's car drive past. Harrah felt that this was certain, and was likewise sure now that the woman was a grief-induced delusion. The woman appeared to her earlier this time, and lingered without moving as Harrah slowed on approaching her, then accelerated just as she made it past.

That second cemetery was a good distance away from the first. How far exactly, Harrah couldn't say, but she was sure she'd been driving for at least ten minutes after the first sighting. She supposed it was technically possible for the woman to have run to a waiting car, sped ahead to the next cemetery, reached it ahead of Harrah, then gotten out in time to be seen again . . . but for what reason? That made infinitely less sense than the probability of her stressed, sleep-deprived, and emotionally tortured brain creating a character meant to help her cope with and confront her heartache and loss.

The mind could do weird things. She thought of stories about phantom limbs. Someone loses an arm and still feels like it's there—feels a pain or an itch or anything else in a body part no longer present—for reasons not completely understood. This woman was her phantom pain. Maybe she was Black because Sarita was half . . .

No, that was stupid. Harrah didn't think like that, even subconsciously. Some of the family thought that way, sure, but not her. The woman was Black for the same reason she wore a red dress and never showed her face, because Harrah's brain just made her that way and that was that. No real logic to how she looked, just to where she appeared. In those little cities of the dead.

Harrah checked her phone for an alternate route that avoided the next two cemeteries and found one that would require her to double back to a road she had already passed, and would ultimately add almost thirty minutes to her drive. Well worth it.

With almost an hour between her and the last sighting of the woman in the red dress, Harrah could again sink into the shallow, potential comfort of being parked at a Lord of the Rings–themed slot machine, drinking one Bloody Mary after another, and letting all the buzzers, voices, fake coin jingling, and more distract her from accepting that her only child was dead. Murdered by some-damn-body. She'd have the rest of her life to dwell on that, and to think of how to get Sarita to pay for whatever part she had in it.

Who was anyone to judge her for wanting to get away from it all? Who was anyone to say she had to step fully into her misery now then shut the door behind her and break off the knob?

By the time she finally made it to Farm Road 481 those questions were drowned out by music turned up to the point of causing static to play like an extra instrument in her old speakers, as well as by a daydream of losing money while downing vodka, tomato juice, and hot sauce. That uncatchable horizon helped as well. It declared that forever was a place, and as long as forever was real and identifiable in some way, then that was proof that some things never ended, wasn't it? Some things go on and on even if the map tries to tell you no, there's an end point.

Frankie was out there in the great forever. One day, far, far down the road, she'd cross the horizon and see him again, and they'd be so far away from where they'd been in life that they wouldn't be able to look back on the old things that broke them apart, and the newer, more heinous thing that tried to keep them apart.

Beyond the short, dry trees, and the patchy grasslands, and all of the sun-bleached dirt that was not quite sand, beyond the edge of visibility, past the limits of her vision and underneath the sky, she could picture a man walking. Her son.

She knew it was him because his head was gone.

Harrah shut her eyes tight and held the wheel tighter. Last she had checked, ahead of her and in her mirrors, there were no other cars nearby. Knowing that, she drove blindly for seconds longer than she would have ordinarily. She had to force that latest image out of her head. Christ, what if that was the next illusion she encountered? She'd steer off the road, target a tree and try to hit a hundred miles per hour before impact if she really saw Frankie like that. Her heart went hollow with the thought of opening her eyes. The gliding sensation she felt with her eyes closed inflated her more practical fear of crashing until it equaled her fear of seeing Frankie in a state that the closed casket deliberately protected everyone from witnessing.

It would only take seconds for a car she hadn't seen previously to come along, especially from the opposite direction, and what if she had drifted into the oncoming lane already? It was a minor miracle that she hadn't hit someone yet, that she'd even been so alone on this stretch of road when she closed her eyes. There was never much traffic on this route when she took it, particularly in the middle of a weekday, like today, but to have absolutely no cars in sight, ahead or behind, was unusual.

Now that she thought of it, there might not have been any other cars on the road each time she'd seen the woman in the red dress. At least that's how she remembered it, but that would have been all but impossible.

Those cemeteries were located in or near towns that were small, but always busy. Full enough with people passing through on their way elsewhere, to say nothing of the locals on their way to work, or lunch, or home, or to a store, or to a pub. It simply couldn't be true that there weren't any other vehicles or people present and visible both times she'd seen the woman, yet in her mind, Harrah saw the woman in red in the cemetery, and no other breathing soul, or even a bird flying by at the time.

Even the wind seemed to have stopped blowing in the woman's presence.

Understanding she was being foolish, assigning credibility to absurd quirks of memory that were trying to scare her more than her legitimately reckless driving ought to, Harrah forced her eyes open.

A quarter mile ahead, to her right, she caught sight of a decrepit, abandoned church standing just above the overgrown grass. Its exterior walls were bleached to the color of bone, its flaked paint almost indistinguishable now from the drywall underneath. The roof looked partially caved, and the steeple above had lost its cross some time ago.

First, Harrah thought, and almost said aloud, that churches aren't supposed to be abandoned. She was never much for religion despite going to Catholic school from first to sixth grade, but she still held on to some vague notion of a higher power, and thought some things ought to be considered sacred in a functioning society. Church buildings were one of those things. Even in an old ghost town, she thought there should be caretakers for the places of worship. That just seemed right to her. Reassuring, for some reason. Seeing this church out here, which was not only abandoned but also remote, like God had picked it up from some other place, dropped it off here meaning to come back to it, and just forgot about it, disturbed her at least half as much as the impossible sightings of that woman in red.

The next thing that came to Harrah's mind was that the building reminded her a little of the old "music building" at St. Francis Elementary, where the students were sent a couple of times a week—sometimes more when they were practicing for one of the school's plays—to learn songs and, for the most part, goof off. Still, a few songs were stuck in her head, either in full or in part, from her youth. One in particular came to her now. Its first line was taken straight from the Bible. The rest she couldn't recall, but she would never forget that line. "If God is for us, who can be against?"

As a girl, she had initially misinterpreted this, thinking it was a statement, not a question. She took it as a warning of sorts, and even now, forty-seven years after her Sunday School teacher had explained it to her, she still struggled *not* to see it that way. She used to imagine the second half of the line in parenthesis, with a footnote added. If God is for us (who can be against)[1] . . .

[1] *God is for you, but it could be the opposite, just so you know.*

Before she could linger on this thought too long, she saw her again as she passed the church. The woman in the Hell-red dress. She stood with her back to the church's front doors and faced Harrah. Her hair was cleared from her face. Harrah saw the woman's focused, dark eyes. She felt the woman's gaze all over her skin as she drove on, determined not to check her mirrors to confirm if the woman was still there, watching for as long as she could until the horizon swallowed her.

"It's okay, it's okay," Harrah said.

This was good, in a way. Confirmation that she was suffering a breakdown, which was in turn validation of her decision to flee from San Antonio, and the source of her distress. Her mind was trying to process things, that was all. This would all go away after—or, better yet, during—her time away. In the meantime, the trauma of something no parent should suffer through was making her see someone who wasn't there, in places that reminded her of death.

Because she'd recognized the flat plain on the way to Eagle Pass and the remote luxuries of the Lucky Eagle casino as a potential, unofficial graveyard, hadn't she? She'd thought of the people who crossed the border only to become food for scavengers, or maybe the discarded cargo of different barely human scavengers that had taken advantage of them before deserting them in terrain desertion was named for.

The woman in red was still walking among the dead out here, even if she wasn't in a proper cemetery. Some people out here were buried by time and nature, others perhaps left uncovered, but all were effectively in the same place as Frankie. God, Harrah had tried to avoid passing those last graveyards, oblivious to the larger, lonelier one she had to drive through to get where she was going.

A sign came into view, along with a few cars, two passing in the opposite direction, one up ahead, in the lane she had thankfully never left while driving with her eyes closed.

EAGLE PASS 28.

Less than thirty miles to her destination. She'd made it this far, she could make it that much farther, even if it meant seeing the woman one more time along the way.

But the woman would not appear to Harrah on the road again.

She would instead await Harrah at Eagle Pass.

8

There once was a woman named Sarah, or Sarai, who married eight times, because her first seven husbands were killed by a demon named Asmodeus on their wedding night.

It could be a coincidence. Sarita wasn't necessarily the half-Black, half-Mexican reincarnation of a Jewish biblical prophetess just because she effectively had a similar name.

The murder of Sarah's husbands by an obsessive demon-king might also be considered apocryphal. Unofficial by even religious standards, to say nothing of historical standards. The slayings were accounted for in the Book of Tobit; as absent from Hebrew and Protestant Bibles as Sarah is otherwise present in those same texts. Catholic and Orthodox Bibles, however, include the book. What did that mean? Little? Nothing? Everything?

Sarita hadn't come across the story in her searches last night because she hadn't thought to search for variations of her own name, or for demons, or to focus on the "wedding night" aspect of what happened to her and Frank. Tori hadn't searched online for that information either, because she hadn't needed to. The story of Sarah and Asmodeus was already in her mind. It was the first thing she thought of when Sarita called her with the news.

After that night in Austin, what happened to Deedra and Candace, Tori had left college to pursue the study of metaphysics and mysticism. Not expressly to become a practitioner, she had assured Sarita years ago—as if Sarita would have judged her for it—but to become more of a scholar in these unofficial, unacademic fields, which would probably necessitate her *incidentally* becoming a minor practitioner as part of her studies. She never told Sarita exactly why, and Sarita never asked because she thought she knew the answer already. If anything akin to the sighting of Angelo happened again in Tori's presence, she wanted to be ready. Better equipped to understand or at least reasonably interpret what a sighting or sign meant, and therefore better able to explain to a friend why they should heed a warning.

Sarita now wished she'd followed Tori's lead, instead of relying on the comfort of feeling protected. Had she been too scared to know more? Afraid of finding out she wasn't as closely guarded as her life experience to that point led her to believe? Had some part of her suspected that Angelo was not as "angelic" as she wanted him to be? Or was she simply contented, and more than a little selfish? Deedra had died. Candace nearly died, and had her life altered irreversibly. That somehow hadn't been enough motivation for Sarita to dig deeper into why Angelo was somewhat mercurial, why sometimes he delivered vague warnings just by appearing, and other times opted for more direct intervention. Like the first time, when he saved her from the water.

And the second time, at the party . . .

After that, the first time she'd seen proof of his capacity for violence, she had been curious to know more about him, but not moved by that curiosity to explore what he could be, or educate herself. She could rationalize her acceptance of Deedra's death and Candace's injuries. She missed them both, loved them both, but was sure of a higher power, a greater intelligence and destiny at work in all their lives. Deedra was gone, but not forever. Someday, Candace would be healed and whole again.

If guardian angels existed, saving certain chosen individuals from horrible fates, then so, too, must a grander design. A world beyond what was known. An "afterlife" likely existed then, some form of paradise. Maybe not a city in the clouds captured by certain painters or poets when they envisioned Heaven, but some kind of peaceful, beautiful state of being that lasted so long it revealed that "life" was mere infancy.

That perspective had made it easier to accept her friends' tragedies as something temporary. Now, her faith departed, she had to rely on expertise she lacked despite being directly involved.

Tori had offered to come over immediately after Sarita called her that morning, but Sarita insisted they meet someplace out in the open, away from the house. Not because she worried about Tori finding the gun, but because she didn't want to be alone again with someone she cared about and risk Angelo attacking them for some unknown reason. She hadn't had a choice in the hospital, with her mother, but she had one now, and told Tori to meet her at a park about a mile away from the house. Tori said she understood Sarita's concern, but then told her that her fears might be unfounded, because Angelo may have targeted Frank for a reason. Then she told her the story of Sarah and Asmodeus.

"So my angel might really be a devil?" Sarita said.

"Not necessarily," Tori said. "I'm just pointing out that there's something of a precedent."

Sarita nodded, bit down hard on any aggravation before it could slip out. What good did it do her to know only that she might not be the first person this ever happened to? Yes, last night she had been looking online for other people who might have also gone through this, but not just to know that her experience was shared. She wanted to see what anyone had done about it. All Tori could tell her was that, thousands of years ago, a woman on the other side of the world who may never have existed possibly went through something similar. Was Tori trying to help or warn her? *You'll have to burn through seven husbands before you find the one that can kill the demon obsessed with you. That's the precedent. Sorry, friend.* If all she had was an old tale with no answers, maybe she should have held on to that.

No, any knowledge was better than ignorance. Sarita understood this as well as she understood how unfair it was to be irritated with Tori, or angry at all with anyone other than Angelo, who did not deserve the name given to him. He deserved no name, only descriptors. Traitor. Maniac. Murderer.

"When does David get here?" Tori said, drawing Sarita out of her thoughts.

"This afternoon. He got bereavement leave."

"Is he still stationed in Alaska?"

"Yeah. Juneau. He tried to come in earlier, for the service, but I told him not to hurry. Not like there was anyone he could save down here."

Tori had no response for this, though her expression told Sarita she was struggling for one. Her friend was more knowledgeable than emotionally connected and intuitive since the incident in Austin.

The awkward silence seemed to push Tori to look away from Sarita, like someone had swept a laser pen past her eyes. Sarita noticed that something caught Tori's attention when she looked back.

They sat on a bench facing a series of divided fields, some with soccer goals, some with volleyball nets, some with barbecue pits, all with limited tree coverage. They were on the side closest to the parking lot and pool, opposite the far end bordered by a small river. A walking track encircled the collection of fields, and several trailheads dotted the perimeter, leading to trails that could take hikers up into the short, surrounding hills.

Across from them, sitting beneath one of the relatively few trees—the one closest to them—were two people. One a short white man with a beard that made him look like he'd just emerged from the woods beyond the river, from the hollow center of a tree bewitched centuries ago. The other was a fit Latina with close-cropped hair. Something about how they sat, and where they sat, made them stand out from the smattering of other strangers in the park, which mostly consisted of senior citizens out for a walk, a few parents with children either too young for school or whom they homeschooled, and a couple clearly out for a hike who had made a beeline for one of the trails almost as soon as they had arrived.

The pair under the tree were dressed like they were out for a run, but didn't look like they had done any running. They reminded Sarita a little of some of the running and hiking groups she used to come to this park with a few years ago. They wore matching outfits: compression pants under athletic shorts; long-sleeve compression shirts; running shoes. These two wore darker colors that made their attire look more tactical than entirely practical, but their clothing alone did not make them look too out of place, if at all.

They could have been resting before a more strenuous walk, hike, or run on an arduous trail. But they weren't. It took Sarita barely a second to understand why she thought something was amiss. It went beyond the ever-present paranoia Angelo had recently instilled in her, though it was not entirely apart from that, either.

These two were not talking to or looking at each other. They weren't blatantly staring at Sarita and Tori, either, or Sarita hadn't caught them in the act, at least. They sat at the base of the tree, not quite next to each other, facing Sarita and Tori enough that they could keep eyes on them without having to turn their heads, and had their heads bowed enough to hide what they might be looking at.

Sarita tried not to be distracted by them, and was starting to think she was making something of nothing, when she noticed a similarly dressed man farther in the distance, closer to the river. He was lightly jogging back and forth along a shortcut through the width of the fields that connected opposite sides of the track. He was tall, lean, blond, and the only difference between his attire and that of the two under the tree was his black backpack. Something about his "running" stuck out to Sarita as an act. It reminded her of the warm-ups she, Tori, Candace, and Deedra would do before softball practice in high school. The high-knee, skipping sort of runs from outfield to infield that their coaches always insisted were critical to a great practice, and that Sarita and Tori could never take seriously, which, hell, maybe accounted for why their softball careers didn't come with them to college. Maybe coaches were right after all.

She could almost hear a coach yelling at the blond man now, telling him to stop half-assing it, to run it right or not at all, and asking who did he think he was fooling with that effort?

It was possible that this trio shouldn't concern Sarita. More than possible, but Sarita sensed this wasn't the case. Which didn't mean she was right to believe something was amiss. Senses could deceive. Sometimes you think you hear someone say something specific when they said nothing at all. Sometimes you walk into a house where food is in the oven or on the stove and think you know what's cooking based on the aroma, only to be proven wrong. And that happened with physical, concrete senses, the ones you learn about before elementary school, so more opaque senses—those of dread or suspicion, for instance—had to be less reliable, didn't they?

She realized, not for the first time, how unfamiliar all of this was to her, how sheltered she'd been by the certainty of having a "guardian angel." She'd never had to worry about being followed, never feared someone might be sneaking up on her, or lurking around a corner, or plotting to break into her home. Was this what it was like for other people—other women, in particular—on a regular basis? Having to look over your shoulder, find the source of footsteps heard behind you, decide how cautious or trusting you needed to be? Angelo's protection shielded her from even accidental dangers. With that shield gone—or at least her belief in it gone—she couldn't tell if her present apprehension and distrust was normal, or an outsized version of what most people felt. How would she even be able to tell the difference?

Nonetheless, Sarita made it a point to be mindful of the trio long enough to mentally store the features she could make out, even at a distance, just in case.

In case of what? she thought, and had no firm answer.

"Okay, so there's a precedent," Sarita said, looking again to Tori. "What can I do with that?"

"I'm not exactly sure, friend," Tori said. "At the very least, I think it could give us an idea about why Angelo did what he did. Just one idea, but it's something. We tend to think of angels, demons, and deities operating on a different emotional or motivational plane. 'God works in mysterious ways,' et cetera. But God also calls himself jealous in one of the first books of the Bible. And Asmodeus is described as essentially jealous and obsessed with Sarah."

Sarita's skin burned like she had a full-body rash brought on by sudden rage. The words behind her tightened jaws wanted to come out as a scream that would reshape her and everything around her the way a prehistoric earthquake altered the landscape. She held on, subdued the scream, and spoke carefully, as though the wrong inflection on a syllable would cast a cataclysmic spell.

"You seriously think he murdered Frank just because he wants me for himself?"

Tori put a hand on Sarita's shoulder, and for a second Sarita could believe things were simpler than they were. A friend was consoling a friend during a conversation while they sat at a park bench. They made commercials out of moments like this. She knew that an outside observer would think they were talking about work or relationships, maybe a health issue, nothing close to the uncanny nightmare of Sarita's current reality.

"I think we can't dismiss the possibility, that's all. That might be it, or it might be something completely different. But just based on . . . based on how you said it happened." Tori paused, her eyes softened, a light sheen of tears covered them. Sarita nodded, giving her permission to say whatever she needed to say.

"The violence of what he did," Tori went on, "what you described . . . he'd never done anything like that before. It's hard for me to think of why he would kill Frank that way if he wasn't furious. And I can't think of what else he could have been angry about."

Sarita was still managing and fighting the idea that Angelo's primary motivation was psychotic jealousy. The angelic being that had carried her out of the water when she was a girl was no more than a pathetic, homicidal stalker. Watching over her unseen for all her life—from childhood, through teen years, into adulthood—not out of a duty to protect her, or a more selfless kind of love, or for some mystical reason beyond mortal comprehension, but because he was a possessive psychopath. That wasn't possible. Tori said it couldn't be dismissed, but Sarita could not stomach this being the reason Frank was dead, the reason her life had been saved even as her friends were kept in danger.

"No, there's something else," Sarita said. "I've never told anyone else about this. Not even my mom. The only person who knows is David, because he was there. Frank wasn't the first person Angelo killed."

Tori's eyes narrowed and she shifted in her seat. Sarita gave another look to the three people dressed in black. The two that were under the tree were walking toward one of the trailheads. The blond man with the backpack was walking to a trailhead farther away. Sarita knew that the trails intersected at multiple points, of course. Did they think she didn't know that? Did they not care?

Was she even on their mind? Was she losing *her* mind?

Maybe she was just doing anything to delay telling a story that needed to be told. It was overdue, she thought. David had been there when it happened, but they had never discussed it, because she knew it would give him another reason to be wary of her guardian, and back then she didn't want to hear it. David seemed to suspect that somehow Angelo was responsible for the incident at Malaquite Beach in the first place, or that at least, if he was a guardian angel, he should have done something to prevent it from happening.

Sarita had always assumed Angelo needed to wait to save her in order to prove what he was. That way, his appearance alone would automatically warn her in the future. Now, however, David's distrust struck her as not only accurate, but prescient. It wasn't about doubting what Angelo had done, but what he might someday do. Sarita couldn't have been suspicious of Angelo as early as David was, but she could have—should have—let her eyes be opened after first seeing the result of her angel's wrath.

9

"This was about four years ago," Sarita told Tori. "A couple of years after what happened in Austin. David was dating this older guy who invited us out to a little get-together at his house. I was actually supposed to meet Frank there. He was coworkers with the guy, I want to say his name was Brett, or Brad. One of those. Anyway, we got there a little early, and Frank never showed because something happened that shut everything down before he got there.

"One of Brett's buddies apparently had been drinking with him earlier in the day and was drunk as hell by the time most people started arriving. And I guess one of the girls who was also there was his ex, or at least they had some kind of history. I don't know. I never really found out. But he kept trying to talk to her and she kept trying to avoid him. It was a decent-sized house, so she was able to slip him for a while, but when more people got there and it got more crowded I guess it got harder for her to push past everyone, or easier for him to corner her. One way or the other, he ended up getting to her in the kitchen, and when she tried to walk away this time he grabbed her wrist and yanked her back.

"I was right there and I wasn't having it. I go over and before I can even get close he's got his finger pointed in her face and I hear him saying something about, 'Somebody should smack you.' I get between them, and I'm like, 'Is there a problem?' And you know, Tori, at the time I was really thinking, 'I dare you to try some shit with me.' Having Angelo in my back pocket made me feel invincible. And there was this part of me that still wanted to make up for what happened to Candi and Dee. I trusted Angelo then. I felt like he knew he owed me one for what happened to the girls. Plus, and I don't know if this sounds crazy, but I used to daydream of doing something heroic, diving right in because I knew he'd protect me. Pulling someone out of a house or a car that was catching fire, knowing he'd save me if it came to it, so, as long I could hold on to whoever else was there, I'd save them, too. Something like that. This was different, but close enough. I wasn't going to let anything happen to that girl.

"The guy says all the stuff you would think he'd say about this not being my business, stay out of it, it's between him and her. But he can't turn off the aggression, and now David sees it, and I see him out the corner of my eye, and I realize I don't even need Angelo right now. My brother's got me. He heads straight for me, and he was home on leave from the Coast Guard by then, and he's wearing one of his extra-tight shirts that are struggling for dear life not to rip in half every time he moves. I swear he'd go into stores and ask, 'Where are your smallest mediums?'"

She stopped to laugh, which gave Tori permission to laugh as well, and it felt as good as it felt forced. It was okay to make yourself laugh, she thought, when it was something you really needed.

"So my brother, who looks like he's Fish-Man's archnemesis, comes up—"

"Uh, do you mean Aquaman?"

They shared another laugh that felt palliative, and Sarita went on, "Fish-Man, Aquaman, The Super-Swimmer. Somebody. Anyway, David walks over to the guy and lets him know he's getting loud with the wrong person's sister. By then we've got almost everybody's attention, so finally Brett or Brad comes over to get his friend and tell him he's too drunk, and he's got to go. The guy says, 'Okay,' but he says it in that way where you can tell he thinks it means something else, and he keeps saying it over again on his way out of the house.

"I check on homegirl, make sure she's okay, she says she is, she thanks me and David, and everybody tries to just get the party back going for a minute. Then we hear this loud bang from outside, sort of like a firecracker, but not quite. Somehow, we all know it's something else. A gunshot has a little more punch or spark to it or something. Maybe that's just hindsight talking. Anyway, right after that bang, there's this insane scream. It cuts right through the walls and goes on a few seconds longer than you'd think. And I don't know how to describe it except that in the moment I kind of thought it was barely human. Like it was a person turning into an animal, or the other way around, and the pain of it was killing them.

"Then the screaming suddenly stopped, and everybody froze. I think we were all wondering if we had really heard what we heard. Then after a bit, Brett went to the front window and opened the curtains to see if he could see anything. Then *he* starts screaming. More people look through the window and there's more commotion, more yelling and shouting, and people who aren't near the window keep asking, 'What's going on? What's out there?'

"David saw it before I did and tried to keep me from looking, but I got close enough to see it. The guy who had just been kicked out of the party was . . . *all over* the front lawn in a few different pieces. His head was a foot or two away from his body, one of his arms was down near his feet, all the rest. The uh . . . the way his body was separated . . . he'd been *pulled* apart. The wounds weren't clean, like he'd been cut up. Whoever did this had used their hands, is what I guess I'm saying. The ripped-off arm was still holding a gun, too. From what we learned later it was a gun he always kept in his car. He must have gone to get it and was planning to shoot his ex, maybe shoot a few other people. Like David and me for getting in the way. Or maybe I would have just caught a stray bullet, considering how drunk he was. No way he was going to be able to shoot straight.

"Even without seeing Angelo, I knew he'd done it. Who else could it be? But even if I had doubted it, David asked me later if I saw him, too. I told him I didn't. By the time I got there he was gone. But David said he saw him across the street, almost blending in with the shadows. Probably no one else saw him because they were looking at the body, and then looking away. But David took an extra second to look for Angelo, because he knew he'd be there. I never asked him what he thought about it or anything, and that was the last time we ever talked about it."

Tori glanced away and back a few times, like she was picking up her next sentence one word at a time from things she saw around her. "That didn't worry you at all?" she said.

Sarita shook her head. "It wasn't like he'd done it to some guy for cussing me out or something. That asshole had gone to get his gun. He was coming back to kill somebody. My angel saved me and who knows who else. And the way he did it . . . I didn't think it was out of anger really. Maybe a little, but I thought he really did it to make sure none of us who were there could possibly get blamed for it. Most of us were barely questioned when the police came. I don't know who they must have thought did it, but they saw that none of us were built for it, and there wasn't a trace of blood on any of us. Kind of the same as . . ."

Sarita swallowed the words, shut her eyes tight, draining the light from the image of Frank's remains in her mind until the scene was black. Then she went on. "Same as in the hotel. He didn't have to be angry to kill Frank that way. It could have just been to make sure I wouldn't get charged, because it's impossible for me to have killed him based on all the physical evidence. The most the detectives think I could have done is set Frank up, and then lied about not knowing his killer. Which is half-true.

"Anyway, to get back to your question, no, I wasn't worried. After that, I couldn't have been less afraid. I actually got a little reckless for a while. That's when I left for a couple of years, tried out being a wanderer and a little bit of a rebel and adventurer, at least my version of it. I went skydiving, rock climbing, skiing, hang gliding. A lot of stuff I used to say you'd have to be crazy to try. I made some friends I normally wouldn't have, went to the kind of bars that used to scare us off, talked to some boys I should have been worried about. Tried ecstasy, did a little coke. Really only stopped because I didn't like either one. Moved on to some hallucinogens and had a better time with those.

"Honestly, the one time I felt even a little afraid of someone or something, I was out in California, and there was this guy who I felt like was stalking me. He would show up at these bars and parties I was at, and I always felt like he was looking at me even though I never caught him. Nobody ever seemed to be talking to him, and nobody knew who he was, or who could have invited him, but there was something about him that made us all just stay away instead of asking him to leave. A few of us gave him the nickname 'Cold Eyes,' because of how it felt when he looked at you. I've actually been thinking about him some lately, because I've been dreaming about him, which is better than dreaming about . . . anyway, it's not *that* much better because, for whatever reason, he always made me think of Angelo, but an evil version. The opposite of him, although I guess I can't really say that anymore. But you get what I mean."

Tori said, "It could be like a barely subconscious thing. Some part of you maybe always equated Angelo with being a little bit of a stalker. I mean he had to be always watching you somehow, right? Following you, basically. And every time he showed up, something bad was about to happen to you."

Sarita started to nod, then tilted her head like she wasn't so sure. "Maybe, but . . . I don't know, this guy also had this weird presence to him, the way Angelo does when he appears, like he's more of a fixture of the place he's in than a living person. Like a tall, pale stone, just shaped like a person, that was given a few days to walk around, pretending to be human. Sort of like that one *Twilight Zone* with the mannequins. You ever see that?"

Tori smirked and chuckled. "Yeah. We watched it together at my mom's old apartment. I'm the one that put you on to pretty much anything in black-and-white, or made before 1995. Remember?" She poked Sarita in her side, playfully, at a point just above her hip, the spot of Sarita's first tattoo, a replication of the Rockford Peaches logo from *A League of Their Own,* which Tori got inked above her hip on the same day.

"Oh my God, that's right. Well, I did mention I've done a lot of drugs, right? It's not the best for your memory. Damn, it's been way too long since we've *really* talked like we used to. Not just showing up at parties and stuff, and sticking to small talk, like we just know each other from work or whatever. It shouldn't take things like this for us to get close again. I just . . ."

Tori put her hand on Sarita's. "It's okay. I'm not going to say I understand, because I can't. You're the only one who's had to go through exactly what you've been through. And then I had my own way of dealing with what happened with the girls. You know, most friends drift apart—and *further* apart—over way more mundane shit. The only important thing to me is for you to know I'm here for you."

Sarita wanted to hug her friend, but could not bring herself to, allowing only for them to hold hands. She kept to herself that Tori's words had renewed her sadness, and not in the way that may have been intended.

I'm here for you.

Perhaps no one could tell her this and earn her absolute faith anymore, no matter what they did to prove it. Maybe her mother and father, maybe

David. Even hearing it from them would make her wonder if they meant it in the way she understood it, or if there was something she was missing, something they were hiding, deliberately or not.

Realizing that the pain of losing her protector felt almost equal to that of seeing Frank killed—being without him—magnified the misery. But it was undeniable, even rational. She had not just known and relied on Angelo, she had loved him almost like another brother, or second father, and beyond even that, she had accepted him as a part of her. Someone she'd known since childhood, and whom she once expected to see from her deathbed, decades later, arriving to warn her not to grow one second older. She would have smiled at him then, assured him that she was ready, and thanked him for all the times he'd been there for her. Then taken his hand and followed his lead into the hereafter.

That was never going to be, and was apparently never meant to be. Every time he'd been "there for her," saving her life, he'd been doing it for secret reasons she couldn't discern. Simple obsession, like Asmodeus with Sarah, or something infinitely stranger. Either way, Angelo had taken more than Frank. He'd taken vital parts of her. The belief and security that had been embedded in her for most of her life was now gone. Ripped away by the strong, cruel hand of something inhuman.

10

In New York, her first stop during her "wandering" period, Sarita met a young ex-con, mid-reformation, who knew how to hide a razor blade in his mouth and push it out without cutting his tongue. When she heard about his skill from one of his friends, she convinced him to teach her. After considerable goading, he taught her how with folded paper "razors" that still nicked the insides of her mouth. She went on to practice with real blades, drawing blood every time, but not enough to endanger herself. Eventually she got pretty good at it, and practiced every so often for years afterward, just to see if she still had the skill, and because she knew Angelo would never let her hurt herself too badly. If she was doomed to accidentally swallow a blade one day, he'd appear to warn her, and she would know to put the razor down.

Her New York boyfriend confessed that the informal lessons he gave her in concealing a small, sharp weapon gave him a greater sense of accomplishment and even peace than his daily affirmations, or the mutually encouraging letters he traded with former cellmates.

Not long after that confession, they drifted apart, her growing desire to seek new experiences interfering with his need to remain sober and focused on his progress.

In Chicago she met an activist who invited her to a gang-leader summit that teetered toward truce then to warfare and back multiple times, yet still managed to be less violent than the protest of police brutality he brought her to, where tear gas was deployed well before the first stone was thrown in self-defense. He managed to pull her away from the worst of it, but she fought to enter the chaos, hoping a bean bag projectile, or perhaps worse, might target her. Then, she knew, in front of cameras from news organizations across the world, Angelo would appear and give whoever had put her in their crosshairs at least a hint of the treatment he'd given the man at the party. How would the world react then? Who could remain in denial of which side was right and which was wrong when presented with an angel's wrath?

It occurred to her later that her desire to weaponize Angelo was reckless. It could have jeopardized people who didn't deserve it, and was unfair to him as well. It was one thing to take risks knowing he would save her whether or not violence would be required, something else to all but lure him into killing for her. At some point in the future, when she had time to be more calculating about deploying him, coming up with ways to set him against those who damned themselves might still prove justifiable, even necessary, but she wanted to remove as much impulsiveness and bloodlust from her decision-making as possible. If she ever indirectly summoned Angelo without a completely clear mind and conscience, and witnessed him brutalize a bystander who only made the mistake of being too close to the target, she'd never forgive herself.

She didn't trust herself to stay with her partner in Chicago without deliberately or inadvertently baiting Angelo into a situation where innocent people might get hurt, so she moved on.

In Colorado and then California she pulled together a small harem of boys—including her first white boyfriends—who were enthused about meeting a Blaxican girl who was far more open to "adventure sports" than most other Black or Latin American girls they had met. She didn't mind being something of a trophy for them because they were the same for her, with the added benefit of showing her how to climb rock faces, navigate rapids, or simply dive into the sky from a perfectly functioning airplane. She figured she was coming out ahead in these fleeting, casual relationships.

They all felt like training for something greater. Despite the recreational drug use, which was consistent, but not rampant, she was close to being in better shape than she'd been in as a high school athlete. She had improved some of her measurables and intangibles, increased her grip strength and physical stamina while also testing her instincts and courage. Those daydreams of heroism she'd long held would never manifest if she was going to solely rely on Angelo to do all the heavy lifting, literally and figuratively. He had already shown that his sole priority was to protect her, and he would let others die or even kill them to secure her safety. If she had ever aspired to be a rescue diver, like David, or even just a lifeguard at the community pool, Angelo might not let her jump into the water to save someone if he deemed the risk too great. Or might pull someone she was trying to save out of her hands to make sure they wouldn't pull her under. Unless she was strong enough to hold on to them, quick enough, physically and mentally, to react before Angelo could stop her.

There had to be something more she could do. There had to be a way for her to harness the blessing bestowed on her. A way for her to prevent the kind of accident that killed one of her friends and altered another's quality of life. She was determined not only to figure out how to do this, but to be prepared in advance for when the realization came to her. One day she was going to be a hero. An angel of sorts in her own right.

Then she made her way back home to Texas, met Frank while he was waiting for a ride outside a party one night, brought him back to her place, spent the rest of the weekend with him, and unknowingly took her first steps away from wondering what her higher calling might be.

The day after their first night together he asked if she would go with him to a small, private library he'd already planned to visit that morning. She had joined him, browsed old and rare books with him, and found herself enjoying quiet, stillness, and lucidity for the first time in several years. Later that night they checked out some small art galleries and museums clustered near one another. Nothing even slightly adventurous until the next day when he proposed an impromptu trip to the coast even though it was late January. He promised he'd have their pick of parties to attend, thrown by "Winter Texans," people who drove south from as far away as Canada to spend three, four, and sometimes up to five months away from the cold. In his experience, he said, they were routinely friendly and inviting.

"A little *too* inviting every once in a while," he said. "If you spot somebody passing around a bowl asking us to put our car keys in it, that's a sign we got picked up to be the young couple at a swinger party."

"You say that like it's a warning."

"And you just said *that* like you're disappointed in me."

"You've just been so open-minded so far," she had teased.

Halfway to Padre Island, they had sex in the passenger seat of her car on the side of the highway while a storm passed through. The rain beating on the roof and windshield almost matched the familiar phantom roar in her mind, which lingered longer than usual this time, as it had each time they'd previously had sex. It had enhanced the experience, depriving her of one sense and driving her to focus more on touch.

When they made it to Padre Island, she realized it was her first time being near the Gulf Coast since Angelo had saved her. She didn't recall consciously avoiding it in adulthood. There just hadn't been that many opportunities to go, or there had always been a good excuse to decline an invitation when one came to her. Even though it was cold and drizzly, she asked Frank, this man she'd known for barely forty-eight hours, if he would accompany her to the shore, and he said yes.

They stayed there for several minutes. She watched the waves curl in and slide out, and thought of being lost in the deep, never coming home, never having this life. Her parents and David missing her, David maybe being too overcome by grief to become a diver. What if someone else in his place would have saved one fewer person than her brother had? She thought of Tori joining Candace and Deedra in the car in Austin, instead of sticking with Sarita and being spared. Or maybe three or more entirely different people would have been involved in that accident instead of them, and they all would have died instead of "just" Deedra and the driver.

What if simply being here, surviving, *was* her calling? What if the questing she'd been doing prior to this had just been foolish endanger-ment? While it seemed improbable for her to have been saved, seemingly singled out, not to lead an extraordinary life, it had to be at least equally improbable for her to be saved by a guardian angel at all, right? And wasn't her life already extraordinary just based on her being alive, when she should have drowned in these waters as a child?

She could not help but to associate the peace and acceptance settling over her then with the man who was with her. Maybe it was a sign that he was meant for her, maybe not, but that felt far less important to her than the fact that she wanted him to be meant for her. She looked at him, smiled, thanked him, kissed him, and in that moment chose him, and did not regret her choice, or question her purpose, or fear for anything in her life again until the night he died.

11

What drink was she on? She remembered at least six, maybe seven, so the actual number was likely between nine and twelve. Harrah still didn't feel drunk. It was possible she was incapable of getting truly drunk anymore. Were she able to, maybe she could have stayed home, or closer to home, and sought escape from Frankie's murder in nothing more than a bottle and a six-pack. Or, if cannabis didn't make her sleepy and produce odd dreams, she could have bought a bag from one of her cousins, smoked a little smoke, and wafted through a cloud of memories. She knew people who stayed high for about half of their waking life, and she envied them. If she smoked as routinely as they did, she would effectively be comatose.

Liquor and beer dulled her senses somewhat, but also slowed and softened her mind enough for unwanted thoughts to linger, soak in, and stain. Drinking lessened the severity of her emotions, but let them hang on in absence of any other distractions. Hence the casino, and more.

She hadn't bought each drink that had been placed in front of her since she had arrived. Three drinks had come her way courtesy of the pudgy man in the decent-looking off-the-rack suit who kept finding his way into her orbit, along with his two taller friends who seemed to be giving him a pep talk every time she looked their way.

He probably thought he was being smooth. Showing interest, but not overzealousness. Goddamn "modern men," some of them had mastered overthinking their way out of a sure thing. She got it, he didn't want to come off as a pest, a harasser, a guy who couldn't read the clues that she was uninterested. But she'd already accepted three drinks, had looked his way and raised a glass to him each time. Christ's sake, did she need to draw him a map? Was he waiting for her to wink, point, and blow a kiss? Did she need to write the word "GO" in glowing ink on the crotch of her jeans? Harrah was on the verge of approaching the man to tell him he needed to make his move, or else she was going to take one of his friends upstairs to her room instead. Well, she wouldn't actually say that, but she wanted to.

Instead, had she gone up to him, she would have used a line that she'd stolen from a TV movie she saw when she was a kid. Not even a chat-up line, really, but a small routine. Approach a man, give her name, let him respond with his. Then turn her back and walk away, not far or for too long, just enough to befuddle him. Maybe circle the bar, mix with a crowd, or turn a corner to escape his sight. Then double back to him and say his name like he was an old friend she hadn't seen in ages. "What are you do-ing here? What have you been up to? What are you doing these days?" It never failed to get a laugh and break the ice when she had used it before.

In high school, the boy she'd gone to prom with said she was "weird pretty," and couldn't explain what he meant when she told him to elabo-rate. It didn't take long for her to like the term and define it for herself. She decided it was born from the collision of certain features. Eyes too light for the darkness of her hair, freckles that went up to her forehead and made her look like someone had flicked blood on her face with their fingers, ears large enough to be prominent, but not enough to invite jokes. A smile that showed off canines just pointed enough to say, *Kiss me at your own risk.* As to the rest of her, in her estimation, her body had only gotten more attrac-tive with the weight she'd picked up with age. Based on the responses of the men she slept with, this was an accurate assessment.

The pudgy man with prematurely graying hair—that or a face too boy-ish for his age—had seen something about her that he liked. He bought her drinks and made himself a satellite multiple times. To be fair, the latter behavior had a remote chance of just being a coincidence, or an in-evitability. The Eagle Pass casino wasn't exactly a main-strip, Vegas-scale attraction. It had a spacious floor, but not so much that it was unusual to run into the same person multiple times as you ventured from one group of slots to another, looking for the machine that was going to be the friendliest.

That, along with the alcohol, was what let her believe that the Black woman in the flowing red dress with a wine-colored scarf around her neck was not actually following her, and certainly wasn't the same woman she'd seen on the road.

For one, the woman on the road's dress had been a more vivid, dark-yet-flaming red. Again, the color Satan would paint his walls with, or use to spray-paint Sarita's name on an underpass if he were a graffitist.

Her hair was similar, but not as . . . active. That seemed the appropriate word. In hindsight, the woman on the road's hair had seemed large and even obtrusive with a purpose, whereas the woman at the casino's hair was more subdued, if not exactly less voluminous.

Most of all, her eyes weren't quite the same as the woman from the road's. Not as intense. Noticeably cooler, and a bit brighter. Harrah had seen gloom and intensity in the woman's eyes on the road, but remembered them now as fiery. A scorched color closer to embers than earth.

Still, the woman at the casino held her attention each time she moved past her. She walked like she had to pretend gravity had any effect on her, and looked like an artist could accompany her and make a fortune capturing her in any given moment.

Other people noticed her as well, walked around her, mouthed "Excuse me" as they passed. A few caught themselves staring at her for a couple of seconds, causing them to nearly bump into someone else before hustling away, embarrassed. This dispelled the idea that this woman was a product of Harrah's imagination, as the woman on the road had been. This was purely coincidental, and with that in mind, while the woman seemed to cross Harrah's line of sight more often than other people at the Lucky Eagle, Harrah presumed this wasn't really the case, and that she only noticed her more because of the coincidence, as well as her grace. She had no reason to be in a place this comparatively humble. Even Vegas seemed far beneath her. Weren't there spectacular, lavish European casinos that showed up in James Bond movies? Those were real places, right? Those seemed a better fit for her.

At least twice, Harrah thought the woman had caught her looking at her. Staring, really. If it happened a third time Harrah was going to leave her machine, approach the woman, and make sure to explain it wasn't some weird race thing. The woman had beautifully dark skin, and Harrah thought about breaking the ice with a "Black don't crack" joke, then thought that probably would be seen as inappropriate. It might already be too much for her to go out of her way to say she wasn't staring at the woman just because she was presumably African—not African *American*, she looked too regal for that, somehow—but Harrah wanted it known. *I'm staring at you because you're gorgeous and elegant as fuck, and I'm so inelegant I say things like "elegant as fuck," and I'm also going through an awful pain right now that I don't want to talk about, but I just wanted to tell you I'm glad to even get to look at you right now.*

Guilt had something to do with this. Harrah was no racist, and nobody could convince her that she was, especially since they weren't psychic and therefore not in her head. Sure, she had sat with some family members and even a good friend or two who'd made jokes she didn't agree with, and she had laughed along for the sake of not starting an argument. That didn't mean she was the same as the bigots in her family. It was one of the things Frankie's father, Don, used to throw in her face when they would argue, before he left her, and even a few times after they separated. He accused her of being something she wasn't just because she knew people like that and didn't "stand up to them" when they said things that weren't worth taking seriously, and she thought that was bullshit. How better to prove that than to walk up to this Black woman who looked like a legendary queen and tell her she "didn't belong here." Not because of her skin color, though, but because she completely outclassed the place. How about that for a swerve?

She wasn't going to say that, either, of course, not because she felt it was wrong to say, but because the woman intimidated her as much as she captivated her. At first, she couldn't understand why, besides the woman's appearance and height. God, was she six feet tall? She wasn't even in heels. She had cheekbones that could sharpen a shiv, bracelets and rings that looked museum-worthy. Something about the scarf, as well, magnified the woman's aura of being a living, mysterious masterpiece. As though the scarf were the ribbon wrapped around a mythical giftbox never meant to be opened.

Careful, you're making her seem like she isn't real. Next you'll tell yourself she really could be the woman you thought you saw on the road.

She pushed the button to spin the wheels of her slot machine, and said a quiet "Thank you" for the odd balance and unexpected clarity provided by games of chance. They gave you an opportunity to hope, and a crash course in cold realism and probability with each roll of dice, or turn of a card, or spin of slot wheels.

She'd seen people blow their mortgage or rent payments on the hopes of a jackpot, then blame the dealers, floorwalkers, and even bartenders and waitresses for conspiring against them and them alone, as if it was a big secret that the objective of "the house" was to take *everyone's* money. So they lashed out and gave every insult they had in their bag to the people who could actually hear them, not the suits in suites who they couldn't get to. And definitely not to the person they might see later in a mirror above the sink in their hotel room.

It couldn't possibly be that they'd gambled too much on something with odds inherently and heavily stacked against them. It had to be some kind of plot that targeted them as though they were important enough to be marked walking through the door and singled out to be bled down to bones.

Harrah wondered how many other things with reasonable, simple explanations dodged this kind of person's perspective. She saw this kind of thinking moving freely through her own family, and it was the exact kind of thing she wanted to get away from now. There was a degree of tunnel vision that could make a person think the whole world was a tunnel. A mindset that could make you think that just because your dead son's bride *seemed* to be hiding something, then that was the only possible truth. And that because of this, because in some way or another she was complicit in that crime—maybe even asked the son of a bitch who killed him to do it—then you should get Joey and a few of your other family members who made a dumb-ass joke or two sometimes to snatch her ass up.

Because things looked one way from your point of view, so that had to be the only way they were, right? Nothing was ever random. No one was ever really just in the wrong place at the wrong time. Chance didn't exist. If you ever subscribed to that, you knew better now, because it had happened to someone you love, and the person responsible had to be related in some way to the person who survived and was within reach. That had to be the case to give you a reason to hurt the person you could get ahold of, right?

No. She wasn't a child. She wasn't a baby in an internet video who cried when they saw Dad without his beard for the first time, because from their minimal understanding of the world Dad had to have a beard, so a man who looked and sounded and smelled and acted exactly like him still couldn't be him, because where was his facial hair? What an infantile way of looking at the world.

To be sure, it seemed apparent that Sarita was hiding something. The question was whether it was her own guilt, or someone else's, someone she feared would come after her if she said too much. She could be protecting someone in her own family, although, as far as Harrah knew, Sarita didn't have any felons or ex-cons in her family tree the way Harrah did. No cousins-by-marriage that made you think, *We've got to stop letting them come over. I don't like the way they're talking about the nice things my boy has because he's done well for himself.*

Damn it, she had to put the hard brakes to this train of thought, too. It wouldn't take much, if she continued down this road, to start wondering if someone in her own family, related by blood or vows, had conspired against Frankie, maybe right along with Sarita.

Harrah pushed the button on the slot machine and heard it trot out a movie quote that was supposed to represent the fortune she may or may not receive. She looked to see if the pudgy man or a waitress was making his way toward her again. To her left, the Black woman stood near the bar. Not *at* the bar. That would be easily dismissible. She would be ordering a drink like anyone else, in that case. But she wasn't at a stool, or talking to a bartender, or even within a raised voice of placing an order. She was just far enough from the counter, just close enough to Harrah, to make Harrah wonder what she might be doing.

The woman turned her head in Harrah's direction and smiled without directing her gaze or smile at her. Harrah wanted to turn toward whatever the woman had to be looking at, but she couldn't look away.

The woman's smile was odd. Not too wide, Harrah realized, but somewhat out of place. It made her think of Frankie's drawings when he was a kid. When he used to sketch a face in profile as part of an art project in first or second grade, and she would have to point out to him that a person's eyes and mouth don't look the same when viewed from the side as from the front.

Holy shit, that's what it was. The woman wasn't really facing Harrah, but somehow Harrah saw her face, her smile, as though she were in front of her. And if Harrah thought her own smile gave off a flirty warning about kissing her, the woman's smile delivered a dire warning about slicing your eye on her teeth if you stared too long.

Harrah blinked twice, and things were normal again. Or close to normal. She saw the back of the woman's head, not even a bit of her face. Maybe she had never seen it. Probably she hadn't. Jesus, how drunk was she? She picked up her glass, inspected the bottom of the last drink she'd accepted from the pudgy man for something that shouldn't be there, something powdery, perhaps, as if she knew what to look for. Nothing but the last small puddle of melted ice. She set it back down, pushed the button on the machine again. A golden ring appeared on the display above the monitor. The roulette cycled through her possible winnings and eventually landed on her getting twenty free spins.

Not bad, she thought, then registered how normal it was for her to notice this. Would that thought have crossed her mind if the man pursuing her had drugged her? She thought not. She'd probably be creeping close to unconsciousness if he had spiked her drink. Presuming he used the same drug someone had slipped her in college, the night Uncle Everett answered her call, drove half an hour to get to her, made sure she got home safe, then made it back to the bar with a few of his friends in tow to beat the shit out of the boy who'd been buying her drinks all night.

"Looks like it might be your lucky day," someone over her shoulder said. She turned and saw the pudgy man in the suit pushing past an older woman who was watching Harrah's winnings as though witnessing someone else's good fortune could be her own rabbit's foot.

"I was starting to think you were allergic to me," Harrah said to him.

"I . . . I'm the one who sent the drinks," he said.

"Yeah. I know."

"Right. Uh . . . do you . . . can I get you another?"

Harrah patted the empty seat of the slot beside her. "They'll come around. Sit down."

"Oh, I'm all done. I've already spent—"

"I didn't say play. Sit down."

He glanced back at his friends who stood within earshot. They snickered and then motioned for him to do as he was told. They were all forty-year-old *boys,* Harrah thought. Was this really the best she could hope for this evening? Should she hold out for better? Prior experience told her it was possible. She had drawn the attention and affection of more confident and capable men before, and even boys who were young enough to make their immaturity excusable, to say nothing of the energy they were likely—though hardly guaranteed—to bring when it came time to shed clothes. The night was even younger than the man and his friends were behaving. There was time, if she didn't want to settle.

Even under normal circumstances, however, she was more willing to gamble with money than potential flings. She could always put in some extra hours to make up for money lost. A wasted, lonely night was only ever going to be what it was. She needed someone to share a bed with now more than ever. She couldn't stay on the game floor all night. Another distraction would be necessary when she got to her room, and here she had a bird in hand that wouldn't fly off even if thrown into the sky.

The man blushed and took the offered seat. After seeming to think over his next line for a moment, then remembering something he'd practiced in a shitty seminar, he said, "You know . . . you're like a goddess."

"I *do* know," Harrah said. "What's your name, handsome?"

The compliment appeared to short-circuit his brain for a second, then she saw him come back online in time to blurt out, "Craig. I'm Craig." Like he'd forget it again in another second if he didn't rush the words out that instant.

He extended his hand for a handshake. She took it, let it go, then made him wait a second for her to introduce herself. "Harrah."

Craig told her, "That's a pretty name."

Harrah laughed. "Prettier than me?"

She relished watching him turn a deeper shade of red and fumble for a response. "N-no. No. I mean, really . . . it couldn't be. You know?"

She wanted to tell him again *I do know,* but just returned his hopeful stare with an assured stare of her own. Like she was a bored, perhaps malicious, professor toying with a student who had given a right answer, seeing if they would break and second-guess themselves if kept in silence long enough.

Craig sighed and said, almost to himself, "I hope I'm not blowing this."

Harrah put a hand on his thigh and felt a level of attraction to him previously unavailable. "*Now* you're not. Not anymore. Craig, pretend I'd walk away right now if you said whatever your friends coached you up to say. I don't have any patience for nonsense today. I've had . . . I've had the worst fucking week. An awful, *awful* week. You really wouldn't believe it if I told you."

She swallowed the sobs that almost rushed into her voice, bit the inside of her lip to keep it from quivering, then muscled up a smile before going on. "Just relax and be real with me, and let's start from there. I didn't ask you to sit down for no reason, right?"

He nodded, and she nodded with him. "Okay, then," she said, "so you know I'm at least interested enough to have you sit with me. You've got a cute smile, and you seem generous. Why did it take you three drinks for you to even get close, though? I mean, I know I'm pretty, but not enough to be scary. Or am I wrong?"

He shook his head, said, "No," then put his hands up like he was preemptively asking her not to leave him. "Wait, not, 'No, you're not that pretty.' Just . . . okay, I'm just going to answer the main part of your question. You didn't scare me. But for a second, I thought the one lady was your friend. The uh . . . the Black lady. She kept walking between us, and she was looking at you, and sometimes me. I thought she was with you and was passing signals or something, and I couldn't tell what it meant."

She was looking at me?

Harrah wanted to interrogate Craig about this, ask what he might have noticed in the woman's look, what he thought of her overall, see if his impressions of her matched Harrah's, but instead she only said, "I'm here by myself. Sounds like you were overthinking it."

"I guess so," he said, sounding as unsure as Harrah now felt about this revelation that the woman she'd been watching had in turn been watching her. Harrah made herself set the potential strangeness of the woman's presence aside before it grew into a fixation. That wasn't the diversion she wanted now.

There would be time to think more about the woman later, wonder why she was present and what she could have been up to. She couldn't have spent much time in the casino's other rooms. The poker tables or craps tables, or even at one of the lounges where the crooners covered jazz and blues standards. Not based on how often Harrah had seen her on the floor near the slots, but never actually seated at a machine.

What was the woman here for, then?

Stop. Save it for later, she thought, meaning days or even weeks later, not the few hours it would take for later to arrive.

When later came, on the other side of midnight, the question of *What is she here for?* became as monumental as the ones Harrah had come to Eagle Pass to avoid.

Why was Frankie dead?

Who killed him?

Was Sarita involved?

Who else might be involved?

When later came, Harrah would become connected to her daughter-in-law in a unique, unexpected way, as she found herself sharing a hotel room with a dead man, and a killer.

12

It might be for the best if Tori's "envious demon" theory was correct, because it might mean everyone else Sarita knew and loved would be safe. If Angelo murdered Frank out of jealousy over their marriage, he'd have no cause to kill David, her parents, or Tori. He would "only" kill any man she loved romantically, and "only" after they were married, committed before God or the law. She didn't want that life, but she would take it over never being able to be around her family and friends without believing she was endangering them.

She had even started to consider how she could put Angelo's envy to good use, make something righteous out of his evil. Revisit those old, vigilante, hero-by-proxy ambitions that she never fully pursued.

How hard would it be for her to find men who deserved what Angelo would do to them—abusers and even murderers of previous wives and girlfriends—seduce them, marry them, and then wait for her "angel" to kill them? It would take patience and diligence, but it was doable, she thought. If she wanted to be extra safe, ensure she couldn't be incriminated after the third or fourth new husband died, she could target convicts. How many stories had she read about serial killers marrying a pen pal from behind bars? Probably not as many as it seemed, but enough to make her think she could lure one—or several, ideally—into her trap.

How could anyone justify suspecting her, no matter how many times it happened, when the men she married were locked up? What would be the argument? That she'd somehow broken in, beaten them to death, and then escaped unseen? That she was some queenpin living an unsuspecting public life while secretly masterminding brutal slayings perfectly executed by her underlings in maximum security prisons? That would be absurd, and moreover unprovable given it would be a lie. She could get away with it, she thought, and make something remotely meaningful out of Frank's murder, and the rest of her life, as well.

It was a grim fantasy, one less satisfying than her dream of killing Angelo. Not just killing him, unmasking him. Revealing a demon disguised as an angel, holding his flayed face for God to see, and declaring, "Look at what I've done for you. Even *you* didn't know you had a devil in your ranks. You owe me for this, and I'm not asking much in return. Just give me back my husband."

She was lost in these thoughts yet again when David broke through, saying, "I really think I should stay."

Sarita looked at her brother and Tori. They sat across from her on her couch in the living room. The couch she and Frank had picked out a month ago.

She wanted them to stay. She wanted her mother and father to be with her as well. As much as she wanted to believe Angelo was Asmodeus himself, she couldn't bet her brother's life on that. Besides, something significant threw off the theory's arithmetic. She and Frank had effectively lived as husband and wife for half a year before getting married, and had been sexually active for almost a year prior to moving in together. Asmodeus attacking Sarah's husbands on the wedding night had a connotation that needn't be in print to be evident. The demon couldn't stand to see Sarah take another man to bed. If Angelo was truly the same, he would have killed the boy she took to the homecoming dance her senior year of high school, and several others along the way. Frank would be alive because he would never have met her, as she'd have accepted hermitage years ago. That, or he'd be alive because she'd have found a way to be rid of her guardian angel, ideally by ridding the world of him, before introducing herself to the man she would fall in love with and marry.

Something else had motivated Angelo. Something she needed more time to ascertain, that she might never completely understand. Unless it was the obvious, and she was still in a denial so powerful the answer struck her as impossible.

Frank couldn't have been planning to hurt her, though. She accepted that her love for him might blind her to signs of something sinister. The world had no shortage of unfortunate women killed by husbands that they believed were incapable of harming them, even after they had threatened or attacked them in the past. Still, Sarita couldn't fathom why Frank would want to hurt her, or why he would wait for their wedding night to do it.

None of the standard motives for murder that came up time and again in true-crime shows and podcasts applied to them. Frank had no mistress, she felt confident about that. No enormous debts he hoped to cover with life insurance money. Even if he did have either of those things, unbeknownst to her, why the hell wouldn't he have tried to kill her when they went camping a few months ago? Or just kill her in the house and try to stage a break-in? Why would he have waited for them to be alone in their hotel suite, where he'd have zero alibi, zero chance to hide a body, zero hope to get away with it?

Even considering those finer points made her feel like she was formulating one of those impractical academic equations that prove why two plus two doesn't always equal four. A problem consisting of imaginary numbers, fuzzy numbers, irrational numbers, and the like. Things that had a place and purpose far removed from what mattered to Sarita.

Frank loved her. *Had* loved her. She still couldn't muster the optimism to console herself by thinking of him in a "next world" where he watched over her. Angelo's action had destroyed her belief in a great, beautiful beyond that belonged to people who lived and loved well. She couldn't presume Heaven as she had believed in it was any realer than angels, as she had believed in them. A world beyond what humans saw and experienced existed, that was all she felt was true, but whether it was idyllic or hellish or anywhere in between was impossible to know. All she could know was what Frank had meant to her. How he had treated her.

He held her like it slowed time down for him, made him live longer. Listened to her like he wanted to, never showing that he was either too tired or too busy, even though she knew he had to be sometimes. When he proposed he was so excited he could barely get the words out. He had been her remarkable man before Angelo reduced him to "used to," and "had been."

"Hey, I really don't think you should be by yourself," David said. "Me and Tori should stay the night."

Her brother's voice brought her back again to the here and now. She shook her head, both in response to what he was saying and to rattle her thoughts into place.

"I'm not safe to be around," she said.

"We've been around you all afternoon. Nothing's happened," David said. He was right. David had made it in that afternoon and had gone with Sarita to spend some time with their parents. Then the two of them met with Tori at a theater to watch the packed premiere of a movie Sarita already couldn't remember anything about.

Public places hadn't scared Angelo off completely in the past, but still seemed safer to her. He could have shown up at the wedding ceremony to murder Frank, appeared at the party to kill the asshole who was going to come back with a gun. Instead, he'd made sure both deeds were done in the proverbial dark.

She had pushed her luck allowing David and Tori to come back to the house with her after the movie. She was still far more afraid of letting them stay than letting them out of her sight.

"He might just be waiting for us to fall asleep," Sarita said.

"Why would he do that? It wouldn't matter to him. He's shown up whenever he wanted to before."

"I don't know, David. I just . . . I just know he shows up around me. It's one thing if we're out around other people, but . . . I don't want anything to happen to you. I *can't* let that happen. Please."

David stared at her, his expression communicating what he kept himself from saying. *I can't let anything happen to you, either.*

You've got to let that go, she wanted to tell him, but knew that if she did say it, she couldn't use the words "let go." Up through his senior year of high school, before he went to North Carolina for rescue training, she'd heard him, from time to time, talking in his sleep over what had happened at the beach.

I didn't mean to let go. I tried to hold on.

David, you were thirteen, she should have told him already. *It was you against nature. There was never anything for you to make up for, but if there was, you've already done it. You're a professional hero. Stop carrying this with you.*

She used to think of it primarily as stupid male pride, magnified by the "machismo" he must have inherited from their father's side of the family. He couldn't stand the idea of a strange male figure—Godsent or not—exposing his "failure" to save his little sister. At times she had felt offended by it, even a little hurt. She didn't think he'd rather that she had died instead of being rescued by someone else, but she thought part of him still resented Angelo enough for usurping his duty that he wished her guardian angel had done something to give him a second chance instead of outright saving her. She thought he wished that the angel had helped him to help her instead of directly intervening, even if that might have put Sarita at greater risk.

It really wasn't about that, however, although that didn't mean there wasn't something beneath the surface of his shame. David felt responsible for not holding on, not being stronger than the wave, even though he'd be blameless to anyone but a fool. More than that, he'd always been suspicious of Angelo, and always worried that a time like this was imminent. A time when Angelo would reveal that he was something else, and now that the time was here, David accepted partial blame for this as well. Because in his mind, if he had just held on, Angelo might never have surfaced, and all of this could have been avoided. It was another in the growing line of insensible things that Sarita found wearying, but for her brother's sake she could endure the fatigue.

"What if I sleep in my car?" he said. "I can keep watch, since the police haven't given you a detail, which is complete bullshit."

"They still sort of think I did it. Or I'm connected to it, or at least hiding something. They've got a guy in the neighborhood, they told me."

"Yeah. Bullshit, like I said."

"Not completely."

"Don't do that," he said.

She waved the rest of the exchange off, seeing it was headed toward a volley of technicalities and facts that weren't really truths.

I am connected to it. I am hiding something.

Yeah, but you didn't do anything.

Even if that was as far as it went, she didn't have the inclination or energy to go there.

"I can stay with him," Tori said. "That way he won't be alone. We won't exactly be here, but we'll be close if you need us, or if we need you, for whatever reason. And, you know, if he does pop up on us, maybe some of what I know can help."

"How?" Sarita said. "You going to pray him away?"

"Who's to say I can't?" Tori tapped her temple. "I have all kinds of invocations, wards, and incantations up here."

Sarita laughed, but was sure that Tori was only half joking. "And you haven't taught me a single one."

Tori grimaced. "If we had the time, by which I mean years—*many years*—I'd take you to someone who might. But the scariest thing about a spell is how easily it can go wrong. I've heard some horrible stories, and I was present once when somebody got it wrong and had a room full of experienced practitioners holding their breath. Best-case scenario when somebody does that is for nothing to happen, and we all got lucky that time."

"What would've been the worst case?" David said.

"I wouldn't even know where to begin listing all of the worst-case scenarios."

"Jesus."

Barely concealing her frustration, Sarita said, "We'll pick this back up in the morning." *You shouldn't underestimate me,* she wanted to say to Tori. *And if you know anything that you truly think has any chance of helping me you damn sure shouldn't keep it from me.* "If you want to stay across the street, that's fine, I guess. I don't know. I don't know if there's like a perimeter, a safe distance or something. I don't know if that's far enough away or not enough, or if it doesn't matter. I hate this. I fucking *hate* this. I hate *him.*"

A painful silence filled the room, like the preacher at a funeral had asked those in attendance to say a kind word about the deceased and no one was volunteering. Sarita broke it with a sigh and said, "Maybe I've been thinking about this backward. I know he won't hurt me, or at least doesn't want to. If I could do it over again, I'd put myself between him and Frank. I'd hold on to Frank to make it where he couldn't kill him without killing me, too. Okay, that's the plan. If you guys stay, we stay in the same room, you both stay right next to me. If he shows up, you stay so close to me he can't get to you unless it's through me."

She pointed at her brother before he could speak. "David, I am so damn serious about this. Don't give me any big-brother crap about needing to protect me or I will throw something at you, I swear."

He raised his hands, palms out, surrendering. "I was just going to say I was fine with it."

Sarita rolled her eyes. "Yeah, but you wouldn't have meant it."

They decided the living room was the best place to sleep in. It gave them room to maneuver if anything happened, and was near the front door if they needed to run. They pushed the couch, love seat, and chair against the walls, placed the coffee table on top of the sofa, then dragged the king-sized mattress from the spare bedroom into the living room. They managed to share a few jokes and soft chuckles as they worked. Then, all of them worn out from being on edge for so long, Sarita most of all, they fell asleep on the mattress together, Sarita in the middle, spooning Tori, David with his back to his sister.

As it had been every night after Frank's death, Sarita dreaded drifting into a nightmare. A reenactment of that night, perverted by the insinuations of the police questioning, the unspoken accusations of Harrah Stallworth and the rest of her kin. Sarita would be stuck in the hotel with Frank again, only this time when Angelo appeared she wouldn't lunge at him, try to pull him away, scream for him to stop. She'd thank him for saving her yet again, then watch with cold satisfaction as his fists erased Frank's face from her memory.

That nightmare sat at the cusp of her mind just before she slept, something she couldn't stop thinking about because she feared it so much, but if she experienced it, she was spared remembrance of it in the morning. What she did remember was the presence of the man she'd told Tori about earlier that day. "Cold Eyes," the stalker from California.

Maybe Tori was right, and Cold Eyes, or Sarita's memories of him, represented something in her subconscious she had always suspected about her guardian angel. That he couldn't be entirely trusted. That if his motive was purely to protect her, he could have done so by different means. Especially if he could predict every life-threatening event in her future. Instead he'd opted to watch from afar, appear unannounced, remain silent.

Tilt the perspective just a little, and those descriptors fit an obsessive, burgeoning killer, not a vigilant sentry.

In a way it fit for her to conflate Cold Eyes and Angelo in her night-mares. The problem was she knew the stalker was a distinct individual. And she remembered now even more clearly—years removed from a rou-tine that involved taking ayahuasca, iboga, or salvia like daily vitamins—sensing something well beyond a chill each time she saw him in California. It had been easy to blame it on the psychoactives back then, harder to dis-miss as a chemically induced overreaction in hindsight. Her *body* had re-acted to seeing him, the way it might to seeing clouds darker and lower to the ground than those belonging to an ordinary storm. Or the way it had reacted to the shadow of the wave that tried to crush and steal her when she was a child. She was sure she hadn't been alone in this. The menace Cold Eyes brought with him became a shared experience among all pres-ent whenever he arrived.

Or appeared.

She never recalled seeing him come through a door. The same applied for most of the people she met at clubs, bars, and parties, obviously, but with the stranger, somehow, it felt wrong. It always seemed like he materi-alized where she was when he wanted to.

Even the version of him that appeared in her dreams felt impossibly conscious and real, like he was deliberately projecting himself into her mind now that she felt she was more vulnerable and vacant. Unable to trust her guardian, barely able to think of another tomorrow without Frank, let alone the thousands of tomorrows to come.

There was an immediacy and knowingness in the gaze and smile Cold Eyes flashed in her nightmares. Part of Sarita wondered if he was out there in the real world, in Texas now, close, and using some of that forbidden magic Tori had spoken of to invade her sleep. To keep her from even remembering Frank's death. Push her dead husband out of her mind. Displace him.

An hour after dawn, the two detectives handling Frank's case woke her with a knock at her door, and when she opened it she almost thanked them for interrupting her nightmare. They apologized for arriving so early, and without calling first, but they wanted to be sure to catch her be-fore she might leave for the day. They said they needed to talk to her about a murder in a hotel room in a town by the border, Eagle Pass, that involved Frank's biological mother.

They spoke for another twenty or thirty seconds before Sarita clenched her teeth, shut her eyes, and asked them to give her a moment. Then she apologized and asked them to repeat themselves.

The phantom roar had flooded her ears as soon as she'd heard the words "Harrah" and "murder." Although it sounded less like a wave, this time, and more like a song of celebration.

13

After Harrah's second orgasm, Craig finished and turned into a snoring lump atop sweat-stained sheets. Craving more and unable to rouse Craig—the liquor, excitement, and release leaving him unconscious as opposed to invigorated—Harrah got dressed, left the room, and went back to the casino floor for another hour. She spotted only a few men she was willing to give a lingering look to—one she legitimately found attractive, two others she found passable. None of them even seemed to notice her looking at them, much less show any interest in taking or following her upstairs.

She had hoped to run into Craig's friends. One of them had been reasonably handsome, and she was sure she'd caught him giving her signs that if she wanted to "trade up," all she had to do was say the word, and he'd step over Craig to give her a better night. At the time she hadn't seized on this, unwilling to chance sparking a fight between Craig and his friend that would leave her empty-handed for the evening, but now, with Craig stuck at least three layers deep in dreamland, and with her still not ready to be left alone to dwell on the worst thing that had ever happened to her, she was eager to accept the unspoken offer. Unfortunately, he was nowhere to be seen, and after an hour of disappointment, with not even additional alcohol having any effect, she grew drowsy and deflated enough to return to the room with the hopes of falling asleep as fast and soundly as Craig had.

When the room's entry light struggled then failed to come on when she hit the switch just inside the door, she should have recognized it as a sign—and not the only one—that something was amiss, and that she'd be better off leaving the room to find help, even if she wouldn't be able to explain what she needed help with. The light had not merely flickered. It seemed to have fought, trembled, weakened, then died.

Still, she moved forward to try the nearest bedside lamp, but was paralyzed by the sense of being watched just before she pressed the button.

Something else was in her hotel room. It had been waiting for her, but had escaped Harrah's notice until now, despite its potency. It tilted the room, placed its center of gravity in an impenetrably dark corner between the television and the window.

Harrah thought that if she could point a flashlight into the corner, darkness would burn the beam to smoke. If she could hold a candle to it, darkness would eat the flame.

This was not a shadow. It was a piece of the night, alive and aware of its eternal war with light. Home to something that would rejoice if the day never came.

"Untrue," said someone hidden within the corner. A woman, whose voice sounded like a grim secret had come to life, learned to speak. "Without the day, what would happen to the rest of you? How long would you survive? And if not long, as I suspect, how would we survive without you? You breathers have little appreciation for your own value. It borders on contempt. It is fascinating and repugnant. I am grateful for every second that separates me from when I was one of you."

Harrah shook her head, trying to free herself from the grip of the shadow woman's voice, as well as her own unusual thoughts. She was not lyrically minded by nature. Not a poet, never one for elaborate metaphors or clever comparisons. Where had all that business about the night and darkness come from, then? Thinking of it like it possessed intelligence?

"I will accept blame for that," the woman said, continuing to pluck thoughts from Harrah's brain. "I sometimes unlock potential in people without trying. Imagine what else I could bring out if you let me try."

As Harrah began to sober up, she discounted the desire to believe she had descended into delirium, or that a bizarre night terror had sprung from her mind while she sleepwalked to that bed, or that this could in any other way be rejected as illusory. This was real. Someone else was in the room with her.

Holy *shit*, someone had broken into her hotel room.

Shit, where was her gun?

In her suitcase, on the floor at the foot of the bed. It would be obvious if she tried to go for it, wouldn't it? Damn it, of course it would, and it was at least as close to the woman in the corner as it was to her, if not closer. And what if the woman had a gun or even just a knife of her own? She wouldn't have to fight Harrah for the .45 in the suitcase; she could just shoot or stab her before it came to that.

She nudged Craig to try to wake him. She'd never needed a man to help fight her fights, but there was a huge difference between "need to have" and "better to have." If nothing else, Craig would give the intruder two people to keep tabs on instead of one. That could only play to Harrah's advantage, right?

The last shred of Harrah's inebriation left her as she registered that the man—the body—on the bed was shockingly cold. She snatched her hand away upon touching him, like a spark had leapt to her fingertip.

The realization that Craig must be a corpse, that he'd been dead long enough for his body to turn icy, readvanced the idea that this must be some kind of dream. The stillness of the moment, however, belied any suggestion that this wasn't reality, as did the unmistakable and rising smell of blood.

Like the very presence of the woman in the corner, the scent of blood seemed to have been deliberately hidden from her until the precise moment when it would startle her dead still. Harrah had read the scent likened to that of copper or pennies in books and articles, but that didn't capture the distinct aroma of human blood. It was sharper, more aggressive, and yet oddly not as disgusting as it should be. Human blood should stink worse than shit, Harrah thought. Its odor should be a dire warning, especially when spilled in significant quantities. *Someone here is hurt, and might be dead or close to it,* it should shout at the brain. *Something has made them bleed. If you're the one bleeding, seek help. If the blood is someone else's, choose quickly: try to save them, or run for your life from whatever has bled them, but do it fast. Don't waste another second.*

It wasn't that bad, however. Unpleasant, but not awful. Not hideous. Not a deathly smell. Why was that?

"Yes, why?" the woman in the corner said.

Harrah made herself touch Craig again and not recoil from his coldness. She pushed him to see if he would react, see if she was mistaken about him being dead. "Wake up."

She shoved him harder, felt for an injury on his chest, then his stomach. Nothing. She stretched her neck and managed to look down at him. His back was to her, and the little bit of light that framed the drawn shade— the light that cowered from the dark corner—was insufficient to give her a good look at his face. She was glad for that. She didn't need a *good* view of it to tell it wasn't there anymore. A messy crater was in its place, and the blood she smelled saturated his pillow. Craig's own mother wouldn't know him from a war casualty.

Just like Frankie, Harrah thought, and a rush of lightheadedness almost made her faint and fall.

It couldn't be coincidental, could it? Well, yes, it could be. *Anything* could be a coincidence, but this one would be extraordinarily cruel. The mother of a man whose face was crushed by an unknown assailant in a hotel room wakes up in a hotel room next to a man who has suffered a similar fate. What were the odds? If left to the flow of happenstance, minuscule. All but nonexistent. If orchestrated by someone, or several people, however, it changed Harrah from being exceptionally unfortunate to targeted.

She drew a slow, steadying breath, held it for a few seconds, then spoke to the person who had broken into her room. "Are you the one who killed my son?"

The subsequent silence felt like an admission, but Harrah needed to hear it. Waiting for confirmation was all that kept her from diving for her gun, because she knew she wouldn't survive the attempt, and was fine with that. She hoped only to live long enough to pump every bullet she'd brought with her into her attacker. Frankie's attacker. The one who had used a bat or a brick or some damn thing to beat her son to death while that girl had done nothing to help him, had done nothing but watched.

"Who are you? Do you know Sarita? Did she set this up?"

"No," the woman said, her tone deep enough to rattle the earth's core, the word a command, not a statement, trying to force Harrah to disbelieve her accusation. Harrah trembled, bit her lip, tried to think of this all being over soon, whatever this was. She'd come here to escape the grief and pain, and soon she'd be as far beyond it as anyone could ever be. All she wanted now was to kill her son's killer.

Kill her. Move, damn it. Get your gun. She killed Frankie. She's the one, you know it. Kill her. Kill her.

The darkness in the corner moved as though lifted and pushed by something within it. Harrah felt the room shrink, felt her fear expand to keep the walls back. The darkness nonetheless seemed to tower over her like something deliberately designed to destroy as much as possible when it inevitably fell. A face emerged from it, allowing light to touch it so that Harrah could clearly see who it was.

The Black woman from the casino floor, the one in the red dress. She was beautiful and familiar even beneath the candy-colored blood that covered her lips, chin, and neck.

The woman smiled down at Harrah, revealing clean teeth that had a reflective sheen, like stainless white metal. The upper fangs, just long enough to be plainly longer than they should be, shone brighter than the rest.

A dazzling delight filled the woman's eyes as she fully emerged from the shadow in layers of diaphanous black-and-red robes, but Harrah was drawn back to her smile when she licked between her teeth, side to side. The woman looked like she'd bitten off a shark's grin just to try it on and might spit it out when she got bored with it, exchange it for a wolf's or a tiger's.

"Kill me?" the woman said. "Please, try."

Harrah opened her mouth to scream, but felt a hand at her throat, holding firmly without squeezing. Yet. The woman shook her head slowly as Harrah held on to her scream.

"You do not want to do that," the woman said. "I will be gone before anyone arrives, and that will leave you to explain the man's body, much like your daughter-in-law's predicament."

So you do *know Sarita,* Harrah thought, then realized how insane such a simple, logical deduction was considering what she faced. The most pressing, necessary thought came to mind.

"What in God's name are you?" Harrah said.

"In God's name? Please. I am The Godmaker. Your son was meant to assist me with that before Sarita let him die."

"She let him?" Harrah said. Furious tears stung her eyes, briefly relieving her of her terror. "I knew she had to have done something to him some way. I *knew*."

"No, you did not. You could not have. But that is immaterial. I have a proposal, and you have a decision to make. Now listen closely. I will repeat myself, if necessary, but I will be displeased."

The hand at Harrah's neck tightened its grip enough for her to feel the pressure at the back of her eyes.

"Are you listening closely, Harrah?"

Harrah nodded, eked out "Yes" after the woman's grip loosened.

"Good. I propose to help you honor your son's destiny and get the revenge I know you covet. I followed you on the road here to feel the hate you have tried to quell. Weigh it for myself. I found it not only present, but impressive. And I have sampled hate in an array of flavors since long before the two halves of the world were aware of one another, so to impress me is an achievement. It would be tragic to let your anger atrophy. I offer you a use for it if you come with me. Alternatively, I take my leave and you can determine what to do next on your own. Consider your options carefully and make your choice."

Might as well have a gun to my head, Harrah thought, and was once again struck by the comparative mundanity of what was on her mind versus what was before her. A gun to her head would not have been preferable, strictly speaking, but would have at least been more comprehensible, and not a new experience. She had, with considerable help from her family, put herself in some bad situations before she had Frankie.

In front of her, however, was someone entirely different. What had the woman done to Craig? Bitten part of his face off? All of it? And not just the skin, either. The woman had gone beyond bone-deep from the look of it.

God, why was Harrah still thinking of her as "the woman," as if she were human? What she'd done to Craig wasn't something normal people could do. *None* of what she'd done was possible for regular people. Carrying the darkness with her, wrapping it around her like a cloud she could control. Her very presence now, the way she looked too tall for the room to fit her, yet too close to be more than a foot from Harrah's face while she was still in the bed, was incomprehensible.

Hadn't the woman said something, too, about not really being human? Or something about how she used to be a person but wasn't anymore?

What was the word she had used? It had sounded strange enough to lodge itself in Harrah's mind like a splinter that sunk all the way under the skin, even as she was focused on there being an intruder in her room, followed by the realization that she was next to a corpse. What was it that she had said? What word had she used?

Breathers.

"You breathers."

She hadn't noticed before, despite staring at the woman's mouth, because she'd been distracted by the sterling teeth, those formidable canines, but the woman did not breathe. She was not merely holding her breath; *she did not breathe.* Harrah watched and listened for signs of inhalation and exhalation she'd never realized she could recognize before. Slight flexes from the nostrils, subtle inflation of the chest, the whisper of air moving in and out. None of it was present near the woman . . .

Like she's a dead body.

Yes, that was why people were built with intrinsic identifiers of whether the person or even animal they were staring at was drawing breath. To help them tell the dead from the living. The woman wasn't dead, though, not by any measure that mattered. So maybe the identifiers were there to help distinguish the "breathers" from . . . whatever it was Harrah saw before her, with its hand still on her throat, in position to choke the oxygen out of her despite promising to leave and let her live.

Harrah was able to picture that hand around Sarita's throat instead of her own. Those teeth crunching through the girl's cheekbones as they must have Craig's. The girl's mother mourning as hard as Harrah had at Frank's "homegoing" service. And at last she felt something more than the anger, fear, and grief that had possessed her for the longest week of her life, so long it might as well have been another life. Something the casino lights and noise couldn't give her, something half-decent sex with a man she'd just met couldn't deliver.

A semblance of satisfaction.

Like she'd been hungrier than she realized before someone prepared a perfect meal for her, and now that's all she could think about. Eating well, feeling full. Sitting back and sighing without a need in the world for a few minutes at least. The best things in life were that simple sometimes.

"What do you need me to do?" Harrah said to the woman.

"Choose, as I said. Come with me or do not."

"I'll go with you."

The woman's smile widened, looked like it wanted to wrap around her head, or was extending to the width necessary to decapitate someone with one bite. Harrah's heart beat like it was doing work for two bodies. There was an odd gentleness to the woman's smile, however, and it settled Harrah. The woman wasn't going to attack. If she'd wanted to do that, she could have done it while Harrah slept. Left her in the same state as Craig.

Poor Craig. Thought he'd gotten lucky tonight and ended up with the ultimate misfortunate instead. At least he wasn't like her boy, though. At least he hadn't thought he'd fallen in love with the one who brought savage, unholy death right to him. Made him a closed-casket service, denied his momma one last kiss goodbye before he went into the ground.

The sympathy Harrah had for him faded as the woman took her hand.

To be wrapped in shadows, she instantly realized, is more a matter of being secreted from light than being consumed by darkness. Anyone who had never experienced it couldn't possibly understand the distinction. Light was a defiant, seeking energy, an explorer and hunter. Darkness was a default state, inherently lazier than its counterpart, so when it became active it was oddly more meaningful. Darkness that moved as though endangered and desperate was the most dangerous thing that could exist.

The air within the cocoon of darkness was clean in an alarming way. Harrah felt like she was being readied for a procedure. She would find out in a moment dominated by nausea and dizziness that she was actually being prepared for transport. Momentum lifted and seized her, hollowed her as the movement surrounded her. She couldn't tell if she was going up or down, right or left or diagonally, but she could tell that she was *going*. It was as though she were caught in a sentient storm that hadn't made up its mind where it wanted to take her.

She reached into the blackness and felt as though her arms stretched into infinity, as though she could have touched distant planets and constellations if they were prevalent enough, but truly so much of reality was made of emptiness that even grazing the cold stone of a planet at the very edge of a solar system was miraculous.

When Jim Morrison sang, "Day destroys the night, night divides the day," he was being unbelievably naive. The day is the smallest, thinnest thorn that can prick the night's finger. Less than that. The sun provided a periodic shield against merely seeing the night. That was the best it could do. The darkness that Harrah was within now should never fear destruction.

And yet, despite its dominance of existence, the darkness still saw the sliver in its finger as a fatal threat. It was profoundly insecure given its position and prevalence. Harrah thought she understood why. She was only human, a "breather," but more aware now than ever of how a stupid, insignificant insect carrying an even less intelligent microscopic germ could end a cherished, sapient life.

Her stomach dropped as the blackness retreated. What she immediately noticed under the moonlight were the blackened puncture marks in her right palm, one just off center, over her heart line, the other nearer her life line. Neither bled, and she only felt a slight sting when she made a fist. They looked like twin bug bites that went untreated for so long the infection they caused ate itself up, necrotizing and numbing the meatiest parts of her hand.

She looked up to ask the woman in red if she had done this to her, and how she had done it, only to see the woman walking away from her already, gracefully moving toward a remote building whose grayed wooden walls were decorated with dozens of old license plates and road signs. The largest sign, which looked like it might have been taken from a long-defunct hotel or resort, read BAJA GRANDE.

Harrah looked around and saw plenty of space to run, but nowhere to run *to*. Not even any shade for when the daylight came. The closest hiding space would have been underneath the elevated pickup truck parked beside the bar, along with just a few other trucks, cars, and motorcycles in the makeshift gravel lot. The truck was sitting on tires better suited to an eighteen-wheeler, raising it so high you'd barely have to bend down to grab and pull someone out from underneath it. That was the best available option.

The unlikelihood of a successful getaway isn't what kept Harrah from trying, however. It was what the woman had said about making use of Harrah's anger. Not letting it . . . what was it she said?

Atrophy.

Harrah couldn't recall coming across that word before but thought she understood what the concept meant based on the context. She saw her anger like it was a withered old man, too weakened by inactivity to move, sitting in a chair, beaten down by his laziness, talking about all the things he could have done with himself if he had ever cared to try. That's what her rage would become, this miserable old thing living within her, aging ahead of her, then dragging her along to catch up with the years it had already accumulated. Unless she did something with it.

She stood and trotted to catch up to the woman in red, who had already entered Baja Grande. When Harrah came through the door she saw everyone present standing dead still, like they were all made of cards and feared falling apart if they twitched. The music coming from a faux-vintage jukebox—a song that she recognized was barely into its first verse—and several mostly full glasses atop the small tables told her that someone had just put a tune on and had ordered a round for the group. It was easy to guess the catalyst for such odd stillness, especially since everyone was staring at the woman in red.

The woman walked past the bartender and the three men who looked like off-duty security or law enforcement with their tucked-in polo shirts and holstered sidearms. Two of them had dates, one was a spare, which added up to five helpless people closest to the door. Near one of the pool tables were two middle-aged men in flannels and jeans, and surrounding the other pool table were four bikers and their "old ladies."

By the back of the bar, close to the jukebox, in a space big enough to dance, was a tall, thin man wearing tight jeans, good boots, and a wide hat. The woman next to him—his wife, judging by the matching bands on their fingers—was, Harrah saw, the only person not standing. She was crouched so low she was practically sitting on the floor, and was almost shivering out of her loose-fitting top. The cowboy was able to move a little. His hand was in his pocket, digging for something that he just managed to pull out as the woman in red got close to him.

Harrah saw that it was a rosary. He held it forth like a riot shield, and the woman in red grabbed the dangling cross and pressed it back into the man's hand like she was returning something he'd lost.

Harrah could see the woman's smile through the back of her head and felt her laughter shift the energy in the bar from dread to doom.

"Eduardo, did you know your great-grandmother gave your grandmother this rosary to protect her from sickness when she became a nurse?" the woman said. "And your grandmother gave it to your father before he turned thirteen to protect him from the sinfulness she sensed could dominate his life. And then your father would keep it in his pocket, much like you, for years. Unlike you, though, he would conveniently forget it was there when he did certain things, such as dangle babies above bonfires to coerce people who did not owe him money to pay him as though they did. Then he would conveniently remember it later, when he expected to be forgiven while lacking true remorse.

"It has had an interesting little journey. So keep it close to you. Your own daughter will want to claim it from your body as you did from your father's."

Eduardo eked out the kind of cry you might make if there was a knife pinning a full scream down in your lungs. Harrah heard the others grunt and whine and make other noises used by people pleading for their lives in the days before language was born.

"I am not going to punish you for your father's sins," the woman said. "Nor will I spare you for the righteousness of his elders. I am going to kill you and everyone here because I have an objective, and because you are all quite convenient."

Harrah made herself watch what took place next, although she had to shut her eyes, turn away, or cover her ears—sometimes all of the above— multiple times. The worst thing about it wasn't the sight or oddly sweet smell of the blood, nor the sounds of ripping and cracking as the woman went to work. The worst thing was seeing everyone wait their turn without being allowed to do what the woman in red was letting Harrah do. Look away. Turn around. Move at all.

14

The officers tried to spare Sarita certain details, possibly attempting to trap her, invite her to divulge something she shouldn't know if she wasn't involved in the killing. Sarita presumed good faith, however, and thought the detectives were trying to be merciful. Keep from her the specifics that would paint a clear picture of how connected this stranger's death was to her husband's. That only made it more apparent to her. The man last seen alive with Harrah Stallworth must have met an end as brutal as it was mysterious. His head destroyed by a weapon as lost as the detectives told her Harrah was now.

"You had said before that your mother-in-law was upset about being uninvited to the wedding," the taller detective doing most of the talking said. "Did she say anything that might have sounded particularly harsh? Anything that stood out?"

Behind Sarita, seated on the sofa in the rearranged living room, Tori and David listened, not having been told to leave by the detectives. The line of the questioning and the fact that Tori and David were allowed to stay and hear it told Sarita she was less of a suspect than Harrah was.

"Nothing too crazy," she said. "Not for her anyway, but she always kind of . . . I don't know."

"Anything you can say might help us." He quickly added, "I mean, help us find her and make sure she's okay. And once we do, we can also question her again and see what more there might be to all of this."

Sarita nodded. The side of her happy to imagine Harrah under closer scrutiny was small but feisty. She was almost warmed by the image of Harrah sweating under interrogation while knowing she was innocent, feeling a modicum of what Sarita had felt at Frank's funeral while being watched and wordlessly accused by the Stallworths. But the chill of fear and uncertainty was far stronger. She could only imagine that Angelo had killed the man they said Harrah was with, and had then done something to Harrah as well. Why, though? She'd thought she was struggling to make sense of things before, but this news made her realize she'd underestimated the density of the obfuscating mist that surrounded her.

She thought of herself as a stone safe in the shape of a person, no combination, no key, only capable of being unlocked by itself. This kept her composed enough to keep her response precise and honest without revealing more than she wanted to. "Harrah never got along with me, or with Frank all that much, and she said some hurtful things when she didn't get her way with the wedding, but nothing really out of the norm for her."

"'Hurtful things,' such as?"

"Look, it all sounds a little ridiculous to talk about considering everything that's gone on, but you know how there's the usual mother-son dance at a wedding? Frank picked Misty—his stepmother—over Harrah for that, and she went off. Pretty much said that since he wasn't treating her like his mother, she wished she wasn't his mother. She said she wished she'd never had him, would've been better off without him. She was just saying stuff, though. I never liked her because she never liked me, but I don't think she meant any of that."

The detective jotted notes in a small pad, gave a single nod. "What about anyone else in her family? Did you ever hear anything from any of them about you or Frank? Anything you think we should know?"

Sarita rubbed her forehead like she had a headache. "Oh, I don't know. Just stuff Frank told me, but he never said exactly what they said. A few times he came home upset after visiting them and told me he'd come close to fighting somebody over something they said about me before his uncle would always settle everybody down. I guess what's weird is that the only thing I really heard straight from any of them was an apology. I've got some texts still in my phone I could find, probably. After Frank would tell me about the fights—or almost-fights—then in about a day or two I'd get a text from whoever must have said something telling me they were sorry about it. Frank always said it was probably because his uncle Everett, who kind of runs the family, he probably made them do it."

"Could you forward those to me?" the detective said. He provided the number and Sarita found the three texts quickly in her phone by searching "Hey Sureta," "Hey Sirita," or "Hey, I'm Frank's cousin." She remembered each incident despite never knowing what slur had been directed at her in absentia, or what joke had been made at her expense.

Growing up half-Black and half-Mexican had inured her to insults and insensitivity to a degree, because she had backward-ass relatives on both sides of the family, young and old, male and female. Black cousins who tried to tell her what they thought about her Mexican side, *tíos* and *tías* who tried to tell her something about her Black side. Sometimes they packaged offenses in complimentary wrapping paper and sincerely thought they were saying something she would appreciate, and she'd chosen in her late teens to let much of it slide.

Sarita smacked her lips and shook her head, then immediately recognized that the detective would read this as something unspoken, so added, "This is just crazy. You don't know where Harrah is at all? Do you think she's okay?"

"We're working on tracking her down," the shorter detective said, finally chiming in. "We'll definitely keep in touch. Please do the same."

They must really think she did something, Sarita thought. They hadn't affected sympathy or comfort for the potential demise of Harrah. Sarita had stated they weren't close, but she had also expressed concern for her missing mother-in-law. If the detectives had an overriding inclination that she was dead or in danger, Sarita thought they would have shown it, even while attempting to conceal it. Their tone, their eyes, the wording of their questions and affirmations, something would have given it away. Instead they spoke of Harrah as though she might be connected to her son's murder.

They brought up her family as well, and Sarita could see them coming up with scenarios that pointed a finger at one of the more disreputable members of the Stallworth clan. Harrah might not have been culpable of anything, she was Frank's mother after all, but perhaps someone related to her had overheard her say something she didn't really mean, something cruel or even threatening, and acted on it. Somehow broke into the hotel suite on Frank and Sarita's wedding night, perhaps wearing one of those realistic masks you can order online, accounting for why Sarita inaccurately identified the intruder as a stranger. They then used a hammer to beat Frank's skull into paste and somehow escaped without being noticed by cameras or anyone else in the hotel.

It was as good an explanation for an unsolvable murder as any for the police assigned to investigate. Except it wasn't the truth.

Sarita's "guardian angel" had done the deed. But now he'd apparently done the same to a man in a city far enough away to be two states over in many parts of the country. A man who had come to Harrah's hotel room.

With their questioning concluded, the detectives left, and Sarita watched them get into their car and drive off. She counted to thirty after they made a turn and left her sight, wanting to be safe beyond certain that they wouldn't come back, in case they were hoping to catch her ... doing what? Dancing in her doorway at the news that the latest part of her murderous master plan had fooled them? Hell, why not? What about that idea was any more absurd than anything that had happened in her life since Frank died? Or anything since she'd been saved from drowning by a mystery man from nowhere when she was nine?

She turned to David and Tori, standing behind her, confusion shaping their faces.

"So ... what are you thinking?" David said.

Sarita stepped inside and shut the door, taking a moment to ask herself what, of import, *was* she thinking? "I don't know. But I feel like Harrah's still alive. I think if Angelo did this ... if he killed her, I can't see why he wouldn't have left her next to this other guy."

"Am I crazy or did they sound a little like they thought she might be a suspect instead of a victim?"

Sarita nodded. "I got that, too."

Tori said, "Is it possible she was involved from the start? I mean with Frank's death, too."

"How could she do that?" Sarita said. "A spell or something? Shit, Tori, you tell me. You know more about ..." She trailed off and rubbed her eyes before tears of frustration could get large enough to drop. "I'm sorry."

"You didn't even say anything," Tori assured her.

"I want to talk more about what you mentioned yesterday. The incantations and all of that. I know, I know, it's dangerous, but just tell me what you can about it if you can't really teach me anything. Is that okay?"

"We can do that. It might help to figure some things out if we talk it through."

"Okay. Let's get out of the house, though. I just . . . I don't feel right in here." She didn't want to say exactly what didn't "feel right" to her, for fear of making Tori more reticent to share. Given her friend's warning about how tricky and treacherous magic could be, however, Sarita wasn't keen to discuss the subject in her home, in case she inadvertently said the perfectly wrong thing that would somehow curse the house and invite demons to inhabit it. With the way things had gone recently, that not only seemed possible to her, but likely.

15

"The most dangerous thing about any legitimate 'spell'—I can't think of a better word—but the dangerous thing is that every little piece of it matters." Tori stayed quiet for a moment after this, letting her information float over the table like a cloud full of unreleased thunder.

They were at The Lantern Café, a restaurant near the downtown that Sarita had known would be busy, but not overly so. They had taken a rideshare service instead of one of their cars after David made an offhand comment about it possibly looking suspicious if they were seen driving from Sarita's house shortly after the police had visited inquiring about Frank's mother being missing. Like they were running out to go meet with conspirators, let them know the cops were onto them. The police probably hadn't fully excluded her as a suspect in Frank's death just because they weren't overtly treating her like one.

It struck Sarita as a bit silly, but then she thought of how much sillier she'd feel if in fact the cops did come back later, asking about her whereabouts at certain hours, why she had left when she did, et cetera. If nothing else, a rideshare-service driver provided instant, independent corroboration of an alibi.

Sarita and Frank used to frequent The Lantern. She had treated him to eggs, steak, and mimosas here a few months ago for his birthday. He'd been in a decent enough mood that night to believe he could weather Harrah's company, but she had declined the invitation to his birthday dinner, as had a few cousins he had invited, hoping to make a little bit of peace in light of the contention related to the wedding. Everett, ever the family statesman, had been the only one to attend.

In fairness to the Stallworths, Sarita didn't think the family's declination had much, if anything, to do with The Lantern being well-known as queer-friendly. To her knowledge, one of Harrah's preferred drinking spots was a gay bar, and one of Frank's aunts was married to another woman, which made her the subject of many jokes among the Stallworths—some that stood at and leaned over the line of outright hatefulness when she wasn't around—but that was the extent of it. Graded on the curve of what she expected of Frank's folks, Sarita thought that made them as close to tolerant as they were capable of being.

She wouldn't have given this any thought at the moment, particularly given what she wanted to learn from Tori, if not for the four familiar faces she had just seen come through the restaurant's front door. She might not have recognized three of them had she not just seen them at the funeral two days ago, but Frank's great-uncle Everett was impossible to forget, miss, or mistake for someone else.

He had a shaved and tattooed scalp, Spanish-moss beard, and the physique of a retired, shorter heavyweight who never minded his diet or invested much in "roadwork."

According to stories Frank had heard and relayed to Sarita, Everett had indeed been an amateur boxer once upon a time, as well as a bouncer, a bodyguard, a professional wrestler, a low-rent stunt driver, and a "bandit truck driver" running goods from East Texas to South Carolina in his heyday. Frank had idolized Everett enough as a kid to once dress up as him for Halloween. Harrah even let him shave his head clean instead of finding a skull cap for him, and helped him adorn his head with a dozen temporary rub-on tattoos of stars, sharks, and tiger stripes to distantly approximate the elaborate, zoologically themed tapestry that crowned Everett. It was the only childhood picture of himself with Harrah that Frank treasured, and Sarita knew it was more a keepsake of his uncle than of his mother.

Sarita thought she saw the host at the door flinch at the sight of Everett and his nephews when they came in. When Everett caught her watching him a second later, spotting her several tables away like he'd known where she'd be seated, Sarita forced herself not to blink.

"Hey," David said, sitting across from her, his back to the entrance. "What is it?"

He started to look back but she wagged her fingers without raising her hand from the table and he understood.

"A few of Harrah's people. It's nothing," she said.

Before he could respond, the waitress came back with their drinks, as well as the steak knife David would need for the "Cowboy Steak Breakfast" he had ordered.

Almost before the waitress left, David said, "That is absolutely *not* nothing. What do you think they're doing here? Do they just come here a lot? That can't be a coincidence, can it?"

Sarita watched the host lead Everett and his party to a booth that gave Everett and the scrawniest of the young men with him the opportunity to stare at her as they pleased. She shook her head, then turned to Tori. "Don't leave us hanging. Tell us the rest."

Tori looked between David and Sarita as though one had given her permission to speak and the other had told her to keep quiet. Seemingly settling on Sarita as the sole authority, she said, "Well, uh . . . okay, I guess I should be clear that there's really nothing I can teach you. I mean, the people I learned from didn't even *teach* me, they just informed me, and I picked some things up along the way. There's a huge difference. I know invocations, for instance, but I wouldn't actually trust myself to invoke anything. I know the words to say, how often to say them, the right candles to burn if that's called for, all the steps to certain rituals, but I'd never trust myself to really try any of them. It's like knowing the lyrics to a song without knowing the tune, and knowing that even if you knew the tune, you still aren't a singer. Except that in this case if you sing even a little bit off-key you might get yourself hurt or killed, or somebody else. Like I said before, it's all very, *very* delicate."

"There has to be a starting point," Sarita said. "People have to practice somehow. The people you learned from weren't experts from day one, right? You're making it sound like it's all or nothing, but that can't be the case. People have to start practicing with something. You don't know any 'starter spells' or anything?"

"You start with small, small protective prayers that I don't think you're really interested in. Little personal things that are just supposed to get you through the day a little easier. They help protect your peace of mind, maybe guide your decision-making. Control your impulses or give you a little more courage for a moment, if that's what you're after. It can take years to even get good at that, from my understanding of it, and it's like anything else where some people have a knack for it and others don't.

"Look, here's the most important thing. On some level, from how I understand it, any spell we can learn is really just asking for a favor. We never have any real power. We're just people. The things beyond us that have the power, and they either listen to us or they don't. A spell is a prayer, a prayer is a pledge, a pledge is a plea, and on and on. The pledges, the contracts, the rules, they're all so old that 'ancient' isn't even the word for it, and they go both ways to a certain degree, but a very limited degree. All of the onus on not screwing it up belongs to anyone trying to defend something, or conjure something, or curse someone, what have you. Do you understand what I'm saying?"

"I think so."

"You've got to know this. I'm serious, Sarita. I can tell you've got that look, and it's making me think I shouldn't have said anything in the first place. I was joking about something I know better than to joke about. Listen, I know you, and I'm telling you, you can't just go online or something and try to research this, thinking you can learn on your own. I mean it. Ninety-nine point nine percent of what you'd find will be fake, but that doesn't necessarily make it harmless, either. And the remaining one in a thousand would probably be more dangerous. Don't play around with that." Tori turned to David. "You neither."

He glanced at her, nodded, then went back to looking at Sarita, as he'd been doing throughout Tori's explanation and warning. Sarita guessed he was trying to read her, examine how tense she was, how concerned. She wanted to ask him if she looked nervous, because she couldn't quite tell how she felt. The last time she'd been scared for herself or even anyone she loved, prior to her wedding night, had been the night of the accident in Austin. Since then, she'd so embraced her presumed invincibility that she now realized she wasn't quite sure what genuine, in-the-moment fear felt like anymore. Even the night of Angelo's attack, she'd been more bewildered than scared. After that she had been paranoid, anxious, but never alarmed the way you are meant to be when a threat is looming and visible.

Everett sat at the edge of the booth, leaning forward, his inside arm on the table, his outside arm on his knee, fingers on both hands flexing, stretching, readying for something. Was he really going to try something here, in public, in full view of dozens of people? She couldn't imagine he was that reckless. Among the many things he'd been in his life, according to Frank, a convict wasn't among them. He had several other relatives who managed to get themselves locked up, some multiple times, but Everett had not only dodged prison time for all sixty-plus years of his life, he'd only ever been arrested once, for a traffic ticket he'd refused to pay or show up to court for on the principle of not accepting a camera's opinion that he'd run a red light. Despite having done his share of dirty work and having lived his share of sin, he had avoided hard time, because, as he told Frank and Frank told Sarita, he didn't have to be a smart man to be a cautious one.

Trying to attack Sarita now would be the height of incaution, but maybe Harrah's apparent disappearance, coupled with Frank's murder, had pushed Everett to do something foolhardy. Maybe he just didn't care what happened to him as much as he cared about making something happen to the person he believed to be at the root of his family's recent misfortunes.

Sarita considered this possibility, alongside the possibility that Angelo was no longer her protector. Even if he was, she no longer wanted him to be. If Everett and his boys had something bad planned for her, Angelo might show up to violently upend their designs, then turn his attention to David and Tori, and then to every other person in the restaurant, for all she knew. She imagined the aftermath of it for a moment, less than a second, the exact frame of time her brain could withstand. So much red, so much silence.

David and Tori . . . incomplete. Spread amongst strangers all likewise torn apart.

She bit the insides of her cheeks, shook her head. To hell with this. It wasn't enough that she was losing sleep, losing weight, stressing herself sick over the chance that an inhuman maniac might pop up out of nowhere and slaughter someone dear to her? She also had to contend with the Stallworth clan's attempt at intimidation, which might provoke the monster she was wary of?

Sarita stood, grabbed a chair from an unoccupied table, brought it back to her own table, placing it between herself and her brother, then motioned for Everett to join her. Everett acknowledged this with a short huff of laughter and a pinched smirk almost invisible under his beard. The young man next to him looked at him, started to say something, but Everett ignored him, stood, and accepted Sarita's invitation.

Up close, his eyes were softer than they had seemed from just a few feet farther away. Sarita could see the fatigue in them now as well. They looked like leaden clouds wanting but unable to release rain. Sarita focused on them, not wanting to look at David or Tori, certain that they would be concerned at minimum, possibly confused. Tori would know who Everett was from the wedding and funeral, and maybe even the party Frankie had thrown where he proposed to Sarita, but she couldn't recall if she'd told David about Everett before. Even without foreknowledge of who he was, or perhaps because of that lack of foreknowledge, David was still apt to be anxious about the man seated to his left, staring at his sister.

Forgoing an introduction, if one was needed, or any pretense that his presence wasn't suspicious at best, Sarita said to Everett, "It's not a coincidence that you're here, is it? Did you follow us?"

In her periphery, she saw David shift in his seat, tense up as he angled himself to fully face Everett, ready to grab the steak knife on the table and attack if the old man even flinched in a manner he took as threatening. She didn't spare David a full glance to confirm this, but broke eye contact with Everett for less than a second, just to see what the boys he brought with him were doing. She still could see only one of them, a pale young man with a hard jaw and what appeared to be a swollen upper lip. He seemed to intentionally keep his head down, his hands clasped before him as his leg bounced with nervous energy under the table. He looked like he might be praying, or just making sure there'd be no chance for him to get caught staring if his uncle turned back after already having indicated he was taking care of this. Both things were likely true, Sarita realized.

Everett held his response long enough to make her wonder if he had no intention of telling her anything, then said, "I understand the police told you about Harrah."

Why would they tell you that? Sarita thought. Were they trying to pit the Stallworths against her? She could have told them not to waste the effort on something that would happen without their help. Maybe they just let it slip while trying to warn the family to stay away from her. Or—shit, why wasn't this the first thing she thought of—Everett was trying to bluff something out of her? Maybe he didn't know if the cops had spoken to her at all, and was just hoping she'd respond with something unintentionally confessional. She considered mimicking his silence, extending it until she saw some flames melt down the affected patience in his stare. Feed him lies, quick ones, monosyllabic nonanswers, until a vein full of burning fuel started to bulge in his temple. Frustrate this man who'd lost his great-nephew days prior and whose niece was now missing, aggravate him right up to the brink of emotional injury just so Sarita could be on the giving side of hurt for a little while.

That was a stupid impulse, and easy to be rid of after she identified what it was. Lying required more energy than she wanted to devote, either to the act or to Everett.

"They came by this morning and told me," she said. "I'm sorry to hear about it, and I've got absolutely nothing to do with it."

"I see. You can understand why I might want to talk to you about it, though, can't you? Could be my family's just going through a hell of a time for no real reason, just the way the world works. Or we're cursed or some-thing. Maybe one of us is Job from the Bible and don't know it, and more of us are going to get hurt or killed just so they can live through it. Lots of could bes and maybes on the table. All I can say for sure is Harrah's gone missing right after her boy died, and those things feel like they're con-nected, and the only person I know who knows anything about what hap-pened to Frankie is you. And I was just hoping to talk to you about that."

"Yeah. Just 'talk.' That's why you showed up with numbers?"

Everett put his hands on the table, palms flat, fingers stretched. A per-formative gesture from a man who'd likely heard "Show me your hands" at least once or twice from cops and fellow criminals alike. He glanced at David and Tori before making it back around to Sarita, and for a moment she felt like he was giving them power, and her most of it, as though she were the head of a criminal enterprise, and he was the head of his own lesser outfit, looking to advance, but accepting, on the surface at least, that this wasn't the time and place to assert himself.

"I come with certain assumptions, and a lack of trust that I'm fighting with, not gonna lie," Everett said. "But I wanted to come alone. Those boys wouldn't let me. They think you either killed our Frankie or conspired to do it. Now, I don't believe that, but you can see why they wouldn't let me come here without backup if they think that way, can't you?"

She wanted to tell him no, but her stronger urge to tell no lies pressed her into silence. Everett nodded as though she'd given an answer.

"Can I tell you something? See that boy back there with the lip?" Everett said.

Sarita looked at the booth again, at the young man pretending to pray. Joey, wasn't it? She confirmed this time that his upper lip was fatter and redder on the left side of his mouth than on the right.

"He got into a fight recently?" she said.

"As recently as on the way here. Not a fight, though. He knows way better than to ever try to hit me back. If he hit me in a dream he'd wake up and put his head through a wall so I wouldn't have to. But on the way here he said something ugly about you that I don't condone, and caught a good smack for it. Then one more to the back of his head to make the lesson stick. Then I told him—because I try not to hit without teaching—I told him, Joey, you must not have loved Frankie enough if what you said about his wife is in your heart. And if it's not in your heart and you were just saying it to be saying it, that might be worse. Either way, if that's all you got to say, then shut the fuck up. Because the only foul word any of us should ever call you, Sarita, is 'killer,' if that's what any of us thinks you are, and the only reason to be mad at you is if that's what we think.

"Nothing else matters. Male or female, skin color, where you're from, what's your background, I don't give a shit about that nor a damn thing else you could think of. You could be my mirror image sitting across from me, and if you killed any of mine, my nephew in this case—my *good* nephew—I'd hate you the same as if you were my total opposite. You see what I'm saying? I'm telling you this so you know what's important to me. How I feel."

Sarita felt a wet burn in her eyes and blinked rapidly to weaken the sensation. She did not want to feel any empathy for this man, or believe he was capable of empathizing with her. She didn't want to think he loved Frank even half as much as she had, was enduring a tenth of the pain she was living with, but was instead more like Harrah, selfish enough to miss her own son's wedding over that damn dance, knowing she wasn't the one who raised him, knowing he'd called her "Mom" a hundred thousand fewer times than he'd said it to his stepmother. Or like the young man with the fat lip in the booth, who didn't even have enough real love in him for Frank to keep from hurling epithets at his widow.

There had to be a reason why Everett was Frank's favorite, however. It wasn't just his ink, his beard, the tough look, and controlled presence. It wasn't because he always showed up when no one else did. He must have felt for Everett whatever he thought his uncle felt for him.

"I didn't kill my husband," Sarita said, "and before you say it, I didn't set him up, either."

"I wasn't going to say that. Deep down, I don't believe that you did. I could be wrong, but Frank is . . . he *was* the absolute last member of our family I'd pick to be dumb enough to marry someone liable to kill him. I think that's why all the rest are so sure you had to do it, aside from the circumstances, even though they don't realize it. But if it could happen to them with any of their wives or girlfriends, why not Frankie, too, since he was one of us? Except he was different. He was the good one. You know, I was looking forward to your babies. Getting a few more good ones in the family. That would have been nice."

David sighed. "Jesus."

Sarita shook her head, held on to her tears as Tori reached under the table to take her hand.

"I didn't kill my husband," Sarita said again. The only thing she could think to say.

"No, but you saw who did it," Everett said. "And I gotta believe you know more than you've told. Maybe you got caught up in something with the wrong people prior to meeting Frank."

"That's not my sister," David said. She hadn't needed to tell him to keep quiet thus far, to just keep his eye on Everett and the other Stallworths and let her speak for herself. But she couldn't blame him for reaching a break-ing point now. Wouldn't have blamed him for reaching it sooner.

"I'm not judging," Everett said. "Lord knows I can't, so I'm not. What I'm saying is that if that's what's going on, you can tell me. I'm asking, hum-bly, for you to tell me. If it's something you can't tell the police because you're afraid of what might happen, tell me so I can help to do something about it."

Everett leaned forward. His eyes shimmered like a lake under moon-light. Sarita saw David stiffen, held her hand to him, asking for one last ounce of patience.

"Sarita, I believed in Frankie, and he loved you," Everett said, "so I've got to believe in you, too. And I think . . . Nah, I have *faith* down in to the deepest part of me that you want to kill the son of a bitch who murdered Frankie just as bad as I do. Am I right or wrong?"

Of all the bizarre, unbelievable things to have happened to her, to have governed her life, Sarita wondered how high this moment must rank. The moment she found herself all but psychically linked to the old white man with a shaved head, gray beard, and hateful family that must have called her every applicable slur in the Big Book of Bigotry when he wasn't nearby. That all seemed immaterial.

He could be hoping to fool her, waiting to signal his kin to jump up, draw knives or guns, and spill blood the second she confessed to indeed knowing much more about Frank's killer. That's what she'd suspected of him when he first sat down and started talking. She tried to hold that in the front of her mind, but it was falling back in favor of another thought. That Everett deserved to know. That it might benefit her to let him know. Because while her parents and Tori and David could give her more love and compassion for her loss than she could store within herself, they couldn't match the fury she felt for the "angel" that murdered her husband the way that Everett could. He wasn't merely seeking answers. He wanted to kill something. He would be willing and eager to help her seek revenge. She wished she'd thought to reach out to him sooner.

"You're right—" she said, barely getting the words out before the light bulbs in The Lantern dimmed, then cut out.

She heard every conversation at every nearby table come to the same quick stop, heard some mutter jokes, others laugh, others make comments to passing waitstaff. She'd lost the luxury of presuming this—or anything abnormal—did not portend something dangerous, and looked around the restaurant for any signs of someone coming. That *he* was coming, summoned not by a threat to her, but by her finally telling someone that she wanted him dead.

She saw no sign of Angelo, but something else alarming. A woman seated at the bar who she'd seen before, very recently. She was the woman from the park. Her eyes met Sarita's briefly, but she appeared too nervous to care that she'd been spotted. She gripped a small charm on her necklace and looked toward a man seated closer to the door, partially concealed by a potted plastic tree. It was the stout, bearded man who had been with her at the park, seated with her under the tree. If both of them were here, then that meant Sarita hadn't been succumbing to paranoia in the park. She'd been right. They'd been watching her, had followed her. What about the third one, the runner? Was he here, too? Looking as anxious about the power outage as his fellow stalkers?

"Does anyone else feel something?" Tori said.

"Like what?" David said.

"Like . . . there's less air in here."

"Little harder to breathe," Everett said. "I feel it."

Sarita couldn't be sure that she felt it, too. The pressure and slight strain on her might be psychosomatic. An odd, dark haze grew within her vision, like a filter blurring reality. As it thickened it reminded her of dreams she sometimes had where a blinding blackness would follow her and force her to avert her eyes, prevent her from looking directly at something she needed to avoid. As if the darkness had transferred the damaging effect of staring directly at the sun to an absence of light too deep and aggressive to be adequately defined by the words "dark" or "black." The haze seemed to be of this element, seeping out of her dreams, polluting the world. While she couldn't begin to process how or why this could be happening, she understood that something was bringing this about, and that as the source of the haze came closer, pushing a sinking dread ahead of it, its effect intensified.

Confirmation that the darkness and foreboding were not confined to her mind came as she saw most of the patrons in the restaurant stand and file for the nearest exit, most taking the front door, but some taking a side entrance near an ONLINE ORDER PICKUP sign. The restaurant staff, save for those in the kitchen, followed suit, and Sarita presumed those in the kitchen opted for a back exit. The uniform confusion and concern on their faces almost made them all look related. They walked as though conducting a planned evacuation drill that had come a day early, and therefore might be the real thing. While they did not run, scream, or display any other signs of panic, they did display an infectious urgency. It made Sarita want to join them, and she questioned why she and those at her table were among the few not leaving. The question repeated in her head several times in scant seconds before the answer came to her.

Something held her in place. Not through force, but a deeper compulsion. It was as if there were a rattlesnake on the table, coiled to react at any perceived hostility, and she felt her best option was to be dead still. She could only wonder if it was the same for Tori, David, and Everett, or if they felt something physical keeping them in their chairs.

The ones who were free to go appeared to obey an instinct, like animals heading for high ground in advance of a tsunami no human could sense coming. When she thought the last of them had left, heard cars starting in the parking lot, she surveyed how many remained. There were those at her table, Everett's three boys, the two who'd had eyes on her at the park, and seated in a corner behind her, the third member of their party. The fake runner. His chest heaved as he stared past her, toward the entrance of the restaurant. She gathered that the crisis that the rest had fled was arriving at last.

She turned as a tall, broad-shouldered man came through the door. The haze obscured his features, but it immediately struck her that he carried himself with the authority of a vicar turned royal, the devious confidence of a trickster. These were impossible things to see, but were nonetheless evident to her, and an instant later, as the dimness dissipated enough to reveal his face, she understood who she was looking at, and knew that the strangeness of her life had at least one more layer than she'd been aware of.

The man came to her table, stood between David and Everett, who could barely turn their heads to see him as he lifted a long leg to step onto the table and stand above and amidst them all.

Outside of recent nightmares, where his very presence seemed designed to make her forget Frank, she had last seen him in California. Cold Eyes.

"What an unkind name," he said, and she could feel his lips brushing her skin as he spoke. Worse, she felt something like a worm in her mind, burrowing to dig out her thoughts, deliver them elsewhere. No, not a worm. A tongue.

He licked his lips. "And I have not been trying to *make* you forget that sad little devil you married. I am trying to *help* you forget him. You surely see the difference, yes?"

"What's happening?" Sarita said. "Why are you here?"

He only smiled, but she knew his answer to the second question at least. He was here for her.

She recalled how he'd seemed beyond human to her. She felt again and anew how that initial impression of him never lessened even after she came down from the mescaline she'd been on the night she first saw him. Not only that, but how everyone who saw him had felt the same thing, but seemed too afraid to speak up about it, like they were keeping quiet in the dark, hoping not to be noticed.

It was impossible to deny, now, what this stranger, this *stalker,* was and always had been. The extremes of hate and trauma could cement a memory more firmly and vividly than love, and so with Angelo's face now clearer in her mind's eye than ever, she could also see how clearly the stalker resembled her guardian angel. Not in the sense that they could be mistaken for twins, or even thought of as distant relatives, but could be identified as countrymen. Gods on holiday who, for some reason, were drawn to her, or who drew her to them.

"Gods on holiday?" he said. It felt less like he was reading her mind and more like he was fusing with it. Bringing his thoughts into her head, so that she could barely tell if he was talking or just making her hear words unspoken. "Gods on holiday," he said again. "I quite like that. It certainly fits me. I think you will be surprised by how well it fits you."

She focused on his unmoving lips and knew that he hadn't uttered those last words.

Because that is not for any of these others to know, he thought, and she heard. *Gods and goddesses are meant to be mysteries to lesser things. It is time for you to shed your lesser self and be with me.*

All those times you saw me before, you thought everyone else could truly see me? No. They sensed something they did not understand. But you, Sarita, truly saw. Because you were not like them. You were not saved, and saved, again and again, to remain one of these breathing, simple, lesser things.

You must have known this always, yes? Suspected it? You had to know you were being saved for a reason.

That sound you could always hear, for your ears only, did you never truly listen to it? That "roar" was never the sound of the sea following you after it could not claim you. Listen closely to it now. Do you not hear the voices?

A shudder almost shook her from his trance and out of her chair. It was as though she was hearing for the first time in her life. Not just the roar, but *anything.* He was right. There were voices. All along, there had been voices.

They sing for you. For us.

"Who?" she said, aware that the question must have puzzled David, Tori, Everett, and everyone other than the stranger. "Who are they?"

Listen and they will tell you. Even if you can't hear their words, you'll hear their hearts. You'll feel their love for you, if you stop to truly listen. They love you so much that simply knowing you hear them fulfills them.

How could she do anything but listen to them? Her head was going to explode, they sang so forcefully, so passionately.

They sang for *her*, and while being heard might fulfill them, hearing them filled her with a bewildering, crippling energy. It was like she'd been suddenly made so strong she couldn't risk moving without snapping every bone and tendon in her body. She needed to quell this, somehow. Better yet, subdue it. Control it.

Then, if it was as powerful as it seemed to be, she could use it to do what she wanted to do.

Kill the one who murdered her husband.

Before that, though, she would kill the one right in front of her now who referred to Frank as a devil. Not immediately, though. Not before she got some answers out of him, because clearly he knew things she needed to know. Even things she ought to have known.

He even knew that some part of her had always believed, or at least wondered about the possibility, that Angelo had saved her because she was meant to do something no one else in the world could.

"It is my understanding that someone recently spoke very rudely of you," Cold Eyes said. Sarita was beginning to find this moment more dreamlike than when Frank was murdered. She'd known Angelo longer, and the urgency inherent in his presence had crystallized that event as it happened.

This surprising arrival was preceded by a haze, and was now accompanied by the unaccountable stillness of everyone who wasn't Cold Eyes, as well as by the presence of two different parties of people who had been following Sarita. She'd just made an unexpected emotional connection with the leader of one of those groups. The other group, comprised of the three who had been spying on her at the park, was still an unknown. The only thing she could gather, when she managed to pull away from Cold Eyes's binding glare to glance at the ones in her field of vision, was that they were as afraid of him as she probably should have been.

Cold Eyes looked to Everett, then back to Joey, Everett's thin nephew who had earlier earned a pair of blows from his uncle. "I overheard that correctly, did I not? The young man here had ugly, vile words for my dear Sarita."

At last, Sarita's heartbeat hastened as Joey, shaking and slack-jawed, eyes so open he looked like a minor-league carnival freak, stood and came when Cold Eyes stepped onto the table and beckoned with a finger.

Everett's fists were clenched watertight. Even without being able to look back, he must have had an idea of what was happening. When Joey came to the table, Everett managed with a pained grunt to grab his nephew's wrist. Cold Eyes flicked two fingers toward him and Everett let go, agony digging into his face like it meant to rip off a mask.

Joey breathed like someone cruel was feeding him air in small portions, often free of any oxygen. He took Cold Eyes's hand and let the tall stranger bring him up to the table to stand close beside him.

With one hand behind the boy's head, held firmly enough to render Joey's weak resistance nearly unnoticeable, Cold Eyes brought Joey's face closer. "What did you have to say about her? Tell me."

From where she sat, Sarita could not read Joey's lips to know what he said, but saw an eager, uncontainable anger shroud Cold Eyes's face. His pale skin reddened, his large eyes recessed. His plainly handsome face, the kind of face a serial killer would wish for, forgettable yet trustworthy, transformed, wizened with fury.

To her left, past Tori, she thought she heard whispering that sounded like a prayer, and wished she knew the words so that she could join, enhance its effectiveness. Its language was foreign, but she heard a pattern and rhyme within the words and thought if she heard them repeated enough she could learn them, echo them effectively, without misusing the accent or failing to emphasize the right syllable, which Tori had warned could bring catastrophe. She had to believe that the person speaking it—the woman at the bar—was using the prayer to try to undo things already done, dispel the present haze and break the untouchable chains binding them. The things Cold Eyes had sent ahead of him, and that emanated from him.

When he showed his teeth, his fangs had lengthened and multiplied. They looked freshly sharpened, and had a metallic sheen that brought them closer to platinum than purely white.

Joey croaked, "Uncle Ev—" just before Cold Eyes's wide bite clamped over the lower half of the boy's face.

Sarita pushed as far back as she could and felt like g-forces pressed her into the chair. Tori whimpered, David gasped, Everett growled. The woman at the bar continued to pray softly, and another voice joined her.

One of her two colleagues. Sarita could not tell which. Everything she heard, including the crack and crush of Joey's faceplate and jawbone, was swimming in a syrupy murk comprising most of her mind.

Cold Eyes ripped Joey's head away from his clenched teeth and full mouth, revealing the red crater his bite had left in the boy's face. Joey would never be able to utter another word again, whether harsh, wholesome, pejorative, or apologetic. Cold Eyes flung him toward an empty booth. Joey crashed through the table, landed upside down and face up, and did not move.

Rather than stare at Joey's remains, Sarita watched the monster standing on the table, watched his throat distend past the width of his jawline and forward to the point of his chin as he swallowed. His food appeared to get stuck halfway down, but then his neck rippled with musculature not previously visible. A crunch worthy of a car wreck coincided with Cold Eyes's neck regaining its previous normal size, as the mass of tissue and bone squeezed down past the neckline of his shirt and out of sight.

"Oh my God, what are you?" Sarita said.

His smile displayed normal teeth again, but it was impossible for Sarita not to see through the disguise now. "I am yours. I always have been."

He reached down for her to take his hand, and she stood. The sound of prayer cast off any gentility, grew into a loud desperate song that brought tears to her eyes, and she thought it impossible for any person who heard it to keep from crying, save for Cold Eyes, to whom the word "person" surely wasn't applicable. Inflexible, invisible steel wires stemmed from his stare and stabbed deep into Sarita, penetrating the back of her skull. That was how it felt. It hurt to even think of looking away, hurt to blink. All that she believed could weaken his gaze was the prayer, which made him wince when he heard certain words, made his smile falter.

The haze drew closer to him as he waited for her, its increasing density transforming it from intense fog to smoke from a wildfire; the difference between something harmlessly inhaled and something heavy and poisonous. His legs vanished within it, then most of his torso. She was an inch from touching his hand—which, along with his face, was all that she could see now, not just of him, but of everything—when she called out, "Tori, *help me!*"

Another quavering, straining voice joined the others. A fourth voice, Sarita realized. Tori sounded almost panicked, as though she were being

threatened to recite these words at gunpoint. Her addition to the agonized chorus proved effective enough to stop Sarita just before the tip of
her middle finger could graze Cold Eyes's hand. Moreover, she could see
that he could not cover this distance, either, though it was too thin to slip
a twig between.

A fury unlike the kind he'd held for Joey blackened his eyes, sank his
prominent cheekbones, tightened his lips over the baby tusks protruding
again from his gums. The shiver that flowed through him looked more like
an unwanted optical effect, a glitch in a frame of footage. Beyond glimps-
ing his fragility, Sarita saw and was strengthened by the sight of Cold Eyes
trying to hide that he'd been shaken at all. She pulled from him, the pain
of the act eliciting an emaciated scream as she fell back into her chair.

Tori's hand clasped her shoulder hard enough to leave a bruise. Sarita
turned to her friend, who had her eyes closed. "Run, Sarita. *Run!*"

Sarita managed to stand without quite stumbling to the floor. The same
could not be said for David and Everett, who both fell flat and toppled
their chairs as they tried to leave. Sarita took a few steps toward the restaurant's front door, feeling as though she was moving downhill, before she
stopped to check for her brother.

David was still on the floor, pointing at the exit, yelling, "Go, go, *go!*"
Cold Eyes stepped down from the table and moved toward David with
a disturbing combination of patience and sadistic intent. Sarita stopped,
reached for her brother despite being several arm lengths away. A different
hand took her arm, pulled her toward the light outside. One of the three
who had watched her in the park. The man near the door. There was no
one else it could be, unless Cold Eyes had allowed someone else to enter,
and why would he?

Why wouldn't he?

Damn it, there was no making sense of what he was, what he wanted,
what he planned, aside from what he had told her. He was here for her. He
wanted her.

He would kill for her.

God, he'd just bitten—*eaten*—someone's face. For all his talk of godli-
ness and mystery, his natural form would make a grizzly afraid to approach
him. That she had to even think of this, remind herself of what she'd just
witnessed, spoke to something else about him. He was a deceiver, a pre-
tender, just like Angelo. A thing that worked to trap your trust just so it

could someday kill whatever it thought you loved too much. Loved more than you loved it.

"Go!" David said again as the stalker grabbed his scalp, positioned his fingers to peel the top of David's head off. Sarita tried to break free of the man holding her, but couldn't, and fortunately didn't need to as Everett and the rest of his boys, freed by the chaos, by the break in the stalker's concentration, rushed the one who had killed their kin.

"Come with me," shouted the man holding Sarita. He sounded like he needed her far more than she needed him to save her. "Hurry!"

She fought to stay with her brother, join the Stallworths, feel one with them in a way she'd never longed to before, but was her entire world now. Those boys had watched some strange, horrifying man kill someone they loved, destroy his face in the process, like he was trying to remove the murdered man's identity. They understood how she felt now, witnessing such a thing while powerless to stop it. They thought they had understood a lust for vengeance before, but now they understood it as she did. Grasped it with a recklessness she would admire if her hands weren't already around it. They had seen how easily Cold Eyes could kill. Knew they stood no chance, and did not care, because the hope of even hurting the source of their pain far outweighed the fear of what that individual could do to them.

Sarita broke away from the man trying to hold her, just for a moment, before the woman at the bar tackled her. She was strong, and evidently trained. She brought Sarita's right arm up above her head and left arm behind her back in a way that no amount of love and ferocity could overcome. All the passion in the world was powerless against sufficient, superior technique and strength.

She screamed David's name as she was pulled through the door. The Lantern's parking lot was nearly empty save for a big white SUV she recognized as belonging to Everett Stallworth, and a black van that the woman was pulling her toward. Her partner was hustling up to the van with his keys out. There were no other vehicles on the main street facing the entrance, nor the side streets bracketing the building, or in the parking lots of two other restaurants nearby.

Dead, Sarita thought, the word landing on her as if it fell from space. The sight of the nearly empty lot in the middle of the day, anomalous as it was, was barely noticeable compared with the absence of cars anywhere near the building. Cold Eyes hadn't just chased away the other people in The Lantern Café; he'd vacated everything nearby for a block or more with the threat of his presence.

In an instant, something else came to her. An old story she'd heard from one of her great-uncles on her father's side. The night the devil impersonated a man to dance in a nightclub and caused the patrons to flee when his hooved feet gave his true nature away. An urban legend captured in any number of books, repeated online in top-ten lists and videos, its origins in San Antonio could be traced to a newspaper article, and a specific night and place. October 31, 1975. El Camaroncito, off Old Highway 90. A place long since abandoned. Long left for dead.

Sarita's great-uncle claimed to have been there that Halloween night. "I know, every other *tío* you ask about it in the city will say they were there, too, or say they got a cousin or somebody who was there, but I *was there,* and this is how you know. This is the part you can't know unless you were there. When I got outside the bar, me and my date, the thing that hit me was that it was too empty outside. There weren't any cars at any of the other places near us, and when we got on the road, I can't say if it took a minute or five minutes for me to see a car that wasn't one of the other ones getting away from Camaroncito, but I can say it took too long. That was a happening area, and it was *dead* dead. It felt like everybody outside Camaroncito knew what was inside way before any of us on the inside knew, or they felt it in their gut or something, and they all stayed away."

The devil—or *a* devil, at minimum—had now come to The Lantern. He'd referred to Frank as though he were demonic, but isn't that what devils do? Pretend to be anything other than what they are, and even try to paint others as the real evil, until they are ready, or forced, to reveal themselves?

A living evil had stalked Sarita for years, invaded her mind in the aftermath of her husband's death, shown up in broad daylight to take her, and killed someone simply to show that he could. Now she was letting strangers drag her away from it all, leaving David and Tori inside to face it.

During the few seconds it took for her to process this, she had fallen still, almost catatonic, and that brief lack of resistance allowed her to take the woman by surprise when she swung her arm and caught her with an elbow flush to her nose. Even then the woman's grip only lessened without fully breaking, and Sarita had to summon the kind of adrenaline rush a mother would use to lift a car off her child to kick free.

The other man had already made it to the back of the van and opened its doors. She glanced back to see if she needed to throw a punch his way, saw the distance between them, and rushed to the front of The Lantern.

The double doors to the entrance broke open as an impossibly mangled body flew through them. Sarita dodged the twisted shape, watched it land a few feet away from her. It took an extra heartbeat for her to understand she was not looking at a single broken, dead body, but two that had collided so violently it would have taken tools to separate them. Neither face belonged to David or Tori. They were the two other boys who had accompanied Everett.

She turned to the open entryway and saw David walking toward her with a semiconscious Everett, bleeding from his head and muttering, leaning against him, one arm draped over him. Tori hovered near, trying to shoulder some of Everett's weight, but when David looked ahead and saw his sister he shouted at Tori, "Go get her out of here!"

Behind them, the blond stranger, the third member of the spy party, stood between Cold Eyes and the doorway. He raised his arms in a position between that of a revivalist preacher and someone standing on railway tracks pleading for the train to stop because the bridge was out. More reminiscent of the latter due to how doomed he was, but his shouted prayer was worthy of a fire-and-brimstone sermon, every word a bomb exploding from deep in his chest. His voice cracked, re-formed, broke, strengthened, then fractured again, over and over with each word.

Cold Eyes towered over the blond man and looked to have embraced his inhumanity. His eyes were a color that you *feel* when your temperature is ten degrees too high. His face and arms were bluish or violet, Sarita couldn't quite tell. She just knew it looked like all the blood in his veins and arteries had burst free and was barely being contained by his skin. His mouthful of fangs had fought past his lips as though they were an army lusting for blood and vengeance and disobeying orders to stand down.

Whatever prayer the blond man was saying, if it ever had a chance of working, it was long past any hope of effectiveness now. Still, he continued, and Sarita noticed Tori had stopped mimicking the chant.

"Who are you?" Tori shouted past Sarita, holding out a steak knife she must have taken from the table. *"Who are you people?"*

Sarita turned, saw the two who had tried to pull her into the black van coming toward them, braced herself to start kicking and punching again, if it came to that, but planned to take Tori by the wrist and rush past them after tricking them into taking a defensive stance of their own.

"You have to come with us," the woman said, her tone like that of a first responder asking for the second time about the victim's blood type. "We're here to help."

"Please, hurry," the man said, more panicked than his partner, reflected in his reedy voice and the pain wrinkling his brow. "We don't have time!"

He reached for them and Tori pushed the knife toward them. "You were summoning something," she said. "Why would you do that? *What's going on?*"

"Oh, Christ," the man said, staring through the women. The blond man's prayer broke into a single long scream made of sheared metal.

"Run," David said. "Run!"

The bearded man took off before everyone else, calling back to his partner, "Myra, it's too late! We have to go, it's too late."

Sarita could not resist looking back toward the scream. The blond man appeared to be levitating. His hands were still raised but were held out wider now, and he looked as if he'd been petrified in this pose. Then he shook, his body rippling like every bone was searching in a different direction for an escape. A vomitous gurgling noise drowned his scream and a splashing cascade wet the ground. Sarita finally noticed that Cold Eyes was holding the man up with one arm, his hand reaching through the blond man's stomach, gripping him by his spine.

The blond man went limp as his killer stood under the outflow coming from the man's opened stomach. Blood rained on the monster's face. He wasted more than he drank.

"Come with us." A hand gripped Sarita's wrist. It was not Tori's, or David's, who had just caught up with her with Everett in tow, but Myra's. The woman she'd slammed in the face with the hardest strike she'd thrown in her life seconds earlier. Myra could have fled with the man rushing toward the van, or ran past Sarita to try in vain to help her other partner, the blond man. Any pain Sarita saw in Myra's eyes had nothing to do with her bloodied nose and everything to do with seeing someone she cared about

slaughtered, mangled, and desecrated. Sarita recognized the pain from reflections she'd spent days trying to avoid.

Here was another unexpected ally. First Everett, now this stalking
stranger whose name she had just learned. Sarita took Myra's hand with
as much thought as she'd give to treading water if she were thrown in the
ocean. Myra pulled and Sarita followed toward the van.

"Where are we going? What are we doing?" David said.

"Come on," Sarita said.

David followed, pulling Everett along, but Tori lagged behind them all.
"What were you doing? You were summoning something! Why?" She lost
a step with each statement. Sarita looked back, but did not plant her feet
to stop, much less go to her friend. The pull to the van was urgent above
anything else that could stop her. Escaping not only meant saving herself,
but saving her brother, who was in the process of saving another. A person
he'd been ready to fight just minutes ago, before the situation changed.

She had to keep going. If she stopped for Tori, who was still slowing,
distrustful of those who could help them escape, David would stop as
well. As it was, he hadn't looked back for Tori yet. Once they reached
the van, once David got inside, then Sarita could break free again, run
back to Tori, but not until her brother was safe. For God's sake, why had
Tori even put her in this position? What could she possibly be so afraid
of? These people had been "summoning" something, she said. Unless that
something was Cold Eyes himself, in his current state, what could be a
more pressing threat?

Unless that something was Cold Eyes.

Had she heard them praying—chanting, *invoking*—before Cold Eyes
arrived, or after? She couldn't remember now. What if they were with
him? *His* allies, not hers. But then why would he be killing one of them?

"Who are you?" Tori asked the strangers, her voice tightened nearly to a
screech, filtered through panic. She came to within twenty feet of the van.
David was already there. After he helped Everett inside, he helped Myra
pull Sarita into the bed of the vehicle.

Inside, the van was decorated with a variety of painted and crafted
symbols, some flat and painted. Some looked sacrosanct and some taboo;
some holy and others malevolent. Crosses with extra appendages stood
out first, followed by curved horns that might have been flames encircling
and adorning spheres, pyramids, pentacles, and more. Directly above her,

a small cluster of silver misshapen skulls crowded what appeared to be an archaic directional map crossed with a bird's-eye view of a world tree.

Behind Tori, Cold Eyes dropped the blond man and closed in with gliding strides that made him look like he was on a moving walkway. In less than a second, he was close enough to Tori to take her by the throat.

Sarita screamed, *"Tori!"* The van's engine cranked to life. Myra and David held Sarita too firmly for her to break away. She watched Cold Eyes lift Tori like she was a lever that would activate a mechanism to draw them both into the heavens. He measured her with his eyes, apparently looking for something, then seized her forearm with his overgrown, clawed spade of a hand, and shredded through muscle and bone.

Cold Eyes watched Sarita while Tori wailed. The van sped up, briefly stopped short to cause its cargo doors to swing shut, then took off again.

Sarita lunged at the doors to open them, to go back for Tori. Something sharp pricked her neck, and she heard a faint fizzling. A bubbly rush turned her cranium to helium. She remained conscious long enough to see Myra holding what appeared to be an EpiPen, hear her brother say, "What the hell—?" before trying to grab Myra, only for her to bring the object to his neck as well.

Whatever Myra had injected her with brought Sarita to a loathsome sleep full of grinning blood drinkers, forsaken angels, and, deeper within impenetrable darkness, things impossibly worse.

16

Cela stopped walking, looked back at Harrah, who followed her through the desert like a captive although she was untethered, and asked, "Have I not given my name?"

Harrah stared ahead stupidly for several seconds. Cela managed not to find Harrah's hesitation terribly aggravating, aware that the burlap bag of hearts Cela carried over her shoulder had stolen much of Harrah's attention, for multiple reasons.

At last, Harrah accepted that it would, hopefully, be safe to answer with a shake of her head.

"My chosen name is Cela. I was given a different name at birth, but selected this one when I was reborn, freed from breath, aging, and other such limitations, so it is all that matters. Just something to consider for yourself, given what is to come."

"What does that mean?" Harrah asked quietly, like she was talking about Cela to someone else.

"Speak up if you will speak to or of me, please. Whispers tend to seek me, for fear that I will eat them if they make me find them first. Of course, I eat them regardless."

Another long, dumbfounded stare from Harrah, finally followed by the question, "What did you mean that I should consider it for myself? What were you talking about?"

"Picking a new name after your rebirth. Not that it is required. Merely a recommendation."

"Rebirth?"

Cela turned completely around and walked to Harrah, who was too afraid even to backpedal. Cela dropped the bag at Harrah's feet, watched her stare and shiver at its contents.

"How long will you pretend not to feel it, Harrah Stallworth?"

"I . . . I don't know what you mean."

A lie that was almost as delicious to Cela as the rumors of her that swirled in the air for generations. Things she would miss if her plan failed and the world was reduced to ash and floodwaters, the remnants of humanity brought down to a basic survivalism even barbarians would find uncultured. Leaving little room for stories, and placing fear of her kind on the same level as a fear of fire or famine.

Her kind.

For too long, Cela's kind gave greater respect to largely dormant forces than they did to themselves. It was behavior they had in common with the breathers, though the epiphany requisite with their conversion to something greater made their reverence for ageless, unseen forces less defensible. A reasonable degree of respect for sleeping ancients was understandable and even prudent, but in excess it contributed to the inertia that would lead to their downfall.

Cela and The Exile, when he was the sole occupant of her inner circle, often debated the best way to address this failing of their kind. The trauma that blinded him before she turned him, his experience with war, prejudiced him against conflict and violence. Her experiences employing both tools convinced her of their ultimate efficacy when used properly. She missed the discussions she had with him, the only individual she came close to considering a friend, in all her years, before he made himself The Exile.

He had seemed to agree with her solution, to utilize religion and prophecy. She had used these to convince many—far from all, but more than enough—that there was a higher calling for them. Their very nature, and the ease with which they could eliminate an entire population of thinking, loving, praying, and feeling beings, fostered a certain amount of nihilism within them. It is harder to believe in purpose and easier to believe in inherent futility when you are an unliving instrument of casual, sometimes incidental, and always complete undoing of a life comprised of ambition, relationships, and potential. When you can reduce a father, mother, son, daughter, wife, husband, et al. to food.

But even the word "food" deserved more reverence. It implied a necessity, even though she had proven it to be a want, not a need, ages ago. Nevertheless, it did not warrant disdain, yet she had heard many of her kind use it scornfully regarding humankind, failing to understand that they were elevating them to something precious and essential. Words better befitting their view of those they consumed—in whole or, far more frequently, in part—were delicacy, or luxury. Things you could do without. Things you could waste. *Things*.

Cela, enlightened as she had become through prolonged fasting periods, knew that humanity was more. They were the balance. The ones who had kept the sleepers resting through the combination of their dominance and fragility. They had overrun the world, yet could eliminate themselves with their abuses of what they needed to survive, including each other. They thought little of themselves, seemed to believe they were worthy of destruction, and too many of Cela's kind—at least the lesser, undisciplined of them—were happy to believe in this convenient lie.

It was married to the belief that the only ones who mattered, who were worth fearing, were the great sleepers, the distant wanderers, and those even higher above, in layers no one could be sure existed. The humans were thought comparatively inconsequential. The sleepers and their gods, and the mothers and fathers of their gods, and possible forgotten, invisible gods of those parents, were all that mattered.

More precisely, not offending them by taking any action they might perceive as attempted usurpation mattered.

Cela was the only one who truly appreciated the value of humanity, and their need and even desire for a visible, active, present god. The same need was present within her kind as well, though most were unaware. Primordial gods were primarily *old,* and little more. Some old enough to be embedded into reality, to effectively be the material of the universe itself. Others were simply decrepit and overdue to be replaced, particularly when they had kept their numerous eyes closed to the needs and even existence of the conscious beings that give them meaning. Hibernating while their pool of potential worshipers grew ever ignorant, and endangered as they poisoned, polluted, and eradicated their ecosystem and themselves.

That the humans now numbered in the billions was immaterial. They remained a commodity. It was far easier for Cela to envision one million comatose ancients embedded in the infinite cosmos than it was for her to picture another Earth, another planet perfectly placed in the optimal orbit circling a supportive star, with no extra moons tormenting the tides, or with tides at all. Water at all. Life at all. It was easier to imagine countless sleepers to whom an eon might as well be a lone night, because the universe was comprised almost fully of night never ending, and what difference did any measure of time make when there would be nothing present to worship and wake them.

The declination of humankind—the loss of the world they created— troubled her more than upsetting any apathetic higher power. A century of travel after her rebirth had convinced her humanity would someday drive itself to hopelessness, and destruction soon thereafter, but she was not given a clear view of the many paths destruction could take until she formed the church, finding and encouraging the likeminded to fast with her. The congregation—those not driven mad by the fasting ordeal— discovered depths that deprivation alone could uncover within them. That was how The Seers obtained an ability thought lost to the dawn of the Bronze Age. A gift perhaps intentionally forgotten given the misery and madness attached to it.

She had seen over one thousand visions of the future, and in fewer than fifty saw civilization survive into the twenty-third century. Cela refused to surrender her future to the infinitesimal chance of living in a world that was not a contaminated, scorched, drowned, and otherwise uninhabitable wasteland.

Many of the breathers could accept such a fate for the world because it did not truly belong to them. They would not survive to see it. She would. Even some of the less enlightened of her own would die off, having never trained themselves to live even a few months without food. One reasonably healthy man's blood could sustain Cela for close to a century. She knew others who could push themselves beyond that, and she was sure that she, too, could live another two or three hundred years from one feeding if she must. But why would she want to?

What good was immortality in a world where all the blood was sickly, and too weak to cling to the palate? Why go on living on an Earth where the seas had swallowed her favorite islands, where winter was no more, where winds carried disease, where nocturnal predators that made eye contact and saw her as family were extinct?

Cela shook her head, stared at the woman she had made The Devil's Mother. "I cannot do this without you."

Her arm lengthened an extra foot to stretch down into the burlap bag, which she had found empty in back of the bar, and filled with several freshly collected human hearts. She took the ripest-looking heart from the bag, held it under Harrah's nose, within an inch of her lips. Held it like an offered apple. Squeezed, released, and repeated, manually pumping the remaining chambered blood through the openings of the dead muscle.

Harrah held for a moment, leaned forward with lips parted, then jerked back, flinging herself to the ground like she was dodging a bullet. When she turned and vomited, Cela knew it was not because she found the heart and blood repulsive. Her body was putting the acrid taste of something disgusting in her mouth in a desperate attempt to save her from temptation.

Cela tossed the heart into the dirt close to Harrah's head. Harrah examined it like it was a half-rotted fruit, and she could eat around the spoiled parts. "What's happening to me?" Harrah whimpered.

"You are being given the chance that I promised," Cela said. "You have seen what I am capable of. Imagine yourself with that power. Killing with such ease. Punishing all who took your son from you. Giving his life as much meaning as his death. More, in fact."

As my new Devil, she left unspoken.

In Cela's crafted prophecy, The Devil was more vital as a catalyst than Sarita and her unborn child—"The Lost Messiah." Even Sarita, in her part as The Martyred Mother, might be less important than the evil destined to be done to her. At least to Cela.

What, after all, did the Christians most prominently and commonly display atop their places of worship, elevated and unmissable to the outside world? An image of their savior? No. The symbol of his suffering. The instrument of his torturous death. The evil done unto him seemed to fuel their faith more than their savior himself. Had the Romans stabbed the

Nazarene to death, every Christian church, chapel, and cathedral in the world would have a massive blade on its steeple.

Sometime after this, Cela would need to visit The Viscount, the "god" she had spent close to six hundred years crafting. Find him before he found her, albeit in a way that let him think he was still in command.

First, however, she had to set one of the two mothers vital to her faith on a path to kill the other.

17

Whose heart was it? Harrah wondered. Then she wondered why she was curious about this. Why it mattered.

Because it belonged to somebody not that long ago. It kept them alive. Now it's just lying there. It's more than just what it looks like.

What it looked like, to her, was a bad, fatty, and chewy cut of raw meat. Something you hardly thought of as having once been part of a living thing, much less the most important part of a human being. Well, second-most. Heart transplants were a thing, while brain transplants weren't. There was a reason for that. One was more delicate and indispensable than the other.

Her boy's brain had been crushed along with his skull, the very thoughts, ideas, and memories that made him who he was pulverized until they couldn't even be scraped up into a paste. As hideous as it had been seeing those at the bar get their hearts torn out, it was a hundred times worse trying not to imagine Frank getting his brain—his *mind*—destroyed, and not just because he was her son. She could see it now, how much more heinous it was to have the thing that contained your identity attacked, as opposed to the thing that merely kept your vessel in operation.

If the thing lying in the dirt before her had been a brain, not a heart, she wouldn't be thinking of taking a bite out of it. At least she hoped not.

Less blood in a brain, too. Wouldn't taste as good.

Her stomach cramped, prompted by this wayward, disgusting thought, and she threw up despite feeling like she'd emptied herself already.

"Stop making me think things like that," she told Cela.

"I am not making you think anything, I assure you."

"Liar. You *are*. Like how you made those people just stand there while you . . . while you killed them all."

"Oh? Like that?"

Harrah glared at the woman, pushed herself up to one knee, surprising herself with the surplus of useful anger she'd gained just from Cela's tone.

"I ain't dumb," Harrah said. "So don't talk to me like I am. I'm not."

"Fair," Cela said, stacking a surprise on top of the one already bringing Harrah back to her feet on legs trembling so fast they almost felt ticklish. "I was rude," Cela continued, "forgive me."

Harrah shook her head, not a refusal of pardon, but a rejection of everything happening to her. How could she be here? How could she have seen what she'd seen? All those people waiting against their will for their turn to die. How could this woman, this Cela, even be real?

How could blood smell so sweet?

How could my boy be dead, she made herself think, actually seeking solace in the plainness of this pain. Thinking of Frankie, missing him, dwelling with the ache of his murder, was somehow preferable to thinking of her present surroundings and situation.

On the road to Eagle Pass she had briefly imagined him somewhere out here, in this openness that had fleetingly felt more like freedom than desolation to Harrah. Closer to Heaven than Hell. Then she'd pictured him with his head gone.

People said he had a good heart—Everett loved saying that about Frankie—but what that really meant was that he was a good, generous person, something he *decided* to be. Something he built himself up to be based on what he saw of the world with his eyes, what he listened to and deliberated over, what he thought about and chose to be.

The family also brought up his blood more than once after his death.

"Frankie was our blood."

"We gonna let someone get away with doing this to our blood?"

Our blood.

Not even *his* blood, now that she thought of it. Community blood.

Family blood. One big well of it somebody had spit in. Dropped an old dead animal into, and now the rest of the family couldn't get anything out of it, which was really what hurt many of them. That what happened to Frankie meant they couldn't get anything from him anymore.

Her boy. "The good one," Everett called him. Harrah used to shush him when he said that. She hadn't liked the idea of him being set apart from the others, but why not? Because those others were more like her than she was like her son? Because they were all "blood" together, so he couldn't be any better or any worse? Shit, she should have taken more pride in what Everett said. Treasured Frankie more, loved him harder while she could.

It's not like she really disagreed with Everett. Not like anyone in the family didn't see it in some way, and early. One of her favorite memories of Frankie, from his childhood, wasn't the Halloween when he dressed up as his favorite uncle. No, it was the *next* Halloween when Joey and two of his other cousins decided to copy Frankie's idea from the previous year. And even though Frankie had wanted to go as something else—a werewolf, if she recalled correctly—he agreed to dress up like Everett again, at the request of his cousins, so they could feel even more like him. They were dressing up as Frankie as much as they were Everett that night. Their parents knew it. Harrah did, too. Their parents thought it was the cutest thing. Harrah was a little embarrassed by it.

God help her, why? *Why?*

There couldn't have been any resentment in her. Any feeling that the better parts of Frankie reflected his father more than her. No, that couldn't be it, she refused to even consider it. She was just . . . just a little inattentive. Thoughtless, as well, maybe. An imperfect mother, not a bad one. Inattentiveness, thoughtlessness, selfishness, those things were to blame for her hurting Frankie those few times she did. Those aspects of her, and not any enviousness of her son's future and goodness. God, no.

Stop talking to God like He gives a damn, she thought.

Then she remembered something Cela had told her in the casino hotel room. It returned to her with such clarity she was certain Cela was making her remember it, but she found herself not caring whether this was true or not. All she cared about was getting an answer.

"Back in the room, before you took me out here, you said Frankie was supposed to help you make a god or something," she said. "What did you mean by that?"

Cela turned her head slightly, narrowed her eyes, mocking confusion. Harrah huffed, clenched a fist, felt an itchy pain from the twin wounds in her palm. "You called yourself . . . what was it . . . *Godmaker*. You said you were a Godmaker—"

"*The* Godmaker."

"—and my son was supposed to help you. How?"

Cela smiled, then sang a song that made Harrah feel like someone had torn everything important away from her—from within her and all around her, body parts and pieces of the world—and left her stranded in a space deprived of everything but Cela's voice. That song.

"If God is for us, who can be against?"

Cela let the silence linger so that the song could echo in Harrah's mind, then, with emphasis that confessed to rehearsal, stated, "*Who* can be against. *If* God is for *whom*."

The old mental footnote Harrah had attached to the lyric came to her again.

> [1]*God is for you, but it could be the other way, don't ever forget that.*

"What are you saying? Who's against Him, who's He for? Who are *you*?"

"*I* am the one here for you now," Cela said. Her long arm snaked down toward the open bag again and picked up another heart.

Whose heart? Why does it matter? It doesn't. Harrah shook her head. "I just want to go home. You're not going to take me home, are you?"

"No," Cela said, startling Harrah. She'd expected something cryptic, or deceptive. A false promise that used the word "home" in a way that was open to misinterpretation somehow.

"Why are you doing this to me?" Harrah said.

"Because you have a role to play. Because I chose Sarita, she chose your son, and my knight chose to sabotage all that I have worked for. So now, here you are. And if I did not do this to you, I would be speaking to someone else asking me the same tiresome question."

Cela's fingers appeared to sharpen. Not the nails, but the bones under the skin. Points and small serrations dotted every knuckle. Her hand looked like a cursed glove that couldn't be removed without amputation, and that would then disappear only to reappear on your other hand the first time you slept.

That's what gave me those marks in my hand.

"Take it," Cela said of the heart, "or else I will take yours. If you will be of no use to me, especially in light of all that I offer you, then I will leave you as I left those others."

"What do you want from me?" Harrah said.

Cela's teeth pushed forward just enough to force her lips to part. They seemed eager to explode from her head like grenade shrapnel that would tear through Harrah in two dozen places.

"What I *want* now, truly, is for you to ask another question to exhaust my patience," Cela said, "and grant me cause to treat myself to your blood. I *want* to savor every drop of terror released into your veins. I *want* to lick the fear from every groove of your brain, it is tastier than you imagined, and then I *want* to clean the inner walls of your skull. That is what I want from you, now. But I long ago mastered my wants and subordinated them to my needs, and what I *need* is for you to understand that you have nothing more in life than what I am offering you. You have no explanation forthcoming that will allay your confusion. You can expect no reassurance to ease your apprehension. You can expect any god you have believed in to be deaf to your prayers.

"You have no son. You have no family. You have no future, even if I were to return you to the place where I found you. I know you cannot appreciate the risk I am taking even consorting with you, much less trusting you, but understanding why you are ignorant to this does not make your ingratitude less frustrating. Do you know what would have happened to you had I brought you to my followers, as I told them I would, before I came to you? I told my congregation that I was going to deliver The Devil's Mother to them to be tortured and feasted upon. I took inspiration from the story of your Christ feeding thousands from a single basket of fish and bread, and promised there would miraculously be enough of you to go around to feed the thousands who call me prophet. I could not have actually made that happen, but I could have made them think it was happening, and I could have made you think it, too. Instead, I am here offering *you* food and opportunity."

What are you talking about? Harrah almost screamed, but she hadn't forgotten the threat Cela had made, forbidding another question, and she pressed fingers to her throat protectively, to guard against an attack if Cela had read her thoughts yet again, and to constrict the space any question might try to sneak through.

"Harrah ... Harrah ... Harrrahhhhh," Cela sang, then tittered. It was almost childish, and her discordant playfulness almost made Harrah pass out from anxiety. "Yes, I heard the question in your mind, but I will not hold it against you. See how wise you can be when you take a moment to consider things? Now take another moment to consider your options. Die here, for no real reason, or accept a chance to become something greater and more powerful. If nothing else, you will be able to exact some measure of revenge on behalf of your son. Take it. Give me what I need, and I will be grateful. Otherwise, I promise to show you how pain transforms time. I will teach you how perfect agony exponentializes seconds into years. Take my offer, Harrah Stallworth. *Take it.*"

The last utterance occupied a space between command and compulsion. An imperative you could override, but only for so long, like your brain's constant instruction for you to breathe. You could defy it for long enough to lose consciousness—lose control of yourself—and then your brain and body would try to operate as they should while you were unable to disobey. A part of her wanted to take this as a sign that Cela might be bluffing about killing her. She had confessed to needing Harrah, after all. Maybe she wasn't truly willing to kill Harrah, or let her die at the hands of the others who saw her as demonic.

A moment of consideration made her realize, however, that what truly mattered wasn't whether Cela's need would save Harrah, but whether there was any truth to what Cela said about Harrah having nothing. The answer to this seemed obvious. It made her sicker than the hardest hangover to admit this, so sick she almost couldn't stand through the aches in her joints, dizziness spinning the world around her, but Cela was right.

Harrah had nothing to live for. Even before all this had happened, she had barely lived for the one person who should have meant everything to her while he was alive, and after he died she fled from his memory and left her family behind, preferring the company of games and strangers to that of kin. *Blood.* Maybe Cela would have gotten to her anyway, even if she had stayed home, but the rest of the Stallworth clan would have at least helped her put up a fight. Now they couldn't help her, couldn't know where she was, and the only thing they might know about her, presuming Craig's body had been found after his friends asked the hotel to check on him in Harrah's room, was that she was missing, last seen with a man who lost his face overnight.

In a way, she chose this. Not to be here, exactly, but to allow this. All of it, even down to her son's murder. She hadn't controlled the drinking and gambling enough to be a better parent, raise him to understand who to trust, what signs to look for in a partner. She wouldn't have had to kick her habits entirely, just keep them in check. Give Frankie just a few more weekends and even holidays than she gave to Vegas, to the WinStar in Oklahoma, and, of course, to Eagle Pass. Pay more attention to whether there was something for him to eat in the pantry and the fridge than to whether she needed to run up to the corner store for more beer. Give up a few more evenings to take him to the movies or a museum or something, instead of taking herself to the same old happy hour spots to see the same old people having the same old fucking conversations that went nowhere.

Maybe if she'd cut back on that and put more effort into showing her boy how much she cared, she could have avoided hurting him those times. Just a few times. A few bad moments where she lost her temper, acted thoughtlessly or was just a little inattentive. And what had Frankie ended up with? A sprained wrist when she had grabbed him and pulled him too hard, the first time. The second time, a scar over his eyebrow because she forgot she had her ring on, and because he had turned unexpectedly when she had meant to hit him in the back of the head. A pretty bad dog bite from the last incident, which, okay, according to the doctor, came close to giving him nerve damage that would have made one hand useless for life. But that last one wasn't even really her fault. Would she have heard him screaming about the stray that got through the fence if she hadn't been drinking all afternoon? Who could even say? Don acted like he knew for sure, like he had all the answers—

(like he was God Almighty, and she was against)

—and that gave him an excuse to take Frankie away to be raised by a replacement mother.

Harrah couldn't even find comfort in believing she knew better now and was more foolish in her youth. She was just as aware then as she was now of what she ought to do, and clearly as liable to make the same decisions now as she did years ago, and those decisions had brought her here.

It's not that simple. There are bigger forces pulling the strings. Cela said it herself. She chose the girl, the girl chose Frankie, then I got picked up . . . This was all some big, strange setup. She keeps talking about a chance, but when did I ever really have one?

That might have been true—was *probably* true to at least some degree—but it didn't matter now. It wouldn't change the fact that she had nothing else in her life anymore except for the offer of a hand that looked like it was made of broken knives, holding a heart that looked as good as a peach.

Harrah came forward, raised her hand to take the heart, to try it. Just a small taste.

Cela dropped the heart and seized Harrah's hand. The grip that closed over her was even harsher than Harrah had feared. She felt like she'd thrust her hand into a bag full of glass shards and hot coals, and then someone had pulled the drawstrings so tight on her wrist it cut off the circulation. She had no chance to scream as, once more, swarming darkness spirited her into a secret passageway in reality, a place that connected two of the innumerable points light did not touch. This time she remained in the dark for longer than before and thought she could feel her blood changing course in her veins as she was whipped through the blackness. Each time she was tossed she waited to make contact with a wall, and for the shadows surrounding her to give way to something somehow darker. The actual color of death.

Without warning she came out of the shadows and could see again. It took her several seconds to understand where she was. She stood among trees adjacent to a large, full parking lot. She had to lean into one of the larger trees as her legs threatened to give out. She looked at her right hand, expecting to see a cauterized stump where it used to be, but it was still there, unscarred, unburnt, save for the two previously inflicted marks. Except, was it a little bit swollen? Actually, that wasn't the right word. Her fingers and palm weren't puffed or fattened, just . . . larger. Were her fingernails longer, too? And, now that she scrutinized her hand more intently, her veins had definitely darkened.

She didn't want to think of what any of this might mean. She looked around less to get a better understanding of her surroundings, and more to simply look at anything else.

Ahead of her, yards away, there was a large building with a bright sign above its doors and carport. A white vehicle with flashing lights pulled to a stop under the sign—EMERGENCY—and Harrah crouched to hide as well as she could while still sticking her head out enough to peek at the proceedings.

The driver and passenger, both dressed in white, jumped out of the vehicle and rushed to the back.

Ambulance. It's an ambulance. You're at an emergency room. Why?

As a doctor and two nurses came out to meet them, the paramedics opened the rear doors.

Unless something happened to Sarita, or . . .

For a second she was sure that she would see her own body brought out from the back of the ambulance. Whoever had broken into her hotel room to kill Craig had tried to kill her, too, probably gave her a severe head injury she hadn't awakened from. All the impossible madness she had experienced since was the product of brain damage, a dying dream, and an out-of-body experience combined. Now she was going to see her own body hauled out of an ambulance, and just like in the movies, seeing her real self was going to put an end to the mad fantasy she was trapped in, force her to accept her death, for better or worse.

The woman on the gurney was not Harrah, however, although she did look familiar. She had tattoos visible through dried blood that caked her shoulder, visible because the sleeve had been cut from her top. The arm that Harrah could see was only half there, missing from the elbow down.

She leaned closer, careful not to make any noise, getting a last good look in before the girl—considerably younger than Harrah—was wheeled into the emergency room. Even through the oxygen mask they had placed over the girl's face, Harrah could hear her saying something. A mantra? No, a prayer, a short one stuck on repeat. Didn't even sound like it was in English. It sounded stiff and overimportant, one of those old languages that gets spoken only when it's being studied and isn't used by anyone as part of their everyday lives anymore.

The dead language wasn't even the oddest thing about the prayer, though. It was that Harrah could hear the girl's voice so clearly from this distance, the volume not getting any lower even as the paramedics pushed her into the building.

Damn, where did she know this girl from? If she could remember that, she could hopefully begin to understand why Cela brought her here. Had that girl been at Frankie's service? Someone he knew from college or work? One of Sarita's friends?

The "witchy one."

That's who it was. The one Joey and a few of the other boys had been crushing on the night Frankie proposed to that goddamned girl. She should have known from those ugly, weird-ass tattoos. From the looks of it, maybe someone else had found them as objectionable as Harrah did, and tried to take the girl's arm off to take that awful ink out of their sight.

Cela wouldn't have put Harrah here in time to see this for no reason. Someone had tried to kill the witchy girl. Someone had attacked her and left her clinging to life.

The same person who had murdered her boy? They'd have to be just as strong, but far less efficient or determined to have let her survive. Harrah believed now that there was at least more than one killer out there with the strength and mean streak to demolish someone's face or head, because the one thing she absolutely trusted about Cela was that she hadn't done to Frankie what she'd done to Craig. There was another one like her out there. Many others, possibly. She had spoken of being the head of a church of thousands, hadn't she?

Harrah started toward the emergency room entrance, then stopped short of stepping out from the coverage of the shade and trees. She didn't want to be seen or found. If Craig's body had already been discovered, then she was either a wanted woman or missing person already. Either way, to get what she wanted, to achieve what she was here for, she had to be careful about being seen.

And what was she here for, exactly? Harrah wondered if whoever had attacked the witchy girl was also Frankie's murderer, and whether Cela expected her to discover this killer, or to finish their work.

It had to be to find the killer, right? What good would it do to kill the witchy girl? Besides making Sarita feel the loss once she found out her friend was dead, and who had done it, what use was there to it?

What more use did there need to be?

Aside from that, it would also let Harrah get some experience with the deed before being transported to wherever Sarita was so she could kill the only person whose face and name were attached to her agony and loathing.

Now that she considered these things, what good *wouldn't* it do to find her way into this hospital, find Sarita's friend, and find something large and heavy to repeatedly drop on her face?

If her hand kept growing, it might be a sufficient instrument for the job.

18

In the minutes that had passed since she had awakened, Sarita's brain had struggled even to accept that she *was* awake. Processing all that had transpired at the restaurant was nearly impossible, but she was just conscious enough to try.

Cold Eyes. The stalker from California was there. Why was he there?

We left . . .

What was he doing there? What is *he?*

We left Tori. We left her arm. She left her arm.

Cold Eyes took her arm.

Where is David?

He's here. He's not moving.

His chest is moving. It is, isn't it?

It's moving.

It's him?

It is. We didn't leave him behind.

We left Tori. She left her arm.

We took the other man. The other . . . Everett. Frank's uncle.

Frank. My husband. He's still gone.

Angelo killed him.

This all started with him.

Don't forget. Don't forget.
Frank is still gone. Now Tori's gone.
No. You didn't see her die. Not like Frank.
But you left her.
Because they took you.
They took you. Who are they?

The soreness in her neck was an odd comfort. The pain sharpened her recent memory, cut through some of her confusion.

"They" were the three people who had been following her. Well, two of them. One hadn't just been left behind, like Tori. He'd been left for dead, and given the state the blond man was in when Sarita last saw him, held high by Cold Eyes like a broken trophy, it would be crueler to hope he survived.

Considering what she'd seen him do to Joey and that blond man, there was no reason to believe Cold Eyes had stopped with Tori's arm. Sarita shut her eyes tight to force any grisly images of her friend's slaughtered corpse out of her mind before they could completely materialize. She hadn't seen Tori die. She'd heard her scream, seen her in pain, but those were both signs that she was alive. Better that than to hear nothing from her, and see her face remain blank when that bastard started tearing through her arm.

The woman who helped take her was still in the back of the van. She must have had confidence in whatever she'd used to sedate the three people in back with her. Or she had a weapon concealed. Maybe she just trusted that none of them would try to attack her for drugging them. She might have only drugged David and Sarita. Everett had been out, or close to it, when they pulled him to the van. Sarita checked on him, saw that his eyes were half open.

"We'll get him looked at when we get home," the woman said. What was her name?

Myra, Sarita remembered.

A sleepless sullenness hung below Myra's eyes. Sarita started to feel steam burning under her skin. *What are you looking so sad about? You made me leave my friend back there. She could be dead. I might have lost someone . . . someone else I love because you wouldn't let me save them. Do you have any idea . . .*

The words stopped as though they'd struck a wall. She recognized something in Myra's eyes, beyond the stern resilience that kept her sadness from melting them. Maybe she did have an idea. Sarita had left Tori behind. Myra, and her partner at the wheel of the van, had left behind the blond man who was definitely dead.

"Who was he?" Sarita said.

A flash of pain crossed Myra's eyes. It made Sarita wince as though she felt it herself, and an instant later she realized how unintentionally harsh, if accurate, her question had been. She'd said "was."

Myra swallowed, straightened her posture as well as she could in the back of a van covering an uneven road.

"You've got to have a hundred other questions in your head," Myra said.

David groaned as though trying to answer. Sarita patted his chest to ease him, then said to Myra, "Yeah, I do."

Myra nodded. "Ask me another, then. Please. Anything else."

"Okay. Okay." She took a second to think of the most pertinent question, then quickly determined that most of them were equally vital. "Where are you taking us? Where's 'home'?"

"We have a base in the hills. It's safe. They won't try to get to us there."

Two new critical questions jumped ahead in line. "Who are 'they'? Who are *you*?"

"They're demons of a sort," Myra said, then paused and seemed to gauge Sarita's reaction to this. How did she expect Sarita to react? She seemed to have at least enough knowledge of Sarita to know where she would be on multiple occasions. Seemed to know more about Cold Eyes than Sarita had, and knew she'd have to intervene to save Sarita after he showed up. It was as if Myra and her small team had been on a mission based on concrete intel. Surely, then, she couldn't expect Sarita to be bewildered by the idea of demons given how long she'd believed in angels.

Apparently satisfied with Sarita's reaction, Myra continued. "They're vampires, although probably not in the way you think of them. You'll learn more when we get home. As for who we are . . . we're all pretty much members of a family. People with a shared history, a lot like yours. We've all been hurt by these things at some point. Now we just . . . we support each other and try to help where we can."

People with a shared history, a lot like yours. We've all been hurt by these things.

Vampires.

This, somehow, was an inch beyond what Sarita was ready to believe.

It wasn't that demons existed, or even that vampires existed as basically a type of demon, that made her shake her head. No, it was the implication that Angelo, all this time, had been one of "these things." As far from angelic as could be.

A significant part of her had still held on to the hope that this was all somehow a grievous misunderstanding. An unthinkable mistake made by the guardian she owed her life to.

If Angelo was, in reality, a devil, and always had been, had she inadvertently given over her soul each time she let him save her? Did she owe him that much?

I don't owe him a damn thing. He owes me. He murdered my husband. He brought all of this on, and now Tori might be dead, too. He owes me now.

"I have to go back for my friend," Sarita said.

Myra sighed. "I'm sorry about that. I truly—"

"Are you guys going to hold me hostage or something? Your 'family'? You're not going to let me leave?"

"For your own good."

"Fuck you. Fuck *you* if you're not going to be honest with me."

"Hey, calm down," Myra said, a hardness that could chip stone forming around her tone.

"No. I left her behind with . . . that *thing*. Do you understand that?"

"Yes," Myra said. An island of grief split the word like a river in her throat, then fell below the tide when she spoke again. "Yes."

"Okay. Then you know how I'm feeling. If you're saying we can't go back, then you've got to give me a real reason for it. It can't be 'for my own good' if I'm telling you I don't give a damn about that, and I *want* to go back for her."

"Fine, call it the greater good, then."

"What does that mean?"

Myra looked down, more exhausted with the situation and embarrassed by her brief vulnerability than unwilling to match Sarita's stare. "You've got . . . You were supposed to—"

"Myra!" called the van's driver, like he was shouting to wake her before she sleepwalked over a ledge.

She turned halfway toward him. "She needs to know, Barnes."

"She'll know. Let him tell her."

"Barnes—"

"Duncan would tell you to stick to the plan."

In the quiet that followed, David stirred again, grabbing Sarita's hand as he tried to sit up.

"Hey...hey...where..."

"We're all right," Sarita said. David looked around as though someone might be holding a knife or gun to Sarita and forcing her to say this. He blinked rapidly, widened his eyes, sniffed deeply. Next he patted his pants pockets, checked for his phone. Sarita hadn't thought to do the same, presuming Myra had emptied their pockets while they were unconscious, a presumption confirmed when David's pat down produced nothing.

Sarita told him, "We're all right." She next looked to Myra and said, "How long until we're 'home'?"

Myra passed the question to the driver. "Barnes?"

"Fifteen or twenty," Barnes said.

"You got anything else?" Myra asked Sarita.

A small part of her considered holding her remaining questions, extending to Myra the mercy and courtesy she would want someone to extend to her after a loss, but what good would that do? That wasn't going to bring anyone back or make anything easier, not when Myra clearly had more she wanted to say. She would let Barnes—the one who'd been screaming and acting like he was ready to leave them *all* behind back at The Lantern—interrupt them if she asked anything Myra wasn't supposed to speak on.

"Were you trying to summon or conjure something back there?" she said. "Back at the restaurant. Tori said you were summoning something. Was that part of the plan?"

"Sort of," Myra said. "Not really, though. We were just...bluffing, I guess. I don't know how else to put it. It would take a lot more than the three of us to really wake up the thing we were talking to."

"And what was that."

"A bigger devil."

"Jesus," David said, still groggy, but evidently lucid enough now to follow the conversation. "Why would you do that?"

"It's a form of protection," Myra said. "Your guy back there—"

"Not my guy," Sarita said.

Myra nodded. "Sorry. Turn of phrase. *Him*...he's a certain type—a lot of them are—where he's more dangerous when he's clearheaded than when his hackles are up. What we were doing was sort of like mimicking a bear call to put a wolf on edge. But pretend we're talking about a wolf that's pretending to be human. I mean, that doesn't really tell you how dangerous he really is, but . . . I don't know. That's what it's like, I guess. That's all I can think of. We tried to tell this killer that there's a bigger killer on the loose that's not going to let him run the same territory. When he heard the call—the prayer—his instincts started taking over. He tried to fight it, but he couldn't, not all the way. And if it weren't for that, you'd have been the only one to make it out alive. Because he'd have tried to take you, and I don't think your brother was letting you go. Am I wrong?"

David's grip on Sarita's hand tightened, and he said, "Hell no. No way. Never again."

"Exactly. But he would've torn right through you and everyone else to have Sarita. Instead, he only . . . he only got through *most* of everyone."

"And *that* was the plan?" Sarita said.

"It's about the best we could have hoped for."

That can't be true, Sarita thought, and then, *But why not?*

"His name was Duncan," Myra said, eyes anchored to the floor again. "The man you asked me about. The one we left."

Barnes cleared his throat, and Sarita knew that it wasn't to quiet Myra, but to loosen a knot of sadness enough to be swallowed.

"He meant something to you," Sarita said to Myra.

"A lot."

"I know what you're feeling."

"I know you do."

For the rest of the drive they listened to the overworked engine, the rasp of asphalt under tires, and the rhythm of Everett's breathing, interrupted intermittently by a gasp or a grunt, like he was still stuck in a fight with a devil. Sarita supposed he was, in a way. They all were.

19

The van pulled into a darkened space, parked, then Barnes exited the vehicle while Myra moved to open the back door.

The garage or whatever it was that they were in was so dimly lit that Barnes and Myra looked to be standing on nothing to Sarita, and she was almost irrationally reticent to join them outside, afraid her feet wouldn't find a floor and she would sink into endless nothing.

She got out nonetheless, ahead of her still groggy brother, because if something as improbable as that were to happen she didn't want it to happen to him first.

Barnes assisted with carrying Everett while Myra led the way to a cracked door, light coming from the other side. When she got through the door, Sarita came into a large, open rotunda carved out of the interior of a hill. A series of darkened entryways to halls dotted the far half of the circular wall. There was an open door to a chamber where she could just glimpse a few benches to her right, and farther to her right, almost behind her, was another long hall easier to see down, with what appeared to be a metal barrier at its end.

The walls and ceiling of the refuge were covered in markings similar to those inside the van, only larger, and so much more abundant that some overlapped with others. They all appeared to have been originally written in white, but most had faded, some to the point of near invisibility, and Sarita surmised that those must have predated everyone currently living in this softly lit sanctuary. None of the "family" members Myra and Barnes walked them past looked particularly young, but much of the age in their faces appeared attributable to hardship, not time. The place looked and smelled so much older than anyone present could be. It had crudely af-fixed electrical lighting wired through rusted torch sconces, and the doors she saw looked to have been made by people with experience constructing forts, if not dungeons or castles.

Three members of the family approached when they first entered. A heavily tattooed, thin white man with strands of gray streaking his red hair. A darker-skinned man, who reminded Sarita of a Polynesian neigh-bor she'd had at her old apartments. A white woman with a strong jaw and stronger-looking arms. The woman and tattooed man brought Ever-ett a stretcher that had seen better days and probably worse-off patients. They placed him on it while the other man checked Everett's pulse, then checked his eyes with a weak penlight.

Everett muttered, "Joey . . . M-Morgan . . . Dex." At least he was talking, even if he was barely getting the words out.

"Everyone else?" the doctor asked Myra.

"These two are fine," she said, pointing to Sarita and David. "Had to knock them out, but they're better now. It's just him."

"*Just* him?"

Myra nodded, and the doctor returned her nod more slowly, before moving with the others to an open room with Everett.

"This way," Myra said, leading Sarita and David past the room where Everett lay on a table. Inside, Sarita saw a washbasin, glass-doored cabinets housing various bottles and vials, a surgical apron hanging on a coatrack in a corner, and what might have been a scalpel and other implements on a different table along a wall, although she didn't get a clear enough look to be sure.

They moved down the wide hall, passing other family members who looked at them soberly, although there were undercurrents of different, competing emotions beneath their expressions. Sadness, hopefulness, wariness, and apprehension. A woman leaning hard on weathered elbow crutches approached Myra, followed closely by another with an entirely whitened right eye.

The woman in front grunted as she shifted weight to the leg that was best able to support her, freeing one hand to be placed on Myra's shoulder. "I don't see Duncan," she said.

Myra hesitated before responding. "Had to leave him. He was gone."

"I'm so sorry," the woman said, then hugged Myra briefly, before returning to the use of her crutches with the assistance of Myra and the woman with the white eye.

"Come on," Myra said. She and Barnes brought Sarita and David to a room to the left of the dark iron door covered in unreadable markings at the end of the hall.

There were two cots inside on opposite walls, as well as a short dresser with a rechargeable battery-powered lantern, and a wicker chair in the corner. Sarita and David sat beside each other on one cot, Sarita putting her arm around her brother, who was still shaking off the effects of the sedative.

"You never really answered my question when I asked if we're hostages," Sarita said.

"You're not," Myra said.

"So we can leave?"

Barnes said, "Look, I know you're upset, but we are, too. We just lost—"

Myra interrupted him. "Go tell him she's here."

If he had any objection, he kept it with him when he left the room. The sound of the metal door right outside opening and closing was as abrasive as an alarm.

"When you hear everything," Myra said, "you won't want to leave."

"I need to know if my friend is alive," Sarita said.

"I'll find out what I can."

"Our parents, too. How do I know he hasn't gone after them after what happened?"

"Because you're here, and not with them," Myra said. "You understand?"

Sarita refused to answer. The insinuation that she was too dangerous to be around, that she was in a way the reason Frank was dead and Tori might be, made her want to charge Myra, strike her in the nose again, break it this time. Do worse if necessary. Then fight her way through everyone else here, dragging David along until they found a way out and a way home. Fight with everything in her, that surge she discovered when Cold Eyes told her that the roaring sound was really a chorus calling upon her to survive. She wanted to show Myra that she was more of a threat—and far more capable—as a protector fighting for those she loved than as some kind of passive, unwilling harbinger bringing violence and death to those close to her.

Of course, she had long suspected the latter about herself, dwelled on it and alternated between denying and embracing the idea. Hearing it from someone else, however, made it feel like a fresh wound. Nothing that had happened since Frank died—and even well before that—suggested Myra was wrong. If anything, all the evidence in Sarita's life pointed to Myra stating something closer to fact than hypothesis.

What if there had been moments where she hadn't seen Angelo, but he'd been there, watching her, patrolling without her awareness and input? Choosing who gets to live, and who dies. What if there were other car wrecks, besides the one involving Candace and Dee? Ones he hadn't just saved Sarita from getting into, but that he had caused to slow traffic at an intersection where she would have died without his intervention? What about everyone else waiting for assistance in that emergency room Tori drove her to in high school? Had one or more of them died because the medical staff gave her the bed and attention they otherwise would have received had Angelo not shown up to warn her? Why hadn't he shown up days or weeks ahead instead of waiting for the last moment? Why couldn't he ever actually just say something to her instead of being deliberately cryptic?

All these years, she'd viewed him as a helpful, living omen, then as a Heaven-sent bodyguard, and even a weapon. She was still coming to grips with the idea that he had made her into a living curse.

"If I'm so dangerous to be around," Sarita said, "then why aren't you more scared of keeping me here?"

"I am scared," Myra said. "But I'm always scared, and always getting over it, every second of every day, from the first time a devil ruined my life. I'm used to it. That's how all of us here get by all the time. You'll get used to it, too."

"I'm not scared."

Myra shook her head at this obvious lie as though she'd heard something so disappointing it made her want to give up. "We're on your side," she said to Sarita.

The crushing echo of the metal door opening again stopped Sarita before she could follow up with another question. Barnes entered the room.

"He's ready to see her," he told Myra.

"Who is this 'he'?" Sarita said.

Myra started to answer and Barnes opened his mouth to cut her off, but she threw a glance like a punch that shut him up before he spoke.

"He's going to look strange to you," Myra said. "I just want to give you a heads-up. He's not human anymore. He hasn't been for a very long time."

"Then what is he?"

"A devil. A vampire. One who's on our side. At least as close as one ever will be."

20

She expected the stairs to lead her deeper underground than they did, and to a chamber darker than it was. Metal door aside, this room did not feel much apart from the rest of the home made by Myra and those she called family.

But the metal door *was* there, heavy and loud, seemingly designed to keep whoever lived behind it from getting out without being heard.

The sconces on the walls here were used as originally intended, holding seven lit torches instead of makeshift electrical lamps. The room was warmer and more humid from the seven small fires cooking off some of the moisture in the limestone walls. A potpourri of cloves, assorted unidentifiable spices, and earthen decay filled Sarita's nostrils even when she held her breath.

In the center of the chamber was a thin-haired, shirtless man seated at a large wooden table, reading from a book that looked like the reason the word "tome" was invented. Behind him, bookshelves stacked with hardcover manuscripts large enough to be used as murder weapons blocked the wall.

From the top of the stairs, Sarita could see the entangled, viny scarification on the man's torso, neck, and arms. It was difficult to tell, but she thought they looked like some of the artwork she saw on the tattooed man, except someone had put away the tattoo gun and picked up a scalpel when they went to work on the man in the chamber. His raised wounds competed with his chilling paleness for his most startling feature. She had been study partners with a man with albinism in college, and the man in the chamber's complexion was nothing like that. This man's paleness looked preserved and hypernatural, like he was born at the bottom of the ocean and clung to his dearth of pigment as a defense against the burn of sunlight.

Sarita descended the stairs, following Barnes and Myra, and holding David's hand. Barnes had tried to suggest it would be better if her brother didn't join her, but Sarita couldn't even finish her refusal to leave him behind before Myra said it would be fine for David to come. When they reached the bottom of the stairs, the pale man closed his book and looked up like he hadn't heard them come in. He stood, but remained behind his table as Barnes and Myra positioned themselves on either side of him, sentries there to either defend or deter him, Sarita couldn't quite tell which.

"Have they told you what this place is called?" the pale man said, every word like a fat, mud-covered reptile crawling through his throat.

"They haven't even told me who you are," Sarita said, barely masking a disgust as primal as that of seeing a dog-sized insect, and a fear big enough to be her hollow clone.

"No? Not at all?"

She shook her head, then shook it again like there was something with feathery legs crawling in her ear canal. "They just said you're some kind of devil."

The pale man gave her a sad smile, revealing dark, metallic plugs over fangs filed down almost to his gray gumline. The smile brought attention to how thin his lips were, and shrank his coal-colored eyes behind his cheekbones and brow.

"Some kind," he said, aloud but mostly to himself. "Sometimes kind. Something. A sum of things."

His smile stretched an inch or two, enough that Sarita feared it would make his face fall apart like a weathered mask, and there wouldn't even be a skull underneath, but a skull-shaped hive of warring wasps and hornets.

"Baby Head Mountain," the pale man said. "The name of this place. Baby Head Mountain. A macabre name. A macabre history. You should know it. They tell me you want to leave. You are safer here than anywhere you might think to go. Understanding why this hill has that name, and what it has invited, will help you understand why people have chosen here, over a chapel or temple, to hide from what they fear."

Sarita licked her lips without wetting them, her mouth dry, her legs straws. She adjusted her hold of David's hand to interlock fingers with him and pull him closer.

"So . . . so we're in a hill? Under a hill?"

"In the hills. Under a hill. Yes, and yes. In a place erroneously called a mountain, which could call into question the fitness of the remainder of its name. But once you know what rests here, you know what must be true."

"What's here?" Sarita asked.

The pale man leaned forward like he was going to transform into a snake and slither over the table. His tinseled hair curtained his eyes, which appeared even blacker now. Sarita took a step back, although David remained planted, his grip strong enough to be painful were it not so comforting. Sarita looked toward Barnes, then Myra. Neither reacted to the pale man's movement. They must have known or at least believed he still posed no threat. This was just one of his eccentricities, then. That, or this was all a setup and Sarita was an idiot for coming down here, trusting people who Tori had been afraid to trust because she recognized that they were summoning something, and who had admitted they were bringing her to see a vampire.

The man sat back, resettled himself, and said, "Baby Head Mountain is named after something found here. Once, there was a massacre here. But once there was a massacre in many places, and in many others a massacre more than once. So, what made what happened here unique enough to lure one of the great sleepers?"

"Sleepers?"

"Massive, ancient evils old and strong enough to be mistaken for gods. So powerful they have grown uncaring, their desire to exist almost calcifying, so they choose to hibernate for decades, centuries, and sometimes longer. One sleeps here because of the hill's history.

"There are competing stories. Some claimed Native peoples slaughtered a small, isolated family—man, woman, child—in the days of settlers, and burned their home. Only the young daughter's charred skull was found in the ashes. Horrible. Enough to welcome a demon seeking shelter? Questionable.

Enough to attract the specific one who dwells here? No, not at all. There is an emptiness in its preferred atrocities. A great space formed by great futility within certain acts of murder.

"The other story says that the family of poor, lonely settlers was slaughtered not by indigenous people, but by wealthier, more powerful men who shared their victims' foreign heritage, but not their class. They killed this family in anticipation of the value of this land. They killed them to dissuade others like them, others that were poor but hopeful, so the wealthy could possess the land and all around it for themselves. They believed that framing the Native people for the crime would not only accomplish this, but also attract the intervention of the government's armed forces, to eradicate the rest of the Native population. These men butchered a father, a mother, and a daughter, then claimed that the savages who had done the deed had left only the child's head behind. Which was true in one respect, but not quite with regard to who the savages were. And it was all so terribly, vastly pointless.

"The armed intervention never came. More impoverished migrants were never coming in the numbers these rich men feared, as there were already other, more hospitable, more welcoming places for them to go. The original people of this land would be driven away by incursive forces regardless. The land itself, which would have been theirs had they done nothing, never grew in value commensurate to what the wealthy men desired. So these savage men of avarice who erased a family, blamed the blameless, and gave this place its name, lost interest. The lie they told has remained well beyond any mark they planned to make here. The true legacy they left, older even than the name Baby Head, but as old as the crime, lives within the spirits."

A steady, cool wind pushed the torches, almost extinguishing them. Sarita heard Barnes sound like he was close to hyperventilating.

"It's okay," Myra said quietly. "It's okay." Who was she talking to? Barnes? Trying to reassure him, do the same to Sarita and David? Reassure them of what?

A needling infant's cry, sharp enough to be felt but small enough to almost go unnoticed, crosscut the breeze, shifting the air in the chamber. Sarita followed the direction of the wind and stopped when she saw a shape at the top of the stairs, caught in a shaded space between the nearest torch and the light of the open doorway. She guessed, from their height, shoulder width, and stance, that they were the muscular woman who had joined the doctor and tattooed man in grabbing Everett when they first entered. Was that who Myra had been speaking to? Because the muscular woman had come to check on them for some reason?

No, Sarita was surer now that Myra had been talking to herself, calming herself, because from her angle she had an even better view of two veiled figures that were now in Sarita's periphery, standing near the wall beyond the stairs. Not near enough to the wall—or, rather, far enough from her—for Sarita's liking, though. Without directly facing them, she made out that the shorter of the two carried something smaller still in its arms. The bundle in that phantom's grasp stirred as the wailing grew louder, more jagged, less infantile. More of a scraping sound.

Before it came to the crescendo Sarita expected—just before she covered her ears to protect her hearing, which David had already done—she instinctively called out, "Stop!"

Not only did the wailing cease on command, but the spirits disappeared as if banished only by the sound of her voice. Before they departed, Sarita noticed that the three phantoms were incomplete in ways she refused to clearly see, though it was still most evident with the smallest of them. They left terror behind, in the void they vacated, and Sarita could sense that it belonged to them, and that she was the source of it. The spirits had appeared, wanting to be noticed and heard by a newcomer, likely hoping for sympathy, or just for a new witness who would care enough to give them attention. Then they had felt something in her voice, in her presence, that made them hide. Not even the vampire that dwelled under the hill with them could frighten them, but *she* could? How was that possible?

She wanted to command them to come back so she could interrogate them. Ask them what exactly they had heard in her voice that made them obey and vanish, so she could start learning how to replicate it. She knew it would be terrible to subject them to this, and felt guilty for frightening these agonized, long-lingering victims in the first place, but struggled to care more about that than about uncovering what she could be capable of.

She forced herself to turn back toward the pale man, ground her teeth as she worked her jaw back and forth to unclench it so she could speak. "How the hell could this place be safe based on what you're telling me? You're doing a bad job of making me not want to leave."

"Safety is relative," the pale man said. "You can hide in the mouth of

Leviathan if it is sleeping, and its presence will discourage sharks from continuing their pursuit."

Sarita sighed. "So . . . in your analogy, who or what is the shark? Is it Angelo? Or the one who just tried to take me?"

"Both of them, and others, too. There are many."

A daze stole her vision for an instant, blood rushing to her head. The possibility of there being others like Angelo and Cold Eyes not just out there, but specifically pursuing her for some damn reason, brought her as close to hopelessness as she had been since this all started.

How had it even started? She could barely think clearly enough to trace it to the beginning . . .

Frank. One of these things killed Frank. Remember it. Remember him.

"You're saying they're too afraid to come here?" Sarita said. "Because of you? Are you the big demon you've been talking about? You seem like the type to talk about yourself in third person."

The pale man shook his head as though he were convulsing. "No, *no*, no. Do *not* say that. I am not the sleeper, nor do I desire to be. I am nothing to it." He lifted his head and called more loudly, "I am nothing to it!"

He then traced the tapestry of his chest scars with his yellowed, pointed fingernails. "I am, in fact, only permitted here because of this. And because of the aroma you have surely noticed. And this, as well." With his index and pinky fingers he drew his lips back to mark where his four fangs ought to be. After this display, he lowered his hands and probed the caps with the tip of his tongue, shuddering in pain as he did so. "I have weakened myself. I have done what I can, short of becoming a breathing man again, so that the sleeper will not sense me and awaken to devour me. Even with that, I hide behind the door to ensure I do not garner the sleeper's attention. The one who has stalked you and thinks you belong to him would be sniffed out within a mile of the 'mountain.' So, too, would The Northman."

"The Northman?"

"You called him Angelo."

An unexpected relief, like a warm, motherly hand on a sick child's chest, came to her. She had one small, new answer to something. Finally. Angelo had a different moniker—a different designation, at least—from the one her mother had given him, and that he no longer deserved.

"What do you know about him? What can you tell me? Who is he? Why did he—?"

The pale man raised his hand to halt her and she fell silent to let him talk, feed her more answers.

"He is not the angel you believed him to be. He was just a man, mad with mourning from what he lost, who then succumbed to the temptation to become something more. I am sorry for ever helping to find him, as I am sorry for ever helping to find you."

"What *are* you? They told me you're a vampire," Sarita said, pointing to Myra, "but that can't be it. You look like a lot more than that."

"We are *all* more than that. You see the modest archive behind me? They are studies and histories. I wish I could give you time to read them all, as I have. They will tell you the truth behind the word you used, and introduce you to hundreds of other names for us that you would have never known. It is likely that all you have learned about us comes from stories, not *histories*. Not from the work of scholars, witnesses, believers, and memoirists. Not from anyone we widowed or orphaned, either.

"Proper, learned authors will tell you that every vampire is, has been, or can also be a witch, a shape-shifter, a phantom, and demon, among other things. We are likely to be some part of all these at any point you may encounter us, or we may be all of one and none of the others, or all of all. Or something else. Whatever, exactly, I am, for instance. I struggle to define myself. I have read and researched, and still have not found a title or definition that suits what I have made myself. Vampire, and vampire-no-more. A man driven blind by barely contained madness, then later a hematophagous horror, and the first disciple of Cela's church."

"What church? Who the hell . . . Jesus, who is Cela? And what did you mean you 'found' me? *What are you talking ab—*" Her body clenched, locking down a scream that would have rivaled the one that almost ripped her apart in the hotel room as she knelt beside her husband's body, grappling with the hideousness of his remains.

His face was gone. His head was crushed. Just tell me why it happened? Why did Angelo or "The Northman" or whatever his name is do that? Why did any of this happen?

She composed herself, then carried on her questioning. "What does all of this have to do with me? Why me?"

"Because someone had to be chosen," the pale man said, solemnity transforming his face so that he looked like someone who never learned to smile. "There were others it could have been, but Cela chose you, just like she chose the one who would be her god, a French Viscount with massive, exploitable delusions. She then guided him to you, and you to him. I am sorry, Sarita. I helped her choose you to be the holy mother of a religion meant to unite us in the goal of vengeance and conquest. You and The Viscount were foreseen as a chance, a mere possibility, then arranged by Cela, The Founder of the church, as a prophecy. You were meant to be the mother of a messiah who would never be born. This child was meant to die in your womb, and your husband, Franklin, was meant to be your killer.

"Then your followers, the voices you have heard since you were first saved from the water, praying to you without you recognizing them, they would have followed Cela's demand for an uprising. A holy war waged to depopulate the planet and enslave the survivors, as part of a mad quest to 'save' the world.

"You must understand, this is not hyperbole. This is not a fable. This is why we must do whatever is necessary to protect you. Your death is the key that opens the way to Armageddon, and Cela already stands at the door."

21

It would have been too dangerous for Cela to return to her church after depositing Harrah, or to travel to speak with The Viscount, after bringing Harrah to the hospital. Not dangerous for herself, but for her congregation, or for the former Viscount she first made immortal, and then into an object of worship. She would have been too tempted to devour them all, and did not trust herself around them, so she returned to the desert, to the same place where she had left the comparatively mundane and unappetizing bag of hearts.

Harrah's blood had been calling to her, and the ache of her restraint worsened in Harrah's absence. She could have fed on Harrah until she sweat blood, left the corpse so desiccated the vultures would have lost interest before landing beside it. Harrah's blood was enriched by her desire to kill her daughter-in-law. The woman her son loved, died believing he was protecting. Harrah's willingness to become the new Devil of Devils—a potentially greater version than her son would have been—made her instantly, addictively appealing.

Nothing tasted better than the blood of a saint or devil.

A man who eats his own child to stave off starvation during an era of famine becomes a ghoul. It can be no other way, and his blood is made more delicious because of this.

And an old woman who wordlessly endures blades and flames that would make warriors scream rather than confess to where she has hidden children that plunderers seek to enslave? How could she not be canonized?

Cela had saved such women from their captors just to make personal blood casks of them.

Harrah's blood would have been more potent. She was now the unwitting catalyst for an apocalypse. The Devil who the end of days could be traced to, as well as the beginning of a new epoch. The Reign of Vampires which would secure the safety and endurance of the planet. Just the thought of how savory her blood must be made it momentarily difficult for Cela to contemplate anything else, and she had far more important subjects to ponder.

But Harrah's blood, spiced not only with wretchedness worthy of legend, but also something else that would make it even more darkly decadent, still clamored for Cela's attention. She could have drunk beyond her fill of it, then gladly trapped herself in a loop of drinking the spillage from her burst stomach. What a lovely indulgence.

That would have suited her want, but not her need. So she abstained. Still, the strength of her thirst made her a hazard. Better to remain alone until she could corral it again. It would work to her benefit in a different way, as well. The only thing more empowering than the blood of a saint or a devil was fasting from either.

In the first years after her conversion, while researching the myriad things that could now kill her, to better develop defenses against such weapons and efforts, Cela observed that starvation was never mentioned in any texts. Her potentially destructive hunger need not be obeyed for her to remain alive. This was a revelation. There must be a reason for this.

All other things that feel hunger *must* eat. When she was a breather, her body demanded sustenance not just to remain in optimal health, but to survive. After drinking a solution comprised of a holy man's bone marrow, soil from her father's grave, and, as a solvent, a pitcher of floodwater that housed a dozen drowned spirits, Cela became something greater than human. Nonetheless, the human weakness of hunger not only stayed with her, it became a knowing thing that relished its influence over her.

It took another decade for her to consider conquering it, in part out of self-preservation. Hunger, like any other unchecked desire, could make one reckless, and had brought her into the path of elder magi who were almost able to behead her, nearly getting halfway through before she escaped with the broken bronze saw blade in her throat, and the hearts of holy men skewered on her long fingers.

She had retreated to the arid, volcanic field of the Bayuda Desert, avoided nomadic breathers and the rare animal alike, and put it upon herself to wander, to test herself. She endeavored to cage, then domesticate, and finally oppress her bloodlust. In the process, she plunged through the previous floors of her agony to find a new abyss of misery. She discovered the cellular and even atomic structure of the physical world when her hunger mobilized the uncountable particles of her being into a contained, voracious universe screaming to be fed. She felt what it was to starve to death without dying, and it was every conceivable hell combined for the first few years.

She first had visions of the great sleepers then, and believed they were mirages of strange giants that she could dine on for eons. She began to shed all her memories, save for those of the taste of blood, the texture of flesh, the faint, satisfying pop of veins when they first yield to teeth. At last, she neared a point when the final thread of her sanity was holding on for just long enough to let her recognize the unthinking beast she had inadvertently made of herself. Nothing more than craving incarnate. That was when the thread became unbreakable, reinforced by the certainty that its failure would leave Cela effectively brain-dead. Her body would go on, but she would become hunger in a mindless husk.

Instead, gradually, she emerged as an enlightened, more godlike version of herself. She saw the giants again on her path back to complete sanity, and recognized these elder gods as though she had known of them all her life, and was closer to being peers with them than they would have wanted.

One evening she raised a hand toward the night sky out of instinct, and was surprised to feel something thinner than silk against her palm, but not as surprised as she ought to have been. That was when she discovered that darkness had substance, was a usable element. She discovered the ability to effectively pull parts of the night away by the fistful. Soon she trained herself to do this without hands or gestures, just with her will. She learned to travel between shadows separated by streams, by rivers, by mountain ranges, and then even greater distances. Later, she understood that spaces untouched by light included the underground, and where she could travel was limited only by her endurance, as well as her pain tolerance, given the strenuousness of the process.

She became the first of a subspecies of her kind, and managed to recruit others over centuries, although for each one she converted, scores more lacked the mental resolve to stave off insanity, and the death of their mind.

She had infected Harrah with two small punctures from her fingertips, enough to grant her more than the necessary skills to complete her tasks, and to even fend off The Northman if he tried to intervene again.

Where was he now? Cela's defiant "angel." The one she had picked to protect Sarita, prove her as the chosen to her flock, until the time came for her and her unborn child to be sacrificed. Sarita had known him as Angelo. Cela's faithful knew him as The Guardian. To Cela he was simply "The Northman." No more a name than if someone deigned to call her The Kushite, inviting her to snatch their voice out with her teeth to address their informality.

Unlike Cela, The Northman never selected a new, preferred name after his conversion, and never remembered the one his parents gave him. In truth, he seemed disinterested in remembering it. Cela had long taken that as a sign of his ultimate selflessness. The trait that made him so perfectly pliable. Had he also known that his lack of a name—the quashing of his identity—would make it difficult for Cela to find him? Had he counted on this keeping him hidden after planning to murder The Devil of Devils prematurely, corrupting Cela's prophecy? Cela did not want to believe this to be true, and held to the hope that The Northman had acted impulsively, traumatized by the thought of Sarita's fate, and was now scared to come home to her and beg forgiveness.

She *could* pardon him if he had acted without thinking or planning. Partaking in a plot, however, would demand execution. Fools acted on suspicion first and foremost, however. She owed it to The Northman to find him, submit him to a proper and thorough inquisition, and sift through his wails to discern the truth.

Despite wanting to believe that The Northman was not a conspirator, she could not help but wonder who the ringleader of such a plot might be. None of the priests she ordained were above suspicion, but the one man that concerned her was no longer part of her church. The Exile, now referring to himself as "Z," had taken residence and sought redemption within a sleeper's lair some time ago. She believed she could strike at him successfully if necessary. She doubted a slothful sleeper would awaken and be wise to her fast enough to pose a threat before she could make off with Z's heart and head. She did not want to kill him, however. He was her inaugural disciple, her first and oldest success, and the only foreteller as gifted as her. It would be a waste of the talent she awakened within him, and of the work and patience required to unlock said talent, merely because he came to mistrust her and left her fold.

True, it was an affront for him to assert she would someday seek godhood for herself. That her motives were not as pure as she had guided him to believe, and that she envied the sleepers, hoping to join their pantheon eventually. That she would burn and ravage the world worse than the imbecilic nuclear god the breathers had awakened, or the ecological hellscape they insisted on manufacturing, if it meant becoming a sleeper. An offensive and grossly inaccurate charge, regardless of whatever vision of such a future he claimed to have. Why would she ever want to be so dormant, for such extended periods of time, that she could be defined by it? What good was such power if it encouraged inertia?

Absurd and objectionable as his charge was, to say nothing of the disloyalty of his departure, she did not think it warranted execution. Active treachery was a different matter. Especially given his knowledge of what was at stake. Not merely Cela's pride and position. The fate of the future. A world probably damned to atomic and climatological ruin, or redeemed by implementation of controlled, if extensive, violence and purgation. Either would claim billions of lives, but only her course would avert a new, prolonged dark age, and instead produce a stronger society.

Why must we hide your true intentions? The Exile had asked, mere days before abandoning her. *Why not share our visions and seek alternative courses that do not require so much death? Why disguise your plan as religion?*

He knew the answers she would give him, she was sure, so she did not bother responding. Despite the contempt they held for the breathers, their kind were just as inclined to individualism, irresponsibility, and a fear of greater ambition. Many were content with a comfortable, often temporary home near a small settlement where they could feed, laze, or engage in assorted baser pleasures as they wished. Any notion of conquest and rule even on a smaller scale sounded troublesome to them at best, and at worst unsafe, as it could alert a nearby, undetected sleeper.

It was difficult not to adopt a laissez-faire philosophy when you are perfectly perched above mortals, but so far below the celestials, and the terrestrial gods, demigods, and demons. That last set especially, as many of them were born so early they were forced to settle for the instinctual reverence of prehistoric beasts, then fell into deep, long slumbers before a sapient species that could properly worship them came to be. These were particularly territorial, almost primitive in their thinking, and wary of being replaced, returned to being worshipped by animals not intelligent enough to understand what worship was. Better not to anger them, most of her kind believed. So she had to make them believe in something else.

Centuries of history had taught her that religion was an excellent tool for mobilizing otherwise unmotivated masses. She taught her flock to resent humanity's characterization of vampires as evil, as essentially devilish. She borrowed from Christianity, the faith that most fascinated her, and Catholicism in particular. She merged her Mary and Christ figures through a single sacrifice. Mother and child, Goddess and Messiah, killed by a petty, possessive man, indicative of the dangerous, intolerable small-mindedness of all humankind.

The prediction alone had inflamed her followers. When it actually came to pass, she had no doubt it would drive them to act. If anything, she would have to remind them that the objective was to dominate, not exterminate.

Concentrating on these things helped her nearly suppress the thirst, when the piercing scent of forbidden blood turned her head. Even before she saw him, and those with him, she knew. He did not just smell of godhood.

Cela had no children, but The Viscount was effectively her offspring, just as Harrah Stallworth now was. All her followers were enlightened because of her, but Harrah and The Viscount were reborn through her. There was nothing more monstrous among thinking beings than devouring what you have given new life to.

Monstrous, stimulating, and uplifting.

"Get away from me," she said, concerned her teeth would be too large and heavy for her to issue the warning in another second.

The Viscount stepped toward her, leaving behind the seven priests standing behind him.

"No, prophetess," he said, "we will not be leaving you. Look at the mischief you get up to when you believe yourself to be alone and unmonitored."

Cela locked her jaw muscles, made herself as still as possible, concentrated on who the man approaching her was, who he used to be, the time she had spent molding him, and how that work, plus much more, would be spoiled were she to succumb to her hunger now.

His aroma sharpened more as he came closer, sawing at her self-restraint.

Later if you must, she thought. *He will be as healthy and ambrosial in one hundred years as he is today.*

"You do not understand," Cela said through clamped teeth. "I am not safe."

"No, evidently you are not, in any sense. You will see that soon enough. I must say I wanted The Exile to be wrong when he visited me. Yet here you are, consorting with The Devil's Mother. *Weaponizing* her, and necessitating my intervention when I ought to be continuing pursuit of my beloved Sarita. To say I am displeased is an enormous understatement. I would be equally disappointed had I not always suspected you had blasphemous ambitions."

This was the most welcome, dreadful news she could have received. It distracted her, made the hunger secondary for a moment. The Exile had visited him? Spoken to him? Warned him about her?

"When?" she managed.

"You need not know. Come with us."

"When?" she repeated, and he froze under the dark chill of her tone. The recognition that smashed through his confidence was unmistakable, even though it lasted mere seconds. Had he been facing the priests in that moment, had they seen the panic in his eyes, their faith in him would have weakened, and might have crumbled. The authority in her tone forced him to feel and acknowledge the strings she ran through him. She had conditioned him to believe himself a god, the latest reincarnation of a promised vampire father, but she could deprogram him almost without trying. She did not want him to remember and revert to what he was before she remade him, she only wanted him to answer her.

"When did he come to see you?" she said again, dulling the edge in her voice this time. It allowed The Viscount to pretend he had only imagined Cela stilling him with a single word. One syllable.

"Shortly after he visited The Northman to advise that your 'prophecy' was, in truth, a scheme, and that my bride and child were not destined to die. He then told me the same, and added a warning that amounted to sacrilege. 'She will kill you,' he told me. I refrained from killing him for saying this as though it were possible, and asked him to specify, but he would only repeat, 'She will kill you.' Now I wonder which of you he meant, you or The Devil's Mother."

I should have killed The Exile the day after he departed. I could have prevented this. Mercy shall be my unmaking.

Even as she thought this, Cela chained every muscle fiber in her body, aware that even a twitch in her toe would ripple through her like a fission detonation, freeing her to kill her "god," the priests, the land itself. For miles in every direction the area would be scarred enough by blood and agony to make clouds wary of passing over it. Watering this land, after what she would have done to it, could only prompt horrors to grow.

She could not surrender to her impulse to kill The Viscount. In doing so, she would lose more than him. She would lose her flock. They would feel his death, know who had done it, and never recover from the shock. So she exhibited necessary mercy, for now, as the priests and god of the religion she founded swallowed her in the darkness of their own shadows to transport her across the sea, to the great, cavernous church, whose construction she had overseen, where her congregation waited to witness her public trial.

22

Everett and the doctor were in the room when David and Sarita returned, escorted by Myra. Barnes had hurried away ahead of them to be by himself, still recovering from the appearance of the spirits. Sarita could not blame him. Were she not feeling so overwhelmed—and were she not so uniquely, freshly experienced in dealing with one new overwhelming development after another—any one of the things she had seen, heard, or learned about would have her looking for a quiet room to be alone in, a wall to stare or shout at, a corner to crawl into.

All these years, Angelo—she still struggled to think of him by any other name—had been saving her just to allow her to be sacrificed. Murdered by Frank while pregnant with some fake god's child. It made no sense. But what about her life had ever made sense? Why else would she be extraordinary enough to warrant divine intervention? She'd been saved from drowning, saved from a medical emergency, saved from the car accident, saved from a drunk asshole with a gun.

Then saved from her own husband before he showed the slightest hint of wanting to harm her.

It was ludicrous. She remembered telling her own mother as much—with different words but with the same adamancy—in the hospital the night of the murder. The few times Frank had even stepped on her heel by accident when walking behind her in a store, he apologized as though he'd almost pushed her over a cliff. He got uncomfortable just seeing her cry at happy endings in movies and television shows, to say nothing of when she was actually upset. But he was, nonetheless, capable of murdering her in the presumably near future? Why?

The one word spoken by the pale man that came closest to making any of it feel plausible was "arranged." It might not matter what was in her heart, what she and Frank would never do, if a higher power was manipulating or outright possessing them.

She couldn't linger on that now. Well, she *could,* and the fact that it would probably do no good made it more welcoming as a time waster. Why not spend a few hours running mental laps around loose concepts of fate, free will, coercion, weakness, and culpability? It would give her something to do without having to go anywhere, try anything, or make a tough decision. Because she felt one was coming, although her mind was almost made up about it already. The hard part was going to be the argument with her brother that it would entail.

The doctor approached after moving a small plastic bucket between Everett's legs, at the foot of the cot where he was seated. He offered his hand and Sarita shook it, accepting any morsel of normalcy she could get. "Sarita, my name is Vai. I'm a doctor."

"I figured," she said.

He raised his eyebrows, shrugged lightly, indicating he'd rather be sure than presume she knew, then said, nodding toward Everett, "He suffered a concussion. He's vomited once, and his pupils are slightly dilated, but he's fairly alert. Not quite as responsive to questions as I'd like, but he's already improving. Based on some of what he's said, and what I know of the situation, I think the primary cause for some of his early incoherence was emotional trauma, not physical. Overall, he'll be fine for the time being, given he made it all this way and hasn't shown any truly severe symptoms just yet. Still, factoring in his age, we can't presume he's out of the woods. I'm due for a supply run back to San Antonio, so I won't be here to monitor him directly, but I'll let you and everyone else know what to look out for while I'm gone. If it gets urgent, we can look into taking him to a hospital. For now, I don't think we need to run that risk."

"Risk?" Sarita said.

"We try to avoid attention, stay off the grid out here," Myra said. "It's not really safe for anyone who wouldn't understand to know we're out here and think they have a reason to look around. Dropping off an injured man who is very, very easy to pick out, and who was last seen at the site of a massacre where three of his relatives died? That's a risk. Even if there are no police at whatever facility we took him to, there could be cameras, or potential witnesses. It's a chance we've taken before, but like Vai said, only when it's urgent. Life or death."

Sarita thought to ask Myra why she and Barnes didn't just leave Everett in the parking lot of The Lantern, but recognized it was a stupid question. Their priority, even above bringing home every member of their team, had been to bring Sarita here as quickly as possible. Everett happened to end up in the van, brought inside by David, ever the rescuer, and it was easier to drive away with him in back than to fight over bringing in an extra, wounded passenger.

Now that she thought of it, they must have ultimately seen David as an unnecessary extra as well. They would have left him with Tori if they'd had the chance. All the more reason to get him away from this alleged haven, the house of a dormant demon that was lured here by the fruitless massacre of a poor family. Myra and her own "family"(that was cultist lingo, wasn't it? Another red flag.) would throw David in front of a threat in half a heartbeat to keep it from getting to Sarita. She would fight for him, scratch and claw to save him, and likely fail.

"When are you leaving?" Sarita asked Vai.

"In a few hours. If any medical issues come up, talk to Rowan. He was with me and Nadine when you all came in," Vai said.

So the muscular woman was Nadine, and the tattooed man was Rowan. Sarita wanted to ask the names of the other two she remembered seeing on the way in, the woman on crutches and the one with the injured eye. She wanted the name of the man—the *vampire*—in the chamber as well, of course, and to then be introduced to every member of the "family" she hadn't interacted with yet. She wondered how many more there were. They all needed to be accounted for and identifiable in case any of them tried something while she was here.

"What about my brother? He doesn't even live here, and doesn't stand out like Everett. Nobody would even know he'd been there."

David, starting to pick up on where this was leading, said, "Wait, hold up."

"I can't see any risk in letting him leave. Can you take him back to the city with you?"

"Fuck no," David said. *"Fuck. No."*

Myra narrowed her eyes as though she'd been handed a present that might be a gift-wrapped bomb. "You want him to go?"

David stepped between them, faced Sarita. "I'm not going anywhere you're not going."

"Stop and think," Sarita said. "I need you to get away. I need to know Tori's safe, and *we* need at least one of us to let Mom and Dad know we're alive before they realize we were there and get worried."

"We can just call Mom and Dad, and call around to find out about Tori. If these people will give us our phones back." He looked between Myra and Vai. "I mean unless you guys have full-on kidnapped us, I don't think it's crazy for us to have our phones. It was crazy for you to take them in the first place."

"It was necessary to simplify things," Myra said.

"You dropped simple when you picked us up."

"When we saved your lives."

"Yeah, the thing is, I actually do that for a living, and I've never taken anyone out of the water and then taken them to God knows where against their will."

"But you've had to strike a panicking person to save them," Vai said. "Am I mistaken?"

David stared at him like he was reading from a stolen page in his diary. The question of *How do you know what exactly I do for a living?* was printed on his face, Sarita saw, but he forewent asking it to say, "That's not the same thing."

"It's something that would look bad to the untrained, inexperienced eye. It might even get a complaint from the person you rescued, but at least they'd be alive to voice their complaint."

Sarita took David's face in her hands, made him look at her. "Hey, we're not going to try to just call Mom and Dad from some demon's den under a hill and convince them we're okay and then hang up. They need to see at least one of us face-to-face to believe it. And you're going to have to leave me because I'm telling you to leave me."

"No. No way."

"We tried it the other way, with you and Tori sticking by me and . . .

and it's like Dee and Candace all over again, except it's so much worse I can't even start to tell you. Tori could be dead, and if she'd just stayed away she'd probably be all right. Frank . . . if I hadn't married him, if we'd never met—"

"Then it would just be somebody else. It's not fate or something, and you're not cursed. It's like that guy down there said, somebody else manipulated all of this."

"Exactly, and they're still out there doing it. And they'll kill anyone I love who's close to me to finish whatever it is they've started."

"They'll try to kill you, too," David said, his voice lowering, yet sharpening on the hard edge of his emotion. "That guy said you were supposed to die as part of this prophecy or plan. They want you dead."

"They wanted Frank to kill me, and he's not around anymore." She swallowed, took a breath, and forced herself to say aloud something she shuddered to contemplate. "Who else do I love, who else do I even have left, that the person pulling the strings could try to have kill me? Mom and Dad aren't here. So who's left?"

She had hoped her words would shock him speechless with one quick jolt, but instead they slid over him like a scaling knife. He grimaced, and when he spoke there was an immature defiance in his tone. "There's no way in the world I would ever—"

"Frank wouldn't have, either, but they planned that for him. Maybe he was going to be possessed or hypnotized, or just framed for it. I don't know. But there's got to be a reason they picked somebody close to me. Who loved me, and who I loved back." She made a sour face and raised her head as though to speak to a hovering, invisible watcher. "Who I will still love, forever. My one and only. And you're my only brother, David."

"Damn right. I'm your brother, and I'm never letting anything happen to you ever again."

He was going to keep pushing back until he put all of his weight on the knives he was making her set out. She had to go right for his heart to get him to understand. "David, if you could do that we wouldn't even be here."

He looked angry, not like he wanted to hit something, but like he wanted to lift and throw something impossibly heavy, then do it again to show it wasn't a fluke, that he could do things thought undoable. Instead, he walked away, just a few steps out of the room, before returning to tell Sarita, "I'm coming right back for you. *Right back.*"

"Check on Tori, make sure she's okay. Tell her . . . tell her I'm sorry and I love her. Go see Mom and Dad, and make sure they're safe. Do that for me, please."

He gave as much of a nod as he could muster, and walked out of the room.

Sarita looked at Everett and asked Vai, "Can I talk to him?"

"Of course."

She went to the older man who she hadn't given that much thought to before her life came undone, and who she'd too briefly bonded with at The Lantern, on a unique level not even occupied by her brother or best friend. The man who saw, or guessed at, her vengeful aspirations, and offered to assist. She wished they'd had more time to talk about it, if nothing else. They might have that now, for however long they would be together under Baby Head Mountain, provided his head injury let him hold a conversation with her. And presuming he wouldn't be furious with her, blame her for the deaths of his nephews. Maybe whatever plot they could concoct would go nowhere. Likely the case, considering what they were up against, but even just working it out with him, sharing the violent thoughts she didn't feel comfortable revealing to anyone else, would be therapeutic, at minimum.

She crouched to just below his eye level and he seemed to barely notice her.

"Everett."

He looked at her, then seemed to look around her, only his eyes moving, still not giving her genuine attention. Maybe he was more out of it than Vai had indicated.

"Uncle Everett."

His eyes snapped into place like he had pushed them back into their sockets, and they locked onto Sarita's. She read a complete, tragic story in his stare before he spoke. "I shouldn't have said what I said."

She gave him time to clear enough fog from his head to find his next sentence. "What I said about Frankie being the good one. I mean he was, but that didn't mean that the others . . . I just shouldn't have said that. Now they're gone. They're gone. I tried to fight for them. I tried. I tried to come see you alone, Sarita. They wouldn't let me. I should've made them stay home. I didn't try hard enough. Now those boys are gone. I saw that thing kill them. I tried, but couldn't even save *one*. Not one."

His eyes dropped to his upturned hands. He looked at his calloused palms like something was supposed to be in them, turned them over to see fresh scrapes and swelling on his knuckles. "I did try, didn't I? When the fighting started? I feel like I tried, but I can't quite remember. Can't hardly see their faces past all the . . . all of it. But I know I must've tried."

"Uncle Everett," Sarita said again. This time when he looked at her, she hugged him, and thought of him at the wedding and reception, icy at first, then loosening up enough to sneak in a dance with Sarita's mom, and tell a joke that made her dad laugh so hard everyone at the table behind them jumped like they'd heard a gunshot. The kind of things that made him Frank's favorite.

She had no doubt that he had tried, just like David tried to hold on to her in the water when they were kids. Just like Frank had tried to fight a stranger he had no hope against. Like she tried to fight an angel for Everett's good nephew, and like she was going to kill a devil or two to avenge him, or die trying.

23

There were fourteen others in the sanctuary, besides the seven Sarita had already met, making for twenty-one in total. Twenty-two if she counted the pale man in the chamber behind the iron door, which she felt for now she ought not to, although she couldn't say why.

After David left with Vai, accompanied by Nadine, Myra came to Sarita's room to invite her and Everett to eat with the rest of the family. Sarita thought of making a remark about having her food slipped to her on a tray under the door, then remembered that Myra was mere hours removed from losing Duncan. She still didn't know exactly what he had meant to her, but Sarita suspected they were close in a way that made Myra her kin in terms of bereavement. Even if that wasn't the exact case, there was no point in saying anything that might upset her. No upside to being difficult or declining a show of hospitality. She also wasn't going to learn anything about her "captors" and her surroundings by staying in the room.

The dining area consisted of seven wooden picnic tables and benches adjacent to a rustic kitchen. The extra seating stood out. Only five of the tables were occupied, and all with room to spare. From the looks of it, each table could seat six people comfortably, and up to ten if they were all closer to the petite side. Sarita sat across from Myra and Rowan, with the silent, almost catatonic Everett to her right. To her left sat the woman with crutches, who was introduced to Sarita as Len. Across from Len sat her companion with the scarred eye, Dottie. Every other table had fewer than five people. Sarita took this as a sign, and understood she might be mistaken, but coupled with Myra's somewhat subdued reaction to Duncan's death, Sarita thought that the family was familiar with loss. No one had had to move out of the room she occupied in anticipation of her arrival. She wondered how long it had been empty.

If anyone was staring at her, watching her like they resented her or were wary of her, Sarita hadn't caught them in the act. Still, she felt like she had brought a cloud with her into the dining area that dimmed the already weak lighting and made everyone quieter. Aside from Myra handling introductions, no one wanted to speak, not just at her table, but at any of the others. Maybe this was how dinner always was, or maybe Duncan's death had understandably placed a pall over their mealtime. Not that Sarita could imagine life was ever joyful here, hiding in the mouth of a leviathan, as the pale man put it.

She and Everett were among the first to receive a plate of thinly sliced lean beef, rice, and chopped vegetables, brought to them by Barnes. Something about the meat made her stomach tighten. When she realized that it brought to mind the ribbons of flesh curling from Tori's rent arm, she nudged the plate away. Needing to think of something other than that, as well as her concern for David, whether he was safe on the road and whether she'd made a bad decision in convincing him to leave, Sarita spoke up.

"Why did you all pick this place?" she said to Myra. "*Did* you pick it? Or were you brought here?"

Myra took time to swallow a mouthful of food and pinch crumbs off her lips with her thumb and forefinger before answering. "A little of both. We've all come from different places, different backgrounds, and different things brought us all together here over time. But this place was picked out a long time ago, like a lot of others similar to it. We're just the latest caretakers."

"Why here, though? Why not like an old church or temple or something?"

"You basically mean like some holy ground? Instead of this."

Sarita nodded. Myra looked at Rowan, passing the conversation to him with a glance. An eagerness to share lifted some of the gloom from his face.

"Hallowed ground is awfully hard to come by," he said, the melody of a light Scottish accent cushioning his words. "It takes a hell of a lot less to corrupt a sacred place than it does to sanctify a bad place.

"That's just one part of it. If it was just difficult to find, and keep, it would still be work going to it if you could feel certain of its protection. You can't, though, maybe on account of what I just said about it being despoiled so easily. Even a tiny crack in your faith can shatter your entire defense. Just look at me." He spread his arms enough to show off even more of his tattoos on his inner biceps and forearms. "I've devoted my very skin to wards, runes, supplications, and symbols, in a permanent fashion. If I could survive the carving, I'd even go further than skin-deep, down into the tissue like old Z down there."

"Z?" Sarita said.

Len said, "The one you talked to in the chamber. That's what people who've lived here have called him since before any of us ever got here. He's been here through at least a few generations of us refugees. He might have helped found the place, although we don't try to get to know him, exactly, so we don't know much of his history. He's originally from Greece, and really, really old. He could have known Socrates, for all we know. That old. Like I said, we don't really dig into his past much. He seems to prefer it that way. The people who were here before us trusted him, and the people before them did, too, back a hundred or so years, so that's about good enough for us."

Sarita wondered briefly whether knowing the ancient man's deeper history might be beneficial to her somehow, then decided it wouldn't be worth pursuing. If he hadn't shared it with the people who'd been here, she didn't think he would be looking to open up to her. Something else about Z, mirrored in less dramatic and violent fashion on Rowan, made Sarita think of another question, however.

"You marked yourself like this for protection?" she said to Rowan, gesturing at the tapestry of ink covering his skin.

"Indeed, but I may have done it all for nothing just as well. The exhibits of holiness, in particular. If my belief wavers in the slightest, I'm no more protected with an ankh or tyet over my heart than some old gangster shot right through the crucifix hanging from his necklace. And I don't get any say whether it wavered at all. No warning, no scorecard to let you know how many of your sins have been wiped clean by repentance, how many more you must be absolved of to be worthy again. Nothing. God, or the gods, determine if your faith is sturdy enough without informing you and allowing you to rebut their decision. No extra chance to prove yourself worthy. On the other side, 'lower powers,' so to speak, can actually be a little more forgiving.

"How a lot of us were raised, we learned that when you commit a sin, confession is in order, to God, or to a man of God, and acts of contrition or redemption are then required, and how successful they may be is a mystery. The many devils we know of, however, connivers and liars that they are, don't expect you to tell ten lies to counter every truth, or anything like that. They don't keep score the same way, and then keep the score hidden from you to boot. You can't trust them at all, yet they're strangely reliable.

"Think of it, you've never heard anybody say 'Satan works in mysterious ways,' or 'Hell only knows.' Devils are . . . I won't say predictable, but they're relatively consistent compared to the other side. You can look through history and see how goodness alters even in the moment. But evil, you can almost always tell what it's about. And one thing you learn fast about it is that it hates itself. Evils hate each other. Devils kill devils. They kill us, too, of course, but once you understand how ruthless they can be with each other, especially the older ones who don't like the idea of anything taking their place, you get ideas about leveraging them against each other to save yourself."

A strong grunt that could have been an objection or affirmation came from Everett. Sarita turned to him, surprised that he was even listening, and not elsewhere, lost in his mind, memories, and recent regrets. A smile curled half of his mouth while his eyes remained under an invisible, low, and impenetrable cloud. He made another brusque sound, could have been a scoff, a chuckle, or just a cough, then looked up at Rowan and said, "I think I get it."

It chilled Sarita that she got it, as well. She was ready to entertain this idea, but she knew part of her was driven by emotion that made her resent the very notion of angels and all that came with them. Angelo was never an angel, but that didn't mean he hadn't effectively impersonated one, and if there was a God, then God permitted that deception. To what end? Rowan had invoked that old "mysterious ways" chestnut, and Sarita could almost hear her mother saying it unironically to convince her to keep her faith, and tell her that goodness was still on her side, watching over her, testing her or readying her for something better.

Despite her anger with a Heaven that, in fairness, she had never pursued any knowledge of and had only presumed delivered Angelo to her, she didn't lose sight of the more critical recent revelation. Angelo was a demon. A vampire. A bloodsucker—no better than Asmodeus—who might have murdered Frank out of pure, petty jealousy. However mad she was at God, or an entire varied pantheon of gods that were supposed to be the keepers and defenders of humankind, the one who had killed her husband was a devil working on behalf of a greater devil. And Rowan had just told her that you could, in theory, get one demon to kill another. She wondered if that, specifically, was what Everett agreed with.

"Are they the only ones that can kill another one," she said, "or can a person do it? Have you guys ever tried it? Are you like . . . vampire hunters?"

In her periphery, she saw Dottie's head shake before she got up from the table and walked out of the dining hall with most of her meal unfinished. Barnes followed her, walking fast to catch up. Everyone else in the room just watched, then resumed eating.

"I didn't mean to upset anyone," Sarita said.

Len said, "It's not your fault. You couldn't be expected to know. Dot knows that. It's just difficult, especially with Duncan gone, now. He's just the most recent. There used to be more of us." She looked to Myra and said, "I figure we might as well tell her, since she'll want to know, but you're at the head now. What do you say?"

"We should eat," Myra said. "I'll tell her everything after we're done."

24

Close to a decade of studying Z's books had emboldened the family, as they identified the myriad alleged ways to subdue and kill a vampire and assessed which stood out as more logical and feasible than others. Festering rage and an urge for vengeance as strong as a bloodsucker's need to drink motivated them. They were going to go on a hunt.

Z tried to dissuade them, but he was also still a demon. It didn't matter that he was repentant, assisting them, warning them of Cela's church and concocted prophecies. It didn't matter that he was supposedly in his fourth century of fasting. For all they knew, he just didn't want them to see that killing a vampire could be done, gain experience in the act. Learn from it and return to teach others that the texts he'd given them were alarmist and propagandist, meant to keep people too fearful to even attempt to fight back.

Duncan had told them all that Z was simply afraid that they would be successful, and maybe he was right to be afraid. Their target was a sickly old worm who'd taken residence in a cave system beneath the defunct train tunnel that used to service the nearby town of Fredericksburg. He had recently converted and made thralls of an out-of-town, vacationing couple that he had plucked from an unsuspecting group of tourists. If they could kill those three, what would keep them from coming home and doing the same to the old Athenian who had filed his fangs to nubs to show he was less of a threat? Nothing but their discipline and mercy, and what right did Z have to expect them to maintain either quality? Why should any remorseful killer, much less one that likely had a small town's worth of victims to their name, expect clemency?

Every member of the family was connected by loss. They had all seen a loved one killed by a vampire, and some of them, like Myra, were sole survivors of a mass killing. They were of different ages, backgrounds, even nations, and had passed through various encampments full of similarly nomadic and victimized individuals before settling at the Baby Head Mountain refuge, but were unified in grief and a niggling, unspoken hope for revenge, even if it came by proxy.

When the trio of vampires nested in the Old Fredericksburg Tunnel came to their attention, Duncan was the first to broach the subject of finally going on the offensive. Previously, any action they took was similar to that of other encampments: sporadic search-and-rescue operations where saving one out of three lives was viewed as a success, and trading one of your own to save a stranger's life was considered acceptable. What more could you expect? These things were harder to kill than any stories made them out to be.

The older accounts made it clear that sunlight was a distraction at most. Yes, they preferred the night, and if skilled enough could harness and deploy darkness, but they were hardly restricted to it. As far as most scholars could tell, vampires liked to operate between sundown and sunrise because that was when most of their prey slept, and why work harder than necessary? When Myra first read this, it startled her how much sense it made. Most predators conserved energy whenever and however they could.

Religious artifacts were only as effective as the ardency of belief in both the person warding off evil, and the evil itself. Garlic, dogbane, hawthorn, and other horticultural repellents were unpleasant to them, sometimes causing brief shocks to their biological systems, but they would suffer through any ill effects if they were determined to get to you.

A stake through the heart was just one step of one possible measure that wasn't guaranteed to work, and was usually most effective on the very young and unseasoned among the unliving, who tended to sleep far more soundly than their elders, especially if no one trained them to listen to the world while slumbering. It was done primarily to pin the vampire in place, preventing it from fighting back as effectively during additional measures of execution and disposal—beheading, extracting the heart, burning these separated parts, and then scattering the ashes, or mixing them into an elixir, or mixing them into grave soil to reinter the unburnt bones. Staking was also far more effective when driven through the heart and into the ground while the vampire was facedown, which presented the added challenge of getting the damn thing into a prone position. Even then, depending on the demon's age and learned capabilities, it might not subdue them long enough for you to complete the remaining acts.

Through the texts shared by Z, the family learned that steel placed near the back of the vampire's throat or tongue—or, more ideally, nailed through the tongue—was a more potent paralytic, but also, obviously, far more difficult and dangerous to attempt. In fact, the metallic, almost platinum appearance of the vampire's teeth was a façade meant to sow doubt as to the effectiveness of this method. If they had "metal" teeth, surely they were accustomed to metal being in their mouths. The fact that they developed this veneer spoke to how effective piercing or even pricking the base of the tongue could be, provided it was done precisely.

Other tactics centered more on imprisoning vampires in a grave. Burying them at a crossroad, hoping they were religious enough in life to believe they were at *the* crossroads when they awakened, and would be too afraid of accidentally taking the road to Hell to wander off. This was typically only temporary, staving off any threat posed for a generation or two before the monster understood this was only a trick and broke free.

Some were buried with sickles over their throats, or consecrated padlocks and shackles secured to their feet. More deception or psychological torment that was better at menacing novice vampires into staying in place than legitimately *trapping* them. Even if they were to never learn this on their own, all it took was a visit from one of their friendlier "kith and kin," as the clergyman Montague Summers once put it, to remove the obstacle to their freedom, or tell them that it was less of an obstacle than they believed it to be before moving on.

The Baby Head Mountain refugees understood all of this, but Duncan, his brother Graham, and his cousin Rowan, had a hatred born from seeing their original family butchered that lurked like an unexploded mine from an old war. Everyone who called the Baby Head refuge their new home would be angry forever, but these three carried a resentment that would burn them out if they couldn't find a release for it.

It took them three or four months to convince most of the family to even consider "hunting" a vampire. After another four to five months of scouting and preparation—during which they witnessed everyone from homeless men to wealthy widows equalized as food for the unliving in the Fredericksburg Tunnel—the majority of the family felt not only confident enough to see the hunt through, but felt that it was necessary.

Of the thirty-three family members who volunteered to go to the tunnel, twenty were selected. They included Myra, Duncan, Graham, Rowan, Dot, Len, and a woman named Ines. They went in armed with modified survivalist multitools that tripled as axes, hammers, and metal stakes. They were additionally equipped with steel anchoring spikes, wooden stakes, gasoline canteens, lighters, and matches. Dogbane and hawthorn, which were stronger than garlic, were worn like leis under their shirts. And they had two people—Rowan and Ines—thought to be well-practiced enough with spells to ensure their operation's success.

The magic was of utmost importance. Approaching the cave at dawn, they planned to softly sing what amounted to a powerful, prayerful lullaby meant to place the vampires in a fog of sleep that made them unable to differentiate between wakefulness and dreaming. It was, they thought, the surest way to prevent them from hearing their attackers coming before they set foot in the tunnel, and waking to defend themselves. The younger thralls, in particular, were supposed to be susceptible to the lullaby.

If you weren't a devil yourself, confronting a devil while they were fully alert and capable was offering yourself up on a plate. Some form of subterfuge and cunning was necessary. Even with that in mind, the twenty members of the raid understood that they might lose two or three people from their group before it was over, even if things went well.

Instead, things went wrong right away.

Much of the earlier discussion and planning had been about whether to try to kill the older vampire, who Z, in his limited contribution to the operation, had confirmed was partly crippled by an ailment new and rare enough to debilitate even a vampire. Radiation poisoning. Z did not disclose how this old worm had contaminated himself. Feeding on disappeared citizens in the aftermath of Chernobyl? Decades earlier, from workers at a nuclear plant in the Russian town Kyshtym? Or later, drinking from patients in Spain or Panama after incidents there?

Every bloodsucker who learned from those who fell ill dining on survivors of the Hiroshima and Nagasaki bombings knew that this new, unintelligent atomic god that humans had unleashed should not be touched, much less imbibed. But certain devils were closer to being "breathers" in this sense; you could give them the information and evidence they would need to make the right decision, and they'll still make the wrong one.

Whatever brought him to his comparatively crippled condition, the senior, centuries-old vampire in the tunnel was less imposing in his unhealthy condition, so Duncan and the others considered trying to kill him first. Without a proper layout of the lair, however, there was no chance that they could get to him before encountering the others. All they had were old maps drawn by earnest spelunkers from the early 1800s, which were helpful, but not enough to base a riskier tactic on. From those maps they had a sense of where the elder would likely position himself, but they could also gather this simply from what was most commonly done, and what made the most sense. The thralls would act as sentries, positioned closer to the entrance, while the "master" who had turned them would rest in a deeper cavity. One of their maps pointed to a narrow crawlway that might give them direct access to that space, but it couldn't be known if a small cave-in had since closed that path, or if that map was more or less accurate than two other maps that didn't show this passage.

So they entered the front of the old train tunnel and never got a chance to stray from the tracks.

Myra was part of the quadrant behind Rowan and Ines, so she heard them praying, but did not see them. She never could pick out where their invocation went wrong, but she also had no talent for magics, and therefore wasn't as versed in them. Later, Rowan would say that Ines's voice quavered for one or two seconds, maybe even just half a second, and that's all it took. Actually, that was more than it would take for everything to fall apart.

From what Myra knew of such things, when a spell relied entirely on words, not on any flames, animal bones, woodcraft, or anything else, then every single syllable had to be spoken with exactitude. A small break in your voice, a slight stutter or slurring of speech, a hiccup, the lightest cough, a stray bit of phlegm caught in your throat, or just the pinch of nervousness pulling your tone a note too high, that would open the door to catastrophe.

Hearing this from Myra, Sarita recalled what Tori had told her at The Lantern, just before Cold Eyes—"The Viscount," as Z referred to him—arrived, and she hoped her friend had brought the appropriate steel to her tone and said whatever needed to be said to banish the devil from the scene and save herself.

Myra realized something was amiss when the entrance to the tunnel abruptly darkened behind them like someone had rolled a boulder over the opening. She withdrew one of the ten-inch spikes in her sidepack, and unsheathed the multitool secured to her back. At the head of the group, Duncan called for them all to cluster together, so no one would get disoriented and turned around in the blackness. No one thought to turn on their flashlight, and it occurred to Myra later how strange it was to be so afraid of the dark—so afraid of what might be in it—that you in turn were afraid to turn on a light. Afraid enough to convince yourself that the light just might draw attention, or illuminate something you'd have been better off not seeing, and that you were therefore somehow safer without it.

Duncan's instructions were barely out of his mouth before a cloudy glow surrounded Ines. It took an extra heartbeat for Myra to realize it was actually not surrounding her, but emanating from her. It was a drained, lifeless color, and something made Myra think of it as an enslaved light, a stray spark shackled and stretched into a cold flame to be used for an occasion like this.

Rowan had tried to continue the invocation, but Myra saw him turn to Ines and shriek when he saw her face. When Ines whipped around and faced the tail end of the group, Myra saw why Rowan had screamed.

Ines's eyelids were closed, but her eyes were still visible behind the skin, the whites grayed, the red-rimmed irises blackened to being indistinguishable from her pupils. She was unconscious and animated by an unseen force. Even in the earliest texts, descriptions of vampiric mesmerism never painted it as this horrific. Myra suspected it was because almost no one who witnessed it survived to tell it, and the few who did were too terrified by the memory to write about it, or driven too mad to write anything.

Myra's own mind froze, lost somewhere in a vast, distant blackness untouched by the heat of starlight, a space of immeasurable cold. By the time she broke free of this, Ines had already taken the spike from her hand and swung it toward her. Dot came from behind Myra, arms outstretched to stop Ines, screaming her name to try to wake her up. Ines drove the nail through the outer corner of Dot's right eye, and Myra knew immediately that the mission was a failure. The vampires had turned one of their own against them before they had gotten fifty yards into the tunnel.

Rowan grabbed Ines from behind and tried to shout a new incantation, a possession banishment that would bring her back, but his voice was sand, and even had it been stone the effort would have been futile. She broke his grip, slashed at him. He fell to the floor to dodge her, and instead of wasting effort on him, she moved to the woman to her right, a woman named Melania, and thrust the nail forward like a fencer, sticking the older woman through the heart. Another man, Horace, tried to grab her from behind the way Rowan had. He was larger and his bear hug on her might have been more effective if he'd been able to secure it. Instead, she reached back with her free hand without looking, the cracking of bone and snapping of tendons echoing in the tunnel as her arm turned over against the natural fulcrum of her shoulder, faster than humanly possible, and speared her fingers through the bridge of his nose and into his brain, killing him instantly.

Rowan recovered enough from shock now to grab her feet, and Myra recovered from her own surprise to rush Ines and help tackle her. Duncan, Graham, and a few others pinned her to the ground. Duncan and Graham tried to shout orders, Rowan kept trying to pray, some of the others shouted that they had to leave now, turn back immediately, while more of them tried to call for help for Melania and Horace as though they weren't already beyond help. Through it all, Myra pinpointed Len who repeatedly asked, "What do we do?" as she cradled Dottie, who was at least alive still, hands covering her injured eye. It's what they all were thinking, even though Len was the only one saying it aloud. But it wasn't the only thought in their heads, not if they all had the same questions screaming through their minds that Myra had.

Why did we come here?

How do we get out?

Is this it? Is this where I die?

Five of them held Ines to the floor, one on each arm, Rowan sitting on her legs, Graham holding her head like he feared she'd have a seizure, and Myra draped across her torso. Ines didn't fight to free herself so much as she seemed to fight for an exit from her own body. She writhed and twisted in the grasp of her friends—her chosen family members—and her bones and joints snapped in directions that weren't in concert with her movements. Her neckbones twisted and telescoped as she rolled her head back until it was upside down facing Graham. Myra could only hope that Ines was already dead throughout all of this.

With a last echoing crack of her spine, Ines fell still and the glow retreated to a place deeper within her. Before it completely faded, it gave Myra a glimpse of a grinning white face hovering just behind Graham's right ear, like it had with a secret to share. The thing's smile was practically falling out of its mouth. Myra was just starting to warn him when the light completely died, and she was immediately drowned out by Graham's bellowing scream, which flew upward, high above their heads. Though she could see nothing, Myra looked up toward the scream just as it was overcome by the uglier sound of flesh being ripped far too easily. A sound that triggered hideous memories for all of them. A drop of liquid landed in Myra's eye just before a cascade of blood and chunks fell to the ground as Graham stopped screaming.

"Something's here!" someone cried out. Myra thought it was Rowan.

"It got Graham," Myra said.

"They heard us coming," Len said. "What do we do?"

Now Myra picked out Duncan speaking among the others, even though his voice was low. He wasn't calling out his brother's name or trying to tell the group to stay close, or retreat to regroup outside. He was repeating, "We've got to get out. We've got to go," softly, as though afraid to be heard. He should have been issuing emergency orders they had discussed and agreed upon should things go awry, but he sounded lost, quietly terrified. Then increasingly distant, and not in the same way as Graham, who had been carried away.

God, Duncan was running.

Later, Myra would convince herself he was trying to lead by example and get everyone to follow him. Myra almost did just that, except she wasn't sure he was running toward the exit. She wasn't even sure which direction she was facing. Based on how things had gone, she thought she had ended up looking back toward the tunnel entrance, where they came in, but the darkness made her unsteady, locked in that feeling of misjudging a stairstep and trying to recollect your balance with one foot in the air.

She tripped almost as soon as she tried to take off, not knowing whether she'd caught her foot on a rail or on an old track tie. She fell chest first into something partially rounded and not hard enough to be a stone. Even through her shirt it also felt fuzzy. No, hairy. She scrambled up and away from it, sure that it was Graham's head.

Beside her, someone in the group finally turned on their flashlight. Myra never saw who it was. A whoosh of air strong enough to knock Myra sideways passed her, the wake of speed that would have been hard to track even in daylight. It targeted the person holding the flashlight, crashed into them, slammed them into the wall so quickly they could not scream, but the bursting of their body against the wall and the flat splash of wetness landing on the ground spoke to their immediate death.

Although it made no sense, Myra thought the flashlight had drawn the vampire's attention, resulting in the swift, violent attack. Later, she would think the vampire did this deliberately to imprint this illogical causation in the minds of its would-be "hunters." Its night vision would have allowed it to see everyone easily, the flashlight would not have attracted its attention, but it wanted to keep its targets blind. Why? Given time to reflect on it—a few years of reflection, now—she maintained her belief that it simply found it more fun to keep them in the dark, play with its food. It was one of the thralls, she would soon realize. Just one. The others hadn't even bothered stirring, and this one might have been enjoying its first opportunity to engage in mass slaughter.

"Run! Everybody run!" That was Len. Her voice and footsteps came from behind Myra. Had she gotten turned around? Were the acoustics of the tunnel teaming with the darkness to throw her sense of direction like a magnet next to a compass? Or had the damned thing that had possessed Ines, employed her to kill two of her friends before it stepped in directly to butcher Graham and another, moved on to another spell designed to keep them all in a maze without walls? What if it didn't need a spell for that? Could that be an innate demonic skill unrecorded in the histories? Damn it, how the hell had Duncan convinced them they were anywhere near prepared for this?

Trusting her gut, which somehow hadn't turned to soup yet, she turned around, followed Len's voice, and ran as hard as she could. More screams bounced off the tunnel walls and ceiling. One shriek surprised her with how close it was, like it was a ghost withholding its appearance for the moment when it could shock someone into cardiac arrest. Right behind that scream came a jet of liquid that hit Myra's feet and ankles, prompting her to instinctively jump to clear whatever might be ahead of her. Her right foot landed on something that cracked like old wood and gave way to a damp space. She heard a weak grunt, stopped to check on whoever she'd stepped partially *through*. She found an arm, then a hand, both slick, and when she tried to pull the person up to their feet, or drag them with her as well as she could, the arm came up too easily, as though not attached to anything.

She flung it aside to see if she could, and it flew from her grip, confirming she'd had an amputated limb—formerly belonging to someone she called family—in her hands, and had thrown it away like it was a garbage bag with something crawling in it. She'd have time to be disgusted and horrified later, provided she made it out of here alive. She kept running.

Up ahead, finally, the summoned shield of darkness blockading the daylight thinned. She saw the mouth of the tunnel and silhouettes approaching it, not too far from where she was. Two . . . three . . . four of them. She could make it to them. She could get out. Fear had spurred her to sprint, but hope discovered a reserve of energy and explosiveness that let her run faster. She felt like she was running at least a half step ahead of her own body, like her spirit was more eager to survive than the vessel containing it. Gliding on the exultation of deliverance as she got close enough to identify the four who had already made it out—Duncan, Rowan, Len, and Dot—she felt weightless. Then, upon seeing the faces of her allies twist in fright and shock as her angle of perception elevated, she realized she really *was*, effectively, weightless.

To the thing bringing her to the ceiling of the tunnel she might as well have been a feather.

She could not tell if it had her by the waist or legs or chest, but she could only hope it didn't have its hand on her throat already, and that she had time for a desperate defense. The family had discussed this in theory, and she'd even had quiet, private conversations with Z about it, where he shared once again how foolhardy they were to consider confronting one of his own. But he also confirmed that vampires can sometimes grow inattentive when frenzied, as their senses become magnified beyond any degree of control.

Take a long nail or spike, hold the base to your neck, pray you've picked the right side, and that the vampire, in its most feral state, hasn't stretched its teeth far enough beyond its mouth to sink into your flesh before the tip of the nail touches the back of its tongue or throat.

Pray that the demon is in such an animalistic craze, whether from ferocity or euphoria, that it doesn't notice what you're trying to do when it lunges in to bite.

Pray that it doesn't simply pull your head off and upend you to drink from the stump like it's emptying a canteen.

Pray that if it's meant to kill you it will choose not to toy with you first.

The heat and stink of its breath warmed her face just as Myra's back hit the ceiling. Then she heard an odd squeal that masked a piercing sound. Next, she dropped several feet to the ground. The impact pushed all the air out of her lungs, but adrenaline gave her the strength to stand. Someone was with her as she made it to her feet. Len. She supported Myra like a crutch under one arm and helped her make it the last twenty or so feet out of the tunnel, assisted by Rowan and Duncan the instant they made it past the darkness.

They weren't fools. They knew that even demons that detested daylight were not stymied by it. They knew that they weren't safe yet, that they had to keep going. But some sense of relief at the minor victory of Myra's survival made them careless for a second too long.

Len dropped from under Myra's shoulder like a sinkhole had opened under her. Myra stumbled, looked back, and miraculously caught hold of Len's wrist before the far larger hand that had seized both of Len's ankles could pull her back into the train tunnel.

The vampire's arm, at least seven feet long now, was all that extended from the dark, all that was visible. Myra heard nutshells cracking, realized they were bones in Len's ankles, lower shins, and feet, and worked her way closer to get a better hold of her screaming friend. Other arms wrapped around Myra's waist, and soon she was in front of a tug-of-war in which Len was the rope. A sick sequence of pops followed, so rapid that the first in line seemed to run over the last. Len's knees dislocated, lengthened her legs and generated nerve damage she would never recover from. Then the rest of the thing they had come to hunt crawled out of the tunnel, looking like it was not trying to pull Len back in after all, but was using her to pull itself out.

It was a woman in a shredded dress. Her skin was taut and purpling against the inflammation of her right side, while her left half, dragging behind her, looked like part of an old corpse recently unburied. Even her face reflected this, her left side stiff and sagging like it turned to stone after a stroke. This wasn't how she had looked earlier, when Myra saw that same face over Graham's shoulder. She was sure it was the same creature, just half-paralyzed, and the thin, long, metal stake skewering the left side of its mouth through the back of its neck explained why. Nonetheless, the side of its face that could move was grinning like it needed to make room for more fangs to grow.

The fact that this thing was once human, and not all that long ago, was all but impossible for Myra to accept. There were numerous ways the master could have turned this woman into the abomination she was now. Feeding her his blood, feeding her a relative's blood, biting her, assorted sacrilegious ceremonies that may or may not incorporate the aforementioned methods. Several others. Myra wondered why this, of all things, flashed through her head as the thing scrambled toward the five of them, but the truth was it was never far from her thoughts at any moment.

She held on to Len, but failed to react as the vampire closed in, the ungodly memory of two people she loved turning into hideous, hungry abominations overtaking her. Her grandparents, after they had been force-fed her mother's blood by a living shadow that turned her favorite cousins and their parents into desiccated corpses. Turned their home, during a small family reunion, into a slaughterhouse. Myra had tried to hide in a closet, but had been found by the things that used to be her grandparents, though they never opened the louvered sliding door to take her. Not out of mercy. They stared with glowing eyes through the door's slats, bared their gleaming teeth with glee, and kept asking her what she was so scared of? Wasn't she still their granddaughter? Didn't she still believe in Heaven? The same God they had asked to bless their food a few hours earlier? They just wanted to send her to Heaven, they said, giggling like they were even younger than she was.

The rest of her family was up there now, and they just wanted to send her there, too. So what was she so afraid of?

She was thirty years removed from that night, yet back there in that closet now with malformed, insatiable death closing in on her new family.

Duncan stepped forward before the vampire got close enough to bite Myra and brought the hatchet end of his multitool down onto the demon's cranium, cleaving it between the eyes. The tool stuck in the vampire's head as it reared back, releasing Len as it turned its face. It managed to stand upright with its strong half, then turn to them, a startled gleam in its eyes, like it had tasted something more piquant than expected and couldn't decide if it liked it or not.

Myra readied herself for the thing to remove either of the sharp objects embedded in its head, but instead it grinned again and let out a stuttering two-note laugh that sounded like it was being looped.

"So brave," it said to Duncan. "Soooo brave. You're soooo brave . . . *now*."

Myra heard Rowan begin to pray behind her, but he fell silent on command when the vampire put a finger to its lips. They soon heard what it wanted them to hear.

Screams were finding their way out of the tunnel. Lost, hopeless cries for help that belonged to people still stuck in the dark. Other survivors. Myra, Rowan, Len, Dot, and Duncan weren't the only ones left. Members of their adopted family were still inside, and all that stood between them and a necessary rescue effort was a half-incapacitated vampire with a hatchet splitting its skull from crown to nasal bone.

"Be brave. *Be braaaave,*" the unbreathing, unliving thing said. It walked backward until darkness poured over it. They heard its voice louder when they could no longer see it, rumbling strong enough to shake leaves from the trees.

"*Beeee braaaave.*"

The only thing they heard more clearly was the screaming of those that they would leave behind.

25

"Do you really think you could have saved them?" Sarita asked.

Myra shook her head, then shrugged. "No. Definitely not all of them, and probably not anybody. But we could have tried, and we chose not to. We ran. We went to that place ready to lose three or four of us to kill three of them. Instead we only got to one of them, didn't even kill it, and fifteen of us didn't make it home."

Everett spoke up, almost startling Sarita, who had forgotten he was in the room with them. "It sounds like it could've killed all of you if it wanted to."

"Probably. Thing is, they seem to like the idea of letting one or a few people live when they can. Let somebody go on to tell the stories, spread the lore. Spread the fear like it's a disease. Like with the . . . the *things* that used to be my grandparents. I think that's why they didn't kill me."

Sarita nodded. Taking advantage of a quiet moment and Myra's vulnerability, Sarita said, "Tell me about Duncan."

She was prepared for Myra to leave the room, or to even lose her impeccable composure at last and lash out, forget that if shared trauma made you a relative then she and Sarita could be sisters considering who they had lost, and how. Myra's lips tightened, her face hardened for a moment, and then she relaxed. Reflexive suspicion and bitterness receded. She drew in a slow, steadying breath, exhaled, then said, "What do you want to know?"

"Anything you want to tell me," Sarita said, then amended this to, "Something good. He gave himself up to make sure we got away. He helped save us today. God . . . that was today."

"Yeah, it was. Get some sleep." Myra went to the door, opened it to leave.

"Please, tell me something else about him."

Myra turned back, and any tears that might have been in her eyes had to fight through ice to break loose. "He was trying to make up for things no one can really make up for. I think that even up to the end, probably, part of him hoped it might be possible for him to kill one of those things somehow, and that would sort of justify everything that happened at the tunnel."

"But you don't think it's possible to kill one," Sarita said.

"It's a tough thing for me to imagine, given what I've seen. At the same time, I've read accounts that claim it's been done before, and it's hard for me to write off *anything* as impossible."

"If you had to try again, how would you do it? More people? Better . . . prayers, or magic, or something?"

Almost managing a miserable smile, Myra said, "I'd just try to be lucky again, like I was the last time."

"You want to know what made me laugh back there?" Everett said when he and Sarita were left alone in the room.

Sarita nodded.

"What that boy Rowan said about evil being predictable and reliable," Everett said. "I can relate. It made me think of when I was a boy. My daddy had a bad leg because of an accident at the factory he worked at. Put him out of work and on disability that was only a third of what he'd been making.

"He was talking with my momma and the rest of the grown folks about what to do, and sent me out of the house to play while they went over it. I knew it must be serious, and I wanted to hear, so I crept around to an open window of the living room and listened. I was too young to really under-stand words like 'mortgage,' 'foreclosure,' and 'bankruptcy,' except I knew whenever they came up, it was never a good thing. And I heard them talk about how it was hard to find good-paying work, and how they were going to have to figure something out soon. Then my daddy said something that stayed with me. He said, 'Well, like Grandpa used to tell us, there's always money in doing some wrong.'

"My people have lived by that for a long time. An honest living might lie to you. Promise you a long career, with raises and promotions and a pension waiting for you at the end of it, then only give you part of that, or none of it, and kick you to the side while the world moves on. A dishonest living is at least up front with you. You might get arrested and locked up. You might get killed. If you're really lucky, maybe you'll make some good money. But you know from the start what this is, unless you're a fool. I know that sounds small compared to what that boy was talking about earlier, but I still felt connected to it. Does that make sense to you?"

"It does," Sarita said. "It makes more sense than a lot of other things that've happened recently. Or even things that happened a long time ago to me." Now she took her own deep-dive breath. "Everett . . . I should have told you all . . . should have told Frank. I never told him that I've basically been cursed since I was a kid. I just didn't know it was a curse. Not until—"

Everett held a hand up and shook his head slowly. "If you didn't know, then it wasn't your fault."

"I'm just . . . I'm sorry for what happened at The Lantern."

"Again, not your fault. If you say you didn't know, then I believe you. If Frank trusted you, what right have I got not to? I definitely don't think I was ever smarter than him. Tried to explain that to the other boys, but . . . ah, goddamn it, why didn't they ever listen? Why didn't we ever *teach* them to listen?"

She crossed the space between their cots to hug him again. When she heard him sniffle, she pulled back. "We've got to try to sleep."

"You're right."

In the ensuing quiet minutes, Sarita rested in her cot and flinched at the suddenness of sleep's eager attempts to take her weary body. Part of her wanted to stay awake, to think through what she could learn from Myra's story, and learn from the ones in the chamber behind the iron door. Not Z, so much. He was protective of his past, from what she had gathered. But the spirits, the dead of Baby Head Mountain, she could learn from them without saying a word to them. If she came upon them again, they would teach her more about what she was, and what she was capable of, if they reacted to her as they had before. And she hadn't even been trying to frighten them then. How would they react if she presented herself as a threat? As a presence willing to embody the reliability of wrong, and evil?

She was not that, was she? She didn't think so, although the song of unseen devils calling for her to join their god, the creation of a devilish mastermind, begged her to be this horrid thing, able to horrify the spirits of slaughtered people who had lost their lives to terror.

Their unholy hosannas and hallelujahs sang her to sleep.

She dreamt of many things. Long dark tunnels lined with teeth. Tori, David, Angelo. Cold Eyes. Even Frank, at last. Before any of these, however, she dreamt of a small mountain under a clear sky growing a dozen massive arms, a hundred burning eyes, and enough legs to support its massive weight as it lurched past screaming multitudes of people in search of a proper, filling meal.

26

What do you do if you're trying to hide from the police? Harrah thought. If you're trying not to be spotted and identified by some-nosy-damn-body who still watches the afternoon and evening local news in this day and age. Or reads news stories off their phone while waiting in line at the grocery store and actually pays attention to the faces in photographs. Somebody like the Harrah she used to be, for instance.

She wouldn't be that person anymore, regardless of how all this played out. Even without the unbelievable events she had experienced, being whisked around by an evil woman who might be made mostly of teeth and who commanded shadows, and even with the comparatively realistic shock of losing Frankie, Harrah would never be the same. Nowhere close to it.

The person she'd been before would have been looking out for the woman she was now. She used to memorize the names and vehicles described in the Amber Alerts that hit her phone, even though the counties and cities also mentioned in those alerts might be hundreds of miles away. She could recite the details from a true-crime podcast like she had been the person doing the initial research and finding the perfect evocative words to bring an unsolved murder to life.

Now, she was on the other side of such sordid, entertaining affairs, but so much further abroad than where she used to be that her old life felt like an unbelievable folk tale, and where she was presently felt like what she had been born into.

After seeing the witchy girl wheeled into the emergency room on a gurney, and then briefly evaluating her options, and *then* understanding what her circumstances really were now that she had been dropped off in relative normality, Harrah decided she needed to get away and regroup. She wanted to kill that girl in the hospital—that inclination hadn't left, and had instead grown since she had first arrived and seen what Cela undoubtedly wanted her to see. But she also wasn't interested in conducting a suicide mission on anybody else's behalf.

She was still wearing the clothes she'd have been last seen in at the Lucky Eagle. Casinos had cameras galore, enough cameras to rival some top-secret facility where the military was testing new weapons and performing autopsies on aliens, she thought. Best-case scenario, she was considered a missing person. Worst case, she was a suspect in poor little Craig Never-Got-His-Last-Name's death. Either way, images of her from the casino had probably been thrown all over the local news. KENS, KSAT, KABB, and WOAI, and that oddball new station owned by the cable network. Even if her face wasn't all over the television, print, and online news, the police would have seen every available picture of her by now. She couldn't change her face, but she could at least change her clothes. Where would she go to get out of what she had on, and into something new, was the question.

There were several different neighborhoods within walking distance of the hospital, but choosing a random house and hoping to find a woman or even man who wore jeans and shirts that weren't too big or small for her posed a significant risk. That was just factoring in the odds of finding a wardrobe with anything nearing the right size, clothes that wouldn't be hanging off or strangling her. What about the possibility of someone being home, and armed? She came from a family that kept guns the way animal lovers cared for pets, and this wasn't unusual in Texas. It was an absurd gamble to hope a random house she broke into wouldn't contain guns that fit right in on a modern war field—some that the soldiers might even envy—and a homeowner who would see an opportunity to kill somebody during a break-in as an answered prayer.

She didn't know a damn thing about breaking into houses, on top of that, much less disarming someone with a weapon drawn on her.

What did she know, then, that could help her?

She knew of one house owned by someone who did not have a gun, and whose owner had specifically told her about times his security system's alarm had gone off and he'd taken it for some kind of glitch. A place where both homeowners might be away, because they both worked odd hours. The man whose name was on the mortgage had volunteered to her that he had only taken a few days off from his construction job after Frankie's death, because, according to him, the longer he stayed away from work, the harder it would be for him to ever get back to it.

As for the woman in his life, his new wife, Misty, the one who Frankie gave the dance to at his wedding like he owed it to her, she was the private caregiver of a wealthy old woman who owned multiple strip malls, and who was, from what Harrah had heard, sympathetic to the loss of a child because she had survived all but two of her seven children, as well as a sister who had died during childbirth. All of this made her compassionate in an atypical way, though. The older woman approached extreme grief and loss as though it were something natural that the modern world had corrupted. She viewed modern infant and maternal mortality rates the way a Mennonite might view a pacemaker. She allowed her employee a few days of bereavement, but expected her to rebound and return to work sooner than other employers might have requested precisely because she thought it would be better for her. She thought you didn't heal by mourning as though you've given up on life, and you didn't honor the dead that way, either.

She wondered now why Misty had shared all of that with her at Frankie's service. Like they were friends or something. Couldn't that woman feel Harrah's disdain for her like a speck in her eye?

Harrah knew Don's address. She had picked Frankie up and dropped him off there often when he was young. Sometimes she had met her ex-husband at his new house to then driven with him to Frankie's baseball or football games, on the rare occasion when she was invited. She had tolerated conversations with Misty about Frankie's potential to be a collegiate pitcher or quarterback during those games. Misty and Don always talked about Frankie earning himself an athletic scholarship.

Harrah had realistically seen in her son a talent that would make him popular with high school girls but wouldn't translate to the next level the way Don's talent had, before he'd broken his throwing arm in a motorcycle accident his sophomore year at the University of Texas. She had spent more time lecturing Frankie about girls poking holes in condoms than congratulating him for striking out seven straight batters who would never sniff collegiate play, or throwing for three hundred yards against a team full of slow, pint-sized defenders that *might* produce one kid who lasted a season or two with Middle of Nothing A&M Episcopal.

She had picked her boy up from Don's house to bring him to choir practice a few times, as well, and had been more impressed by his vocal range than his arm strength. That was where he truly stood out, and showed he had a future. He couldn't have been a lead on Broadway or anything, but he could have been a background singer somewhere, or a bit player who got one great line in a pretty big show if he was lucky and the producers really liked him. He could be a reliable, professional vocalist, as long as he practiced, committed himself to it, and understood the limits of his range. Nothing at all wrong with that. People made a good living doing that.

Had she ever shared that with him? She didn't think so. Damn, why hadn't she done that? He probably never would have met Sarita if she'd told him that. He'd have gone to a different college, might've even gone out of state, and had a whole different life, and none of this would have happened. Damn it, it would have been so simple to tell him that.

Get out of your head, Harrah. Focus. You've got things to do.

She walked along the highway, head lowered and pace quick, from the hospital to the nearest bar, which was closer than any of the surrounding neighborhoods. The rideshare drivers parked there weren't supposed to pick up unscheduled riders, like a taxi, but she knew that they were accustomed to making exceptions for drunks who might stumble out of the bar midway through happy hour, much less later in the afternoon and into the evening. Some were stringent rule keepers, others, not so much.

She found one of the rule breakers with the first car window she knocked at. A car with the soft, illuminated sign of the service they were contracted with sitting in the lower left corner of their windshield.

She pulled some twenties from her pocket, cash she'd been saving for day two at the Lucky Eagle, and showed it to him. "I'm just trying to get home," she lied.

The driver's eyes darted around, not like someone outside of the car or working for the large "saloon" they were parked near might spot and report him, but as though the car itself might be bugged with a hidden camera and microphone. Like his display of suspicion could somehow act in his favor should his employer pull footage later. *See, I was worried about it. I wasn't just happy to do it right away or nothing. That counts for something, don't it?*

"All right, get in," the driver said, after appearing to count the number of bills in her hand. He had a rough, damp beard and greasy hair and small dots that raised the topography of his forehead, and honestly if she were her past self, genuinely trying to get a ride to her actual house, Harrah would have also tried to make his day by telling him to pull over to live out a porno fantasy on the side of a road. She liked the character of his face, and his youth, the gruffness of his voice. He smelled good, too, in a woodsy way, and from the fit of his clothes he looked like one of those puffy muscular types who'd be stronger than his physique initially suggested.

She wasn't worried about him recognizing her, either. He seemed young enough to treat local news as though the concept of it should be reserved for high school class curriculums, and specifically taught on the same day as senior skip day. Did younger people still partake in a "skip day"?

All of this was dashing through her mind because she was feeling wistful about her past self. About even *having* a "past self." God, why did whoever or whatever made human beings give them a desire for so many things they could never get? Why was the concept of rewinding time even something they had access to? It should have been an idea so outlandish no one in their right mind would think of it. Like how, she was sure, no person, no matter how thirsty they were, even if they were dying parched in the middle of the desert, probably ever thought, *Damn, I wish I could drink sand.* No, you'd just keep praying for water. The same should apply to the past.

But here she was, allowed to dream of undoing all the hardship and heartbreak that led her here, of traveling back in time to well before she'd lost Frankie, to even before she'd met Don, to the time when she didn't think twice about measuring up a stranger, getting in their car, and paying them to drive her from one bar or party to the next. Back then it wasn't a formalized service, and instead you were handing them gas money. Simpler times. Easier times.

He didn't notice or pay any attention to her right hand when she got into the car. Didn't see her unnaturally lengthened fingertips and hardened fingernails, or the fact that each finger now had a superfluous knuckle. Why would he look for such things? He was probably used to people—male and especially female—judging him as the potential threat based on looks alone. He was probably more concerned with the potential risk of them trying to ditch without paying, or of looking like they might throw up in his back seat, than anything else. If she hadn't shown him the cash already, or looked sickly drunk, he probably would have turned her down, obeyed the rules and regulations of the company he was contracted with. But he let her in, she gave him all the money she had, then an address, and it must have never crossed his mind, or mattered to him, that the house he was taking her to wasn't hers.

She was almost too excited to sit still. This might really work, and then she was going to come back for the witchy girl. First, though . . . well, she was thinking that the first step would entail stealing some things from Misty's closet. Don had a type. He'd moved on to someone who not only looked a good deal like her, but had aged like she had aged. Filled out a little in the same places that Harrah had. She figured Misty couldn't be more than a size or two off from being her twin, wardrobe-wise. That would certainly do.

There was a strong possibility that rumors about Frankie's murder, accompanied by her own vanishing in conjunction with the discovery of the dead man she was last seen with and had taken to bed, would be making the rounds and even a second lap by now. Nonetheless, she had faith that the man driving her to her ex-husband's address was clueless to this, or at the very least wouldn't suspect her of being the woman people might be whispering about. He was just a young man trying to earn extra money, maybe for a bouncy castle for his daughter's birthday party, maybe for the last few dollars to buy his fiancée an engagement ring, maybe just to buy himself the newest hard-to-find gaming system.

Harrah was going to use her lovely, deadly new right hand to rip the poor boy's throat away at the last stop sign before reaching their destination. The hand that had grasped Cela's, and was learning to transform into a talon-tipped claw from that devil's example.

Harrah glanced at her hand several times during the drive. Its mutation did not scare her. What alarmed her was the ease with which she carried on the conversation with the driver. He asked if the music he played was okay with her, and she said yes, she could listen to almost anything. R&B. Country. Reggae. Oldies. Even a few songs in languages she didn't understand. He expressed surprise at this, then asked her what her favorite song was from a foreign language, and she said it was hard to pick between two Japanese "city pop" tunes. He asked her what "city pop" was and she tried to educate him on the genre as well as she could in the limited time the drive provided.

As they got closer to her ex-husband's house, a constant voice broke into Harrah's thoughts.

The throat or the mouth, it said.

The throat or the mouth.

The driver said, with sincere enthusiasm, that he was looking forward to searching for more city pop tunes besides "Plastic Love" and "56709," and Harrah barely remembered giving those song titles to him. Where did she even know them from? Some boy she had dated twenty years ago. No, not that far back, just a decade ago. God, her past self was so far away that the difference between ten and twenty years felt like the difference between one and two days.

They pulled to the curb of the house across the street from Don's, and she saw one car in the driveway. Someone might be home. Was it his car or Misty's? It didn't matter. It was too late to change course.

"Hey, what was that one song called again?" the driver said, his tone so bright it changed his face, brought boyishness past his hirsute, weary exterior. "Five-nine-seven-what?"

"Five-six-seven-oh-nine," Harrah said, leaning forward. She held his eyes with her own in the rearview mirror. An understanding of danger floated into his pupils and shrank them ever so slightly when he realized she had stuck pins into his gaze that would not even allow him to blink. Surprise filled her own eyes. She didn't know she had this power. The same that Cela had exhibited at the bar in the desert. It would prove useful, she imagined.

If God is for us.

The words popped into her head and seemed random, divorced from the current situation, until she took a nanosecond to truly consider them, and what they meant to her now.

If God is for us.

He is not for me. He let my boy die. He let that woman take me. He let all this happen.

Who can be against . . .

He is against me.

"If God is for us . . . who can be against?"

It really isn't a question. It's not the *question, anyway.*

"If God is for us (who can be against[1]) . . . then what? What other choice do you have?"

The way she was brought up, she knew that God forgave and God loved. No, God *was* love, and God *was* good. She said that before thanking Him for her food ahead of every meal. He embodied goodness and love. Without Him those things couldn't exist, and without them, what else was He?

Love and Goodness had allowed her son to die. To be murdered so savagely she couldn't get a last look at his face. Then it allowed her to be taken from the hotel room where another man was similarly savaged. It let her witness the meticulous murder of several people at a bar. Goodness and Love were, at best, disinterested in her. And at worst were antagonistic.

Who can be against . . .

What then?

Goodness and Love had let her son die in the name of an evil religion that had made him its Devil. That's what Cela had told her. So what did that make Harrah?

The Devil's Mother.

Her clawed right hand came around and took the driver's throat.

The mouth or the throat, she thought. Then consolidated this into, *The voice.*

She did not understand why, but understood that this was crucial. Sever anything attached to the voice—the vocal cords, the mouth, the *tongue*— and you eliminate any resistance. Bite it out, rip it out, do whatever you need to do, but sever it. Destroy it. Cut the voice at its root.

The blood on her hand called to be licked clean. Her stomach growled as she thought of it. The dashboard, steering wheel, radio console, and windshield were all either flecked or splashed with blood, but the red on her skin, drying into a thin, grim glove, was most alluring.

She drove the car now, having dragged its owner into the back seat after he stopped twitching, though he gave one last leg kick that smacked the car horn and raised Harrah's heart rate as she repositioned him. More accurately, she figured, *he* didn't kick the wheel and set off the horn, his *body* did. His surprisingly light body.

"So much for deadweight," she had muttered while moving him, then was sickened enough by the cruelty of that comment that she had to choke back a surge that almost breached her gullet.

This poor boy hadn't done anything other than give a ride to the wrong person. Now he was gone, and his body had been tossed to the back like an empty bag of fast food. Harrah hoped his parents were already dead. She hated the idea of putting some other mother through what she'd been through. At the same time, she couldn't change it now, and there wasn't much point in dwelling on it or getting upset enough over it to second-guess herself. If anything, backtracking on her original plan now, and making this stranger the only casualty of her endeavor, would be the worst thing she could do to him. Dying how he had was bad enough. Dying for nothing would be worse. If she finished what she started, there would at least be a purpose to what was done.

She doubled back onto Don's street, debating whether to park along the curb a few houses down, or to turn around and park in the driveway of the house with the FOR SALE sign she saw two streets back. Then she saw Don come out of the house, walk to his car, keys in hand. He must have come home to get something, or maybe today was his day off and he was headed out for an errand. It didn't matter why he was here at this moment, it just mattered that he was, and that this would save her the trouble of breaking into the house.

None of the pride and confidence that made her fall for him in the first place was present in Don's stance and stride. That golden boy gorgeousness was gone. He looked like he was draped in invisible chains. She'd been in too much of a daze and too focused on Sarita to pay much attention to him at Frankie's funeral, but seeing him this way made her want to spare his life. Why should he get to check out and move into the next world, whatever that entailed, leaving her to live on with the full weight of their loss?

Don't overthink it. Do what you came to do. Now's the time, go, GO, do it!

She gave a quick scan of the street as she pulled up behind his car, blocking him in his driveway. No other cars were coming. She got out of the car almost before placing it in park. She saw in Don's expression that his mind was running a second behind everything happening, which gave Harrah ample time to close in on him before he could react.

He was still wondering why a stranger's car had blocked his exit after Harrah stepped out of the vehicle. Then he was still trying to make sense of recognizing her, and the fact that she was here when she'd been reported missing, while she was coming toward him. He had barely gotten her name out of his mouth with a question mark attached to it when she raised her right hand, inviting another question that would never make it to his lips, but that she read in his eyes.

What is that? he asked without speaking. There were probably several other questions queued behind that one, each arguably more urgent. *What are you doing here? What are you going to do? What's happening?* And behind them all a statement that must have been screamed a million times in every language by murder victims who had the misfortune of seeing their fate coming.

Stay back!

Harrah thought of what a waste it was to let those be your final words, then considered holding off for just long enough to let him get that scream out of his chest. She wanted to hear him say it. Tell her how he really felt one last time before it was over. "Stay back." "Get away." Different ways of saying you don't want someone around. That's about what he'd said when he left her, and then said it on Frankie's behalf when he took their son away from her. Like she was so irredeemable, so awful for either of them to spend too much time with. What good had that done their boy?

On second thought, she didn't want to hear him say anything ever again. She wanted him to die with words stuck in his neck, right under her thumb, which she drilled through his Adam's apple and out through the nape.

She held him that way, her arm fully extended and strong enough to take him an inch or two off the ground, though her elbow hyperextended slightly with the effort, as she moved quickly toward the front door of the house. She should have been well beyond caring if a neighbor caught her in the act and called the cops at this point. She wasn't some ordinary killer. The things she had seen, the things she now knew, along with what she was capable of . . . there was no way it wouldn't be apparent to anyone who saw her. In fact, it wouldn't surprise her if there was an old man across the street looking at her through his dining room window right now, convincing himself that he'd lost his mind and just needed a drink and some sleep, any excuse not to get involved.

Harrah didn't recall hearing Don's keys hit the pavement, but saw that he'd dropped them when she looked at his hand once they reached the entryway. Without thinking, she grabbed the doorknob with her free hand, turned it, felt a pop and vibration that came from the breaking of metal bits meant to keep the door locked. She pushed the door open and noted that even now, after what had happened to their son, Don still wasn't in the habit of locking the dead bolt. But she was the irresponsible one . . .

She brought him to the kitchen floor and straddled his weakening body. When she unplugged the wound she'd driven through his esophagus, a jet of blood struck the corner of her mouth. Her tongue snaked out to steal a taste before her hand could wipe it away. Small explosions of disgust and wonderment blitzed her brain. She kicked her head back and shut her eyes. The flavor was immediately astringent and addictive. A little bit like alcohol in that the acridity that made it unpleasant was just sugary and warm enough to also make you crave another sip before you swallowed the one you just took.

The first thing she noticed when she looked back down at Don were the bubbles accompanying the red stream flowing through his puncture wound. The next thing she saw was the dullness in his eyes that made her regret not having savored the panic that had been there seconds earlier. Then she saw the last thing she expected to see, and her heart ripped anew.

Whenever people would talk about recognizing certain features of a child as belonging to one of the parents, Harrah used to think they were full of shit. "He's got his mama's eyes." "She's got her daddy's smile." No, he doesn't, and she doesn't, either, unless you're talking about something as obvious as eye color or hair color, in which case, wow, the kid has something in common with their folks and a hundred million other people. Even as they got older, unless the similarities were blatant to the point of extraordinary, which did happen, but was rare as far as Harrah was concerned, all the talk about kids looking so much like their parents or even their grandparents was exaggerated. Naturally, there'd be some resemblance, but the way some people talked you'd think they'd struggle to tell the daughter apart from the mother in a police lineup.

Maybe it was the lighting, the moment, the vestiges of her disintegrating humanity trying to get her to see anything that would make her more afraid of what she was becoming, and what she was doing to complete the transformation that Cela initiated, but as she watched Don grow still and release his soul with a sigh, she saw what Frankie would've looked like in his forties.

She wanted to kiss him, heal and resurrect him with some fairy-tale magic, only Don's soul would still be gone and Frank's would occupy this body instead. Why couldn't this be possible? If bloodsucking monsters could exist, then why not fabled mothers whose kisses or tears could revive murdered sons?

They can both exist, but you're already the first one, Harrah thought, and absently licked the blood from the back of her hand. Some of it had dried already. She let it dissolve in her saliva and shivered.

Before she could stop herself, she was tearing through Don's neck, alternating between drinking from the burbling fountain she made of his jugular and carotid artery, and lapping up the puddle spreading on the kitchen tile.

27

She had come for a change of clothes and received a change of appearance that made a disguise pointless. Nevertheless, before she left, she traded her jacket and top for one of Misty's shirts, and switched out her jeans for a pair of Misty's as well. Prior to leaving she looked at herself once more in the oval mirror hanging on the foyer wall. It still surprised her that she could see herself.

After drinking so much that her stomach was nearly bursting, she'd left Don's body where it lay and went to the bedroom. There was a full-length mirror on the back of the door that she sat in front of for a while. Could have been fifteen minutes, could have been an hour, she really couldn't tell. She was in a daze of shame and delight, the latter gaining size as the former evaporated.

There was no way to make sense of what she had just done, other than to accept it, and accept what her actions and thirst told her about herself. With that in mind, she waited to turn invisible in the mirror. Vampires don't have reflections. That was one of those things she felt like she'd known all her life, like it was one of the first things you learn in school. *I* before *e*, Columbus discovered America, vampires don't have reflections.

Of course, that grammar rule had a ton of exceptions that had nothing to do with coming after *c*, or rhyming words, and Columbus never made it to America itself and died lying to himself about finding the back half of India. Sometimes you learn something early and hold on to it as fact only to find out years later that it's bullshit.

Vampires weren't pretty, refined things, either, judging by the woman she saw staring back at her, but she'd seen a wide enough variety of movies to know they weren't always the picture of goth glamour. Still, she wasn't sure she'd seen anything—in a movie, an illustration in a book, a painting, anywhere—that suggested vampires had teeth so big Red Riding Hood wouldn't be dumb enough to comment on them. Okay, that was an exaggeration, but that's how large they felt in her face. Like a psychotic genius of a surgeon had replaced her mouth with a bear trap.

Now that she thought of it, she might have caught a glimpse of something like this once before. She recalled walking in on her cousin Hampton—the one Joey and the others teased for his obsession with Asian girls—while he was watching one of those violent Japanese cartoons he liked so much. He said it was about an "original" vampire who was also a vampire hunter, and while Harrah watched with him, there had been a moment when one of the bloodsuckers changed from looking human to being something closer to a gargoyle. Harrah thought that if she could find that video now and hit pause on it during the first or second frame of the transformation, when the monster was still mostly human, but clearly turning into something else, it would resemble her now, at least in the face.

Her right hand was considerably further along, and still the largest giveaway that she was something extraordinary. Even cleaned of every speck of red, there was no hiding that it was as much weapon as appendage. Probably better suited to causing injury than any other function. She tried to think of how she would react if she saw someone who looked like her coming down the street, with those long, bent tines for fingers, but it was already getting hard for her to think like an ordinary person.

Like a breather, she thought, then immediately inhaled to test the sensation of air in her lungs. An odd, sickly heat filled her chest, bringing to mind the days when she'd stayed home from school drinking orange juice for extra vitamin C at her late mother's behest. The later days when she, as an adult, powered through illness to clock in on time. Days that didn't feel like they belonged to her anymore.

Can't go back. No point wishing for it. No point thinking about it, except for the one thing.

The one thing.

She'd had a son. She and the man lying half-decapitated on the floor after being turned into food in his own kitchen. They'd had a son together, but Frankie had always been her boy the way all boys belonged to their mothers. Their *real* mothers, no matter who tried to interfere with that bond, or raise them as if they had given birth to them.

A humming sound grabbed Harrah's attention. The garage door was coming up. When they were married, Don had always let her park in the half of the garage that wasn't taken up by rarely used dumbbells, a treadmill they didn't have room for in the house, boxes full of stuff from before they moved in together, tools and other junk. He apparently gave Misty the same privilege. Good old, chivalrous Don.

Either Misty wasn't terribly attentive, or Harrah hadn't left enough of Don's blood in the driveway for Misty to notice. Maybe she was just distracted, still in a fog over the death of her stepson. Harrah never doubted that Misty loved Frankie. Had she ever thought the woman was bad for her boy she'd have cashed in on Joey and the other boys' offer to do something awful to Don and his new wife. Harrah never truly disliked Misty as a person, she was just against the idea of any other woman playacting as her son's new mother. She didn't care for Misty, but the same would have been true of any woman raising Frankie in her place, and overstepping their bounds to take a once-in-a-lifetime moment away from Harrah at her only child's wedding.

She heard Misty come in through the door that led to the garage, and knew the smell of Don's blood and waste would hit her early, if not right away. She would come in anyway, because most people aren't built with an animal's intuition to literally sniff out danger. She'd run into Don's body, and honestly, wouldn't that be bad enough already? Walking in on your husband's mauled remains in your own house. Then seeing his barely human killer emerge from your own bedroom. Wouldn't that be a terrible enough revenge to inflict on someone you didn't even fully despise?

Yes, it would be. And, knowing this, Harrah could walk away from Misty, leaving her petrified, stupefied, almost seizing with panic.

She could, until she *couldn't*.

When she came out of the room and saw Misty, all Harrah really saw was a nice tender sack of blood that would have made her pant with excitement if breathing weren't already becoming optional for her. And, although she had felt overstuffed a second earlier, as soon as she saw the woman whose clothes she now wore, and whose husband's blood caked her chin, Harrah grew famished, and surrendered to her craving.

28

Sarita suffered through a troubled yet deep sleep. A series of nightmares pulled her by an invisible string through the night with the patience of a seasoned torturer. People spoke to her in these awful dreams, their words like shredded poems demanding to be read and reassembled. Waking came in stages as she drew herself link by link from the chain trying to bind her consciousness to these visions.

Even after she sat up in her cot and focused on drawing air into her lungs, she felt like she was in a darker place than a room under a hill, barely lit by two shrinking candles. She knew where she was, but reminded herself of it, just to reassure herself. She was at the sanctuary built into Baby Head Mountain, home of Myra's "family."

Myra's name came to her easily. Yesterday's turmoil and revelations were too traumatic not to be crystalline. This wasn't like waking up after a night of drinking and smoking, wondering about the unfamiliarity of your surroundings, and needing a minute to remember you had crashed on someone's sofa, or in their spare bedroom. This was, she guessed, closer to waking up in a war zone, knowing you're far from home, and just needing time to firmly identify the border that separated the horrors confined to your head from the horrors alive and thriving in reality.

David was gone. She'd sent him away for his own good, and to check on their parents, as well as on Tori. The guilt stemming from abandoning Tori began to creep back in, but Sarita shut the door on it before it could come all the way through. She still thought it a valid emotion, but also thought it unproductive. She couldn't help her friend, her brother, her parents, or anyone else by wallowing in remorse over something she couldn't control.

What could she control? Right now, the first thing she could decide was whether to stay in bed and in the room, or get out and see where exactly she might be able to go unsupervised. She recalled thinking that the family hadn't treated her quite like a captive yet, and maybe that was only because she hadn't tested her boundaries. For all she knew, someone was standing guard right outside the door of her room now, tasked with preventing her from leaving. Hell, for all she knew the door was locked or barred from the outside.

She walked to the door, grabbed its handle, and pulled it open with no resistance. There was no one on the other side. She looked back to see if she had awakened Everett. He breathed heavily, with a slow and constant rhythm, and did not stir. She wondered if she should try to wake him. It might be good to have someone else along to look out for the others, and he might worry if he woke up while she was gone, but she couldn't bring herself to disturb his rest. It also might be for the best if she did this alone, with no distractions and only herself to worry about.

She stepped into the corridor, looked first to her right to see if anyone was at the far end, watching, and saw no one. She then looked to her left. The metal door to the lower chamber, Z's den, all but called to her to test it.

She went to it, noticed for the first time the raised markings on its face. She read them more with her fingertips than with her eyes. The many glyphs and sigils were mostly foreign to her, although several matched some of Rowan's tattoos and Z's scarring. She recognized loop-headed crosses, stars, and crescents, even if she wasn't entirely sure of the significance of each. Other emblems struck her as being from certain regions based on appearance. A sun with multipronged beams and a solemn face in its center, that possibly had a quarter moon in its forehead, seemed Mesoamerican to her, while a tree with long, drooping branches that circled down to connect with its equally massive roots looked more druidic. Still others appeared Egyptian or Asian, while the rest were well beyond her limited ability to even speculate.

Was she supposed to feel anything in the presence of this metal piece of protective craftwork? She thought she felt light sparks of electricity tingling through her fingers, but that might have been a result of anxiousness, or nothing at all. A placebic charge generated by her expectations and awe. The door amazed her, not only because it existed, but also because she was here with it.

Was it just two weeks ago that her biggest worries were caterers and whether Harrah might try to crash the wedding? Things she didn't even have to worry about much, because Frank's friend and coworker was a terrific chef who had catered larger events before, and because Frank assured her that the worst that Harrah could do was make things a bit awkward before Everett promptly settled her down and convinced her either to make peace if she meant to stay, or go back home.

Now Frank was dead, Harrah was missing, and a troupe of vampire-attack survivors had brought her to the grimmest-sounding place in Texas, home to a haunting and an unnamed ancient demon. She stood in front of an old metal door behind which, she knew, was a vampire who didn't want to be what he was any longer.

Compared with all those things, all that she now understood was possible, the act of merely pushing this door to see if it would open felt more commonplace than risky or foolish. The hinges groaned and the bottom of the door lightly scraped the stone floor, but Sarita didn't have to put her full weight into it to move it. She didn't close it behind her after stepping inside. Better to leave it open in case she needed to run from the chamber.

What if *she* wasn't the one who would need to escape? She wondered if she might encounter the family of phantoms again, and if she could once more chase them away with a single word. She didn't want to do that, and not entirely out of compassion for them, but because a small part of her wanted to get a better sense of how much fear she inherently instilled in them. She had called out "Stop" to silence them, more a reaction than an outburst, but they retreated as though she had promised to make them suffer if they lingered another second. Thinking on it now, while she found no pleasure in scaring off the spirits, she was eager to find out whether she could do this again. Do it at will.

Inside the chamber, in the center, Z still sat at his table, more books piled around him now, stacked three and four volumes deep. He was hunched over the book directly before him, which looked like it might

DEVILS KILL DEVILS • 213

be open to largely blank pages from what Sarita could see at the top of the stairs. Z held a pen in his hand and was scratching ink so quickly in lines across the top of the page that Sarita was sure he couldn't be writing anything remotely legible. Without looking up, he paused his scribbling long enough to motion for her to come down, then resumed what he was doing.

Sarita thought of what he'd told her yesterday about making himself less of a threat to placate the "sleeper" that called Baby Head Mountain home. The greater devil that took comfort and power in the act of point-less brutality that inspired the hollowed-out hill's name. She remembered Z's capped fangs. Even if her nostrils were plugged with cement and her taste buds burnt to nothing, she would still notice the aggressive aromatics packed into Z's quarters. All of this told her not only that Z wouldn't at-tack her, but also that he'd be afraid to even look like a threat to her.

He was here, presumably, to hide from others like him. He'd worked for a woman who was a leader. A "Founder" he had called her. Cela. She might still be looking for him, and he was effectively in witness protection. Even if they knew where he was, they would apparently be afraid to come for him here. The menace of the sleeper was that strong.

Even so, Sarita came down the stairs cautiously. She had to presume Z was dangerous. He belonged to the class of things that killed Frank, and that had, at minimum, severely injured Tori. Angelo—The Northman—didn't need his fangs to kill her husband. Cold Eyes—The Viscount—might have bitten Joey's face off, but it looked like he tore open Duncan with his bare hands. Neither of them had the scarification that Z had, but Cold Eyes had been physically altered by Myra, Barnes, and Duncan's summoning bluff, and if his transformation was as painful as it looked, he didn't show it. Not the same thing, granted, but still a small clue, as Sarita saw it, that any discomfort, distortion, or even pain caused by spells might not be deterrent enough when devils were determined to kill. Myra's story of what went wrong in the tunnel also lent credence to that theory.

When she reached the bottom of the stairs and came within a few feet of the table, Z looked up at her, shutting the book on his pen as he did so. The thick tome closed with a thud almost loud enough to pop Sarita's ears.

Z stood slowly, slumping his shoulders and keeping his head partly bowed, aware of and trying to mitigate his inherent capacity to intimidate. He slid his chair toward the edge of the table, in Sarita's direction, and turned it so she could sit and face him as he retrieved a different chair closer to the shelves along the wall behind him.

As Z sat and faced her, Sarita leaned forward in her chair and built a wall around her trepidation. She had come here on something of a whim. The fastest, most brazen test she could come up with to see what her boundaries here might be. Now that she was here, and this inhuman thing that could end her life with a swipe was treating her like an expected guest, she recognized that her visit with him could be more purposeful. Before she could ask him anything, Z told her, "You must be careful. You are more dangerous than you realize."

The incongruence between what she expected him to say after the first sentence and what he actually said demanded she take a moment to reboot her brain. She squinted at him like he'd just awakened her. "What's that supposed to mean?"

"It means you must remember what you have been told, and must not pretend you are not curious about what more you could be. An enormous *horde* of extremely powerful, aged minds, with a belief so strong they would die for it, still sings to you, do they not? These things that conquered death hundreds of years ago have spent centuries worshipping you. Waiting for you, praying for your survival. I was once among them. I know the ardency of their faith. You are, to them, the mother of their messiah. What would you say that makes you?"

The word was instantly on her lips, waiting for her to speak it. Cold Eyes had told her what she was at The Lantern, but she still struggled to accept saying it about herself. "A . . . goddess, I guess. Some kind of dark version of . . . I don't know."

"You *do* know. You were told it, and now you have just said it. No guessing is necessary. A goddess is what they have made you."

"I don't really care what they think I am."

"You *must* care," he said forcefully, then bit his tongue, dropped his head, and whined as thunderous rumbling loosened dust and sediment above them. "I am sorry, but *that* is exactly why you must care, and be careful. That thought you had when you opened the door, of wanting to see the spirits and test yourself against them again, it was careless. Do not entertain such things. A show of such power would be unwise here."

"You're worried I might wake up the thing you were talking about earlier."

"Correct. And your boldness in coming to me alone speaks to a nascent recognition of what you can become. This was inevitable, but it is happening much sooner than I expected. It does not matter if you refuse to believe in this, or do not care to acknowledge it. No, no, that is wrong. It absolutely matters, in the sense that your denial could prove calamitous. Or not, perhaps. I am still struggling with a vision I was struck with this past night. But you must listen to me.

"You are no longer simply the chosen one to your believers. Nor are you merely The Godbride. You are even more than the mother of their savior now. You, along with your guardian, are the unmakers of prophecy. You are—"

"Who is he?" Sarita said, not interested in being told more things about herself that were ultimately beyond her control. "Who is Angelo? The Northman. Why was he called that? Who was he before he turned into what he is?"

Z hesitated to answer, still startled by her interruption. Sarita couldn't imagine he'd been cut off mid-speech too often, and certainly not by anyone he would have sized up for dinner in the distant past, but there wasn't any indignation, much less anger, on his face. Instead there was an odd . . . What was it? If forced on the spot to put a word to it, she might have gone with "hope."

"I was not entirely forthcoming about that with you earlier, was I?" Z said.

"Not at all."

"Do you have something in mind that you can do with this information, should I decide to share it?"

"I just want to know who I've trusted my life to the most since I was a kid. More than my grandparents, more than my mother and father, more than my brother. Even more than my husband right up until he killed him. I grew up sure that I had a guardian angel, and now it's all upside down. You want to tell me about everything else. Tell me about *him*. I need to know. He killed Frank right in front of me. Beat him to death and then left without saying a word. Beat him like he hated him."

"He did. He was taught to."

"Yeah, fine," Sarita said, even though it wasn't "fine," and her tone belied the word. "I was there, you don't have to convince me he legitimately hated Frank. And I get the why. I mean, I don't 'get' it. I'll never get it. If he loved me so much, if I was this 'goddess' to him, then why not talk to me first, say something to me? If he had just asked me about Frank I could have . . . you know what, that's not what I'm after right now. I don't think you can really answer those kinds of questions the way I'd want them answered. But you can tell me who he really is, or was. You can give me direct facts. That's all I want. Doesn't it make sense that I'd want to know who he is? I feel like I deserve to know."

Z nodded. "I would not disagree. It is difficult for me, I will say. I was the one who told Cela where to find him. I saw and recognized a man destroyed by terrible loss and I . . . I was once a blind man. She restored my sight so that I could only see her plans as she wanted me to see them. It took far too long for me to recognize what she wanted to become, and then longer to break away. I digress. I apologize. You do deserve to know who he is.

"My visions of him never showed me his name. When Cela reached him, he could not tell it to her, as he had not spoken to anyone for some time, and had stopped thinking of himself as anything beyond being the man who lights the fire and rings the bell.

"It was the time of the Great Mortality. The Great Pestilence that would later be known as the Black Death. This was during the plague's second great wave. The first wave was devastating, but the second proved even crueler and more crushing. Many at the time believed it was truly the end of all things.

"Where The Northman lived, Scandinavian land as it came to be known, there was enough time to anticipate the calamity as word of the Great Mortality reached villages before the pestilence found their country's shores. Throughout the afflicted lands there were omens and beliefs that begat atrocities that Cela could exploit for the furtherance of her church. However, in the North in particular, were stories of plague precursors, and old, preventative practices that could save an entire village, so they believed, through adequate human sacrifice. Many convinced themselves that to stave off the pestilence they needed to sacrifice a child, often by way of live burial."

"Tell me he didn't do something like that," Sarita said.

Z gave her a sad grin crossed with a grimace. "No, he did no such thing. But he encountered it along the route he took to save one of his sickened children.

"Wanderers of all stripes were common during the Mortality. In the northern lands it was not irregular for entire communities to leave their homes together to outrun the pestilence, typically unaware that they were already carriers, now spreading the illness elsewhere. Once the plague began to kill in earnest, survivors in some villages were scarce, and unable to do anything but continue to roam in search of help. Sometimes these were children, and they need not always reach another community to be taken up as sacrifice if they were encountered on the road by other travelers.

"When the plague came to his town, it struck The Northman's oldest daughter first. Their local physician would not touch her, and whispers reached The Northman that certain other townsfolk wished to do something evil to him, his wife, and their other children, under the assumption that they must also be sick, even without symptoms. There was a city within traveling distance that had a school for learned men, which was at least minimally more invested in new ideas than old ways. He tried to take his daughter by horse and cart to this city in search of better medicine. He left behind his wife with their other two children, who had yet shown no signs of illness.

"Two days into his trek, almost midway to his destination, with his daughter's condition worsening, The Northman encountered a group of survivors, mostly men, from a different community. They were full of grief and delirium, but most of all a deep-seated misery, which you could not scrape clean from the soul with the sharpest blade and all the time Hell will hold you for. The kind of misery that helps men mistake destruction for accomplishment. This is not to excuse them. I am a monster. It is easy for me to identify others. Still, their actions speak to the deterioration of their reasoning.

"They could see that the girl was sick. They saw the marks on her skin. This should have sent them running as fast and far away from her as they could. Instead, they allowed the loudest and least sane among them to proclaim she must be buried to bring their departed loved ones back, and they were swept up into his mania. In a moment such as that, a man can become a storm that some will shelter from, and others carried by.

"The Northman fought them with the ferocity expected of a desperate father. He was a larger man, naturally stronger than his attackers, and doubly so given his comparative health. A dishonorable history belonging to his grandfather was all that kept him from the soldiers' class of society.

He always traveled with a hatchet to help fend off bandits on the roads, and wielded it well in his daughter's defense. He managed to kill two of the madmen, and maim six others, but there were fourteen of them, and the remainders managed to subdue him while overturning his cart to take his child. When he continued to fight, the mob's leader struck him in the head with a large stone, and he fell unconscious.

"Later, when I came to know The Northman, I always wanted to speak to him, to tell him that his child was spared the awfulness of live burial, because the disease took her before the mob first stuck a spade into the ground. Cela forbade the sharing of any information that might grant him peace, however, and I did not possess the courage to resist her. Even today, I know I could do more, but . . . I simply cannot. I . . ."

He clenched his teeth, sucked hissing air through the spaces left by his missing fangs, settled himself, and continued.

"When The Northman woke, a day had passed. He was left only with the bodies of the men he had struck down. His tried to find his daughter. He searched for three days in the surrounding woods, barely sleeping, hardly remembering to drink water or forage for food. When he found the road again it was by accident, and he accepted it as a sign that he should return home.

"On foot, without his horse, it took him five days to get to his village. When he arrived, he found it vacated. As a collective, the community tried to outrun the plague without realizing it was too late. Many fled to the mountains and tried to form new villages that often died out. Perhaps that happened to The Northman's village. Or it is possible they survived and thrived without him. I do not know this. I am not all-seeing. I saw The Northman's life because his immense pain and his . . . *usefulness* . . . brought the vision of his suffering so clearly to me."

Z took another moment to subdue the shame that Sarita could almost see coiled around him like a constrictor snake covered in cool slime. She would never have imagined herself capable of pitying someone like him, who had admitted to using despondent people, even targeting them precisely because of their despair. But she felt needles piercing her heart when she thought of the remorse he lived with, and, more impactfully, how long he lived with it. His pain was deserved. He'd done what he'd done and could never change it, but that didn't make him entirely unworthy of sympathy.

"He searched each house," Z went on, "for any signs of life, or just a sign that his neighbors might be coming back. He found some dead bodies in beds, some on the floors, and one in the doorway of a house, all left behind along with things too heavy or cumbersome to be carried. No notes were left to tell him where they had gone, whether to wait for them or join them, or even just to tell him to stay away. Not in any neighbor's house, or in his own home.

"Days passed, and as he waited for them. With no other direction of what to do or where to go, The Northman grew obsessed with the idea that his family was trying to come back for him, even if no one else was. But they had gotten lost. He had just been lost in the woods and only found his way to the road by happenstance, so he convinced himself the same had happened to them. For that matter, his daughter might have escaped her attackers, recovered from her illness, and be searching for him as well, wondering where her father was, too weak to call his name as he had called hers.

"He did not want to risk going to find her only to be absent when his wife and other children returned. So he went to the church and the tower. His community was not prominent, but they had these buildings that looked armored, made in part from wood of an older temple torn down at the behest of Christian emissaries. A shallow cauldron built to house signal fires had been a feature of the old temple, and was now housed below the bell in the newer tower, more so a symbolic decoration than functioning beacon. But The Northman found use for it.

"He rang the bell at morning, midday, and evening, so his family could follow the sound home. At dusk he lit the cauldron, tending to it through his restless nights, to provide his family a light closer than the stars to guide their way. He did this religiously. That is the appropriate word. The whole of his faith was compacted into his ability to will his family home, regardless of where they were or what condition they were in. He stopped thinking of them as alive or dead, only as lost, and in need of help to find their way home.

"This is the soul I led Cela to. I do not believe I have properly explained Cela to you. It would take so much time to do so, but I will tell you that she is The Founder and Godmaker of a great and terrible church. She is quite possibly the first of us to see greater gods, the first of us to conquer the bloodthirst, and certainly the most ambitious of we, the unliving.

"Her intention, she claims, is to save this world from human avarice and destruction. She gave me, through her guidance, the power to see futures as she could, and I in turn shared with her visions of variant wastelands. Futures much like that of the Great Mortality, but unending. Worlds she did not want to endure, that she could avert using the tyranny of the unliving, provided her fellow devils were willing to abandon their permissiveness of human folly, and trust that the sleepers would not rise en masse to quell what they might mistake as an uprising.

"Cela used me to foretell of a goddess to be chosen by her selected god. The Viscount. Chosen for his vanity and malleability. Nothing more. She crafted her prophecy around you, him, and The Northman. You are The Godbride, destined to be martyred with your unborn child. The Viscount was your true love who you would come to eventually, and father of said child. And The Northman was the guardian who would save you time and again, proving that you were divinely protected, which would make your death—at the hands of an ordinary man you were gracious enough to have once loved—a greater, more unforgivable tragedy. Her followers—your believers—would be driven insane by this, and annihilate much of mankind as revenge.

"She convinced The Northman that he could make amends for his failure to protect his family by being your guardian, until the day the prophecy would be fulfilled, and The Northman was eager to play his role. But she miscalculated the effectiveness of her manipulation. Two thousand years of success reinforcing your own genius and infallibility gradually makes it easier to miss flaws in your design and execution, especially when that flaw is a product of doing your work too well. She made The Northman believe in you as his entire world. His full spiritual reclamation, and sole purpose. She instilled in him a paternal, protective love for you that survived dozens of generations. Then she expected him to stand down when she called him to, simply because it was 'prophecy.'"

A numbness that made her feel drugged clung to Sarita. She realized she had hoped to hear that Angelo was more like the demon Tori had told her about. Obsessed and jealous. A supernatural stalker. Somehow that would have been less troubling, likely because it would have justified her hatred of the being that had repeatedly saved her life.

Hearing that he loved her the way that he did, even if that love was also, in part, a means to the end of personal redemption, made what he'd done more painful. He'd believed he was doing the right thing, and worse still, despite wanting to deny it, Sarita could just barely understand why he felt that way. His entire priority was saving his new surrogate daughter. Not her friends, not her family, not anyone else she loved. No one mattered to him the way she did. He had no intention of being a hero, only a guardian.

She stood up without speaking, turned toward the stairs to leave, and saw Myra sitting on one of the steps halfway down. She saw in Myra's weary eyes that any chastisement for venturing into Z's chamber, or any attempt to strong-arm her back into her room, was not forthcoming. Still, she waited for it, out of instinctual respect for the person who had, just the day before, come to save her, even at the expense of someone she cared about.

She thought again of the lasting love Z said Angelo felt for her, then thought of how she had never felt anything close to that for him, despite all he had done for her prior to killing Frank. Sarita had valued him, relied on him, developed a faith in him. But she had never come close to loving him in any capacity. She thought that shouldn't matter to her, but for some reason it did, as though she could have prevented most or all of this if she had just told Angelo that she loved him almost like a brother, almost like a father, and just like some of her aunts loved the saints they prayed to when a family member was in the hospital.

Hell, why even start with "I love you." She had never even told him thank you. Never said it in the moment, although that was excusable. Things had always happened too fast, or she had been too frantic or concerned while it was happening. But afterward, she could have spared him a small prayer under the assumption he was listening. Why wouldn't he be? He was always watching. But she had never given him a simple, "Thank you, Angelo."

Angelo. Not "The Northman." That only reinforced that he had lost his name when he had lost his daughter. He deserved a name, didn't he?

No, he still deserves to die for what he did to Frank, she thought, feeling weakened by the idea of forgiving him, and reflexively rejecting it. *And, fuck it, I should kill him for letting Deedra and Candace get in that car. For putting me through all of this. For putting Frank's family through it all. Even Harrah. Hell, even Joey and those other boys. Everett's boys. Everett was there for me today—no, yesterday,* damn, *yesterday—talking to me, asking me if I wanted his help. Angelo never asked what I wanted. He never spoke up.*

222 • JOHNNY COMPTON

How was I supposed to know anything about him if he never said any-thing? If he had just talked to me I could have told him to save Candace and Dee. I could have told him to leave Frank alone. He could have told me about Cela and the rest of this, and then I could have told him that if he had to kill anybody, that's who he should kill. Or how about killing Cold Eyes—"The Viscount"—when he came for me at The Lantern? For God's sake, where was Angelo then?

She turned back to Z. "Where was he when everything went down yes-terday? Is he done with me?"

Z shook his head. "Your life was not at stake. The Viscount would not have killed you. We could not let him take you because, eventually, you *would* be in danger. Closer to Cela, she would seek new paths to kill you to hold on to her power, fulfill her plan, and then billions would die in her followers' crusades.

"This is why you are here, to be kept from her. As I said, if we allow her to kill you, it will bring about catastrophe. She may be able to convince her followers to still attack mankind, or they may rebel against her de-ception and engage in a global slaughter to compensate for their extended abstinence. They may split into factions and embroil the world in their religious war. I have seen all of these futures, and in each, millions die, if not billions, and nations are laid to waste. The only way to prevent this is to ensure your survival. Which is also why you must be careful. You must accept what you can become and control it. If the sleeper awakens to find a *goddess* in its abode, nothing will be able to protect you."

Sarita shook her head. *I didn't want any of this,* she thought, but what good would it have done to say it? Besides, now that she had it, this bur-geoning power, she at least wanted to see how to make use of it. She turned back to the stairs, where Myra stood now, her hand offered kindly.

"It's earlier than you probably think," Myra said, "and you don't look like you slept much."

"I actually slept harder last night than I have in days," Sarita said, ap-proaching Myra, accepting her hand before they went up the stairs together.

"Breakfast won't be ready for a couple of hours," Myra said. "Even if you can't actually sleep, it might help to just rest up some."

"What else is there to do around here if I'm not that tired?"

"Chores. Play cards. Play chess. Read. We do lots of reading. Want to see our library?"

"Could I help cook?" Sarita said as they exited the chamber and approached her room.

"If you can put up with Rowan. It's his turn today, and he gets a little—"

Sarita stopped dead at the open doorway to her room in the Baby Head Mountain encampment. Myra followed Sarita's sword-sharp stare to Everett, who was awake and sitting up in his cot. He asked, "What is it? What's wrong?"

"You don't see her," Sarita said, intending it to be a question but transforming it into a statement of fact when the answer—"No"—became apparent to her halfway through. The apparition in the room was not visible to Myra or Everett, only to Sarita.

She recognized the blurry figure of a young woman from one of the nightmares she had suffered the night before. One of the dreams she could not quite remember until now. The figure before her appeared almost like a body floating inches below the surface of murky water. Its back was turned to her.

It was missing part of its right arm.

I know you, Sarita thought before the specter turned around. *Oh God, please no.*

When she saw Tori's face she thought that it was impossible she hadn't recognized her sooner. In actuality she had, but had also refused to accept it. She'd give anything not to have anyone else get hurt just because they knew her. It was one thing—horrible enough as it was—to lose someone you knew to a random act of violence, but something else, and worse, to lose people when you were the epicenter the violence rippled from.

It didn't matter how much she prayed for Tori to be spared now, though, because Tori was there in the room, unseen by anyone else. There had to be a reason for that.

Tori faced her with her eyes still closed. She raised her hands like she was feeling for a wall in the depths of a cave.

"Sarita? Can you hear me?" Tori said, her voice coming from every direction. "She took David."

Sarita felt like she was struck by lightning and launched into the sky at the same time. She marched into the room, reached for Tori, and saw her hands pass through her friend's spirit. Still, she held them there as though she could hold Tori in place and shake her into solidity somehow.

"What do you mean?" Sarita said, her voice almost a chirp, her anxiety so high. "Who took David? Is he okay? *What are you saying?*"

"She took David," Tori said again, struggling with the words like she was relearning to speak after a brain injury. "Can you hear me? She *has* David."

"Who?"

Tori's eyes snapped open, finally hearing Sarita, and a pained relief came to her face. Less than a second later, the relief was gone. "The mother," Tori said, then repeated herself, her darkened, heavier tone giving her words a title, authority, and inherent warning they warranted.

"The Mother. Harrah."

29

David waited with Nadine in the windowless cab of the van while Vai drove. He presumed she was there to keep an eye on him, and while he had sized her up and thought he could defend himself adequately if she tried anything, he also had to presume she might know something he didn't. She might have a weapon on her, or might know how to use one of those crazy spells to incapacitate him. Who knew what she or any other member of her "family" were capable of?

He was being paranoid, and rightly so. His younger sister's "guardian angel"—whom he'd always been suspicious of—had revealed himself to be a psychotic killer just over a week ago, and things had only gotten stranger since then. Years of quiet distrust had rushed into the present to prove itself justified, then stuck around to make a point: "Actually, all along, it was a lot worse than you thought."

Apart from the occasional ask of, "Are you okay back there?" from Vai, and a few offers of a water bottle from Nadine, the last of which he accepted, some old soul singers on the radio did all the talking for most of the drive to San Antonio.

When they made it to the city, they took David to Sarita's house, where Tori's and Sarita's cars were still parked in the driveway, and his rental car was still at the curb. Nadine finally gave him his phone and he got out and went to his car without a word, because what were you supposed to say to the weird little cult that was holding your sister to keep her safe from an infinitely weirder, more dangerous, more incomprehensible cult? He looked back and gave Vai a small goodbye nod, but kept his mouth shut for fear he'd blurt out what he was thinking. *You'll see me again real soon. I'm coming back for her as soon as I'm done here.*

He drove to his parents' house, not wanting to call in advance in case the police were there feeding his folks things to say so they could find out where he was. The cops weren't anything to be afraid of compared with all that he'd seen yesterday, but they could still make themselves a nuisance if they wanted to detain him. He wasn't sure if he was wanted for questioning, if he was even on the cops' radar with relation to the massacre at The Lantern, which was all over the local news feed he had pulled up on his phone, even making it to some national news outlets.

David was relieved to see no patrol vehicles at his parents' house, and only slightly less relieved when his mother didn't reflexively slap him for worrying her to death by not answering her dozens of calls or messages as soon as he could, instead of just arriving unannounced. His parents had been terrified by David and Sarita's radio silence after news broke about the killings at The Lantern, given not only the shared last name of all those killed, but the first name of the sole survivor found at the scene.

David explained as much as he could and tried to reassure them that Sarita was safe where she was, an almost impossible task since he didn't actually believe that last part. Janelle was more willing to buy into the uncanny elements of the story David told them. José, who had always tried to explain away the incidents involving his baby girl's "guardian angel," was stunned mostly into silence. He didn't have to fully believe everything David told him to believe that his son—a Coast Guard rescue diver who could keep a cool head within a literal tempest—wasn't so emotionally scarred by what he'd seen that his mind had broken, resulting in him resorting to fiction to maintain sanity.

What neither of them could accept was that David wasn't going to take them with him when he went back for Sarita. Both became almost frantic in arguing—demanding—that they come along.

David saw them the same way he saw people panicking in the water, flailing about, threatening to kill the diver trying to rescue them along with themselves by way of their freakout. Sometimes, as training authorized and required, just as Vai had said, you had to hit somebody hard enough to subdue them to protect them from themselves. Obviously, he wasn't going to hit his parents, but he thought he could strike some sense in them with the right words.

"Listen, just think about her how you've always had to think about me," he said.

"What? What the hell does that mean?" José said.

"When you hear about some big storm headed my way, or if it just crosses your mind for some reason that I'm out there putting my life on the line with what I do, and that I might not come back from going out to save somebody someday, how do you deal with that? How do you go on about your day, every day, thinking about that?"

His mother and father looked at each other. Angry tears burned in Janelle's eyes, while José looked as confused as he was hurt. "What are you saying? Are you serious right now?"

His mother shook her head stiffly, and spoke with a startlingly sudden calm, sounding almost as if she were speaking coldly to a stranger who had just threatened one of her children. "You are not about to sit here, right now, with all of this going on, and tell us you think that we don't care what happens to you. This isn't about you—"

"I know that, Ma, come on," David said. "I know you both care. I know you both care so much you can't let yourselves think about it or you'd drive yourselves crazy. That's my whole point. You wouldn't have any room in your heads for anything but worry if you let yourselves think about it too much, and I wouldn't want it any other way. Because if I knew you two were that worried about me, I wouldn't be able to do what I do. And that's the way Sarita wants it . . . that's what she *needs* right now. Do you get what I'm saying? She's already scared enough for herself *and* for the rest of us, but the one thing she's counting on is that we're all safe if we're not around her."

"But *you're* going back," his father said, voice cracking with ache.

"Dad, I'm trained to go back for people. I do it all the time for people I've never met before. Damn right I'm going back for Sarita. And I'm not going to risk either of you getting hurt by bringing you with me. You'll want to help without knowing how to help. Shit, I barely think I know what I'll do, and I'm actually trained for . . . not exactly *this,* but . . . look, I'm CPR & First Aid fully certified. I'm used to the sight of blood, and things a lot worse than that, and I've already seen the things that Sarita's hiding from. Think of it this way, if she was out in the deep waters, you'd trust me to go save her, and you wouldn't get in the way by jumping in yourself, right?"

This did not settle the argument, but curved it in the direction he needed it to go. An hour later, promising to call and message them frequently, he was able to leave without worrying they would get into their own car and try to follow him as he went to his next stop.

The latest news stories he'd browsed indicated Tori was in critical but stable condition at the Methodist Hospital Metropolitan. He didn't know how he would get in to see her, but figured he'd start with claiming to be her brother, giving his name, and praying she'd be alert enough to know it was him and go along with the lie.

Ideally, she'd even be alert enough to tell him more about one of those spells she never got around to telling Sarita about at The Lantern. Right now, even if recent events had sapped what limited faith he'd had in a higher power, he had faith in himself that he wouldn't stutter, misspeak, fail to suppress a cough or do anything else that could make an incantation go wrong. If there were words he could say to shield his sister from the demons who set sights on her, he needed to know them, and Tori needed to know he would say those words precisely as directed, as often as necessary, and with the conviction of a missionary.

Tori was not in condition to see anyone, the nurses told him, not even immediate family, and they could not release any further details about her progress at this time. David didn't insist because there was one cop lingering in the waiting area, along with the hospital's security guard. He didn't even want anyone else to hear that he was asking about the young woman who had survived one of the most bizarre and sensational attacks in the city's history. The nurse welcomed him to wait in the lobby, and told him that someone would come to get him if Tori's situation changed, and David said thank you, then took a seat against the far wall.

He spent the next half hour trying not to be noticed as he kept an eye on the nurse he spoke to—a younger woman with an earnest but direct manner of speaking and holding eye contact—and the cop, an older male whose frequent glances at his watch gave away his preference to be off the clock and elsewhere. Eventually, the nurse, a doctor—or at least someone wearing a doctor's coat—and a second officer approached the first cop and had a brief conversation with him. David saw the nurse nod in his direction and the new cop take a quick peek at him. He wondered if coming here had been a mistake. Lying about being Tori's brother would make him look like he had something to hide once the truth came out. He supposed he *did* have something to hide, but nothing like what the cops would presume.

He wasn't sure whether to remain seated or get up to go speak to the police, nurse, and doctor together. If he were Tori's actual brother, wouldn't he do that? He would be more impatient and ready to insert himself into a conversation about his sister's status if Sarita were in this hospital instead. The only thing that kept him from standing and walking toward them was his concern that they might think he was trying to leave, since they were on the opposite end of the lobby, and he would have to pass the entrance to get to them. That might make him look more suspect.

Nonetheless, he found himself standing abruptly, even as he was contemplating what exactly he should do, how best not to arouse suspicion.

Why was he standing? Why was the person beside him, an older woman, also standing, and why was she clutching the pendant on her necklace so tightly it had to be cutting her palm if it had any edges at all? Why were her eyes so wide? Why was he backing away toward the corner behind him, absently moving chairs to get there, as though he knew a lion would be walking through the doors to the ER in the next few seconds?

David noticed two other people standing, and also noticed a loose darkness like smoke tendrils clouding the overhead lighting. It was a bit like the darkness that had preceded the arrival of the demon who came to The Lantern. Not as strong, not as concentrated, but unmistakably similar.

Here he had been worried about his parents following him, the cops looking out for him, and the people he had left Sarita with being untrustworthy. Somehow, he had prioritized those concerns over another encounter with the undeniable danger that he had seen tossing men like toys and ripping them like tattered cloth just the day before.

No, actually he had not subordinated his fear of seeing that thing again, or another of its kind. Like his parents with respect to their worry over the dangers of his job, he had just compartmentalized his dread because what else was he going to do with it? Convincing his parents to stay put, trying to think a step ahead of the police, returning to Baby Head Mountain, searching for the entrance to the encampment, getting back to Sarita, those were actions he could take.

Surviving another vampire attack would be like trying to survive a natural disaster no one previously knew existed. He'd rather go through an earthquake or a tornado. There were at least steps you could take to maximize the survivability of those kinds of catastrophes. Drills that people went through to better their odds of making it out alive. But this . . .

This.

He never realized the power in that simple four-letter word until now.

This.

It conveyed proximity. Immediacy.

This was about to happen to him and everyone else in the building, and there was nothing to be done about it.

This could not be averted, because it was already here.

This was a monster walking through the sliding doors of the ER, slowly outgrowing the human suit it had on before everyone's eyes, and saying in a tone darker than organ music, yet impish as a child who likes killing ants, "I think there's something wrong with me."

30

Harrah walked through the emergency room's automatic sliding doors, her right hand so large and heavy it could have torn her shoulder out of its socket were her muscles not strengthening accordingly.

In the waiting room, some people stood and backed themselves from the doors even before she entered. Without looking, she saw that some of the ones standing wore rosaries, others crosses on gold necklaces. One wore a hijab. Another, holding an infant, had no apparent religious affiliation. Perhaps they had someone praying for them elsewhere, unbeknownst to them, or they were just inherently and unknowingly in touch with forces undetectable by scientifically recognized senses.

Were any of them, or anyone they knew, a practitioner here in San Antonio of Santeria, brujería, or even Palo Mayombe? Did they have some ink on their skin that they thought was meaningless, that their aunt or uncle had suggested to them just because it would "look good," but that was really a talisman of sorts, which could never fully protect them but could at least alert them?

Harrah was genuinely curious to know why each person who stood and backed away from her before they could see her did what they did. How could they sense something was coming without even knowing that they knew? But she would have time to track any of them down, or others like them, later. Whenever she felt like it.

"Later" was becoming as much a luxury to her as money or influence were to the wealthiest people in the world. Something that others could not count on, but that would always be there for her. Even as her flesh was distended, and trickles of blood from two bodies wept from a dozen pores and splits in her overripe skin, she felt fuller with time, which was infinitely more valuable. A certain recognition of her riches accompanied her conditional immortality, which was her reward from the tiny gods of hunger, thirst, and blood living within her, which some might mistake for parasites. She saw them as symbiotes at worst. Things that could help her as long as she helped them, and they only had one directive: obey the drive to feed.

Fortunately for Harrah, this drive coincided with her desire to kill. It did present one conflict, as her overriding hunger fought against her want to hold off killing and eating until she found her intended target, but she thought she could navigate and balance these related, competing longings in the short term.

She threw her hand onto the counter at the reception area and said to the wide-eyed nurse, "I think there's something wrong with me." Her voice possessed by an earthen croak, but also a devilish delight.

To her left, a man screamed and ran for the exit. An older woman crumpled into a fetal position on the floor, shielded her eyes with one hand, tore at her necklace with the other, hard enough to break the clasp, and extended the closed fist that concealed whatever ornament she hoped would protect her.

Another man in the corner farthest from her stood and watched her. Did she recognize him? He looked familiar.

She had neither time nor inclination to bother with matching his face to a place or event of any significance to her. When she was done with who she came for, if he was still there, mimicking a statue, maybe she would ask him directly where he knew her from, and if he couldn't bring himself to speak up, maybe she'd bite what she wanted to know out of his brain.

To her right, stepping away from a doctor, a nurse, a security guard, and another cop, a police officer approached her, reaching for the Taser at his side. He was transfixed by Harrah's hand, which probably didn't even look like a hand to him. Harrah may as well have walked in holding five curved knives, and he had probably taken her statement that something was wrong with her as a confession that she was unhinged and needed to be put down. It wasn't an inaccurate assessment on his part, but being correct based on bad presumptions didn't exactly make a person "right."

An ounce more of caution and consideration might have saved his life. Instead, as he lifted the Taser and ordered her to step back from the counter, she whipped her long arm toward him, her hand almost squid-like until her fingers connected with his wrist and severed his hand cleanly.

Before the shocked officer could drop his damaged arm, Harrah seized his forearm with her left hand—which was growing stronger by the second—and yanked him closer, the pop of his elbow dislocating like that of a firecracker. She had bitten through his clavicle, clumsily missing his throat in her eagerness to bleed him, before it occurred to her that she needed to save some room for the person she was actually here for, especially since she had fed twice recently.

She twisted the officer's head backward, snapping his neck and silencing all of his hollering. This got everyone else screaming properly from every corner of the room, though it was hard to hear them over the gunfire.

The other cop drew his gun and put three bullets through Harrah that she barely felt before she closed the gap between them and shot her arm like a harpoon through his chest.

Even people who couldn't or hadn't seen any of this shouted to the others to tell them that they all had to get the hell out of the building. There were several sick or hurt people among this small crowd. People who were infirm in various ways. The only ones who didn't move on their own to the exits were an elderly man confined to a wheelchair, and that young man in the corner. God, where did she know him from?

You're not here for anyone else but that girl. The "witchy one." She's here somewhere.

Harrah followed the doctor and nurse as they pushed through the double doors that led to the critical care rooms. She moved urgently, but did not run, though she was tempted to chase them like they were her last chance to eat before starvation set in. God, she was hungry. It made it hard to focus.

She rooted herself in place for a moment to concentrate on a voice that sliced through all the others. The voice of the witch girl. She remembered it from earlier, when she'd heard her uttering that weird prayer in an unknown language after she first got to the hospital. Harrah still didn't know what the prayer meant, but the words were even more distinct and archaic to her now than when she had heard them hours before.

She followed the voice around the first corner she came to and was met by a security guard, a would-be hero charging toward the screaming. He froze at the sight of her, and she proactively slashed open his neck instead of wasting seconds waiting for him to get his bearings and reach for a weapon. The arterial spray painted the wall near to her on the right, and she couldn't pass the five-foot streak of red without licking part of it, although she barely broke stride to do so.

Past the short hall and another set of double doors was a large horseshoe-shaped counter that she could tell two orderlies were hiding behind based on their breathing.

You breathers, she thought with contempt, and walked behind the counter to find not two, but three orderlies hiding as low to the floor as they could get. The one woman who was petite enough to do so had also cleared space from the lowest shelf and placed herself halfway onto it, as though it would fully conceal her or act as a protective cocoon.

A blur of ferocity and red passed before Harrah's eyes, and it took her several seconds to realize she was the source and center of this whirlwind of motion, by which time there were two bodies at her feet, a third crushed within the makeshift cubby they had hoped to hide in, and a half-chewed heart in her left hand.

She dropped the heart, shut her eyes tight, smashed her ballooning hunger as far down as it would go, and rushed to follow the witchy girl's voice to the bed before she was overwhelmed by hunger again. She thought she could feel the excess blood sloshing in her swollen veins and engorged organs, and under her weeping skin as she ran to the smaller room the voice led her to.

Beyond her peripheral vision, down the hall behind her, in a space she shouldn't be able to see but could nonetheless envision, she noticed one of the men from the lobby coming toward her, fighting through the throng of people trying to get away from the carnage. It was the man she still couldn't recognize. She couldn't worry about him now. Let him catch up and catch his death if that was what he was after. First, though, there was the one on the bed right in front of her. At last. The one that Cela had brought her here to kill.

The witchy girl didn't look Harrah's way as she came inside. She only continued to pray, and if it was a prayer meant to keep the devil away it was wholly ineffectual. Seeing her objective gave Harrah a much-needed, relative calm and focus that she didn't trust herself to hold on to for very long. She'd come here wanting to take her time with Tori—that was the girl's name, she suddenly recalled.

I think I've got a shot with that girl Tori, she remembered Joey saying at the party where Frank proposed to Sarita.

Who's that? she had asked him.

The witchy one.

Oh, good luck with that.

"Good luck with that," she said aloud now to Tori, in reference to the futility of her prayer. Still, Tori did not acknowledge her. She stared at the ceiling and repeated her mantra, which was only a few sentences long at most, as though possessed by the incantation itself. This only made Harrah want to torture the girl more, but she wasn't going to have time for that. Though it had been easy to tear through everyone she had come across in the building so far, she still didn't want to get caught trying to fight half of the SAPD, who had to be on their way to the scene. There was a chance, probably a good one, that Harrah could win that battle, but why risk it when she didn't have to?

She turned the light out in the room, shut the door behind her, and stepped toward the bed which she could still see clearly in the dark, as though it were irradiated. She lifted one of her lengthened legs high when she got close and stepped up onto Tori's chest. Then she crouched down and compressed her weight above the girl's heart and felt the sternum and ribs crack under her feet. Tori shuddered and blood from her punctured lungs sputtered through her lips as she tried to continue the prayer, but getting the air squeezed out of her didn't permit her much of a voice anymore.

Harrah leaned closer to Tori's face, feeling her neck stretch. She wanted to bite the girl's lips off. Top, then bottom, preferably, but she wouldn't be able to keep herself from taking them both at once. She wanted to see the pain spark and crackle through the girl's face, freeing her from the spell that even crushed bones and pierced lungs couldn't break. She needed to be able to tell Sarita later, when she caught up with her, exactly how her dear friend died so terribly, far worse than Frankie did, and she didn't want to have to lie about certain details. Like the girl's apparent lack of awareness of what was happening to her. No such mercy had been afforded to Frankie, Harrah presumed, and she was in no mood to let Tori have it.

The door to the room opened, a man stood silhouetted against the light behind him. Not just her eyes, but Harrah's entire body instinctively adjusted to the sudden brightness by drawing every available darkness in the room toward her, from under the bed, from every corner, and from the shadow hiding the man's features.

He charged her to knock her from her perch on Tori's torso, and Harrah held out her hand to jab her pointed fingers through his heart, opting at the last moment to instead seize him more safely by the neck. Finally remembering who he was made her spare his life. For now.

He was Sarita's brother. Another attendee at that party where Frankie doomed himself by asking that girl to marry him. God, why was she wasting time on the witchy girl when she could have taken Sarita's brother instead? He hadn't been at Frankie's funeral. When had he come to town? Had she known he was even here she would have been out in the city trying to hunt him down. Perhaps this was the way it was meant to be, the reason why Cela dropped her here. Maybe she didn't know where exactly the brother was at the time, either, but knew that he would show up here at just the right moment.

Or, for all she knew, Harrah had somehow drawn him here herself. She needed to stop thinking of herself merely as Cela's agent. How much more evidence did she need to believe that she was a power unto herself?

The Devil's Mother. Cela had called her that.

Who can be against?

I can.

I am against.

The girl was as good as dead, and was unwilling to give Harrah the satisfaction of even a soft squeal, much less a chest-cramping howl of pain. The brother might give her more to work with if she could subdue her bloodlust for long enough. He could even bring Sarita to her, instead of making Harrah work to find her. All she had to do right now was get away with him.

She pulled him into the cloud she had gathered around herself and tried to think of a suitably dark and distant place to abscond to with him.

The abandoned church.

The one on the road to Eagle Pass.
That old, dead church.

Of course. That derelict chapel that she had driven past on the way to the Lucky Eagle. She could picture it easily, and knew the shadows of its forgotten past waited behind its boarded windows. She knew immediately that this was where she wanted to go, and why she wanted to go there.

She heard the brother gasp like he was about to dive deep and swim through an underwater grotto before coming up for air. She was glad for this. This being her first time, she didn't know how long it would take her to get from one point to the other. Cela seemed capable of crossing great distances swiftly, or dragging the process out if she saw fit, and carrying as much oxygen as any passenger might need along with her, but Harrah wasn't entirely sure she would even be able to get to where she wanted to go. It could take her enough time to navigate this darkness for Sarita's brother to suffocate. What a disappointment that would be.

A weak light framed a rectangular shape before her, and the body in her arms drew a ragged breath. Harrah tittered with relief, glee. That had happened so much faster than she had anticipated. Were they really already here?

She was exhausted, and it felt as though all her skin had been rubbed off with sandpaper, but her giddiness at having used the darkness so effectively on her first try nullified some of the pain and fatigue. She reached out and pushed the old door in front of her open, and it fell off its hinges after being used for the first time in years. Out of a dark storage closet she stepped into the church's chancel, looked past the altar and over the rows of long-empty pews. She glanced back at Sarita's struggling brother only to confirm it was still him held firmly in her hand, and not some other person she had picked up by mistake like someone else's luggage, if that was a possibility.

Why wouldn't it be? Why would anything be impossible? Not long ago she drove past the same strange woman multiple times while trying to get away from the greatest tragedy of her life, and nothing approaching explainable had governed her life since. Now she was beginning to get used to an entirely new life, an existence where she would never feel powerless, never be at risk of losing a loved one again.

But she could give the pain her past self had experienced over to others. She could be the monster they all feared, instead of being the helpless mother wondering what kind of monster could have taken her son away, and what kind of God could allow it to happen?

A deadbeat, neglectful God, she thought, and getting her start here—her proper, more calculated start, not the impulsive rampage she had just indulged in at the hospital—was fitting.

It was why she wanted to come here, to fully embrace her role as The Devil's Mother in this space that God had vacated and forgotten.

31

"Where did she take him?" Sarita said.

"She wants you to find him," Tori said. "She'll let you know. She wants you to come for him."

Tori's voice weakened, sounded like it came through a thin tube. She faded for a moment, as though the message she had just delivered was all she had come to say, or all she was allowed to say before she was snatched away. Sensing her departure might be imminent, Sarita called her name like it might wake her up, keep her present.

"Tori!" When her friend came closer to solidifying, as close as she could come, Sarita felt a jolt of optimism that what she'd done had worked, and could keep working if she needed it to. Still, she felt an urge to keep talking, press her for where Harrah could have taken David, as if any stint of silence might invite Tori to depart.

"You don't know where he is? Tell me what happened."

"He tried to save me, but it was too late, and she took him."

"He tried . . ." Sarita said, then hesitated, finding herself having to speak around a knot of grief in her throat. "Tori . . . are you . . . dead?"

Tori nodded.

"Tori, no. I'm so sorry."

"It isn't your fault."

"All of this is my fault," Sarita said. "This is why I didn't want anyone near me after—"

"*Stop it,*" Tori said harshly, her hair briefly flaring like a flame caught in a gust, her eyes flashing violet before she resettled into her more placid appearance.

Fearing she would disappear, Sarita rushed to ask, "Tell me what happened."

Her calm restored, Tori said, "She found me at the hospital. David was there. I could feel she was close before she got there. I could tell she had turned into something. I started praying. I knew I couldn't stop her, but I hoped I could find you and warn you. I prayed with everything left in me for my soul not to be held down, or claimed, so that I could be free to tell you what I could about Harrah. She's turned into something..."

"A vampire," Sarita said.

"Vampire," Tori said, looking like she would spit on the word if she could. "I only knew she was infected by something demonic. She's given herself over to it. Her hatred for you is like a god to her. She's devoted herself to it. She's going to use David either to bring you to her, or her to you. I felt it, all of her hatred, and all of her plotting spilling out of her head. I breathed it in, even when I could barely breathe. Even after I couldn't breathe. I saw it flooding out of her like smoke from a burning building. I saw it. I took it in. I died with it." An intense sadness shook her voice and form. "*I died with it.*"

Sarita wished she could hold her friend, comfort her. She wouldn't say sorry again. She understood why Tori reacted the way she had to Sarita blaming herself. She had died in the palpable presence of someone else's invasive hate. It had to be an emotion she loathed and found hazardous now. It was destructive, at least in the form Harrah had nursed, adopted, and consumed in place of her lost son. The hatred Sarita had carried with her for Angelo and, more quietly and perhaps more potently, for herself, had been unproductive at best, as well.

"I love you, Tori," Sarita said.

She saw Tori's mouth move, and she read the word "love," or it might have been "live," on Tori's lips, but heard nothing. The fade overcame Tori more swiftly and inexorably this time, and Tori was gone before Sarita could think to say her friend's name again. Gone, just like that. Gone for good.

Sarita immediately felt sick, like swamp water was swishing in her stomach, but also like she was at the onset of a fever, the unpleasant internal heat filling her head with haze. Knowing she didn't have the time or energy to mourn Tori properly intensified the sickness, like her body was trying to compensate for the emotions it knew she couldn't supply right now.

Myra stepped closer, and Everett stood up. It was his turn to come to Sarita and console her. Sarita felt his hand, warm and gentle, on her shoulder, and felt a different part of her, on the shore opposite her grief, hate the idea of anyone trying to comfort her.

This isn't what I need you for, Everett, she thought. *Don't you remember what we talked about at The Lantern? I need you to get those hands ready for some killing. And, honestly, I don't even* need *you, or anyone else, for that anymore.*

She wondered whether tension in her muscles or some form of telepathic messaging told him that he should step away. Either way, she thought it was good that he understood he ought to move back.

She reached into the space where Tori's spirit had just been, and closed her fingers over a lingering iciness. She wished she could take this remnant with her and use it somehow when the time came to take Harrah's life.

"Were you talking to your friend?" Myra said. The sound of another living person's voice, asking the closest thing to a practical question as someone could ask under the circumstances, proved an odd, unexpected salve.

Sarita just nodded, then made the decision and effort to speak calmly and assertively. "It was her. She said Frank's mother got turned into one of those things and abducted my brother."

She turned to Myra and hoped the burn growing behind her eyes made them glow. She hoped Myra would flinch at the sight of her, as Everett did. While Myra didn't do that, she did narrow her eyes and put her weight on her back foot like she was prepared to run away, regarding Sarita with a newfound wariness.

To Sarita, Myra looked like she was standing before a massive wall and just noticing water leaking through the mortar between the bricks, and in turn realizing the wall was a dam. That a flood was coming to destroy everything it touched. When Sarita imagined bodies battered, tossed, and helpless in the enormous wave of her living anger—a wave worthy of an enraged, ancient goddess—she felt better than she had since before Frank died.

"I need to get to my brother," Sarita said.

"I'll get everyone up," Myra said. "We'll get together, we'll think of something."

"I'm not waiting on you. I'm going to get him. I need my phone. She could have had him calling me already."

"Hold on. I understand that you want to—"

"You don't understand," Sarita said.

"I *do,* and you know that," Myra said, her legs more evenly under her now, though she had to step back from Sarita to regain that balance. Still, she spoke with at least some of her confidence and command of the situation renewed. "We brought you here because it's dangerous for you to be out there, for yourself and everyone else. *Everyone,* your brother and parents included."

"I'm going to David whether you help me or not," Sarita said.

"Listen to me. It doesn't help him for you to just charge out there with no thought to what could happen. There's a reason we couldn't let them take you. Do you understand what happens if—?"

"I know. Z told me about all of that. He told me something else, too. I'm not just Cela's 'Martyred Mother.' Angelo changed everything when he did what he did, and I don't have to be happy about it to use it. I'm a violation of Cela's prophecy. Z told me there's an entire faith that sees me as their goddess. They made me a goddess before I was even born. Before my parents, my grandparents, or their parents were born. I've been worshipped by *devils* for hundreds of years. They've been in my head for almost my entire life, calling out to me. Why can't I use what they've given me? If Harrah can get turned into whatever she is now, I should be able to turn into something that can kill her and save David."

Myra shook her head, but she didn't have a rebuttal to Sarita's proposal that she could verbalize beyond, "Z also told you why it's not safe—"

"You can either help me or get out of my way."

The crack of breaking stone and an accompanying rumble stopped Myra short of saying anything else. Instead she looked around the room like she expected creatures to start coming out the walls and the ceiling.

The flood is coming, Sarita thought.

"Myra, please don't stand between me and my brother. I don't want to do anything to you or anyone else. I just have to leave."

"Sarita, you need to be very careful," Myra said, her voice low and stern, her teeth close to clenched. "Remember the sleeper?"

A massive groan that emanated from seemingly a mile underground shook the hill harder, staggering Myra. Sarita was unmoved, and only gave a cursory glance downward, toward the apparent restlessness of the sleeper of Baby Head Mountain. She no longer hoped that her eyes were glowing, but believed that an aura must be emanating from her. A darkly radiant stencil of her, large enough for her to grow into it, allowing her to see from its greater height. It was comprised of centuries of pure reverence dedicated to her, written, spoken, and sung by things that were unholy.

The flood she had pictured arrived, but was internalized. The leak in the dam had been the first hint of belief, picked open by her weakness and desperation in the wake of seeing Tori's ghost, hearing that David was abducted, knowing that she could not withstand another loss. Not one more. She would do anything to prevent it. Even become a goddess to the godless.

"You should get away from me while you can," Sarita said to Myra. Then to Everett, "Please, while it's safe."

Everett shook his head uncertainly, while Myra did the same more forcefully. "I'm not giving up on you," she said. "I didn't lose Duncan and everyone else just for it all to lead to *this*. Sarita, you have to get this under control. Please. If you wake this thing up—"

"It isn't her," said Z, appearing in the doorway behind Myra. "Get the others. You must all evacuate."

Myra turned to speak to him, but he was already walking away, toward the main chamber of the refuge. "What do you mean it's not her? What is it?"

She and Everett followed Z while Sarita trailed them all. Z's call for an evacuation would give her a chance to get away and figure out how to find where Harrah was holding David.

In the rotunda, several people had already gathered, though Barnes was the only one Sarita recognized. She wondered which room Dottie and Len were in. The strongest quake yet came, cracking and tilting the ground, knocking everyone save for Z and Sarita to their hands and knees. The sound of crashing plates in the dining area, falling and fragmenting stone throughout the refuge, and concerned screams from the other halls turned the rotunda into an amphitheater of chaos and fright.

244 · JOHNNY COMPTON

The screams were especially alarming, even to Sarita. She hadn't given up her heart to gain her fledgling power. If that trade-off was to come, it was still well ahead. Only two more people—one of them Rowan, draped in several charm-laden necklaces—had come from one of the halls in the aftermath of the latest quake. Sarita hadn't taken an official head count yesterday, but thought that there were at least ten others missing. Still in their rooms, and maybe trapped in them now if their doors had warped and jammed due to the shaking, or if large enough parts of the place they called home had dropped onto them, or into their way of escape.

"What's happening?" Barnes said.

"You must all leave," Z said.

"We have to clear out," Myra said. "Barnes, you and I can check the rooms for anyone who isn't already out here."

"You do not have time for that," Z almost shouted. "Those of you who can must leave *now*."

Everett said, "What's going on. Are we going to be safe out there?"

"Safer than within the mountain. Get out and get as far from here as you can. The sleeper is stirring."

"What? Why?" Barnes said.

"Because she is here." Z pointed toward a corner of the ceiling, where strands of every shadow in sight were collecting into a small funnel cloud. The cloud flattened like it feared the one who had summoned it, but could not get away from them, only behind them.

The woman revealed by the receding shadows clung to the ceiling, her back to it, her fingers penetrating the stone. She surveyed those in awe beneath her. She bared heavy, gleaming teeth that spoke to the strength of her bite just by existing in jaws muscular enough to contain them. She looked abnormally tall, or long, as it were, eight feet or more, with arms that stretched out disproportionately wide. Her eyes, the color of the sun through ash clouds, found and fixed on Sarita. Her grin could make death dig a pit to hide in while she passed.

The sleeper was not awakening because of Sarita's burgeoning apotheosis. It was coming to because this great abomination had arrived.

Cela, Sarita thought, with no doubt that this was the woman's name, and that she was here to kill her own creation.

32

Impatience had proven her undoing. Not The Exile, the priests, or The Viscount. The only one who could come close to defeating Cela was Cela, and she had managed this without realizing she was fighting herself.

She had allowed The Viscount and the priests to bring her to the temple. She let them bind her with dogbane, hawthorn, and steel woven rope to a large stake placed at the altar. They summoned her congregation to witness what they believed to be her humiliation, and their triumph. As though they had done anything. As though they did not owe their continued existence to her monumental mercy.

After Franklin Stallworth was killed, Cela should have given herself time to plan, relied less on improvisation than strategy. Instead, she had been rash, and worse, overconfident in her imprudence. There would have been little risk in delaying a month or more, at minimum, before deciding on a direction. She could have gathered her thoughts, gathered more information, determined her options, and weighed them all twice to find out which were slighter, which heavier, and which had enough gravity to stop the turning of the Earth.

She had taken greater offense to The Northman's defiance than she had admitted to herself. She was similarly insulted by the collusion she suspected was behind it, and appalled by the audacity of anyone thinking they could oppose her. *Her.* The one who had taught them all to subdue the hunger that would have mastered them. The Founder of the church that made devotees of demons, all in the name of saving the future, with none of them—or almost none—aware of her design.

Her.

The Godmaker.

This was her second failing; she had conditioned them too well. The Northman could not think of himself as anything other than a guardian, and acted accordingly. The faithful loved Sarita too much to believe her rescue was anything other than a miracle. How could they understand it as the danger it was if Cela had deliberately kept them blind and dumb to her plans? As for The Viscount, she had selected him precisely because his foolish arrogance made him moldable, and more susceptible to taking credit for acts he took no part in. She had deconstructed and rebuilt his mind and personality with a perfect balance of deific ambition and self-satisfaction. Now he stood before her, believing himself her god, as if he was important. As if he couldn't have been replaced by a thousand other men at various points centuries ago. Just as she had intended. How angry could she be at him for turning into what she had made him?

Considerably, it turned out, although not because he had helped bind her and dared think he had a right to interrogate her. What angered her was his ignorance of his vulnerability. His unawareness of the threat posed to him.

She thought of what he told her in the desert, and who The Exile spoke of.

She will kill you.

Who was "she"? It could not have been Cela. Tempted as she was to end him now, she had enough control of her emotions not to succumb to them. As for Harrah, how would she even discover who The Viscount was? How would she ever get close enough to try to attack him?

That only left one other.

"Children," The Viscount said to the silenced, overawed gathering, "I trust that none of you have mistaken my absence for neglect." He was close enough to Cela for her to sniff the faintest bouquet of anxiousness on his skin. He reached back toward the priest standing nearest to him, and the priest handed him a thick, metal nail long enough to punch through Cela's body, into the post she was tied to, and out the other side.

"I trust that none of you believe I ever abandoned you to this false prophet for all this time," he went on. "This plotter and deceiver who has even tricked those with actual power to calculate the future into thinking that she, or The Devil's Mother, could actually kill me."

It was hard for her to fathom what a fool he was. How could he have even the slightest grasp of her plans and intentions without also understanding how much she valued him? He was part of her life's work—spanning scores of human lifetimes. All she wanted was to prevent its derailment, and the death of the god she sculpted from ego and hedonism would be a debilitating setback. She had failed to account for too many disruptions already. This was the one thing she absolutely could not let happen. The one thing she was sincerely afraid of. And the idiot she would do anything to protect nonetheless thought she might want him dead.

"Children, I was never truly gone from you. I have been here all along, even when I was unseen, reborn time and again, as you well know, and all the while I watched. As much as you prayed to me, I prayed for you. I prayed your eyes would open to the lies and treachery right in front of you, but I waited until now, until it was impossible for me to wait any longer, to finally appear. I tested you. I had faith in you. And as disappointed as I am that you did not see the obvious lie before I brought it to your attention— the lie that I would somehow fail to save my bride, and my only child— disappointed as I am, I *still* have faith in you. But do you have it in me?"

Pleas and proclamations of fealty rained on him from thousands of voices, each hoping to be heard above the others. No longer truly unified, but individuals competing for their god's attention, afraid that he might single out the one voice not screaming with enough conviction and use the nail in his hand on them.

Smiling, The Viscount asked, "Are you certain? Because you have let Cela tell you for centuries that I would let your goddess die with my son in her womb. Killed by an ordinary, breathing man elevated to antigod by your belief!"

Now came protests struggling to balance between cautious and earnest. *I never doubted you, Lord. I never believed the priestess, Lord. The others did, yes, but never me. Please forgive me.*

"I."

"Me."

"The others."

What was he doing to her flock?

Cela trembled with anger she knew The Viscount might misinterpret as fear, but she did not care about that. She cared that he was undoing her work with an inelegant, performative speech whose true purpose was shouting down the niggling terror in his own mind. Because he saw when he turned to face her, as he had seen in the desert, the power that only she had.

She was the one who taught her kind what they could be. If any among them deserved to be exalted, it was her.

But she did not want that. She would assume the responsibility if necessity demanded it, and presumed that someday she would be called upon to take the role, but she never sought reverence for herself. And now this fool who was infatuated with a girl that Cela arranged for him to be obsessed with, based on her knowledge of what he would do with his life ages before he was conceived, was chipping stones from the foundation of her creation without understanding that he was part of the structure itself. That he would be the heaviest piece to fall and shatter should it all collapse.

"That you seek their praise at all speaks to your inadequacy," Cela told him. "You are aware of that at least, are you not?"

The congregation could not hear her, but saw that she spoke to him and grew louder, overflowing with jeers and abuses after she spoke to the god they thought she betrayed.

The Viscount wanted to retort, but opted instead to stab her through the heart with the nail, driving it up to the head into her sternum. A shock of intensity that she would not quite call pain rigidified her body, but only for a moment. When she freed her arm and reached for the nail to withdraw it, albeit stiffly, silence covered the church like an occultation. The Viscount reached to pull her hand away, but stopped short when she pointed her clawed fingers toward his hand like she meant to snatch it from his wrist.

"Stop all of this," she told him. "I am still on your side."

"She means to kill you, my Lord," one of the priests said. "She has always meant to."

The Viscount held his hand up to silence him, raised his voice to give it an illusion of power. "Which is the truth, Cela? Have you always meant to kill me, or did you mean for The Devil's Mother to endeavor the impossibility of deicide? Which of you is the 'She' that The Exile warned me of?"

"Neither of us, you simpleton."

"Obstinance is unbecoming on you," The Viscount said, garnering a pathetic, placating laugh from what was no longer a congregation, but an audience. When she was close to completely pulling the nail from her chest, he darted his hand out to take the nail before she could finish.

A child playing at being a god, she thought, and felt a grief that could generate a decade of rain. Her disastrous impatience had not begun with choices made after The Northman killed her chosen Devil. It started when she chose this impudent man-child to be the object of her flock's undying fidelity. She chose him out of convenience. She chose him because he was predictable and shapeable. She chose the wrong one. A mistake it was far too late to unmake.

He was a more essential piece of her plan, as evidenced by the groveling he inspired by the believers at the suggestion that they had lacked appropriate faith in him. The Godbride could still be replaced. She was designed to be expendable from the outset. It would take decades that she and the world did not have, however, to groom another god.

"Where did you send The Devil's Mother off to when you freed her?" he said.

Cela answered, "She is not the one you ought to worry about."

"So you admit that it is you?"

"I am not 'She.'"

"No? Who else is there, then?"

"The Godbride, you damned *child*. Sarita. *She* is going to kill you!"

Cela knew that The Viscount did not love Sarita as much as he loved the concept of "The Godbride," but it was evident in his reaction that he loved this concept enough to go temporarily insane at the suggestion of Sarita killing him. Seconds before, he had been afraid to touch Cela's hand, but now he gripped her jaw and tried to pull it down, open her mouth to drive the nail into her tongue.

This final threat, Cela could not abide. Steel piercing her heart was not strong enough to paralyze her, something she had tested on herself previously and knew already, but metal impaling her tongue might trap her inside her body for several days, if not longer.

She flexed her muscles through her skin, instantly pushed through her reserved form, and stretched her arms wide, snapping the remaining ropes that had held her. Her monstrous hands met around The Viscount's

250 • JOHNNY COMPTON

head like two huge spiders trying to mate through his skull. How easy it would have been to decapitate him and then launch his head—mouth still agape—like a ball into his adoring crowd. She would love to see whether they tried to catch it in the hopes of somehow reattaching it to his body, or avoid it as they were overwhelmed with the impossible horror of their headless god.

You still do not understand, she thought, staring fire into his eyes. *All that keeps me from killing you is that you still matter, because* I made you matter. *You are still the plan. I need you not to die. Even now, what I do is done to save you.*

She tossed him aside, then pulled all available darkness toward her until she was covered.

The Godbride. Sarita Bardales. Another one who owed her life to Cela. She would have been a dead girl found too late to push the water from her lungs if Cela had not selected her. Instead, she was now a goddess because Cela had made her one. What objection could she make to Cela removing the gift of life and divinity that she had never earned?

Cela knew where to find the girl. The Viscount must have known as well, or could at least surmise where she might be, given his previous meeting with The Exile. He could inform others of her whereabouts, but Cela doubted he, the priests, or anyone else would be fearless enough to follow her to the sanctuary under the hill. An almost perfect fortress for those who knew that every vampire, even the feral maniacs consumed by their thirst, dreaded drawing the attention of the sleepers.

Cela was beyond fearing the sleeper of Baby Head Mountain, however, or any other. The only thing that frightened her was the threat to her life's work. All that drove her, screaming across the darkness and directly into the heart of the sleeper's abode, was the need to kill Sarita Bardales.

33

What if I let her kill me? Does that save everyone?

This notion, partly a product of her mind trying to cope with the immediate threat and grandiose terror of Cela's presence, faded so quickly it was almost as if it never existed.

If I die here, David dies, too.

That was all Sarita needed to know to understand that sacrificing herself wasn't an option. Still, she did not run from Cela, even when the magnificent, menacing devil dropped from the ceiling to land on all fours on the floor.

Coming to grips with her survivor's guilt, which Tori inspired her to do, meant understanding that she *was* a survivor, and that this meant more to her now than mere continuance of life. It meant capability.

When she got to David and saved him, she wanted him to do more than survive whatever would happen after she and Harrah warred with each other. She wanted him to emerge as capable as he had been when she sent him away, which meant she needed to be capable of making that happen. She didn't want to count on finding that courage, in the face of fear so present and solid that you could carve a statue out of it, at the last moment, when she was face-to-face with what Harrah had become. Here was a much greater, older vampire, whose very presence was summoning something closer to a god, disturbing its rest.

Be brave, Sarita thought, remembering the taunt issued by the young vampire from Myra's story.

Be brave.

She turned to Myra, who had looked to her, of all people, for assurance—maybe because Sarita was not, strictly speaking, "people" anymore, but something worse and greater. In Myra's eyes she read a resilience bolstered by the strength Sarita had embraced. Cela landed in a place between Myra and the other hallways—dark and reminiscent of tunnels—that she needed to reach to save others.

We could have tried, and we chose not to. We ran. Sarita could almost hear Myra repeating those words, and could tell that, even more than Duncan's death, this is what haunted her. It had haunted Duncan as well, and was part of what brought the two of them closer. They had found a strange, unique love formed by mutual regret.

Whatever Myra and Duncan had been to each other before their disastrous expedition into the old train tunnel, their survivor's guilt had brought them closer. Sarita understood that. She had felt the same about Tori after Deedra and Candace's accident, and now, oddly, wanted to experience the same sense of closeness and regret with David. Tori was gone, but they could still make it.

They would spend their remaining years wishing they had done something differently, noticed something sooner that could have helped them save Tori, but they would at least have those remaining years together. Tori would at least have survivors to remember her. First, though, Sarita had to prove to herself that she was a survivor, and not solely because of Angelo's intercessions.

Myra and Barnes rushed past Cela, heading toward the leftmost hall while the others, save Rowan, rushed past Z toward his chamber beyond the iron door. Sarita heard Everett call her name, glanced over to see him being pulled away by two other evacuees, and told him, "Go." If not for his injuries, he probably would have had the strength or will to break away and try to make it to her side, but instead he let the others take him away.

Z stepped toward Cela intending to be a distraction, as well as a shield between Cela and Sarita.

Rowan came forward to form a front line with Z. Sarita tried to join them, but Z stuck his arm out to prevent her from stepping between and ahead of them. Together they walked forward like a couple who had formed a suicide pact. Z moved ahead of Rowan and pushed the man away to safety when they came close enough for Cela to touch them.

Sarita heard Z say, "I am sorry—" before Cela swooped him up, one hand on his torso, the other holding his legs, and tore him in two at the waist. Cela's jaw unhinged to take the Greek in, eating him from the open end of his upper half. She bit through enough of him to get chunks of his heart caught between her teeth before spitting the rest out to survey the wreckage.

She shrank into something closer to a normally proportioned human being as she stared down at Z as though realizing for the first time who she had just attacked. There was anguish in her face that made her seem susceptible, but Sarita did not take this as an opportunity to try to attack, instead moving past Cela, as well as past three other members of the family who had just made it out of their rooms, to join Myra and Barnes in one of the halls.

"All that I gave you," Cela said to Z, "and how did you repay me? I gave you so much, and you betrayed me!"

"I am sorry you became so lost," Z said weakly, his long life ebbing as he lay halved and heartless.

"Lost?" Cela said, her voice a whipcrack that would have shaken the sanctuary if the sleeper's invisible lurching weren't doing it already.

At the end of the hall, Myra and Barnes tried to pull away a heavy, triangular chunk of stone that blocked the doorway to a room. Sarita heard Dottie and Len shouting for Myra and Barnes to go away, save themselves, and she ignored their words just as their adopted family members did.

She went to one end of the rock, letting Myra and Barnes continue to pull from the middle of the obstruction. She hoped to help them rock the stone enough for them to be able to roll it away from the door. Instead, she was able to lift her end of it up high enough for Barnes to drop to the floor, reach under the stone, and take Dot's hand as she crawled forward while also pulling Len through the gap.

Sarita felt the weight of the stone. It was not light to her, but put her in touch with a degree of strength she otherwise wouldn't have known she had. After Len made it through and Dottie helped her to stand, Sarita dropped the stone and the impact widened a crack at her feet that she hadn't previously noticed. She turned to help the others, then went ahead of them when she saw Cela waiting for them at the mouth of the tunnel.

The part of her thinking, *I can't die here,* could only be shouted down by the part of her declaring, *No one else dies because of me.*

She didn't know how, but she was going to save everyone, herself included. She felt closer to her younger self now, the one who had ventured from home after the incident at the party and wandered in search of ways to utilize the gift of her "guardian angel" for the benefit of others, before she lost course.

Cela started to come down the hall, her first step faster than a twitch, but something invisible grabbed her from behind and lifted her up and out of sight before she could make it halfway to her target. A bone-rattling bellow, almost too baritone to be audible, accompanied the act.

"Move, now!" Myra shouted. Sarita led the way and the others followed as closely as they could.

Outside the hall, in the central chamber, they saw Cela held aloft, and Sarita wondered if the others also saw the shimmering, barely translucent shape that she did. Part humanoid, part octopod, and also arboreous, like a living oak tree with a bulbous trunk and extra limbs that doubled as roots, the thing hunched to fit within the rotunda, and appeared to Sarita more like a bulge in reality, an optical effect, than the present and fearsome ancient demon that it was.

Sarita thought it must have multiple mouths, because as it made the struggling Cela disappear into what she took for its head, it also grabbed the two halves of Z with its tentacular lower limbs and drew them into other openings in its body. A crushing of bone and leak of fluids onto the floor followed.

Sarita didn't realize she had stopped to see all of this until she felt Myra pull her arm and heard her shout, "Come on!"

The others had already gone ahead into the lower chamber. Rowan held the metal door open for everyone to make it through. Sarita followed Myra toward the door when a tremendous fissuring sound came from behind them, along with a roar like a pod of whales trying to generate a tsunami with their song. The entire hill seemed to raise up several feet and drop back to the earth. This threw Myra off-balance and onto the ground. Sarita lifted her up and they both turned to see what was happening.

Cela fell from the hole she had torn in the sleeper from the inside—

from what Sarita guessed was the creature's midsection—and crashed into the ground. The sleeper slumped and staggered, continuing to emit painful, mournful cries that must have been audible for miles.

Acidic burns covered and discolored Cela's steaming skin. Patches of her clothing were cooked into her flesh. Her eyes were bleached completely white. Puncture wounds and serrations from her consumption left parts of her flesh in tatters that jerked like they were electrified as her body immediately began an arduous regeneration. She looked like she was well past dead, and like her corpse had been desecrated and mutilated, yet she also somehow looked stronger than she had previously.

She had just ripped herself out of the great awakened sleeper. Burst forth from the god that had devoured her.

As Cela crawled forward, it was difficult for Sarita to tell if the sleeper was following its freed prey, or if Cela was dragging the behemoth behind her by strands of its viscera that entwined her.

Any idea of confronting Cela fled from Sarita, and she now led Myra away, practically carrying her along as they ran to the door. Rowan regained his footing, waved and shouted, "Hurry! Don't look back!"

They rushed to the door, trailed by the thumping sound of pursuit and a dragging and cracking that caused a furor worthy of a demolition project. Sarita pushed Myra through the door first, then turned to help Rowan close it after she made it through. She saw Cela lunge at them just before the door shut.

Her impact with the door buckled the entire wall it was attached to, and knocked Rowan from the top of the stairs down fifteen feet to the floor below. Sarita put her shoulder against the door and looked down at Myra, who ran down the stairs where an escape waited.

The bookcases behind Z's table had been pushed aside, revealing a tunnel reserved for such an emergency evacuation. The family must have believed they would have more advanced warning of an impending threat, and that a secret escape route that they could close behind them might buy them some time, leave any intruders—human or supernatural—momentarily at a loss for where they had gone. They had never expected a vampire to arrive in their sanctuary so boldly, unconcerned with being caught in the proverbial and literal mouth of their protective leviathan, and certainly did not foresee anything as powerful as Cela was, able to cleave her way out of a minor god's stomach.

Instead of running to the exit, Myra turned to Rowan, whose right shin was bent backward at an angle just severe enough to make the fracture unmistakable.

Sarita shouted, "Go! I can get him out!" Before she could say anything more, as if solely to refute her idea of rescuing Rowan, another stronger impact against the door broke it in half, sending metal slivers flying into Sarita as she was thrown off the landing and down to the floor, near where Rowan landed.

Cela descended over the landing's ledge, partially suspended by the elastic, viny, nearly invisible guts of the behemoth she had disemboweled. Within this lower level of the chamber, now close to the exact place where she had seen the ghosts of Baby Head Mountain, Sarita heard a father screaming, a mother wailing, a child screeching.

Discordance. Madness.

The greatest power Sarita possessed now was keeping her sanity from bursting and fizzling into nothing like a firework. Adrenaline numbed her almost entirely to the pain from tiny bits of metal embedded in her skin, one dangerously close to her right eye, another having pierced her mouth, creating a tight pocket in the inner wall of her cheek. She licked at it to loosen it, putting the taste of blood on her tongue.

On one good leg, Rowan pistol-squatted to a standing position, assisted by the wall behind him, before Sarita got back up. Myra made it to Sarita's side while Rowan moved toward Cela, hands raised like he was waiting to catch the ceiling when it fell.

He called out a prayer with loud, fanatical force that initially made Sarita think he was frantic. Quickly she realized that while he must have been terrified—unless he was out of his mind—the way he spoke the incantation did not reflect that, instead capturing the desire for redemption pouring from every ounce of his being. Sarita wanted to reach out, pull him away as he limped closer to Cela, but couldn't risk interrupting him mid-prayer.

Though her eyes were entirely whitened, Cela's gaze was clearly fixed on Rowan. His spell commanded her attention. Sarita thought she saw the tattoos on his skin darken—highlighting how little of his skin wasn't illustrated—as he continued to all but shriek his prayer at a pitch and volume that would shock a thunderstorm into silence.

Sarita could not tell precisely how the spell was impacting Cela, or to what extent, but it seemed to at least hold her for a moment. Then, with an agonized wail of her own, Cela imploded and disintegrated into black mist.

For a second, no more, Sarita thought that Rowan had miraculously spoken the exact words with the exact tone necessary to vanquish something as powerful as Cela was. But when the mist didn't dissipate, she immediately realized that Rowan had not done this; Cela had done it to herself.

Sarita reacted too late to save him. The dark particulate cloud, now free of the entrails that had held Cela up, formed into hundreds of fine points and speared Rowan through every space of untattooed skin available on his body. Attacking his eyes would have sufficed, but the cloud wanted to do more damage than that. It wove through him, turned him into a standing corpse with countless entry and exit wounds, then let him drop when it was finally finished with him.

There was no way to fight this if it came for her, Sarita realized, but after killing Rowan the cloud started to disperse, then re-formed tenuously—still more cirrus than cumulous—as it pooled along the ground sluggishly, as though weighed down by every drop of Rowan's blood it had just extracted. The cloud took on a relatively human shape, elongated limbs notwithstanding, and pulsed erratically as Cela's body reconstituted itself. Her grinning face, marked by mania, immense torment, and what Sarita took as a deranged joy, emerged from the dark fog.

No longer needing to tell each other to get away, Sarita and Myra turned and ran together for the exit through the moved bookcases. Cela was in no condition to follow yet, but her laughter bounded after them, and her words were right behind it.

"Darkness is a force," Cela declared. "Darkness is its own matter. And we are all dark *on the inside*. I am a *world* of *darkness* under my skin. And I can make the dark do whatever I please. Let me show you. Let me show you what you are *innssiiiide*."

Loosened dirt fell from the walls and ceiling of the tunnel as Sarita and Myra ran its turns, inclines, and drops. The support beams were visibly weaker, some having splintered. The tunnel had withstood the quakes caused by the sleeper's awakening first, then the violence between the god and the supposed "lesser" who was far closer to being its equal than the god must have known. Like the rest of the refuge, the age of the wood used for the beams and the old sconces being used to prop up electrical lanterns made it clear that the structure was older than any member of the family. Now the tunnel was on the verge of a cave-in encouraged by the shock waves that carried Cela's words, and by the sleeper's continued agonized bleating.

Myra led now, being more familiar with the old tunnel, which made Sarita the rear guard. She looked back frequently to see if Cela had reassembled herself enough, or gained sufficient control of her mist form, to give chase again. Not that there was anything Sarita could do if she saw the cloud rolling toward them, but she would rather see it coming than not.

They came to a shaft that had a ladder leading upward. Beside the ladder was a burlap bag, partly opened, beside two other bags, one entirely empty, one untouched. There were three multitools in the partially open bag. Sarita took one and saw up close how they had been modified. The metal ends, extending beyond the rubber grips higher up on the handles, had been sharpened to create stakes, adding to the chopping and bludgeoning properties the tools already had.

Sarita glanced back once more as Myra started up the ladder, and saw darkness vacuum the light out of the lanterns into the deeper end of the hall. A void of not quite darkness but antilight trailed Cela, who looked like she'd been through a teleportation mishap involving her clone. Her four arms and three legs rotated behind her stretched neck and enlarged face as she moved down the tunnel, as though trying to emulate a drill. Her oversized teeth gnashed at nothing as she came forward, although Sarita suspected she was trying to bite all the light still ahead of her, eat it and smother it with the immense darkness she proclaimed was within her.

The sleeper's multitudinous, translucent tendrils punched through the tunnel's walls to block Cela's approach, forming a web that seized her once again. Even as she fought with the wounded old god still that wanted to consume her, Cela watched Sarita, focused more on killing her than fighting for her life.

Sarita followed Myra up the ladder and through an open hatch that let in gray daylight.

It's the daytime, Sarita thought. *How is it daytime?* She worried it was an illusion, a trap. She'd been in the belly of Baby Head Mountain for less than twenty-four hours, but still felt that a permanent nightfall should have covered the world in that time. Knowing that this was an absurd thought, she kept going, and made it to the surface right behind Myra.

The members of the family who had escaped ahead of them waited outside, along with a handful of other individuals—not human—most of whom Sarita did not recognize. But even with malice on his face and predation in his bloodstained smile, she recognized Cold Eyes. The Viscount. The false god who thought she was his bride.

34

The escape tunnel had brought them to the Baby Head Mountain Cemetery, the hatch being an old grave marker. Beyond the cemetery gates there was a road, hills, and nothing else. Not one bird was in the sky, not one house or ranch was in the distance. They were by themselves out here, at the mercy of The Viscount and his party. Barnes lay still at The Viscount's feet, eyes wide and throat torn. The Viscount held Everett by his neck with one hand.

"Hello, my love," The Viscount said. "I truly wanted to wait for you to come to me on your own, but present circumstances demand extremes. I do not want to hurt anyone else, but if I must, I must. I tried to set this example before, with your friend, but was not able to make my case due to my condition at the time. I am quite, *quite* close to that now, and I will turn all your new little friends into mulch if you delay, and you will then join me regardless, or—"

"I'll come with you," Sarita said through tight lips, dropping the multitool.

She was tired. Fleeing Cela's misshapen, transformative madness would have been enough to exhaust anyone, physically and emotionally, even if they were well rested and fresh, but she had been broken down for days already. Broken by death and confusion and revelations about herself and the entire world that were too enormous to be digested in the amount of time she'd been given to try to process them.

Beneath her feet, two vile demons warred with each other, and when either of them won, Sarita and the family would be thrust once more into a fight for survival. Meanwhile, somewhere out there, David was Harrah's hostage, and that was all she wanted to care about, but in the moment she could barely consider the possibility that anything existed beyond this graveyard, these people, and this devil with delusions of godhood demanding she reign with him. It was more dangerous to the others—and likely futile—to resist him now. Safer to simply go to him.

The family must have seen the uselessness of fighting with The Viscount and his entourage as well, because none of them, not even Myra, tried to dissuade Sarita from moving toward him. They watched her wearily, nervously, and she had sympathy for them. She understood what they had lost already, and how that made them fear what else they could lose even more. She didn't expect or want any of them to intervene as she went forward, and none of them did.

A different figure emerged to come between her and The Viscount, however, as she passed under the shade of a large tree that covered a gravestone topped by the sculpture of an angel.

Where have you been? Sarita thought when she saw him. *It's too late now, Angelo. It's too late for you to make up for anything. You can't help me, and I don't want you to.*

"Guardian, you are not needed here," a robed man beside The Viscount said. "You seem to have misread the situation, but you have already served your purpose. Move aside."

Angelo, The Northman, turned his back on his god and the priest who told him to stand down. He faced Sarita. Rage boiled the tears she saw trapped in his eyes. She shook her head at him as soon as his lips parted. *Now* he was appearing to her? *Now* he wanted to talk to her?

"I am sorry," he said, his voice hard but unimposing. Something old and rarely used. "I made a horrible mistake. They told me that he would kill you."

Again, Sarita shook her head, keeping her mouth shut.

I know they did, but that doesn't matter, she thought. *You cut my heart out. You started all of this.*

He hadn't actually started it all, and she knew. She couldn't say what

262 · JOHNNY COMPTON

would have happened had Angelo not killed Frank, but it was likely that Cela, whose fight with the sleeper continued to send tremors through the ground, would have taken a more direct approach if—when—Frank didn't behave as she needed him to for her prophecy to be fulfilled. Or, for that matter, when Sarita didn't fall for The Viscount's seduction and rejected him to stay with the man she loved. One way or another, Angelo would have had to do something if he was going to save her from the fate Cela had prepared for her. And it was likely that if Angelo had not killed Frank, one of these other devils would have. But Angelo *did* kill Frank, and knowing his history and reasoning, and the forces that influenced him, didn't make it easy for Sarita to forgive him.

That wasn't why she walked past him now, though. She genuinely did not want or need his help, and the latest shock wave that cracked multiple headstones in the cemetery reminded her that she didn't have much time.

She approached The Viscount and felt an unexpected glow of love and fulfillment, not from the egomaniacal monster she was raising her arms to embrace, but from her followers. The roar of the devout returned. Her believers had, for hundreds of years, prayed not only for the day when their god and goddess would be united, but also for a future in which she would not be murdered by The Devil of Devils. A future that did not demand her sacrifice as The Martyred Mother, did not demand that her child, their messiah, would be slain as well. She felt the intense, searing energy of their love and dreams flowing through her now as she reached out for their god. He let go of Everett to put his arms around her, and welcome her kiss.

The power surging within her came from every member of Cela's church sensing that everything they had ever hoped for had come to pass. The gates of their paradise were opening before them. The energy of their hope, joy, and love was almost too immense for her to withstand.

What would it be like for them when that faith was brutally severed? When their goddess turned into a truer, greater devil than they ever imagined could exist? Sarita would soon find out.

She had loosened the piece of metal that was stuck inside her cheek, but never spit it out. Metal from a door full of carved wards. Metal that did not harm her, because while she was the desired bride of the vampire god, she was not vampiric herself. Whatever she was now, she was not susceptible to the same things that The Viscount was. She was relying on that. Hoping that, in his haste to have her, he would not realize what she was doing until it was too late.

When he opened his mouth to kiss her, she used the skill she had learned from that young man she had been with years ago in New York, who taught her how to conceal a razor in her mouth and slip it out with her tongue. She pushed the sharpened metal bit into The Viscount's mouth, tried to cut into his tongue with it in the hopes of temporarily stunning him, buying her enough time to kill him. This did not work quite as planned, but something even more effective happened.

The Viscount reflexively tried to swallow the fresh blood—her blood—when he tasted it. The metal bit slipped back like a sharpened pill and was pinned between the back of his throat and the base of his tongue.

She felt him convulse, pulled her mouth away from his before his teeth snapped shut. He was not entirely stiff, but was immobilized by spasms. While his priests were still trying to understand what might have happened, before they could begin to come to grips with the possibility that The Godbride—the one whose life they had prayed so hard for—had used an act of love to betray and attack their god, Sarita turned back, pointed to the multitool she had dropped, and shouted, "Myra!"

While even the other family members appeared too startled to grasp what was going on, Myra knew that understanding wasn't important. Acting was. She grabbed the multitool and threw it to Sarita.

Sarita caught it in one hand, brought her other hand to the handle as she swung, and with the strength of a vengeful goddess she beheaded the paralyzed Viscount clean under his jawline.

His body dropped as his head tumbled toward one of the priests, who dumbly knelt to pick it up like it was a precious artifact he wanted to dust off.

Behind her, Sarita heard an explosion as Cela burst through the tunnel hatch and rose high above them all, screaming like there was a nation of banshees caged in her chest. Her presence turned the overcast sky into a midnight with the moon and stars too close, eerily illuminating the graveyard with enough white and bluish hues to make the shadows more pronounced.

Sarita did not turn around. She raised the staked end of the tool and brought it down into The Viscount's body, driving it through his spine, through his heart, and into the earth.

The communal torment of screaming believers afflicted by the sensation—the *certainty*—that their goddess had killed their god, almost blinded Sarita. She saw the priests' faces turn into melting masks of horror and hysteria. They were torn by the immediate desire to attack their god's killer, by an opposing, entrenched allegiance to The Godbride, who they had truly loved and prayed to more than their god, and by an equally powerful need to do nothing, because reacting in any way would validate that the impossible, the inconceivable, had occurred. As long as they did nothing more than try in vain to quell their amazing grief, their god might resurrect himself, their goddess might hold him again with sincere love this time, and this atrocity would be revealed as a final test of faith, weeding out those who had believed this could ever be real.

Sarita felt like the queen of the deepest dungeon of Hell. What else could she be? She now reigned over a place reserved for the faithful who nonetheless sinned egregiously, and were now stuck in a realm with shattered parts of their supreme being, told that its broken state was their fault alone, and that its return to glory depended on them completing the Sisyphean task of piecing their god back together with no tools, no blueprint, no way to find all the remains. She had plunged the flock she never wanted into this infinite place. Their misery clung to her, and strengthened her.

As darkness descended closer, Sarita turned to acknowledge Cela, and welcomed the awe of the spectacle.

She won, Sarita thought. *She killed the sleeper, and she ate it instead.*

The cloud that Cela turned herself inside out to become, still streaming from under the soil like a Plinian eruption, was large enough to be confused for space itself at this proximity. Her white eyes were twirling, burning celestial bodies, and there were dozens of them now. Sarita only felt one eye fixed upon her. The others circled the remaining vampires like satellites.

Sarita stood and spoke to the substantial piece of Cela's attention that she held. The part that she could feel still wanted to kill her, though it would serve no purpose now.

"I'm all that's left," Sarita said, not blinking as she stared down the great pallid eye. More forcefully, she said, "*I am all you have left.* What else is there? *What else?* The god you made? I killed him. The 'Devil' you made . . . he already died. And 'The Martyred Mother' died when he did. What's left of all your work except for The Godbride? I'm all that's left. What do you have to show for your whole life except for me?"

From the stygian atmosphere, a detailed impression of Cela's original human form pressed forward, resembling a living statue carved of onyx half-embedded in a massive black wall. "I have another Devil," Cela said, her voice chiseling her words into history and legend. "The one who has your brother."

"Not for long," Sarita said.

"I have her for as long as I want after you are dead."

"You'd rather have her than me? You'd rather keep a devil you had to make on the spot over the goddess you built everything around?"

Cela's silence would have concerned Sarita more had it lasted longer. She only had a couple of seconds to wonder if she had misread Cela's thoughts, misjudged the situation.

In a flash of darkness, Cela proved Sarita's gambit was worth it. Not only was her manufactured "god" dead, he'd been killed by the goddess who was never supposed to survive. The goddess who had shown herself to still be in love with the deceased, alleged "Devil" of Cela's religion. There was no salvaging her prophecy now. Killing Sarita, or even her lifelong "guardian," at this point would only serve to drive her congregation deeper into its unique and unrelenting hell, instantly fracturing their minds and spirits well beyond repair, and Sarita could sense that Cela didn't want that.

What Cela wanted was to directly punish every member of her church, from the clergy to the laity, because they had turned on her. She wanted to savor their suffering. She wanted and needed, for the first time in ages, to indulge herself.

The cloud and its many eyes spread over the cemetery, and while cries came from human and vampire alike, only the ones who had come with The Viscount were taken away when the cloud vanished, along with the false god's corpse.

35

Within the swarming blackness, Cela listened to her captives beg for forgiveness.

She chewed through them meticulously, each of the countless grains of her body being a galaxy of teeth.

She acted patiently and purposefully, and so time swelled with the pain of the sufferers, until every moment of their torment became an individual epoch. The era of the lost arm. The period of the eaten eyes. The age of the swallowed heart.

When she made it at last to her church to appear before the lamenting faithless, she assumed the form of a gigantic, living obsidian memorial to herself, and the masses that had called for her to be staked not an hour before now sang her praises and implored her to show them the new way, the way out of their hell, whatever it was, and they swore this time not to question their Founder.

The New Way. She would show them.

Her veins were full.

Her stomachs were full.

She had consumed one older god live and whole, then ate her false god's remains. The dead body of her own creation. How perfectly monstrous of her. In doing so she achieved godhood herself. She was a true, magnificent, vicious, and vindictive deity, who was so weighed down by her enormity that she could not fend off becoming listless and feckless, but not before she consumed the entirety of her congregation.

As Sarita Bardales had declared The Martyred Mother dead, so, too, could Cela now declare her past selves dead. She was no longer The Founder, or The Godmaker.

She was Cela, the sleeper.

She needed to do nothing more to prove this, but she *wanted* to finish her banquet. Her church was still full of those who had so recently distrusted her. Lost, foolish, shuddering little devils who all deserved to be devoured.

After her feast, she closed her many eyes, listened to the congregation's lullaby of lament, and slept.

36

"I have to go to my brother," Sarita told Myra.

"I know you do," Myra said.

"Take care of Everett for me. I'll come back to help when I can."

"Just go," Myra said, then turned to attend to the injured survivors among her family. Sarita couldn't afford to feel any regret for leaving them to fend for themselves for now. Nor could she feel guilt for what she planned to do to Everett Stallworth's niece. For not even telling him what she planned to do, explaining what Harrah had done, and giving him a chance to come with her, possibly talk Harrah down. There was no time for that.

She hoped they would still be here when she was done, but she didn't know how long this might take, and whether the family had a contingency for an invasion of their home that called for them to move on as quickly as possible. They had lost the protection of the sleeper, and once all of them realized that, she was sure they wouldn't want to stay. For now, though, they hadn't even had a chance to pick up the literal pieces of their home and family, and still probably had the echoes of the attack floating in their ears. Sarita certainly still heard it all, and preferred to focus on that over the unceasing chorus of her followers' screams, their voices congealing into a rush of noise that steadily crested and fell.

Torture and vengeance were truly all that Cela had left, and had any interest in. She was going to fill herself with it until she couldn't move, couldn't remain awake. Sarita no longer factored into Cela's plans. So Sarita didn't have to concern herself with anything keeping her from David, except Harrah.

She picked up the multitool she had killed The Viscount with and approached Angelo. He braced himself, expecting and possibly hoping she would strike and kill him as well.

"Somebody took my brother," she said. "Did you know that? Did you see it?"

Angelo nodded.

"Do you know where he is? Can you send me there? I don't know how to do that thing you all can do. Can you teach me? Or just send me?"

"I will take you."

"No, I don't need you there for this. And I don't know if I can trust you not to . . . not to kill somebody else I love. Make another 'mistake.'"

"Please. I know I have no right to ask, and I know you do not need me. I need it for myself."

Arguing over this would only waste more time, and while she didn't think she needed Angelo's help to fight off Harrah and save David, she did need him to bring her to their location. She reached her hand out, took his, and told him, "Let's go."

The words were barely out of her mouth when her own shadow rose and scaled her body, fitting her like a skintight cocoon. She could no longer see Angelo, but sensed him in the dense, immaculate blackness they passed through. More than that, she sensed the consciousness of the darkness, and the strange insecurity that made it yearn to be used like this, to be given importance and purpose that light had. That made what Angelo was doing easier to learn. Already, Sarita felt like she could use the darkness to find her way anywhere, because it would be so eager to assist her.

This was good to know, in case she needed to make a fast exit with David.

They emerged on the shadowed side of an abandoned building. An old, small church alongside a lonely stretch of highway. Through a small gap in the boards nailed over one of the tall windows, she saw her brother kneeling between the front pews, on the floor, a sprinkling of what might have been blood in his lap.

Crouched before him, holding one of his hands close to its lips, was a thing that looked like it had crawled into Harrah Stallworth and stretched her from the inside to see when the seams would split.

Empowered as she was, Sarita felt extraordinarily normal and unsure of what to do for a moment. Should she shout David's name, make sure he knew that she was here? That would let Harrah know that she was here, too. Was that better, or worse? Would that help or hurt her chances of saving her brother? Should she try to lure Harrah outside, get her away from David? Would that even work? Or would Harrah go into a frenzy when she saw or heard Sarita, overcome by the anger she had for her, and would that make her forget about David, or prompt her to kill him immediately since he would have already done his part in drawing Sarita here for this showdown?

What was she supposed to do?

Just as she narrowed down her potential courses of action, something darkened the front entrance of the church. Angelo went inside, taking the decision out of Sarita's hands.

"Harrah Stallworth," he said, "I am the one who killed your son."

37

Relative to what she had done to Don, Misty, Tori, and many others in the last several hours, Harrah had treated David Bardales gently. She had bitten the tip from his forefinger, primarily to show just how sharp her teeth were, and peeled the fingernails off his thumb and pinky, but even that minor damage had been confined to a single hand. Beyond that, she bit an earlobe off, ripped one of his molars out, and cracked one of his anklebones like an eggshell after he tried to run once too often. She didn't even wake him up when he passed out. She figured that exhaustion, more than pain, had made him nod off. Whichever it was, she let him sleep it off and come to on his own before starting back on him.

To his credit, none of the pain or threats of more grievous harm convinced him to text or call Sarita as Harrah commanded him to. He never even screamed, though the raggedness of his grunting and growling, particularly when she peeled his thumbnail back while pinning him down with her other arm, told Harrah he was using more of his strength to lock down expressions of pain than to try to pull away from her. Still, he never gave in to Harrah's demands. His sister did not deserve him, and he didn't deserve what was going to happen to him if he continued to hold out. But it *was* going to happen. If Harrah couldn't draw Sarita to her to try to save her brother's life, she would do so by inspiring Sarita to avenge his death. And the deaths of her parents, if need be.

After killing David, she would drop his corpse off in front of a police station or at a hospital. Ensure he was found and identified. Sarita would surely come out of hiding then. Harrah hadn't seen the girl since Frankie's funeral. It would be fitting for them to meet again at another service. Maybe that was the route to take, and she was wasting time trying it this other way first, but she wanted to give her brother a chance. Frankie never got a chance, not even to live up to being the devil he was supposed to be.

Harrah had taken his place, and there was no going back to who she had been. She had slaughtered far too many people, many of them having nothing to do with her rage and revenge, to ever be a normal person again, even if such a conversion was possible. So why was she putting on a show of humanity when she was no longer human? Why not just eat David Bardales and forgo all this fair play, "give him a chance" nonsense?

The bodies piled up in her wake were the exact reason why she wanted to slow down now, show some restraint, prove that she killed when she wanted to, not because she had to. It would be an injustice to Frankie to just keep killing people she didn't have to in his memory. Now, if Sarita's brother insisted on being stubborn and refusing reason, that would change things for him. In that case he would be choosing to die as much as she would be choosing to kill him.

When the door to the old church opened, she expected to see Sarita entering, having somehow found them, maybe brought there by Cela herself. Harrah wondered whether she should let David survive after ripping his sister limb from limb, or spare him the pain of living with a loved one's murder, knowing you couldn't have done anything to save them, but still feeling like you ought to have done something. Before she could think much on that, however, she realized that Sarita was not the person standing in the aisle, coming toward her.

This was a tall man with a papery pallor and a deep solemnity on his face.

"Harrah Stallworth," the pale man said, "I am the one who killed your son."

Harrah tilted her head and stared at him like she wasn't sure he was even there. She stood up and walked past David to get a closer look at the man.

"I am the one who killed your son," he said again, his unstated apology present in the deliberate meekness of his voice. "I alone am responsible. I know the pain that I have caused you. I endured it myself, long ago, and I can never ask for your forgiveness."

This is a trick, Harrah thought, then turned her face to a window to her right when she thought she saw a shadow through the nailed planks. There might have been someone there before, but no one was there now, and her heart jumped before she turned back to where the man was, sure that he would be charging her, revealing fangs as sharp as hers, claws just as large, fury just as frightening and deadly. She'd have fallen for a trick sprung mostly by herself, and would be in for her first true test, her first good fight, since becoming a monster.

The man was not coming in to attack her, however. He stood with his hands raised wide and just above his head, as if to show he was unarmed, and was no threat. She dared to get closer to him, still primed for him to pounce.

"You're the one who killed my boy?" she said.

"I did."

There was too much that she wanted to say, including questions that had already been answered. She knew "Why?" for instance. The woman in red had told her. Her boy had been caught up in a prophecy and conspiracy he'd never even known about, and this man had killed him to keep him from doing something he never would have done, at least not without good cause.

Even so, she wanted to ask him why he'd done it. Likewise, she wanted to ask him if Sarita had set him up to do it, even though she already knew that Sarita was probably ignorant of the bigger scheme she was involved in. That didn't make her innocent, in Harrah's eyes. She had to have known enough to give Frankie a warning, at least. Frankie probably would have thought she was crazy, and maybe wouldn't have married her because of it, which would have saved his life.

Instead of asking either of those questions, or launching into the extended, barely coherent invective boiling at the bottom of her brain, all she managed to say was, "You . . . *you* . . . ?"

"Yes. I am the one. I alone."

"You killed him. You *really* killed my boy? You . . . *you killed my son!*"

Red saliva foamed in her mouth as her teeth grew, splitting her gums. Flaming redness filled her vision. Her hands grew so heavy she had to swing them up like the striking ends of flails rather than lift them, then use that momentum to launch herself at the man, who remained still and waiting. She didn't care if it was a trap or an illusion, nor did she care that, behind her, she heard wooden boards breaking.

Now or never, Sarita thought. While Harrah tore into Angelo, Sarita hacked through the boards on the window with the multitool. Inside the church, she immediately went to David, brought him to his unsteady feet and hurried out with him through the way she came in.

She ran with him through the dry, tall grass, to the highway, where the only two cars she saw sped past like they were trying to outrun the blast wave from a bomb. Just before the gravelly shoulder of the road, she sat him down, checked his injuries to make sure nothing appeared serious. His shirt wasn't torn, there was minimal blood on his jeans, some on his neck, but that was from his missing earlobe, not anything severe.

"You're good?" she said to him.

"I'm good enough."

"You're sure?"

"I'm fine."

"All right. Stay here, I'll be right back."

He started to stand up, but she put her hand on his shoulder and told him, "I mean it. I'll be right back. I know what I'm doing."

He saw something in her, she could tell. He saw that she was more than who she'd been when they last saw each other. More than human. What he saw frightened him, but also did not change the fact that she was his sister.

"I'll give you a minute," he said, then shook his head. "Thirty seconds. I'm for real, I'm going to be counting."

This almost got her to smile. She had just saved him, and he was in no condition to even fight an ordinary person, much less a vampire, but what else was he supposed to say? He was her brother.

"Let me go," she said. "Trust me. I'll be right back. Just stay here."

She took the multitool and turned away before he could say anything else.

Bestial snarling and wet scraping sounds came through the open doorway of the church. Sarita walked in with the tool held up, ready to swing.

On the floor of the church, Harrah knelt over Angelo's shredded remains, clawing into the concrete floor under the stained carpet where his head used to be. From what Sarita could see, Harrah had torn his torso open, pulled his heart out, and ripped his head to pieces, and now she had broken two of her fingers while continuing to tear into the unforgiving foundation of the church, lost in her effort to destroy every bit of Angelo's face and skull.

Sarita watched her do this until it became apparent that Harrah wasn't going to stop, and that she hadn't even noticed someone else enter the church. Sarita considered leaving her here like this, but knew she couldn't afford to, not with the looming threat Harrah would pose to her brother and parents. She knew that it would be cruel to do so, as well.

"Harrah," Sarita said, then said it louder when Harrah did not look up. "Harrah."

This got her to stop, although she still did not lift her face to see who had called her name.

"He killed Frankie," Harrah said, giving a last long look at what she had done to Angelo—what he had let her do, what he needed done for himself—before she looked at Sarita. Tears poured down her face, and Sarita wondered if Harrah could cry all the blood and evil packed within her out if given enough time. Sarita's eyes welled up, and she thought that it shouldn't have taken all of this for the two of them to come to this point. She couldn't say that this was how it ought to have been because Frank should have never died, but this was a moment they should have shared earlier, at the funeral, under far different circumstances.

"He killed Frankie," Harrah repeated. "He said he killed Frankie. He killed my boy. He killed . . . he killed our Frank."

Sarita nodded, then waited. Harrah's eyes hardened. The bond of grief evaporated, as she knew it would. Perhaps because Harrah's heart, deluged by the blood of her many recent victims, and charred by the desire to blame Sarita, resisted reconciliation. Or, maybe, because she wanted to give Sarita a reason to end things for her without having to ask to be killed.

You can ask, Sarita thought. *I'll do it for you. For what you did to Tori, and for hurting my brother, and for Frank, too, if he's out there somewhere, because he wouldn't want you going on like this.*

Harrah bared her teeth and screeched. Sarita flipped the tool's stake forward. Harrah must have seen her do this before she moved, but she leapt at her anyway and impaled herself through the mouth.

Sarita set the immobilized, twitching Harrah headfirst against a pew, then went behind her to grab the end of the stake sticking out the back of Harrah's skull. She put her foot into Harrah's back for leverage, and pulled as hard as she could. She thought this would bring the axe-head all the way through, separating Harrah's skull at the jaws, but she instead ripped Harrah's entire head off, where it remained stuck to the top of the multi-tool. She drove the stake down through Harrah's back and into her heart, then left the church alone to soak up the blood of innocents and devils alike.

David was limping toward the church when Sarita came out.

"What did I tell you?" she said.

"I heard a scream."

"Hers, not mine."

"So you got her? It's over?"

"It is today."

Hearing this gave him permission to sit back down, almost falling to the ground, and he nearly hyperventilated with equal amounts of relief and sadness. He blinked back tears as he started to tell Sarita, "Tori . . . she's—"

"I know. But Mom and Dad are safe?"

He nodded. Sarita dropped down beside her brother. He put his head on her shoulder and reached over for her to hold his hand. She did so gingerly, and he still winced from the pain, but tightened his grip like he was afraid she would let go of him.

"Just give me a minute and I'll get us home," Sarita said.

She stared into the clear sky, knowing that there was a universe of darkness beckoning her beyond the blue. She squeezed her brother's hand, kissed the top of his head, and imagined that they were at the beach, that life was simpler, and that the distant screaming that would live forever in her head was the roar of the surf.

Author's Note

ABOUT BABY HEAD MOUNTAIN

Baby Head Mountain and Baby Head Cemetery are real places in the Texas Hill Country. The stories about how Baby Head got its name, shared in this book, are genuine (if very likely inaccurate) gruesome legends.

I tend to agree with TexasEscapes.com's explanation of why the place was given such an odd name: There are two creek heads, one large and one small, in the general area. The smaller, "baby" head runs closer to the hill and other landmarks nearby. That makes more sense than naming the area after the grim remains of an unnamed child after she and her unnamed family were victims of an unsolved slaughter, which is not documented in the historical record, but for the purposes of a horror story I went with the macabre legends, of course.

ABOUT MY VAMPIRES & DEVILS

In a long tradition of storytellers that includes Octavia Butler (*Fledgling*), Brian Lumley (*Necroscope*), Bram Stoker (*The Shoulder of Shasta*; something else, probably), and many others, I used different elements from preexisting vampire (and even non-vampire) lore and fiction, discarded other elements that I didn't find as interesting or as much fun to work with, and made a few things up.

The biggest influences were (strap in): older, pre–Lord Ruthven vampire folklore; the writings of Antoine Augustin Calmet, Dudley Wright, Montague Summers, and Agnes Murgoci; the anime films *Blood: The Last Vampire* (2000) and *Vampire Hunter D*; the OVA series *Hellsing: Ultimate*; and the Hammer vampire films of the '50s, '60s, and '70s.

For some examples, the physical appearance of the vampires in their more savage state is largely inspired by *Blood: The Last Vampire,* while the metal through the tongue and bloated-to-near-bursting appearances were among many interesting things I found in older lore that aren't featured often (if at all) in popular, modern vampire fiction. (So much of the bizarre lore I really wanted to include, even as just a passing reference, I chose to leave out, like the Russian vampires that are identifiable by their pointed tongue and lone nostril.)

Even the repeated biting of mouths has a source of inspiration. I got the idea for it after reading the Romanian tale "A Story from Botoşani," as translated by Murgoci, in which a charming vampire invites himself to a party and woos a woman who flees when she reaches down for her dropped distaff and sees he has "the tail of a vampire." In another version, instead of a tail, the vampire's true identity is revealed by the girl seeing he and his vampiric companions have horse hooves instead of feet. This is reminiscent of the classic urban legend, born in San Antonio, of "the devil in the dance hall," which also features a dashing, diabolical party crasher whose cover gets blown when the woman he's charming looks down and sees he has either chicken feet or goat hooves, depending on which version you've read or heard.

Devils and vampires. Not so different.

Anyway, about all that mouth-violence, when the other partygoers in "A Story from Botoşani" can't find the young lady who escaped the vampire, or tell him where she ran off to, the vampire cuts everyone's lips off (ahead of several other acts of carnage).

And just to let you know what comes of him, he continues pursuing the young lady, and isn't stopped until he gets into a fight with another vampire whose sleep and home he disturbs. No real reason is given for why they fight each other immediately instead of trying to talk things out. You get the impression, though, that territorialism and conflict come naturally to two vampires who aren't previously acquainted, or, perhaps, even if they are.

Devils kill devils.

Acknowledgments

Thanks to my editors for this novel, Daphne Durham and Kelly Lonesome.

Thanks to my publicist, Ashley Spruill.

To Saraciea Fennell, Michael Dudding, Jordan Hanley, Kristin Temple, and the rest of the Tor Nightfire team.

To my agent, Lane Heymont, as always, thank you.

And to anyone reading this far, thank you as well.

About the Author

JOHNNY COMPTON is the author of the Bram Stoker Award–nominated *The Spite House*. His short stories have appeared in *PseudoPod, Strange Horizons, The NoSleep Podcast*, and many other markets. He is a Horror Writers Association member and creator and host of the podcast *Healthy Fears*.